REBECCA SCOTT

A Novel

JOE KELLEY

ISBN-10: 1493661167
ISBN-13: 9781493661169

For Melanie

CHAPTER 1

FALL 1994

A bby Whitman pointed across the bar at the Kennedy volunteers. "Take the signs outside. Now."

The kid with the beard spread his hands in supplication. "Aw, come on."

She pushed two pints of Bass Ale toward the grad students from BU and pulled the Harp tap down hard into a frosted mug. "Make up your minds, boys. It's either you or the signs." She nodded toward one of the tables by the window. "The Romney people left theirs outside. Same goes for you. No politicking."

"But what about the beers we ordered from Sean?"

"They're not going anywhere."

She slid four Harps along the bar to the house painters from McPhee's and then quickly poured three pitchers of Bud for Sean to serve to the football team filing in from Friday night's game on the Cambridge Common. With an eye on the retreating Kennedy workers, she placed two Chardonnays in front of the saleswoman from Marathon Sports and the hair stylist from Carol's Salon. Slowly, full of smiles and apologies, and conspicuously missing their signs, the trio of amateur Democrats trudged back in and took their seats. It was only when she glanced behind her that Abby noticed Jeannie Devir. Jeannie's right elbow was propped up on the bar, and she was shading her right eye with her hand.

Abby turned and looked at her. A red welt bulged under Jeannie's eye and the young woman's hands shook uncontrollably. Abby touched her arm. "Are you all right?"

"I'm alive."

Most of the time, Abby enjoyed bartending. It helped pay her way through Stanford, and she kept at it while making her fortune in Silicon Valley. To Abby, tending bar was like watching a play where you were peripherally involved with the actors. You served them some alcohol and before long, they began presenting you with little dramas. Sometimes, like the yelling, brawling football players, they put on comedies, and other times, as in the case of the two Chardonnay drinkers, they acted out scenes from what could only be described as a maudlin little soap opera. There was no question, of course, that what she saw working itself out in the life of Jeannie Devir was a tragedy, but it was a tragedy Abby had allowed herself to get involved in, and that was against her better judgment—against, in fact, all the rules of successful bartending. The nature of the job, as everyone knew, involved a certain level of sympathetic listening. But that was as far as it was supposed to go. The problem was she was letting her sense of outrage get the better of her. Once, she had even walked Jeannie home after closing time because she was afraid to go by herself, and a week later she met her on a Saturday afternoon for coffee at the Starbucks across the street and listened to her talk about her marriage.

Jeannie was twenty-nine, a year older than Abby, and had been married for ten years to Chuck Devir, a pipefitter, whose main interests, from what Abby could see, were weightlifting, drinking and beating his wife. Jeannie was a shy, working-class girl from North Cambridge whose only hope in life was to escape this monster and find a nice guy somewhere who would treat her like a human being. After all, why shouldn't Jeannie Devir have a chance at some happiness? Why should she have to go on like this?

On that Saturday at Starbucks, Abby listened with sympathy for as long as she could, but finally, she began telling Jeannie that she had to take control of her life. The questions poured out of her. Why would you want to stay with a man like this? Why haven't you called the police? Why don't you leave the jerk? She kept hearing her mother's voice in the back of her head warning her not to get involved, not to interject her strong opinions into the minds of others, not to try to change people who refuse to change themselves. But in this case she just couldn't help herself. It was intolerable that this sweet, pretty young woman should have to spend the rest of her life being abused by a sub-human.

Abby got herself so worked up one day that she even told one of her professors about it. Like many of the young women in Professor Mark Stevenson's seminar on the political history of Boston, Abby had a bit of a crush on her instructor. He was an older man in his late forties, but there was something about him that intrigued her. For one thing, he was very handsome. Tall and lean and rather aristocratic looking. He had blonde hair with a touch of gray at the sides and a blonde moustache, and he was always well dressed. He was a striking contrast to some of the younger instructors in their thirties who showed up in jeans and an old sport coat, or the nerdy ones with their wrinkled shirts tucked tightly into polyester slacks.

But it wasn't just his good looks and neat attire that attracted Abby. And it wasn't just because he was witty and charming. He spoke calmly, soothingly, and somehow this enhanced his ability as a teacher. There was nothing egotistic or arrogant about him. He never showed off in class or used his intellect as a weapon as so many academics did. He worked hard too, correcting his students' research papers himself and still managing to publish his own scholarly work as well as several commercially successful travel books. Abby had seen a number of them in the Cambridge bookstores and bought the one with the guided tours of Boston's neighborhoods so she could get to know the city.

Another thing she liked was his kind, almost courtly manner, and it was this quality that made her feel she could talk to him about Jeannie Devir. So last week she stopped him as they were leaving Robinson Hall. "Professor Stevenson, do you have a moment?"

"Certainly, Abby. What is it?"

"Well, it's kind of an odd request. You've mentioned in class that your wife's a lawyer."

"That's right."

They walked down the steps together and strolled into Sever Quad. It was a lovely fall morning with a cool breeze blowing off the Charles River. "What kind of a lawyer is she?"

He smiled. "She's a troublemaker."

They paused for a moment by the pathway in front of the Appleton Chapel and she laughed. "Don't you mean a troubleshooter?"

"No, I mean a troublemaker. She spends about half her time on criminal law, which is what she's supposed to be doing, and the other half helping elect liberal Democrats."

"Well, I'm a liberal. I hope you won't hold that against me."

He laughed good-naturedly. "Of course, I won't. I wouldn't have lasted this long at Harvard if I couldn't peacefully coexist with liberals. Besides, you're a California liberal. You guys are into vegetarianism and boycotting lettuce and banning smoking from your restaurants. She's one of those East coast liberals. One of those dangerous ones that really wants to change things."

Finally, she told him about Jeannie Devir. He became very serious and she noticed a spark of anger in his eyes, an expression she had never seen before. "I'll speak to my wife tonight, Abby."

So now, with her hand on Jeannie Devir's arm, Abby looked deeply into her frightened eyes. "I may know someone who can help."

Jeannie glanced nervously at the door. "I don't know. He may come after me tonight."

"Do you want me to call the police?"

"I don't know if I'm ready for that yet."

Abby felt like shaking her and telling her to come to her senses. Instead, she reached under the bar, scooped out some fresh ice and wrapped it in a clean towel. Then she placed it gently on the welt near Jeannie's eye.

Suddenly, the door flew open and a bear of a man burst into the bar. He shouted at Abby and she jumped, instantly hating herself for the panic that seized her by the throat. He thrust his ugly face into hers. "What the fuck are you? A nurse? Is this a bar or a fuckin' shelter you're running here?"

"I'm just trying..."

"Don't try shit, little girl!"

He grabbed Jeannie's arm, yanked her off the barstool, and pushed her toward the door.

One of the football players yelled at him. "Hey! Leave her alone!"

Devir shoved his wife against the wall and went for him. The guy was barely out of his chair when Devir punched him in the face, sending him sprawling to the floor. Devir turned to the rest of them. "Anybody else? Anybody else want a piece of me? Huh? Come on, you fuckin' pansies!" He began pointing at every man in the bar. "You? You? You? How 'bout you? None of you can touch me! There's nothin' you can do to me!" He stopped and gestured with a wide sweep of his meaty arm. "Anybody here think they can take me? Nobody can take me!"

Abby watched him preen and hulk his way around, challenging everyone in the bar with absolute impunity. She watched him rage and spit and threaten, and she wished—for the first time in her life—that she could be a man, a bigger man, so she could crush him. Grab him by the throat and throttle him. Smash his head against the wall and crack his dim-witted, Neanderthal skull. She felt she could kill him without a flicker of remorse. But like everyone else, Abby felt frozen in place, her heart pounding but her body immobilized. As he shoved the door open and dragged his wife out of the bar, Abby caught the expression in Jeannie's eyes. It was a look of defeat. An empty gaze of utter hopelessness.

Three of the football players knelt on the floor, trying to bring their friend to consciousness. In another minute, everyone would forget about Jeannie Devir. She waved Sean over to the bar. "Take over for me! Use this phone and call the cops. I'm going outside."

Sean stared at her. "Jesus, Abby. That guy'll kill you. Maybe you should wait until they get here."

"Maybe that'll be too late."

She ran out the front door to Mass Ave and stopped for a second. Then she heard shouting in the alley between the bar and Canterbury's Bookstore. She stepped around the corner. Devir had Jeannie pinned against the brick wall, his left hand around her throat and his big finger in her face. "You don't ever walk out on me! Ever! You hear me? You fuckin' bitch! You..."

"Leave her alone!"

Devir turned and glowered at her. "You really are a dumb fuckin' broad, aren't you? Didn't you see what I did to that asshole in there? You're gonna be next, little girl."

"I've called the police. They're on the way."

"Fuck the police!"

Jeannie tried to twist away, but he slapped her hard across the face.

Abby jumped at him and pushed him away and for a second, he lost his balance. But then he came at her in a rush and smashed her in the face and she was on her back in the alley staring up at the evening sky, a sharp burning sensation flooding her nostrils and hot tears streaming from her eyes. She tried for a moment to get up but fell back, feeling something warm and moist on her upper lip. She put her hand under her nose and when she took it away, it was covered with blood. She heard him slap Jeannie again and heard her cry out in pain. Struggling, Abby forced herself up on her elbows and tried to focus through her tears.

Then she saw someone. Standing on the sidewalk at the entrance to the alley was a woman. She was tall and blonde, and she was wearing a silvery dress that shimmered in the streetlight. The woman stared into the alley. Then Abby heard the woman's voice. It was loud and strong. "Take your hands off her!"

Devir pushed his wife to the ground and faced the stranger. "Who the fuck are you? How many fuckin' dumb bitches do I have to take out tonight, anyway?" He paused for a second and looked her up and down. Abby could see she was quite beautiful. A woman in her thirties or maybe a little older. From where Abby lay, Devir looked about eight feet tall. He started to taunt the woman. "Nice dress there, honey. Why don't you come a little closer and I'll take that silver thing off and show you something you'll never forget."

He took a few menacing steps toward her. But she didn't move. "You can't stop me, lady. Nobody can. I just wailed the shit out of a very big boy in that bar there, so there ain't a damn thing *you* can do. So whaddya say? Think you can take me? Think you're gonna call the cops like this other bitch back here? Think you can take me that way? Try it. I'll just find out who you are and come after you. I've done that before, you know. And I can do it again. Nobody ever takes me. I can beat anybody. Anytime. Anywhere. Get it, bitch? I can take anybody."

Abby waited for the stranger to turn and walk away rapidly before he could get to her, and she wondered if the woman had been out there when she said the police were coming. Wondered if she were just stalling things until they arrived. But then the unimaginable happened. The woman took several steps into the alley, her silver dress shining in the darkness. Devir roared in his rage. "Didn't you hear what I said? I can take anybody!"

Through watery eyes, Abby saw the woman raise her right hand, holding it out at arm's length. She was pointing at him. "Can you take this?"

An explosion rocked the alley and Devir staggered backwards. Abby saw the look of shock and disbelief on his face. A second explosion dropped him to his knees, and then a third tore off the top of his head and knocked him flat on his back.

Abby saw the woman slip something into the silver purse that hung from her shoulder, and in the distance, finally, she could hear the wail of a siren. The woman stared at them for a second. "It's over. He'll never hurt you again. Ever. You won't miss him at all."

Abby glanced quickly at Jeannie and their eyes met, and when she looked back, the woman was gone.

CHAPTER 2

U rsula McGuire leaned back in her chair and observed the two girls carefully. They were young women, of course, not girls, but to Ursula, they were in the flower of youth. It didn't really matter how often her husband or her male friends praised her beauty; the fact of the matter was that she was almost fifty, and sitting here this morning in her office, facing these two young things with their short skirts and flawless legs and pretty faces, she felt like an old bat.

The blonde girl, self-assured and perceptive, had no trouble meeting Ursula's gaze. The other, dark-haired, was just as attractive, but she avoided looking Ursula in the eye, constantly glancing at the floor while telling her side of the story. She had a sensual look about her, too, that set her off from the gleaming, clean-cut appearance of her companion. And then there were the bruises, especially the large purple welt under her right eye and the swollen lower lip. When the young woman reached forward to shake her hand, Ursula saw more bruises on her neck, marks that could only have been made by a large strong hand.

The two young women told their story together in a rush, alternating back and forth like frightened, excited children, the wounded, dark-haired girl gesturing a great deal with her hands and speaking in what Ursula's husband, with his gentle but nevertheless still Waspy manner, insisted on calling a Dorchester accent. But to Ursula, who knew Dorchester well, there was little variety in the speech of the working-class people of Boston. It didn't matter if they were from Brighton or Southie or Dorchester or the North End or East Boston, or, like this poor, battered young woman, from North Cambridge. The real distinctions came from class and education and exposure to money at an early age. Then you could hear the differences in the intonation of people's voices, and the words they chose to express their thoughts and their hopes and their fears. Obviously, it was the other girl, the blonde from California, who had been given all the advantages.

Finally, she had to interrupt them. "Hold on for one second. It's clear to me what happened in the bar and in the alley. But I'm having trouble with the description of this woman. She appears out of nowhere and fires three shots into your husband and then disappears into thin air."

Jeannie Devir bit her lower lip and winced at the pain from her swollen mouth. "Are you...are you saying you don't believe us?"

"Not at all. But if you want me to help you, you both need to slow down and describe what happened a little more clearly. Now was this woman a blonde or was she a brunette? She can't be both."

The girls glanced at each other, and Abby Whitman leaned forward. "What we're trying to say is that something happened between us from the moment the police arrived to the beginning of their interrogation."

"Something like what?"

"Like an unspoken communication. An innate under-standing of what we were going to say. I can't think of any other way to explain it."

Jeannie Devir leaned forward in the exact same posture. "The thing is, we didn't agree to say anything together. We didn't whisper or anything. We didn't plan it. It just happened. The cop looked at me and said, 'So what did she look like? Gimme a description.' And I looked at Abby and she looked at me, and we just *knew* what we were going to do. I didn't know which one of us was going to do it or how we were going to do it, but I knew it was going to happen." Then she sat up straight in her chair as if what she was about to say was a matter of pride. Her whole demeanor, defensive, wary, and frightened, seemed to change. Abby Whitman smiled at her friend and placed her hand on hers. Jeannie looked right back at Ursula, and for the first time in the conversation, her voice seemed steady and confident. "I lied to the police."

"You lied to them?"

"Yes, I did."

Abby interrupted her. "And if they had asked me first, I would have lied to them too."

Ursula looked back at Jeannie Devir. "And what was it you told them?"

"I told them she was a dark-haired woman, around my age, wearing a red dress."

"When in reality..."

Abby sat back. "When in reality, she was a tall blonde woman, stylish, sophisticated looking, definitely not our age, older...my...my eyes were still tearing from the blow he had given me, but I could see that much. Her dress was silver, not red, and she was...she was a very beautiful woman, really, the remotest possible image of someone who would do something like this."

Ursula folded her arms. "How do you feel about what you did?"

Abby sat back up. "We feel we did the right thing."

"And you, Mrs. Devir?"

"He was going to kill me. If he didn't kill me that night, it would have been another night. I knew it was coming. He was getting worse and worse all the time. And the thing is I never knew why. I tried to be a good wife to him. I tried to..." Suddenly, she began to cry and her voice rose. "You don't understand! You don't know what it's like to be afraid every single night. You don't know what it's like never to sleep! Do you know what? Up until Friday night, I couldn't remember the last time I slept through the night. And you know what? On Friday night I slept for ten hours. I guess that's a terrible thing to say when your husband has been killed, isn't it? But for three nights in a row now I've realized what it's like to be able to sleep again. You can't understand what that's like after so many years. That woman gave me my life back. If we told the cops what she looked like they might have found her...don't you see?"

Ursula nodded, the emotional force of the young woman's words making her pause. "Yes, Jeannie. I do see. I see why you feel that way. But as a lawyer, I have to look at things a bit differently. I have to look at things from the point of view of the law."

Abby Whitman ran her hand through her short blonde hair and a wild look came into her hazel eyes, the first sign Ursula had seen yet of any loss of self-control in this very contained, confident young woman. "Where was the law when that pig Chuck Devir was smacking us around the alley? Where was the law when Chuck Devir kept disobeying the law, taking the law into his own hands? Where was the law then? The police hadn't shown up yet. *The police were not there.* This woman was. What this woman did may have been illegal, but it was right. It was...it was *moral.*"

Ursula stared at her for a second, and then suddenly, although she instinctively tried to ward it off, a strange sense of pride seemed to swell up in her soul. These two young women had acted boldly, courageously. Acted just as she would have acted at their age. They had come to her for help, for advice, possibly for legal service, yet she felt as if they were enlisting her in a cause, a cause that could not but help to attract her allegiance.

By this point in Ursula McGuire's life, professionalism came naturally. It had been a long, long time since she had experienced the need to shake herself free of a strong emotional attraction to a client's actions. Her own moral cases were too far behind her, back in the late sixties and early seventies, when every battle seemed a clear choice between good and evil, progress and reaction, idealism and apathy. It had been a simplistic view of the law, of course, and she had grown wiser as she had grown older, yet she missed the way it had made her feel. "All right...so what happened after the cops showed up?"

Abby sighed. "By then, the whole bar had emptied out into the street. The football guys were all staring into the alley and then more cops arrived and the sidewalk was crawling with people, and cars were slowing down along Mass Ave to see what all the excitement was, and finally I told the cops I had to get back to work. So two of them came in with us and took down our story. They questioned everybody who had witnessed Devir's assault on the football player and his treatment of Jeannie while he was inside the bar, and then they told us that we had to come down to the station with them."

Jeannie Devir took a deep breath. "That's when it got scary."

"At the station?"

"No. Before the station. See, when we got outside again there were other cops still talking to people, trying to find out if anyone else had seen the woman, but nobody had."

Ursula frowned. "That's kind of strange, wouldn't you say? I mean a mild Friday night in September and this woman fires three shots into a man and nobody sees it happen, and nobody even sees a woman running or at least walking away from the scene of the crime?"

Jeannie glanced down and then looked up at her. "Well, somebody did. We were about to get into the patrol car when this old guy starts telling another cop that he a saw a woman in a silver dress walking down Mass Ave and then around the corner of Wendell Street. I looked at Abby and her face turned white, believe me. But after the guy kept talking a while it was obvious he was drunk. He kept slurring his words and saying the same thing over and over, and when he turned to point at the corner of Wendell Street where the ATM is, he staggered and almost fell down."

Abby shifted in her seat. "Everyone in the whole neighborhood knows this guy. The cops see him all the time. They're always taking his bottle away from him and moving him along. He hangs out at the corner next to the Bank Boston ATM and waits for people to come out so he can beg for money. He kept telling the police over and over that he saw this beautiful blonde lady wearing a silver dress walking around the corner."

Ursula smiled. "So the cops didn't believe him, did they?"

"No."

"You lucked out."

Both girls nodded quietly and then Abby pursed her lips and stared at her. "We...what we're worried about is what happens if someone else saw her and didn't come forward and then decides to come forward later. The cops really grilled us carefully at the station. Especially Jeannie. They wanted to know if she had ever obtained a restraining order against her husband, if she had ever taken him to court, if she had ever owned a weapon, if the two of us were close friends, if I knew how her husband had treated her and on and on."

"Sure. Those are natural kinds of questions to ask. Jeannie had a perfect motive."

Jeannie Devir looked her in the eye. "Do you believe us?"

"Yes, I do."

The young woman sighed deeply and sat back in her chair. "So what should we do?"

Ursula stood up and began to pace back and forth over the large Persian carpet that covered the floor of her office. "In the first place, stick to your story. If you change one iota of your testimony, you open yourself up to a whole new kind of interrogation. Keep telling yourself, over and over, that all you're guilty of is protecting the woman who saved your life. Because that's what you did. Finally, if the police get in touch with you again, call me. Right away. Understood?"

Jeannie Devir rose to her feet and held out her hand. "Understood. I have to get to work. Thank you, Ms. McGuire. Thank you, again."

Abby Whitman waited until the door had closed behind her friend. "Do you think the police have a chance of finding her?"

"Not if they're looking for a young brunette in a red dress. She left no evidence, no prints, no weapon. All they've got is the identical testimony of two intelligent young women and the drunken rantings of an old bum. Not much to go on. There are the bullets, of course."

"What can they tell from those?"

"Not a hell of a lot. Ballistics will show what kind of a gun it was fired from. If it's a rare kind of weapon, it might help them under certain circumstances."

Abby's eyes widened. "You mean if it were a special kind of gun, they could call all the local gun shops and see who bought one?"

Ursula smiled. "Well, it wouldn't be quite that simple; nevertheless, by the description of your lady, she sounds like someone who might have purchased a gun legally. She doesn't sound like the kind of person who would buy a weapon on the street. If she's got an odd kind of gun, the police can trace it to the number of people who bought it. On the other hand, if it's a commonly owned pistol that people buy for protection, then the cops don't have much to work with."

Abby looked around the office for a second. "There's something else I'd like to ask you."

"Sure."

"When I spoke to your husband outside of class, he made some amusing remarks about your political work. About how you spend too much of your time helping elect liberal Democrats. But I see from the business card here on your desk that your firm is an investigative one. So do you do criminal or political investigations?"

"We do both. In the late sixties and seventies, I worked for the district attorney's office here in Boston, and for the past fifteen years, my two colleagues and I have run our own firm. The office as a whole focuses on criminal work, but my specialty involves political investigations, what used to be known as opposition research in more innocent days. Politicians or their people come to me if they need to get information about an opposing candidate, or if they think the opposition is going to use something against them. Mark's crack about liberal

Democrats is wholly justified. When I work on criminal cases, I work for anyone. But when it comes to political cases, I work for the party I believe in."

Abby glanced away and then looked back at her. "If most of your own cases are political, what makes you choose particular criminal cases?"

"If the case itself is inherently interesting, or if I believe someone has been the victim of a clear injustice."

"How do feel about this case?"

"I think you know how I feel. If I didn't think you and Jeannie had done the right thing—the *moral* thing, as you put it—I would have advised you both to go right to the police and give them the correct description of that woman." Ursula smiled. "Abby, I can see that you're getting at something else. Why don't you just put it right on the table."

"Well, Ms. McGuire…"

"Ursula."

Abby laughed softly. "OK…Ursula. I guess what I'm getting at is something more substantial than a little free legal advice. First of all, I want to thank you once again for seeing Jeannie and me on such short notice. I know you're a busy woman. But secondly, as I sat here this morning and realized what it is you actually do for a living, something else has occurred to me. I wonder…let me put it bluntly. I wonder if I could hire you to find this woman."

Ursula stared at her. "Find her? I'm not so sure that's a great idea, Abby. I mean I can imagine the fascination you must have for her, and then, of course, there is the fact that she saved you from bodily harm…"

"That's exactly what I'm thinking. Maybe Devir wasn't through with me either. Maybe she saved my life too. I want to do something for this woman. I think it's pretty obvious she's been a victim herself."

Ursula nodded. Her instincts had told her the same thing. "What makes you say that?"

"Because she did not kill without reason. She killed to save another woman. And right after she saved that woman, she said it was all over, that he would never hurt her again. Then she said, 'You won't miss him at all.' Ursula, I think…"

"You think this woman is speaking from experience."

"Exactly. And that she might need help."

"But Abby, even granting the logic of your suppositions, what kind of help do you think you can offer her? You're studying to be a historian like my husband. You're not a psychiatrist or a social worker, and even if you were, you know nothing about this woman."

"That's where you come in."

"Well frankly, I think you've done her a great favor already by lying to the police. You've put yourself in a risky position. Maybe you've done enough. Maybe there are legal and even moral consequences to what you're thinking about here that you haven't considered—to say nothing about the financial aspect of this kind of investigation."

"Finances are no problem."

"No problem? Abby…"

"I know. I'm perfectly aware of the expenses surrounding legal transactions. I've been involved in a number of them. When I graduated from Stanford, I wanted to make some money so I didn't have to be one of those poverty-stricken graduate students when the time came. Right after graduation, I spent a summer working for a start-up company, and in the fall they were bought out by Cisco and I went with them. At first, the salary wasn't the greatest but they gave me a lot of stock options. In four years the company let us sell the options, and I invested about a quarter of the money into part ownership of a bar I had worked at during my senior year, a quarter in the stock market and half in Treasuries. I arrived in Boston this summer with assets of more than $300,000."

Ursula shook her head. "In the sixties the stock market was the last thing we ever thought about."

"Well, you had Vietnam and civil rights and the cultural revolution and God knows what else."

"Mmm…well, it wasn't just that. We were abysmally ignorant of economics. It wasn't until I started this firm in the late seventies that I began to understand what business and money were all about. But we're getting off course here and I've got another client in ten minutes."

Abby stood up and smiled and slung her purse over her shoulder. "Another client? Does that mean I'm a client?"

Ursula laughed at the young woman's persistence and held up her hands. "I didn't say you were my client, young lady." It struck her immediately that she had never called anyone "young lady" before, and she wondered what made her do it. It was something one of her maiden aunts might say. "Let's just say I'll think about it."

But Ursula had already thought about it, and the second Abby closed the door, she buzzed her secretary. "Lily, can you call Mr. Rosario at his work number?"

"Right away, Ursie."

A minute later, one of her phone buttons lit up. She picked up the receiver. "Hello, Ursula. Rob's in class right now, but I'll have him call you. Any message?"

"Yes, Linda, there is. Tell him I have a job for him. She's blonde, beautiful, and dangerous. Sounds like a bit of cliché, doesn't it?"

Linda laughed. "Well, yes, but it also sounds like something that might pique his interest, although you never know. With all the complaining he's been doing recently about getting old, I don't know if a blonde will be enough of a draw anymore."

Ursula stood up and stepped over to the window and looked down across Beacon Street at the Common. "Ah, he goes through that every fall, especially right before his birthday."

CHAPTER 3

Robert Rosario paused at the corner of Ash and Brattle Streets and looked up at the evening sky. A flock of red, yellow and dark green leaves twisted and turned in the wind and blew across the steeple of St. John's Memorial Chapel. He breathed deeply, inhaling the crisp, clear autumn air and followed the old brick sidewalk along Mason Street and crossed over into the Cambridge Common. All around him, young men in their twenties and thirties raced back and forth across the field, running football plays and tossing long, leisurely passes. One of them flew off course and sailed high over Rosario's shoulder. Instinctively, he ran back and pulled it down. Then he turned quickly, sidestepped an imaginary tackler and drilled a spiral into the hands of a stranger downfield. The kid laughed and gave him a thumbs-up.

When he reached the corner of Chauncy Street, Ursula McGuire was waiting for him. "Right on time as usual, Rosie."

"That's right."

"Everything's always scheduled right down to the last minute."

"You got it. And coming out on a Monday night is not on my schedule."

"You sorry?"

"Nah, I needed a break from all the correcting. I spent half of Sunday on kids' papers." He looked at her and smiled. "You seemed excited on the phone. It's been a long time since I've seen you step outside the boundaries of your professional responsibilities."

She nodded. "Maybe a little too long."

"So where do we start?"

"Right here." She pointed across Mass Ave at a row of five small stores. "The first establishment on the left, Fancy Fingers, is open until 8:00 on Friday nights."

"What is that place, anyway? Chinese take-out?"

She stared at him in astonishment. "Chinese take-out! What the hell are you talking about? It's a nail salon! Gee, I'm really glad I asked you to help me out on this one. I thought you knew every inch of the area around the Square."

"Well, I guess I just never spend any time on that block."

"Well, you should. There are some thoughtful gifts in Looks in case you ever decide to go out with a woman again, and The Three Aces has some of your favorite beers on tap."

"I'll take the beer."

She looked at him and frowned. "What's going on with you, anyway?"

"What do you mean?"

"I haven't seen you with a woman in a long time. A real long time."

"I'm downsizing my life."

Ursula laughed out loud. "When did you ever upsize?"

24

He ignored the question. "So Fancy Fingers closes at eight. From what you said on the phone, that was the time of death, right?"

"Approximately."

"So what about The Three Aces?"

"Open late, naturally. But no one there recalls seeing our blonde."

"Well, that doesn't surprise me. If the drunk guy was right, she walked down Wendell Street away from Mass Ave. Now, that makes sense. Coming back to Mass Ave doesn't. Why would she walk away from Mass Ave, cut over behind all those houses and apartment buildings, and then re-emerge here?"

"Because she had to cross Mass Ave somewhere to get home."

Rosario stared at her. "Home? Are you telling me you already know where she lives? In one day you found that out? So, what the hell do you need me for?"

She smiled and then looked back across the street. "I don't *know* anything yet. I'm simply eliminating possibilities. Now bear with me for a moment. The Central Barbershop closes at four, the Crimson Cleaners closes at six, and Looks closes at seven."

"All too early. So there you go."

"Not quite. Although Mrs. Tang, the lady who runs Fancy Fingers, closes at 8:00, she was still in the shop cleaning and locking up at 8:30."

"And?"

Ursula glanced away from the row of buildings and looked into his eyes. "And that's when she saw her."

"Saw her for sure?"

"Well, nothing's ever for sure. But she saw a beautiful blonde woman wearing a silver dress pause in front of her shop around 8:20 or so and then cross Mass Ave toward Chauncy Street. Then the blonde woman paused once again at this corner, and after glancing back over her shoulder toward the scene of the crime, she walked rapidly down this sidewalk toward Harvard Square."

"Half of Cambridge lies beyond the corner of Chauncy Street and Massachusetts Avenue. Just because she slipped away from all the chaos back at the scene of the shooting and emerged here doesn't mean she lives in the neighborhood."

She put her arm in his and they walked along together. "I've covered every store and business from Jarvis Street to Linnaean Street on both sides of Mass Ave except one. The only person who's spotted our blonde was the proprietor of Fancy Fingers."

"What's the place you missed?"

"Chez Henri."

"Why Chez Henri?"

"Because that's where we're going to dinner this evening. I'm going to mix a little business with pleasure. Besides, Mark invited Abby Whitman when I told him I had asked you to join us."

He shook his head. Ursula McGuire had a long and unfortunate history of trying to fix him up with women, and he always knew when she was headed down that road. Luckily, he had become an expert in heading her off at the pass. "Oh, is that so? *Mark* invited her, right?"

She smiled enigmatically. "Yes, he did."

"You mean after you suggested it to him." They crossed Langdon Street. "Look, Ursula. This kind of thing was tolerable when we were in our thirties, but..."

"Our thirties? You found it quite intolerable when we were still in our twenties!"

The rush hour traffic heading into Harvard Square was louder along this section of Mass Ave and he raised his voice. "But we're almost fifty now! You said this girl was still in her twenties. I'm old enough to be her father. What are you thinking? I'm not interested in women that young and you know it."

"Abby's twenty-eight. That's almost thirty. Besides, you know how some of these graduate students have a thing for older guys."

"Yeah, well not *this* old."

"Will you cut it out? You're forty-nine, not eighty-nine."

"Look, Ursula. It's way too old for a kid that age, and since when have you been an advocate of hooking up older men with young women? This is a new wrinkle, isn't it?" He stopped and grabbed her by the shoulders. "Wait a second here. Hold on. Now I get it. You didn't call me to help you with this case. You're trying to hook me up with this little chickie because you think she's got the hots for Mark. And you're jealous. I've never seen you jealous before."

"OK, OK! I've never been almost fifty before either."

"Oh, so I'm not the only one who's concerned about my age."

"Concerned? You call that neurosis a concern? I think a pathological obsession would be more like it!"

He laughed. "I can't believe you're jealous. Come on, Ursie. Forget about it. Everyone I know thinks you're beautiful. Didn't you see those two guys just check you out when they walked by?"

"What two guys?"

"Those two fat guys in the sweaty undershirts."

She leaned back and laughed. "You bastard."

"I'm kidding. I mean those two yuppie guys in the suits who just crossed Mass Ave."

"Those two? The ones with the Romney signs? They're pretty cute. What am I hanging around with a couple of old geezers like you and Mark for?"

"Beats me."

She looked back again and folded her arms. "Listen, in the first place, I did not tell Mark to invite this young lady. Secondly, I'm not trying to use you as a decoy to ward off any case of middle-aged jealousy. I really do want you in on this case."

They walked a little more and then stopped at the corner of Shepard Street in front of Marathon Sports. Rosario looked across Mass Ave at the corner of Wendell Street where a line of people waited at the Bank Boston ATM machine. To the left were The National Bank and the popular local bar where this Abby Whitman worked. Next to the bar was Canterbury's, an old used bookstore he and Mark had frequented for years. And between those two buildings was the alley where this blonde stranger, this woman Ursula was after, had fired three shots into one Charles Devir. Ursula had only given him the bare outlines of the case over the phone, and so far, based on what he had heard, he couldn't work up much of an appetite for tracking the woman down. From what he understood about the victim, the son of a bitch got what he deserved.

She grabbed his arm again and led him down Shepard Street toward the dark red facade of Chez Henri. "After we finish dinner, I'm going to rely on you to get Mark and Abby out to the street so I can talk to the bartender."

"Why?"

"Because I think this was where the killer was before she shot Devir."

He opened his hands in exasperation. "Based on what?"

"Based on what she was wearing." She stopped and gestured around them. "Name one other place in this neighborhood where people dress up to dine on a weekend evening."

"Well, you've got me there, but she could have been at a party."

"Possibly." They reached the front door and she turned and lowered her voice. "Just remember. Don't say anything in front of this girl about what we've discussed."

"That'll be easy. We haven't discussed a hell of a lot. Except your jealousy, that is."

He laughed and opened the door for her, and she snarled at him in a fierce whisper. "Knock it off, Rosario. I am *not* jealous."

At the bar people sipped drinks, waiting for their tables, and in the dining room against the far wall, he saw Mark and his graduate student drinking wine and talking. He wasn't particularly impressed. She looked like a million other pretty young women. But he decided to play her up to get Ursula's goat. "Wow!"

"What do you mean, *Wow*? She's not *that* great."

"Are you kidding? She's something else. Man, am I glad you set this thing up."

"I did not set anything up."

"I apologize for everything I've said about you trying to fix me up over the years. By the way, she's really showing a lot of leg in that skirt, isn't she?"

"Shut up."

Mark saw them and waved and Rosario waved back. "Am I imagining things or does Mark have his hand on her thigh?"

She went to dig her elbow into his ribs but he grabbed it and steered her toward the table. Mark rose from his chair and kissed his wife. "Rob, this is Abby Whitman, one of my students. Abby, Rob is a history teacher. You have something in common."

Abby Whitman took his hand and he sat down next to her. Before he could say anything, Ursula waved the waiter over. "I've just spent ten minutes in the company of an old fool, and I need a glass of wine as quickly as possible."

Mark smiled at him from across the table. "I see there's been the usual clash of personalities."

Rosario shrugged. "Not really. Just a little disagreement about Ursula's current state of emotional well-being."

Ursula shot him another look and flung her hand into the air as if she were dismissing an annoying child. "That will be enough of that." Then she smiled at the waiter. "I'll have a glass of Chardonnay, and that elderly moron over there will probably want a quart bottle of Bud to gurgle on."

Rosario smiled. "I'll have a glass of your Pinot Gris." When the waiter left, he turned to Abby Whitman. "You'll have to forgive Ursula. She gets a little testy after 6:00. It's part of the aging process."

Mark held up his hands. "OK, you guys." He looked across at Abby. "They've been fighting for over thirty-five years."

Abby's eyes widened. "That's a long time. Do you always argue about age?"

Rosario looked at her. "Just recently."

Ursula snorted. "Yeah, like the last twenty years. Rob had to be sedated on his thirtieth birthday."

Abby smiled at him, and now that he had a good look at her, he had to admit that she really was quite attractive. She frowned a little and said, "I guess your whole generation is kind of hung up about your age now, isn't it?"

He nodded. "Except for your professor over there. He seems to glide through decade after decade with hardly a wistful moment."

"And is that what you are? Wistful?"

She was certainly very direct. He shrugged again. "At times, sure. Who isn't?"

"I think that's because your generation lived through such interesting times. Actually, I thought my times were pretty boring. Until last Friday night."

When the waiter returned with the wine, he asked if they were ready to order. Rosario chose the grilled lamb chops and Mark selected a halibut stuffed with curried Caribbean crab, but Abby seemed undecided, so she allowed Ursula to guide her through the menu. Rosario observed the two women as they talked and went through the small physical gestures of a dinner discussion, and he suddenly realized he was comparing them. There was no denying Abby Whitman's young, athletic, all-American looks. Her tanned skin, her clear brown eyes, and her sunny, straw-colored hair were all enough to attract any man. Yet there was something missing that Rosario could not quite put his finger on. At first, he thought it might have something to do with that combination of beauty and intelligence and independence that was so much a part of Ursula's appeal. But Abby Whitman certainly appeared to have those qualities as well, and after all, it was hardly fair to judge her after a five-minute acquaintance. He was having a hard time trying to put it into words for himself. Ursula leaned toward Abby, her black hair touching her shoulders and her blue eyes focused intently on the menu. He had to smile. He couldn't imagine why she should ever be jealous. The younger woman, attractive as she was, simply couldn't hold a candle to her.

CHAPTER 4

U rsula was still on top of him, leaning back with her hands planted firmly on the bed. Mark opened one eye and smiled at her. "I guess I'll have to take you to Chez Henri more often."

She pushed herself forward and pressed her open palms down onto his shoulders. "Next time without the little chippie."

He laughed. "Little chippie! I thought she might like to meet Rob."

"Rob's too old for her, and so are *you*."

He leaned up on his elbows and looked into her eyes. "What is this? Jealousy? After all this time?"

"Not really. I guess I just get a little tired of seeing all these adoring young women circling around you year after year like shapely little satellites."

"Me too," he grinned. "It's awful! So what about you? What about all the men who've lusted after you? The horny clerks at the courthouses. The attorneys. The pols."

"Boors every one, and you know it."

"You know what else I know? Jealousy does not become you." He chuckled. "By the way, Rob did a pretty smooth job whisking Abby and me out on the street after dinner. So are you going to fill me in or not?"

"Well, you haven't given me much of a chance. I was hardly through the bedroom door when you assaulted me."

He laughed. "Why do I remember it the other way around?"

She ran her hand through his hair and kissed him. "The elderly often remember things backwards." Then she stretched out on her back and began her story.

———

U rsula had deliberately chosen Monday night to eat at Chez Henri not only because she was eager to move quickly on her investigation, but also because she knew that Karl Hamilton would be tending bar.

"Hey, Ursula. I didn't see you come in. The bar's been packed solid. I think it's the election. Nobody gets too worked up in the off years, but this challenge Romney's throwing at Kennedy is exciting people. He's really giving your old pal Teddy a run for his money. The latest poll I saw has them dead even. When's the last time a Republican ever did that? And all this scuttlebutt about Clinton coming to town to campaign for him? That shows he's in trouble. So, what'll you have?"

Under normal circumstances, Karl's needling would have elicited an instantaneous response. But tonight she needed to be nice. "A glass of Sauvignon Blanc and a little information." She leaned forward. "You still work Friday nights, don't you?"

"Sure—oh, it's about Friday. My God! You know it was so noisy in here we didn't even hear the shots."

She smiled and patted his hand. "That's not what I'm interested in."

He poured her wine and leaned on the bar. "The cops sure were. Two of them in here looking for a brunette in a red dress."

"So I hear. No, actually I'm looking for a blonde, and from what I understand, an extremely beautiful one."

Karl smiled. "Actually, there was a really dynamite woman in here Friday night. Is this one of your political cases? You know I can't help you there. True to my Reaganite principles, I never speak ill of another Republican."

She laughed. "I have no idea which party this woman belongs to. This is purely non-ideological. It's just a missing persons case, and from what I've learned it's really all a big misunderstanding. One of those stories where a wife isn't really missing at all but took off for the weekend in a huff. That kind of thing."

Karl frowned and shook his head. "Well, this one was with two other women. On the way out of the dining room, one of them suggested a nightcap. So they each ordered a glass of wine and sat at the bar and talked shop. They were in some completely incomprehensible business from what I could gather."

"Incomprehensible how?"

"At first I thought they might be computer geeks or high-tech folks from some Kendall Square company, but these ladies worked in Harvard Square. That much I did understand. And they had something to do with medicine or hospitals."

"Hospitals? Not in the Square. Did they mention the name of a company or an organization of some kind?"

"Nope."

"Anything else catch your attention? Anything odd or significant in any way?"

He burst out laughing. "Actually there was. One of them, a chick with curly red hair, plopped a gigantic book the size of the Manhattan phone directory on the bar. I started kidding her about it so she opened it up and spun it around and gave me a peek. Not exactly bedtime reading, let me tell you. Lines of numbers alongside bunches of phrases. I only caught a glance in between mixing drinks, but they were medical phrases. I do, however, remember the name of the book. It was a catchy title."

Ursula tried to contain a swell of enthusiasm. "And the title was?"

"ICD-9-CM."

"What?"

Karl laughed again. "You got it. I was actually curious by this time, but the redhead and the third woman had to leave."

"This was around what time?"

"Oh, probably quarter of eight or so. The blonde stayed behind for a while to finish her drink. I tried to strike up a little conversation, but she wasn't exactly pleasant."

"Was she rude? Antagonistic?"

"No. Just cold. And it wasn't just me, either. A guy came in alone right after her friends left and tried to pick her up. Laid all kind of compliments on her and got nothing in return. I mean *nothing.* He was a pretty suave, sophisticated guy, too. Didn't use obvious pick-up lines. The way she stared at him stopped him dead in his tracks. Whew! If looks could kill, believe me. Then she paid her bill and walked out."

"And that was it?"

"That was it."

Ursula paused for a second, deciding exactly how to phrase the next question. "One more thing, Karl. Was this woman wearing a light blue sweater and black pants?"

Karl pushed himself away from the bar. "Well, that does it, Ursula. She's definitely not your woman. This one was wearing a silver dress. A damn sexy silver dress, too. I'd recognize it anywhere."

———

Mark smiled down at her and put his hand on her hip. "I'll bet you were just smiling ear to ear when you left Chez Henri."

"You bet I was, professor. You bet I was. Except, of course, for the mysterious ICD-9-CM."

"An easily solved research problem, I would imagine. Now I just have one question."

She raised an eyebrow and stared up at him. "And that might be?"

"Do you think this is an isolated event?"

"You mean do I think she's some kind of a stalker? A woman who goes around knocking off abusive men?"

"It has occurred to me."

"Uh, huh. Me too. But for that you need some more bodies, don't you?"

He laughed softly. "Yes, I guess you do." He slid his right thigh between hers and kissed her behind the ear. "Maybe I should concentrate more on this body."

She laughed and turned away from him on her side and looked back over her shoulder. "Well, maybe you just should."

———

O n Wednesday evening, Ursula McGuire left her office at 6:00, walked home to her townhouse on Chestnut Street, changed into shorts, T-shirt, and walking shoes, and hurried down Charles Street and up the stone stairway to the MBTA stop. She was just in time to leap on board the Cambridge-bound car as it lurched forward and started across the Longfellow Bridge. Fifteen minutes later, when the train reached Harvard Square, she dove into the crowd as it rushed for the doors, walking swiftly along the platform, and then climbing the stairs to Church Street.

Rosario was waiting for her in front of the old Unitarian church at the corner, and they walked quickly down to the end of the block and crossed Garden Street into the Common. He waited until they had passed the playground. "OK, counselor, what did you come up with? You sounded pretty exhilarated on the phone."

Circling around, they saw the Hotel Commander on their right and then the playing field where a football game was in progress. "I'm getting close, Rosie. Damn close. I started with the gun. With Arturo Suarez at the Middlesex County Medical Examiner's Office."

"Suarez do the Devir autopsy?"

"Not personally, but everything goes through him. The cause of death was gunshot wounds to the heart and the brain. A third bullet was found in the lower abdomen. All three were .380 caliber bullets, meaning they were fired from a semi-automatic pistol which, of course, helps us a great deal."

"Why?"

"Because most people who buy guns legally for protection go for the revolver. The chances of malfunction are practically nil. This information narrows the field of inquiry consider-ably. So what I needed to find were women who purchased firearms in the last few years and who live in Cambridge. We have to start somewhere, and I can always work backwards if necessary."

"You didn't get the Cambridge police to give you that information. They're already looking for a woman like that. They'd get to her before you and you'd look suspicious as hell running a parallel investigation, and gun sellers won't cooperate with you either. They can't give out that kind of information."

"Right."

"So who the hell..."

"In the Commonwealth of Massachusetts all requests for gun ownership and gun license renewal go directly to the town or city police chief; however, most of that data are then forwarded to the Firearms Record Bureau of the Public Safety Department, where it just so happens that..."

"Yeah, yeah, yeah...I just remembered. Where Anne Marie Donnelly works. Is there any place in this state where you don't have some Irish Catholic bureaucrat hanging around just waiting to give you information?"

She glanced over at him and laughed. "As a matter of fact there is. The Cambridge Police Department and local gun sellers for two. But back on track. I now learn that there are eighteen women living in Cambridge who have purchased a gun within the last two years. Furthermore, I have their names, dates of birth, addresses, and occupations. What I don't have, unfortunately, are the makes of their weapons or the reasons they gave for purchasing the firearm. That info remains in the hands of the town or city chief of police. So for the moment I'm screwed on the gun front. But I've got five women in their twenties, three in their thirties, and seven in their sixties."

"What happened to the ones our age?"

"The police wouldn't approve the permits. All the ones approaching fifty were so depressed about getting old, the cops figured they'd turn the guns on themselves."

She looked at him again and saw that he was laughing. They finished the full circle around the Common and he picked up the pace a bit. "So you've hit a dead end."

She smiled. "Dead end via the gun route. Another route leads us to Rebecca Scott, age forty-six, clinical data manager at Pharmaceutical Data Research in Harvard Square, lives on Chauncy Street, which is the street, you'll recall, that Mrs. Tang at Fancy Fingers saw the beautiful blonde lady head toward as she crossed Mass Ave."

"As I recall Mrs. Tang's words, as reported to me by one Ursula McGuire, a great stickler for detail, the lady in question *paused* at the corner of Chauncy Street and headed toward Harvard Square. She could have been heading for her car or for a cab that could have taken her anywhere."

"Well, that's where Chez Henri comes in."

By the time she had finished telling him about her talk with Karl Hamilton, they had been around the Common two more times. "So this book is...ICD what?"

"ICD-9-CM is a numerical classification of all the diseases in the world. It's used by hospitals and contract research organizations, called CRO's. Basically, pharmaceutical companies outsource clinical research trials to CRO's so they don't have to manage them in-house. Since the bartender told me the three women work somewhere in Harvard Square, it was pretty simple to find their place of employment. The company is right around the corner of Brattle on that little street where the upscale furniture store is."

"Story Street."

"That's it. PDR's offices occupy the floor above them. So I did a little fake furniture shopping and learned that PDR has no cafeteria. No cafeteria means the staff eats lunch in the Square somewhere. Further fake shopping led to the discovery that most of PDR's employees break around 12:30. I simply waited for this Rebecca Scott to come out for her lunch hour."

"And?"

"And Bingo. Out comes this lovely looking blonde woman..."

There was a hint of annoyance in his voice. "All dressed in silver with a silver purse packing a very convenient gun."

"Stop making it seem as if this whole thing is falling into my lap."

"Look, you did your groundwork. I'm not disparaging you. But just because she's a nice looking blonde doesn't mean..."

"She's a little better than nice looking. She's drop dead gorgeous." Ursula paused a moment. "The strange thing is she looks like Eve. In fact, when she first stepped out of the building I thought it *was* Eve. At any rate, she's gorgeous."

"Fine, fine. She's gorgeous. That doesn't prove..."

"Rosie, listen to me. I've got her leaving the bar at Chez Henri wearing a silver dress minutes before the shooting."

"But that's not proof."

"No, it's not. Not yet. That's where you come in."

"Where I come in?"

"Uh, huh. I want you to meet her. Casually, of course. I need to know if Rebecca Scott ever lived anywhere other than Cambridge during the past several years."

"What for?"

"Because if she's our girl, she's either carrying an illegal piece, or she purchased a gun in a city or town other than Cambridge."

"It strikes me that an enterprising investigator who can almost wrap up a case in two days ought to be able to find out something as simple as that without involving one of her best friends with an apparently very dangerous woman."

She laughed. "Obviously, I don't want you to get involved with her."

"I won't. Don't worry."

"It's just that I may want to know a number of other things that a personal encounter or two might yield."

"A personal encounter? I'm certainly not going to ask her anything that might compromise her position at work or in any other area of her life. So if that's what you're after, forget it."

"Have I ever asked you to compromise someone's position?"

"Yes. Many times."

She laughed again. "You must be thinking of some other investigator."

"I don't think so. Besides, women are dangerous enough without guns."

"Oh, here we go. Women are dangerous. Women are..."

She tripped over a loose brick in the sidewalk, and he grabbed her by the arm to steady her. "And *some* women are pretty clumsy."

She pushed him away, striding ahead and sidestepping several slow-moving pedestrians. At the corner of Chauncy Street and Mass Ave she turned left with Rosario right on her heels, and as they approached the end of the road, she nodded to her right at a small, neat, two-story wooden house tucked away between a tall brick apartment building and a pink Victorian. "Look fast, Rosie. That's her place right there."

They turned right on Garden, headed out toward Huron Avenue, and then doubled back until they had rounded the corner of Brattle and Craigie Streets. He glanced over at her. "How did you find out where she lived?"

"I followed her home. She's so close to work she goes home for lunch."

"Lucky for you."

"Why do you keep stressing the luck angle here? What about skill?"

"Because you need to remain humble. You need to keep that big brain of yours in check sometimes. So now, as I understand it, it's all up to me."

She shook her head impatiently. "No, it's not *all* up to you. But I would like your help. So what do you say?"

"I think I can handle it."

"Good. I figure it fits right in with your plan to stay totally uninvolved with the opposite sex now that you're an old guy."

"I never said anything about being totally uninvolved."

"Well, tangentially involved. How's that?"

"That's good. I like that."

"I don't know, Rosie. Sometimes I worry whether you still have the capacity to allow yourself the possibility that someday you might fall in love again. That's about the best way I can put it."

"You know what?"

"What?"

"You're a hopeless romantic. You talk as if people our age have the same emotional capacity to go gaga over each other that they did at seventeen or twenty-seven. Well, I don't think they do. You're blinded by the fact that you've been in love with the same person for your whole adult life. Most of us haven't had that experience. Most of us have had relationships that—no matter how intense for the time they've lasted—have ended, and it colors the way we look at things and eventually makes us less capable of that kind of blind faith you need to really fall in love again."

"I think that's sad."

"I don't. It might have been sad when we were younger. But now? Now it's just a question of accepting life for what it is."

"You just don't want any personal responsibilities anymore."

"Well, you're right there. I like my life just the way it is."

"You like your life. But do you love your life?"

He stopped at Berkeley Street and stared at her. "Love my life? What the hell are you talking about?" A seedy-looking academic in a rumpled suit with a backpack and an armful of books strolled by them. Rob accosted him. "Do you love your life?"

He took the question completely in stride. "Of course, I don't. What an odd notion."

Rob grinned at her. "See?"

Ursula watched the man amble away. "Nice example, Rosario. A real representative sample of humanity if I ever saw one."

"Well, remember, you're in the general vicinity of Harvard Square. He might be more representative than you think. Now, come on. We've got three more miles to go."

CHAPTER 5

For many years now, Rosario had used the solid, spacious tables of Harvard's Gutman Library to correct student papers, develop curriculum and plan lessons. But danger lurks in the Gutman. A languid line of dark red couches beckons from the big windows overlooking Brattle Street. Shaped like chairs so as to give the illusion of functional furniture, they are really more like cushy sofas—wide, soft, and absurdly comfortable. Anyone foolhardy enough to leave the purposeful atmosphere of the tables and venture forth to this area must relinquish the notion of serious work. Any intention of studying or even indulging in casual reading, leads to a kind of contemplative stupor, where the unwary victim sits ape-like and slack-jawed, gaping at the endless parade of humanity moving in and out of Harvard Square. Within seconds, eyelids grow heavy. Within minutes—oblivion.

Today, however, one of these couches afforded Rosario a perfect view of the corner of Brattle and Story Streets, where, he calculated, Rebecca Scott would most likely appear on her way home from Pharmaceutical Data Research. According to Ursula, PDR closed around 6:00. According to the big clock on the wall of the Gutman, it was now 5:40. He had plenty of time. He removed the *New York Times* from the newspaper rack and settled in to wait. Sometime later, as he emerged from a soporific state, he saw it was 6:07.

He was outside in a minute, walking rapidly down Appian Way, taking a left on Brattle and then stopping at the corner of Farwell Place. He crossed Brattle and stood near the corner of Story Street in front of Cafe India. Turning slightly to his right, he caught the smell of tandoori chicken, and that made him think of the chicken tikka masala and the samosas at Bombay Club, his favorite Indian restaurant. Then he thought of the cold white wine he always drank there, the Riesling from Washington State, and he had half a mind to forget this whole thing and go indulge himself. After all, he had worked out hard at Mike's Gym last night and put in his five-mile walk the previous evening with Ursula. She had gotten so indignant after their argument about love and romance in the declining years, that she outdid herself and they walked an extra mile at top speed.

He smiled to himself and when he turned, Rebecca Scott was heading straight at him. There was simply no chance it could be anyone else. She was blonde, she was stunning, and she was carrying two large flat rectangular packing boxes stamped with the initials PDR in big block letters. Her purse hung from her left shoulder, and the expression on her face, as she got closer, was one of barely controlled anger, as if lugging these big unwieldy packages was turning out to be the last straw on a particularly bad day. She was six feet away now, and he still couldn't take his eyes off her. She stopped right in front of him and let the big flat cartons touch the sidewalk. "Didn't anyone ever tell you that it's rude to stare? Do you always look at women like that?"

"Actually, I don't. I apologize." He wracked his brain for an excuse, but all he could come up with was a cliché. "But you look so much like someone I used to know."

"That's an old line."

"Well, I'm an old guy."

"Look, I don't have the time for..."

This was ridiculous. Beautiful or not, he didn't need this. Not at this age. "Me neither. So I apologize for staring at you, and I hope you have a good evening. End of story, OK?"

"OK."

As she hoisted the giant rectangles off the ground, a young couple, arm in arm and deep in conversation, hurried past them. The young woman carried a box of Romney stickers and her companion clutched several signs. Inadvertently, he bumped into one of the rectangles. Rebecca Scott glared at them. "Watch where you're going you...you religious fanatics!"

The couple stopped and turned, utterly unaware of what they could have done to incur such hostility. Finally, the girl opened her mouth. "What are you talking about? What do you mean, religious fanatics? Because we support a moderate Republican, we're fanatics?"

Rebecca Scott snarled at her. "He's a Mormon, isn't he? They're pretty fanatic. You might want to check out their attitude toward women."

"Listen, lady. I'm a Catholic. I grew up hearing about all the religious prejudice directed against JFK. This election will be decided on issues, not prejudice. Ted Kennedy's been in office too long. It's time for some new blood."

Her companion stared at Rebecca Scott. "I'm curious, madam. Are you a Kennedy supporter?"

"Certainly not."

"Yet you dismiss Romney on the basis of bigotry. What's your case against Senator Kennedy?"

"It's rather simple, young man. He's just another liberal blowhard. OK?"

The couple backed off, retreating in the face of her unrelenting animosity. It was time for Rosario to leave, and yet something held him. Against his better judgment, he spoke to her again. "Well, I must say, you certainly articulated a reasonable rationale for the independent voter. Would you like some help with one of those things?"

She sighed. "Look, you don't seem like a bad guy, OK? I'm just trying to get home, and I'm also just trying to find a way to tell you not to try to pick me up, because it isn't going to work."

"I'm not trying to pick you up. You're way too angry for me. When I offered to help you carry whatever the hell those things are you're carrying, that's *all* I meant. It seems to me that one more block with those two crates, and you're going to have a major temper tantrum."

She stared at him for what seemed a long time. Then she handed him one of the boxes. Not an ounce of tension had disappeared from her face. Not a sign of a softening in her features. Without a word, without an exchange of mutual glances, they started to walk down Brattle Street together. Inside Cafe of India, normal people were laughing and talking and enjoying their dinner. They passed the Blacksmith House where several couples, looking even more normal than the last group, sat outside in the cool autumn evening enjoying a cup of coffee and a quiet conversation.

They crossed Hilliard Street and walked along the brick sidewalk in front of the Loeb Drama Center. Finally, she spoke to him again. "So, what's this woman's name? The one you think looks so much like me?"

"Eve Taylor." The name came quickly to Rosario's lips, for he had been in love with a woman named Eve Taylor many years before. Like Rebecca Scott, she was both blonde and beautiful. But the resemblance ended there.

"Maybe I should look her up to test your story."

"Maybe you should."

"Do you just hang around Harvard Square trying to pick up women?"

"No, I live around here."

She stopped in front of the expansive lawn of the old Greenleaf mansion. "Really? Where?"

He glanced at her hands and noticed there was no wedding ring. Then he looked into her eyes and pointed over her shoulder across the yard. "Back there."

She turned and looked. "Back there?"

"That's right."

"Now I know you're a liar."

"Really. Why is that?"

"Because the president of Radcliffe lives in that building."

He laughed. "I can assure you I don't live with the president of Radcliffe. I said back there, as in back of the president of Radcliffe's house. A little road called Ash Street Place. That's where I live." He pointed across the grass through the trees. "So, you see? No lie."

She nodded her head. "Do you like arguing with women?"

"Sometimes, but you're a bit much. Women normally don't pick fights with me in the first two minutes of conversation. They usually wait until they discover all the personality traits that rub them the wrong way."

It was difficult to tell what she thought of this last remark. There was no reaction. Not a hint of anything in her eyes or her mouth or the way she carried herself. She simply looked at him with a kind of potentially explosive wariness and then gestured toward the other side of the street. They crossed Brattle and went into the soft green beauty of Radcliffe Yard, passing Buckingham House. Suddenly, a crowd of women, clutching books and briefcases, bustled out of the Schlesinger Library and swarmed around them, talking excitedly. Rosario waited to see if another collision with the rectangles was imminent, but the chattering scholars navigated skillfully and flew up the steps to Longfellow Hall.

Rebecca Scott sneered. "A flock of feminists, no doubt."

Rosario laughed. "What makes you say that?"

"Isn't that what they do in The Schlesinger Library? Talk and study about women's issues while the rest of us women work for a living?"

He looked into her eyes again. They were beautiful eyes. *Arresting* was the word that flashed through his mind. At first he thought they were pale blue, but now he realized they were gray with an almost silver tint to them. He smiled. "Well! This has been a productive outing. We've taken care of the Mormons, Ted Kennedy, predatory middle-aged men, and now the feminists. Whose next?"

"Well, you never know." She tossed her blonde hair and glanced at him. "Give me a second and I'll come up with someone else."

Ahead of them, across the Common and looming up out of the trees, the stone tower of the Harvard-Epworth Church rose into a violet sky. They walked down the path through the gate and turned left on Garden Street, crossing Mason and passing the First Church in Cambridge and the Hotel Commander. All the while, not a word was spoken between them. At Berkeley, she nodded and they crossed Garden near the Longy School of Music and came to a stop at the corner of Chauncy Street.

"Well, thank you, Mr...."

"Rosario. Robert Rosario."

"Thank you, Mr. Rosario. My name is Rebecca Scott."

"You're welcome, Ms. Scott."

Suddenly, something down the road caught her eye. She glanced at him quickly. "Please...could you watch these cartons for just one minute?"

She grabbed her purse and ran swiftly down the road to where a teenage boy and girl stood shouting at each other. In an instant, Rebecca Scott forced her way between them and pushed the boy off the curb, sending him stumbling into the street. Then he was back on the curb yelling at her. Rosario grasped both packages. All he heard as he moved in on them was Rebecca Scott's warning to stay away from her daughter, and the boy's cocky, defiant, obscene threats that he could do whatever he wanted. Rosario leaned the cartons against a tree and went after him.

He grappled the kid by his left arm and spun him around, bending his wrist behind his back and frogmarching him down the sidewalk. The boy struggled under his grip, craning his neck to look back at Rosario, his rage building as he swore and screamed and tried to break away. But Rosario held him tightly and kept prodding him along Chauncy Street toward Mass Ave. "Let me go, you fuckhead!"

"Sorry, I don't respond to bad language."

"I can do whatever I want to with..."

"Not with me around, you can't."

"Who the hell do you think you are? You aren't her father. He's not around. Who are you that you think you can..."

They reached the corner of Langdon Street and Rosario shoved him to the ground. "I'm her uncle."

The kid sprawled on the sidewalk glaring up at him. "What uncle? From Newton? I never heard of any uncle."

"Uncle Fuckhead. I'm surprised they never told you. And if I see you anywhere near that house again or if you so much as touch that girl, I'll kick your ass all over Cambridge."

"Maybe the cops would like to know about how you assault minors."

"Maybe they would. But I've got two witnesses back there. What have you got?"

Rosario stood over him, waiting for any challenge, but the kid rose slowly and then retreated to the crowded safety of Mass Ave.

Rosario walked back down Chauncy Street where Rebecca Scott was waiting alone. She crossed her arms and looked into his eyes. "What happened?"

"I just pushed him around a little. Told him he'd have to deal with me if he touched your daughter again."

"You shouldn't make threats you won't deliver on."

"What makes you think I won't?"

"Because you're a complete and utter stranger to me."

"Well, you're right there. But since I've already threatened him, I guess I've sort of backed myself into a corner, haven't I?" He reached into his wallet and found a card from Bombay Club. He wrote his name and phone number on the back and handed it to her. "If he gives you trouble again, call me. Or try the Cambridge Police Department."

She shook her head. "Not the police. The police are not much help when it comes to protecting women from violent men. Look, I don't quite know how to put this, but first of all, thank you. I appreciate your pulling him away from me like that, and secondly, and I hope I don't sound ungrateful—because I am grateful, believe me—but I hope you don't think that because of all this you can..."

"I can what?"

She looked up at him, a fierce beauty shining through her hard, gray eyes. "That you can use this as an opening."

"An opening? You're a tough one, aren't you?"

"I guess I am. I wasn't always. But I am now. I've had to become tough, and if that means meeting men is not a part of my life anymore, well, then that's the way it has to be. Let me be honest with you, Mr. Rosario. I'm not interested in relationships anymore."

"Fine."

"Fine? No argument? No macho, egotistical statements about how much I'm missing by not getting to know you?"

"I'm afraid not, Ms. Scott. I'm not too interested in relationships anymore myself."

"Really?"

He nodded. "I think so. But I haven't given up because of any deep, tragic impulse. You know what it is? This is going to sound awful, I guess. But frankly, it's just too much goddamn trouble."

For the first time that evening, she smiled. "You're right. It is way too much trouble. Far more than what it's worth. Goodbye, and thank you again. I am grateful for what you've done." They shook hands. "And thank you for helping me carry these charts."

"So that's what those things are."

"That's what they are. They're necessary, but at the same time they're overly complicated and exceedingly troublesome. Good night."

"Good night, Ms. Scott."

He had almost said, "Rebecca," but he caught himself and turned and walked away down Chauncy toward Garden Street.

At the corner, in the fading light, a man in black stood stiffly, glancing around as if he were lost. The man turned toward him and Rosario saw that it was a priest. There was a hard cold look to him, piercing, ice-blue eyes and white hair brushed back severely into a military style crew cut. He reminded Rosario of the Irish Christian Brothers who had slapped him around in high school back in New Jersey. The hitting, kicking, punching brothers, as an old friend still called them. Rosario couldn't resist slipping into a brogue. "Top of the evening to ya, Father."

The priest recoiled. "Christ Almighty, do I look *that* Irish?"

Rosario dropped the accent. "As a matter of fact, you look a little lost. Can I help you?"

The priest paused for a moment and stared at him, almost as if he didn't understand Rosario's words. He looked away for a second, and Rosario could see the man was making a concerted effort to seem polite. "Uh…no. I don't think so. I think I'm heading in the right direction. Thank you."

The priest nodded and started to walk away down Garden Street. Rosario called after him. "Father! Sorry about the Irish thing. It's probably just the darkness. The shadows. I'm sure in the light of day you look like a beacon of multi-culturalism."

The priest granted him a grudging, rueful laugh and moved away.

Rosario headed back to the Square, and as he walked, he found himself hoping that Rebecca Scott was not the woman in the silver dress who had gunned down Chuck Devir. He wasn't quite sure why he felt that way. There was not a lot to like about Rebecca Scott. But he was impressed with her, and he hoped that his good friend Ursula McGuire was wrong.

CHAPTER 6

It was Rosario's turn to come to Boston for their walk, and Ursula waited in front of Savenor's Market until she saw him coming down the stairway from the MBTA. "Nice job last night, Rosie."

"Thanks, but I don't think she's your woman."

"You mean now that you've met her, you don't want to believe she's my woman."

He shook his head. "No, I didn't say that."

"You did say on the phone, however, that you were impressed with her."

"That's right. I did say that. She has a certain strength of character that struck me right away."

"Strength of character and the ability to kill are not incompatible."

"If she's the killer. But I wouldn't extrapolate all kinds of meaning from the one conversation I had with her. Let's move."

They started down Charles Street toward Beacon, dodging the pedestrians along the brick sidewalk and then moving out onto the side of the road for better footing. She glanced over at him. "Now let me tell you what I think after hearing what you had to say on the phone."

At the corner of Mt. Vernon Street a truck thundered past and Rosario called over to her. "Let me see if I can guess. It has only convinced you even more of your initial impressions."

She smiled. "Why, how did you know?"

"Because I know you!"

Rosario looked over his right shoulder at the Charles Street Meeting House and stared at it for a moment. She laughed. "Years ago all you did was stare at the women walking around here."

"That's right. And now I stare at the architecture. Your husband has taught me well. Contemplation of the fine arts can give a man a sense of serenity."

"Well, you don't want to become *too* serene."

"I don't think there's much danger of that."

They moved quickly down Charles and crossed Beacon into the shadows of the Public Garden. As they picked up their speed, she raised her voice. "Based on your own account, we have two examples of a woman with pronounced tendencies toward violent action."

"I don't call running to the defense of one's daughter a tendency toward violence."

"But you said she shoved this kid into the street. I doubt very much that would be the average woman's first move. Calling for help? Sure. But shoving a male assailant into the street? Pretty unusual. Secondly, you said a young couple bumped into one of her packages, and instead of just looking annoyed, she called them religious fanatics because they support Romney. Sounds pretty unstable to me." She could tell that he was thinking it over.

Finally, he glanced her way again. "And from this you reason what?"

"I reason that she is quick to rage. I reason, based on what that kid said when you were shoving him down Chauncy Street, that she no longer has a husband, and I reason, lastly, that the explanation as to why she no longer has a husband is that he abused her."

"And you reason that because..."

"Because when you mentioned the Cambridge Police, she told you that the police are not much help when it comes to protecting women."

"Well, sure, but all women know that by now, don't they?" He stopped suddenly and put his hands on his hips and laughed. "You have incredible recall for someone pushing fifty. Last night I opened the refrigerator and couldn't remember what I was looking for."

She smiled and pulled ahead of him, passing Washington's statue and the entrance to Commonwealth Avenue. The point of these walks, as Rosario had so often reminded her, was not just to exercise but also to take their minds off work. So by mutual and silent consent, they dropped the subject. Stepping up the pace, they went around the Garden twice, the Common twice, and then headed down Beacon Street and over to the esplanade along the river.

Later, sweaty and tired, they walked up the stairs to her office. Once inside, she reached into the refrigerator next to her secretary's desk, pulled out two bottles of water and handed one to Rosario. She took a long drink and led him into her inner office. "Now back to our reasoning."

"Whoa! Enough reasoning. I thought we were going to relax."

"We'll relax at dinner. Mark's making veal scallopini. So here's the deal. The kid you knocked down wanted to know if you were her uncle from Newton. So assuming Rebecca Scott's daughter transferred from the Newton Public Schools…"

"An assumption on your part."

"Yes, well assumptions sometimes turn out to be accurate, and based on that assumption I did a little digging. Rebecca Scott, it turns out, is renting the bottom floor of that two family house on Chauncy Street and has been since April. She was—I know this thanks to a brilliant assumption on my part—a resident of Newton up to that time. She has, it turns out, two daughters, both of whom attended Newton Public Schools until their transfer to Cambridge. Scott is her maiden name and Warner is her married name. Obviously, some form of separation has occurred between husband and wife." She stopped and studied his face for any reaction, but he simply stood and listened. "Now to the gun. I've already talked to Chief Flanagan in Newton."

"Wait a second. Hold on. That wouldn't be the Flanagan you defended in that police corruption case, by any chance."

"That's right, Rosario. Connections, connections, and don't give me that look. He was found innocent. He is also grateful. Be that as it may, Robert, Chief Flanagan faxed me a list of Class B carry licenses going well back to the sixties."

"Hmm…that was certainly helpful, wasn't it? I wonder how many other private investigators get cooperation like that."

"Just shut up. In life you deal with the cards you got."

"And you appear to have a few aces."

"That's right, wise guy. Now let me lay them on the table for you. David Warner, Rebecca Scott's husband, purchased and registered a Colt Python .357 back in 1969."

Rosario smiled. "Well, that lets Ms. Scott off the hook right there. Have you ever fired a Python?"

"No. Have you?"

"As a matter of fact I have. Last time I was in Denver, Tom Keller took me out to a desolate area near the Flatirons, and we fired every weapon he owns. I had to use both hands with the Python. The recoil and muzzle blast are earthshaking. Few women could shoot a gun like that. Not even a tough old broad like you. Besides, you said the bullets used in the crime were from a .380 semi-automatic."

"They were and if you hadn't interrupted me in your rather transparent effort to clear Rebecca Scott of a crime you don't want her to have committed, then you would have learned about the second gun. That gun was registered in 1979. The Beretta .380."

He walked over to the window and looked across Beacon Street at The Common. "Well...I guess that might complicate things a bit."

"Guess so, Robert. You know, it just hit me. One of Romney's chief fundraisers is a guy named Warner. Wouldn't that be a kick in the ass, huh? Hey, let's get out of here. I'm starving."

She locked up the office and they walked around the corner to Charles and then up Chestnut Street. When she opened the door, the smell of veal and sizzling garlic and mushrooms filled her nostrils, and behind her she heard Rosario groan with hunger. They walked into the kitchen where Mark stood by the stove tilting a frying pan to one side. He looked up and smiled at her. His hair was still wet from his post-running shower, and he was dressed in his faded blue jeans and a black T-shirt. She went up to him and patted his ass and kissed him. "Smells great."

He laughed. "Me or the veal?"

"Both."

Mark turned to Rosario. "Robert, how was the walk?"

"Good. The old lady keeps right up with me."

She made a face at him. "Yeah, yeah, but it's not the same as the old days when you could run with Mark, is it?"

Rosario smiled. "Stop it. I adjusted many years ago."

"Uh, huh. You're a paragon of adjustment." Behind her, Mark slipped his fingers into the elastic of her shorts and pressed them softly into the small of her back. It meant, as so many of his gestures meant, knock it off. Calm down. Let it go. Stop arguing. And with that simple gesture, she felt herself being drawn back into his orbit. Into that peaceful, sensible, restorative world he had somehow created for himself. She knew no one else like him. No one who could make her feel the way he did. Rosario was one of her best friends—certainly her best male friend—but they always seemed to be in conflict, and after a while, despite the excitement of the relationship, she always longed to be back in Mark's company.

Mark picked up a long wooden spoon. "Rob, if you want to shower, there's a clean sweatsuit in the linen closet next to the towels."

Rosario put his hand on Mark's shoulder and grinned at Ursula. "How'd you ever find a guy like this, anyway?"

She leaned back into her husband, and Mark put his free arm around her waist. She laughed. "It was easy. He was a pushover."

She felt his lips behind her ear. "I was. I was a pushover, wasn't I?"

Rosario headed for the shower. "All those willowy Waspy girls after you and you settle for the Irish scullery maid."

She called after him as he made his escape from the kitchen. "Says the Italian peasant. Listen, Rosie, after your shower, be sure to clean up all the olive oil and grape stains from the tub, OK?"

Then she heard his voice from the top of the stairs. "You mean this tub up here that's all filled with potatoes?" She heard him chortling with glee as he slammed the door before she could respond.

After dinner, Rob finished off his glass of wine and looked across the table at her. "What's with the legal pad? I thought we were all through with work this evening."

She looked up at him. "I'm listing the hospitals most convenient to Newton."

Mark ran his thumb under his moustache and then wagged his finger at her. "You're not going to pull one of your medical record deals, are you? You know how I feel about that kind of thing."

Rosario held up his hands. "Hold on. What are you doing? Going after her medical records?"

"I'm trying to find out if this woman has been abused or not. I certainly cannot find out by walking up to David Warner and asking him, now can I? So what do you suggest?"

"I don't know, but people's medical records are their own business."

Mark swirled the wine around in his glass. "Not to Ursula, they're not. Did she ever tell you about the Upton case back in the early eighties? Ah, hah. I see that she hasn't. When Bob LeClerc was interning at Mass General, he told Ursula that medical records departments in most urban hospitals were so chaotic that all you had to do was put on a white coat and walk in, and you had a damn good chance of getting at any patient's files. He said he had done it himself. No one questioned him. So that's exactly what she did in this Upton business years later. She got herself a white jacket and walked right into the file room at Brigham and Women's."

"And by doing so, I resolved the case in favor of my client, who was the aggrieved party. Do you deny justice was done?"

"No, I don't. In that case, justice was done. Barbara Upton was innocent and you proved her innocence. I'm questioning the means to that end."

"The means, my dear, brought the end about. Besides, I'm not going to pull that stunt again. My company was a fledgling firm back then, and I didn't have a hell of a lot to lose. I'm not going to risk everything we've worked for. Relax."

Rosario was still staring at her. "So what are you going to do?"

She put her pen down on the pad and leaned back in her chair. "You know even now, even in a city like Boston, some parts of the health care industry still rely on paper, but the whole trend is toward electronic systems that are only going to benefit people like me and work against individual privacy. Computer software vendors have developed technology to streamline record keeping, which means that more and more people are going to be able to get their hands on your records. So one thing I can do is take a look at hospitals, with Newton-Wellesley at the top of my list. My next step is to look at all the people who have access to medical records besides physicians. Obviously nurses, but also billing clerks, medical records personnel, people in the emergency room, X-ray technicians and others."

Rosario interrupted her. "Among whom I'm sure are lots of friendly bureaucrats named Keenan and O'Brien and O'Toole and Flaherty."

She smiled. "Not exactly, Rob. Actually their names are Connelly and Hardy and McCarthy and Sweeney; but unfortunately, none of them work at Newton-Wellesley, and even if they did, I would not put their jobs in jeopardy by asking them to ferret out medical records."

"But if one of them just happened to be looking at medical records all day as part of the job, it would certainly be an easy matter to just glance…"

"That's correct, Rosie, but since I don't have an in at that hospital, I can't play that card, can I?"

"Thank God, you can't."

"So I think my only opening here is the most direct route. Going right to the family doctor."

Rosario frowned. "That's a little ballsy, isn't it?"

Mark poured himself some more wine. "She's done that before too, although with a feminist twist. In both cases, the doctor was a woman, and in both cases, the person being investigated was a woman who had been abused. So there was a natural sympathy among women that worked in her favor." He pointed at her with his glass. "What if Rebecca Scott's physician is a man? What if he's a chauvinist pig? What then, my dear?"

"In this business, as you know, one must take risks. Finding the Warner family physician is the only method I can think of that might yield me evidence of abuse."

Rosario shook his head. "Are you telling me those two doctors allowed you to look at patients' private medical records without their permission?"

"Neither of those patients knew I was investigating their backgrounds. Neither one of them was my client. Both of them were in fear of their lives and didn't want anyone to meddle in their personal business. They believed that their husbands would be even more violent if they thought they were disclosing information about them to anyone. What I did was to tell the physicians that I suspected abuse and asked them to review their own records to see if they or a colleague had treated these women for anything that would be indicative of abuse. Both agreed."

Rosario stood up and went over and leaned against the doorway. "And just how do you propose to find out who the Warner family doctor is?"

"That's the least of my problems. You've told me yourself every teacher at Liberty High School is handed a list of kids' names every year to alert them to their medical problems. School nurses and secretaries have access to those lists and from those lists to the attending physicians is a hop, skip, and a jump. If I can't bullshit my way down that road, I go to my sources at the HMO's."

"You can't get medical records from an HMO. That's impossible."

"Impossible to get at medical records. Not so impossible to match the names of patients with their primary care physicians."

Rosario glanced over at Mark. "I'm not so sure I like this end of your wife's business."

Mark pointed at her again. "You're completely shameless. When we argue politics, you tell me I'm morally obtuse. That I don't feel for the downtrodden masses and the victims of corporate greed. But when you want to get your own way on a matter of business, well, then the hell with morality."

She pointed right back at him. "Wrong again, my dear. In this case I am acting for the greater moral good."

"The greater moral good? You are concealing the identity of a murderer, and you are about to embark upon an invasion of a family's private life. And that's just for starters. Greater moral good, my ass!"

Rosario stood up. "And on that note, I'm off. Ursie, we're going to have to talk some more about this. Thanks for dinner, Mark. It was delicious."

After he was gone, she looked across the table at her husband. "Sure as shooting, he's going to bail out of this one."

He nodded. "A poor choice of words, my love. But I think you're correct. And I don't blame him one bit."

CHAPTER 7

Robert Rosario sat in his study and stared at the framed photographs on the wall. In the one directly in front of him, the sun was rising on the edge of Massachusetts Bay. Orange, white and purple clouds floated over Marblehead Harbor, and the dark rocks below the big tree on the headland were just becoming visible. That was the place to be right now. Sitting on one of the benches near old Fort Sewall at daybreak, inhaling the cool sea air, his hand wrapped around a warm mug of coffee. Not here at his desk on the phone telling Ursula McGuire he had decided to bail out.

He kept telling himself that her investigation of Rebecca Scott was still in its early stages. That it was perfectly clear to both of them that Ursula could get along without him on this one. Furthermore, there were precedents for what he was about to do. He had bailed out of other cases that had taken him down a road he preferred not to travel, and Ursula had always understood. It was not as if he were letting her down.

But her voice seemed quieter than usual. "May I ask you something?"

"Sure."

"Are you...do you find yourself emotionally drawn to her?"

"After one meeting? Come on, Ursie!"

"Is it sexual?"

"Man, are you ever nosy."

"I'm sorry. I shouldn't have asked that question."

"No, you shouldn't have. But that's never stopped you before." He listened to her soft laughter and then leaned back in his chair and smiled. "It's not sexual either. At least I don't think it is. She's a good-looking woman. No question about it. But I'm not on fire with desire or anything. I'm not thinking about her that way."

"Well, how are you thinking about her?"

"I'm not sure. This woman seems so negative. So cold. So fierce, I guess. She..."

"Fascinates you."

"Right...but...well, look Ursie. Here's the deal. I have to tell you that I just don't feel right about it. I'm not convinced that she's your shooter, and I don't feel right about fabricating some token friendship with her so I can gather information for you. OK?"

"OK."

"Still friends?"

He heard her laugh. "Do I have a choice?"

"Do you want one?"

"Not after all these years, Rosie. And don't feel bad about bailing out. You're probably doing the right thing."

"Thanks."

He hung up the phone and took a deep breath. It had been important to get that out of the way before his walk—his "old guy" walk—as Ursula liked to call it. He didn't want it hanging over his head, infesting his mind while he was trying to exercise and sweat and loosen up. Tonight was Thursday. Tonight was the night he walked the extra mile. The night he looked forward to as a way of flushing out any strain or tension or dull fatigue that had crept up on him after a week of work. He had learned long ago how important it was to go into the weekend with a clear head and a calm heart, and now it seemed even more important than usual.

It had rained for most of the day, but now, as evening approached, a fine mist hung over the Square and a light fog drifted through the streets. Rosario put on a heavy Liberty High sweatshirt to ward off the chilly wind that blew in from the river and headed toward Brattle Street. At Huron Avenue, he picked up his pace, zigzagging his way up one street and down another until he reached Fresh Pond. Then he walked around twice at a good clip and emerged just beyond the chaos of the traffic circle by Concord Avenue. He waited until there was a break and then jogged across the parkway to the other side. He was sweating heavily now and about to pull his hood on to sweat even more, when a dark blue Honda Civic pulled over by the side of the road a few yards ahead of him. The window opened as he approached, and a woman with her hair pulled back in a ponytail leaned across the seat. The last thing he needed at this point was someone asking for complicated directions. He wanted to keep sweating and moving swiftly through the darkening, foggy Cambridge streets with his heart beating and the blood flowing smoothly and efficiently through his veins.

But when he leaned down he saw it was Rebecca Scott, wearing a black sweatshirt and red spandex leggings and a red headband, her face flushed and vibrant. "Hi!"

"Hello!"

"I thought that was you. You ought to be more careful running across Fresh Pond Parkway like that, you know. You could get killed."

For a moment he was taken aback, wondering what Ursula would have made of a comment like that. "I've been doing it for many years, I'm afraid. No injuries yet. You look like you've been working out."

"I have. Can I give you a lift?"

"Well, actually, you've caught me in my own workout. I have about twenty minutes to go."

"Oh...OK. I'll let you go. Listen, Mr. Rosario, I want to thank you again for the other night, and I want to apologize for seeming so...well, so cold. My daughter and I very much appreciate your helping us." She looked away for a second, staring out the front windshield, but with her right hand still resting on top of the passenger's seat. Then she glanced back. "Would you like to join us for dinner?"

He paused for a moment, thrown off balance by this sudden show of friendliness. "That's very nice of you, but I don't want to put you out. I'm sure you've had a long day at work and then the gym. You hardly have time..."

She smiled, waving away his objection. It was almost as if she were a different person. "We do take-out on Thursdays. The girls are in charge of that operation. So I'm afraid I can't tell you what it will be. They love Asian food and it's usually Chinese or Indian or Thai. Well, think about it."

"All right. I'll think about it."

She turned back and put her hands on the steering wheel. He knew he should stick to the polite refusal. He knew he should stay away from this woman. This could only be trouble, to say nothing of the difficult situation it might put him in with Ursula. His regimen called for another twenty minutes of walking and sweating. A long hot shower. A healthy, relaxed meal with no alcohol. The last two hours of the evening in his big armchair reading the *Times* and the *Journal*, followed by a good night's sleep. But somehow the regimen wasn't standing up too well against Rebecca Scott's invitation. He leaned back down and looked at her. "Shall I bring wine or beer?"

She smiled again. "After that workout? Definitely beer. 8:30 OK?"

"8:30 is fine."

On his way to Chauncy Street, Rosario stopped off at University Wine Shop on Mass Ave and bought two bottles of Singha, two bottles of Kingfisher, and two bottles of Tsingtao. Whatever cuisine Rebecca Scott's daughters selected, he was ready.

When the door opened, a tall thin girl with short brown hair and big brown eyes greeted him. "Are you Mr. Rosario?"

"That's right."

"Hi, I'm Emily."

"Hello, Emily. Nice to meet you."

She showed him through the front hall to the dining room where Rebecca Scott and the older daughter were peering warily into a plastic container of food. Rebecca glanced up at him. "Hello, Mr. Rosario. I see you've met Emily. This is Elizabeth."

Elizabeth, with her mother's gray eyes and blonde hair, looked up at him. "Hi. Hey, thanks for the other night."

Rosario smiled and nodded. "Has he caused you any more trouble?"

She wrinkled her nose. "Not really. Just a few dirty looks in the hall. One of his friends told me you said you were my uncle."

"That was the best I could come up with at the moment. I figured it might be better if a relative were pushing him around rather than a total stranger."

Rebecca looked at him for a moment and then glanced back at the food. "Speaking of strange, we're trying to make sense of what we've got here."

Elizabeth rolled her eyes. "Mom? Come on. I didn't do it on purpose. I got the shrimp and ginger. I got the chicken and hot basil. I got the beef satay."

Rebecca placed her palm affectionately on the top of her daughter's head and smiled. "And now if we can only figure out what this is. Kang something. What do you suppose that means?"

Rosario took the six-pack of assorted beers out of the bag and placed it on the table. "Did you order the Duck Choo Chi at Siam Garden?"

Elizabeth's eyes brightened. "Yes, we did. We thought we'd try it."

"Well, Kang Ped Ped Yang is Duck Choo Chi."

Elizabeth put her arm around her mother's neck. "I *told* you, Mom."

Rebecca held her daughter's wrist. "OK, OK. Luckily, Mr. Rosario speaks Thai."

Emily motioned toward a chair for Rosario and then sat down next to him. "So how come you can speak Thai? Were you in Vietnam?"

Rebecca sighed. "Don't interrogate Mr. Rosario, Em. He's hungry."

Rosario laughed. "It's perfectly all right. In the first place, Emily, I can't speak Thai at all. It just so happens that I eat at

Siam Garden a great deal, and I'm a big fan of Kang Ped Ped Yang. And yes, I was in Vietnam, but only for a month."

Emily stared at him. "A month? I thought the tour of duty was a year."

Elizabeth rolled her eyes again. "You'll have to forgive Emily. She's the brain in the family. A's all the way. History's her big subject. You can call me Lizzie, by the way."

Rosario shrugged. "It's easy for me to forgive her, Lizzie. I teach history."

The older girl seemed shocked. Then he remembered that her only contact with him had been as a stranger who had assaulted someone out on the street in front of her house. But Emily seemed unfazed. "Where do you teach?"

Rosario poured the cold Singha gently down the side of one of the glasses and handed it to her mother. "Liberty High."

"That's a terrific school. Your debate team is like the best in the state. I do debate at Cambridge. So, fill me in on how you only spent a month in Vietnam. We're studying the Tet Offensive in my honors history class and..."

Her mother gave her a look. "Emily, maybe Mr. Rosario doesn't want to talk about Vietnam right now. Maybe he doesn't want to talk about it at all."

Emily stopped chewing her food and her big brown eyes widened. "Oh, my God. I'm sorry. Maybe you were wounded or something. Maybe that's why..."

Rebecca and Elizabeth spoke at once. "Emily!"

Rosario laughed again and then took a long drink of the beer, that first, deep, soul-satisfying draft after the exercise and the sweat and the hot shower. He placed the glass on the table and looked back at the now-chastened younger daughter. "Emily, you can ask me anything you want. The fact of the matter is you're right. Draftees did do a year's tour of duty in

Southeast Asia during the war. The only thing is that when Uncle Sam drafted me back in the late sixties, he sent me to South Korea instead of Vietnam. That's where I did my year. At the end of my tour of duty, I had a chance to go to Saigon before I came home."

Elizabeth stared across the table at him. "There wasn't any fighting in Korea then, was there? Wasn't the Korean War before that? Why would you want to go from a place where there was no war to a place where there was?"

Rosario looked at her. Most kids had no idea there even was a Korean War. At least this one knew it had happened. "Well, Lizzie, sometimes young guys do crazy things. Sometimes there's no accounting for what they do. But at the time, I felt that Vietnam was the biggest thing that was going to happen to our generation, and I wanted to see it. I had a friend who was in the navy and ran a PT boat on missions up the Mekong River. My superiors in Seoul OK'd my going and I went. I guess it was history, Lizzie. I wanted to see it in the making. That's what made me do it."

"But you might have gotten killed."

"Well, you can get killed anywhere. There's probably a higher chance of my getting killed running across Fresh Pond Parkway than there was in some of the places I ended up going to in Vietnam."

He glanced across at Rebecca. It was evident she had been listening intently to what he was saying, and now, as he finished his last remark, the bare hint of a smile crossed her face.

Emily leaned forward and dug into the shrimp and ginger. "So what did you do in South Korea for a year?"

Rosario put down his fork. "I had done some reporting and writing for my college newspaper, so I ended up working for *Stars and Stripes*."

"The army newspaper?"

"That's right."

"So that must have been interesting, huh? Did you…"

Rebecca raised her hand. "Em? I asked Mr. Rosario over to dinner, not to explain his entire life story to us."

After they finished eating, the girls cleared off the table and pulled out their books and homework. It was obvious their mother wanted to check their assignments, so he signaled to her that he would be on his way. But she insisted that he stay for another beer. For a moment, he felt uncomfortable, the odd man out, and he tried to think of a polite way to disengage, but then Emily asked him a question about a paper she was doing, and soon they were deep into the presidential campaign of 1968. Before he knew it, he had finished his second beer and it was past ten o'clock. Now it really was time to go.

Emily looked up at him. "Hey, thanks. I get it now. So the whole Democratic convention in Chicago that was supposed to help Humphrey beat Nixon turned out to be like one big attack ad for the Republicans."

"Exactly."

Emily closed her books and got up from the table, and Rosario took advantage of the moment to say goodbye. Rebecca Scott walked him to the door, and they stepped outside into the cool mist. He turned and looked at her. Ursula was right. She was drop dead gorgeous. He laughed. It sounded like a line out of a thirties detective novel. She looked into his eyes. "What's so funny?"

"Nothing."

"Eve Taylor again?"

"No. I see now that you're quite different from her."

"Is that good or bad?"

Good question, he thought. "Neither good nor bad. Just different."

"I apologize for Emily's inquisitiveness."

"Nonsense. Teachers like inquisitive kids."

"I mean about asking if you were wounded in the war."

"Well, I wasn't. I emerged unscathed."

"That's an interesting word, isn't it?"

"*Emerged?*"

She laughed, the first real laugh he had heard yet. "You bring a kind of comic sensibility to life, don't you?"

No one had ever said that to him before. At least no one had put it into quite those words. It was as if she possessed an almost instinctual understanding of what kind of a man he was, and he found it a bit unnerving. "I don't know. You might have a point there."

"What I meant was the word *unscathed.* "

"I know."

"Many people don't get through life unscathed."

"I'm well aware of that."

She shook her head. "I'm sorry. I didn't mean to imply that you take life too lightly. I can see by the way you helped Emily that you're very serious about your work. I guess what I mean is that I sense that you…"

"Don't bring a tragic sensibility to life."

"That's right."

"Well, you're correct. I don't. I don't find it to be particularly helpful."

"Helpful for what?"

"For living. The most miserable people I know are the ones who dwell on their suffering. Who think and talk about it all the time. It paralyzes them. Imprisons them in the past so they can never learn to cope with the future. I know one guy who takes a kind of perverse pleasure in it. He's in his mid-fifties and still blaming his parents for everything that's gone wrong with his life."

"Maybe he didn't emerge unscathed."

He looked at her, drawn in by her beauty, while at the same time all the important lessons he had learned in life bore down on him, focusing his mind with a power and clarity that surprised him, and warning him to stay away from this woman. They were still looking at each other, standing there together at close quarters, yet each one very much alone. And then they both smiled. It was, Rosario thought, a moment of complete honesty between a man and a woman, and he suddenly realized that it could only have happened at this stage of their lives. For they were basically communicating, without saying a word, that they were utterly unsuitable for one another. They had both lived long enough and been through enough to see it at the beginning of a relationship rather than at the end, and this realization, rather than saddening him as it might have earlier in life, seemed a kind of victory over impulses that could only bring both of them to grief.

He tried to think of something to say but failed. She glanced away for a moment and then looked back at him. She reached out her hand and he took it. "Good night, Mr. Rosario."

"Good night, Rebecca. And the next time we run into each other, you can stop the Mr. Rosario business, OK?"

She smiled and nodded. "OK."

"And if you ever need any help, call me. I'm just a few blocks away."

"Thank you."

He turned and walked away and headed home, gratified that he had finally reached the point in life when he could do the right thing without regret.

CHAPTER 8

D r. John Crust, a small, round, pink-faced man, pushed back his chair. "What do you mean coming in here and making such a charge? I have treated Mr. and Mrs. Warner and both their children for over ten years! There have been no complaints whatsoever either from Mrs. Warner or her daughters and absolutely no physical sign of even the most superficial of injuries on the patient. Why should I believe you?"

Years ago, in an attempt to help his wife gain control of her Irish temper, Mark had invited her to meditate with him and had showed her how to focus her attention on inanimate objects. The purpose of this exercise was to empty her mind of thoughts and her soul of feeling and thus to calm her intemperate spirits. In the silence of Mark's study, it had worked out well. So now, she took a deep breath and glanced for a second at a dark blue coffee mug sitting peacefully on top of a stack of medical journals. Then she leaned forward and folded her hands on his desk. "You shouldn't. I wouldn't either if I were you. What I'm going to ask you to do, even if it flies in the face of everything you know about this family, is to review your records and satisfy yourself that there is no medical condition or accident or report of any kind that might mirror the symptoms of abuse. As an attorney, I would never take such an extraordinary step as this if I did not think it was a matter of extreme importance. I'm well aware of how important your time is and even more aware of the sanctity of the doctor-patient relationship."

To Ursula, her voice had sounded calm and reasonable, and her last two sentences had reached her ears, at least, as especially convincing. So she was not quite ready for the swiftness of his response. "Get a subpoena or get out!"

Looking at his coffee mug again, and now, with every last vestige of meditative self-control gone, she seriously considered bouncing the thing off his florid little head. Then she tried to think whether she could possibly need this man for anything ever again. She decided that she wouldn't and rewarded herself. "You know what you are?"

Reddening, the little physician jumped to his feet. "This interview is over!"

"I can see you're dying to know. Which is good because I'm more than happy to tell you. You're one of those doctors who are simply unable to believe that this kind of thing goes on in comfortable middle-class homes. You're psychologically incapable of even imagining it. Or worse, you just don't want to get involved."

Dr. Crust's face turned scarlet. "Get out of this office at once or I will call the police."

On her way through the reception area, she paused at the secretary's desk. "He must be a real gas to work for, huh?"

The secretary looked puzzled. "What makes you say that?"

"Because he's such an old fart."

This was exactly the kind of behavior Mark had always warned her about, but sometimes she just couldn't help it. Sometimes, it just felt too damned good.

U rsula spent the rest of the morning putting the finishing touches on her investigation of Congressman Kevin McNamara's Republican opponent, and at 1:00, right on time, her secretary showed Abby Whitman into the office. Dressed in a gray business suit, looking prim and efficient, the young woman held out her hand. Ursula took it and smiled. "You are certainly not coming from your last class at Harvard."

Abby laughed and sat down. "I certainly am not. I've been to see my lawyer on State Street and an old friend of mine from Stanford who's a portfolio manager at Fidelity."

"Sounds like a busy morning."

"It has been. My partner at the bar has been making noises about selling me his share, and I needed to take a look at all the legal and financial ramifications. Do I look too formal?"

"Not at all. You look very professional. If this were an interview you'd get an A for first impressions."

Abby smiled and leaned back in her chair. "Hard to imagine interviewing for a job like yours."

"Why?"

"I'm not sure, exactly, but I think it's because your work is so different from anyone else's I know. I mean on a regular basis."

Ursula shrugged. "I guess it is...in some ways."

Abby glanced at some of the photographs on the wall and pointed to one of Ursula and the senior senator. "When was that?"

Ursula turned in her chair and looked over her shoulder. "That was in '88 when Joe Malone was Teddy's Republican opponent. It was a cakewalk."

"And now?"

Ursula turned back. "This is a tougher one. Much tougher. But we'll win in the end."

"I've been reading these articles in the *Globe* about those Indiana workers being fired from their jobs. Is it true Romney's company did that?"

Ursula nodded. "It looks that way."

"That's really going to hurt him in a state like this." The young woman laughed softly. "I suppose you're hard at work making sure that it does."

Ursula raised her hands in mock innocence. "I'm hard at work on many things, Abby. Hey, have you eaten lunch yet?"

"No. I haven't had time. As a matter of fact, I'm starving."

"Me too. Come on. I'm buying."

Ursula led Abby out of the office and down the steps to Beacon Street. Around the corner, a gaggle of tourists held up foot traffic in front of DeLuca's Market, and she waited until they passed. Then she nodded at the entrance. "Robert Rosario's great-grandfather worked in that store at the turn of the century. He was a grocery clerk, an immigrant from Venice."

"That must explain the blue eyes then. The northern Italians."

Ursula chuckled. "Hard to tell. His mother's side of the family is all Irish. Galway people. So he might have gotten them there. Rob's a half-breed."

Abby smiled at her quizzically. "And you?"

"Full-blooded Irish all the way. My father's side is from County Louth and my mother's people from Cork. The

McGuires crossed over during the great famine in the 1840's. Rob's family on the Italian side came in the 1880's, so they're newcomers."

"I like that."

"What?"

"How so many easterners seem to know about their background. Their history. No one can seem to remember anything in California. Everybody's from somewhere else, and they can't remember where they came from in the first place."

"I'll bet the Mexicans remember."

Abby nodded. "Well, you're right there."

"In this city, less than a hundred years ago, the Irish and the Italians were treated just like the Mexicans by the white Anglo-Saxon Protestants. So the historical memory stays with us."

"The Boston Brahmins."

"That's right."

"How ironic that you should end up married to one of their descendants. The old class enemy."

Ursula laughed and took the young woman's arm and they walked down Charles Street together. "He is the old class enemy. But don't you see, Abby? It's all part of a plot. I'm sure you've taken some courses in women's history, haven't you? They seem to be all the rage these days. Well, this is your first lesson in *Irish* women's history. First, we out-reproduced them, then we took their city away from them, and then we started marrying all their young men."

They crossed Chestnut Street and Ursula took her into Toscano. A waiter seated them at a table for two by the window. It was late enough so much of the lunch crowd had departed, and there was no need for Ursula to lower her voice. "Let me tell you what I've found so far."

Abby sat up straight. "Is it much?"

Ursula smiled. "I think so. I don't have everything, but I'm close."

Abby gazed into Ursula's eyes with a look of youthful admiration, and it made her wonder what life might have been like had she and Mark had children. There had been no doubts on either side during the heady days of the 1960's and 1970's. They had enjoyed their independence and their freedom and had lived life to its fullest. She had never been the maternal type, and all those years when her friends were dealing with crying babies and messy children and surly teenagers passed without a single regret. But now, looking at this intelligent, successful, charming young woman, she began to think of what it might be like to have an adult daughter. Someone she could talk to and share things with in a way she couldn't with her contemporaries.

The waiter came over and Abby ordered an arugula salad with walnuts, pears, and Gorgonzola cheese. Ursula smiled. "That's way too California for me. I'm going for the linguini and mussels marinara." When he left, Ursula leaned forward. "I certainly think you were correct in my office the other day when you told me what the woman said after she shot Devir. It certainly does sound like something someone would say who has been a victim of male violence. And subsequent information I've been able to gather only reinforces that notion. By the time Rob and I met you and Mark at Chez Henri on Monday night, I had spoken to every merchant in the immediate vicinity of the crime. While the Cambridge police were busy searching for a young brunette in a red dress, I was conducting a parallel investigation for a beautiful, blonde woman in silver."

"What did you tell them?"

"I said I was looking for a missing person. I framed my questions in a way so they were totally unrelated to the shooting. Only three people spotted her."

Abby's eyes widened and she spoke in a hushed whisper. "You mean there are *witnesses?*"

Ursula put her fingers on the young woman's hand. "Calm down. The only people who witnessed the shooting were you and Jeannie. The local drunk you mentioned was not taken seriously by the police. A Mrs. Tang, who runs a nail salon a couple blocks down toward Harvard Square, saw a blonde woman dressed in silver crossing Mass Ave toward Chauncy Street about twenty minutes after Devir was killed. Finally, Karl Hamilton, the young bartender at Chez Henri, saw an identically dressed woman at the bar on Friday night shortly before 8:00. From Karl, I was able to learn what line of work the woman was in and where her place of employment was. The following day, I found that place of employment and followed her home. Once I had the address, I was able to discover her name."

"Which is?"

"Scott. Rebecca Scott."

Abby leaned forward and stared at Ursula. "Up until this moment, the whole thing was like a dream. But now that you've given her a name, it's suddenly real."

"You can still back out, you know. You've certainly done enough for her already."

Abby sat up straight again. "No. No, I want to see this through. Go on."

"Before Rebecca Scott lived in Cambridge, she lived in Newton. Luckily, an old friend happens to be the police chief in that town and faxed me a list of gun permits—none to Rebecca Scott. Two, however, are registered to her husband, a

Mr. David Warner. I then discovered through a source of mine that the daughters of this Rebecca Scott now attend Cambridge High School. Now the next step is to try to find any medical evidence that Rebecca Scott has been treated for injuries."

"How's that going?"

Ursula laughed softly. "That's the part of the investigation that's not going so well."

"I wouldn't wonder. You can't get into people's medical records."

Ursula took a sip of her mineral water and didn't answer. She didn't want to go through all that again, and there was only a certain amount of information any client needed to know. "You're right there. That's a tough one."

"But we do know that Rebecca Scott had access to a weapon."

"That's correct. But while I'm convinced that Rebecca Scott is our woman, I cannot prove it to you. That will have to wait until you identify her."

"How do you want me to go about doing that?"

"By doing it with me there and by letting me guide you as to the manner in which we do it."

"Which I assume we will want to do without her knowledge."

"Absolutely. Any attempt on your part to meet this woman would put you in grave legal danger. If the Cambridge police ever have a breakthrough in this case, there can be no connection between you and this woman. You understand this, I hope."

Abby nodded. Then the waiter was between them serving their meals, and when he withdrew, Abby was still looking into her eyes. "I…I have to admit, Ursula, many times over the last few days I've wondered what it would be like to meet her. What she would say. How we would talk to each other. Whether she would talk to me at all."

Ursula put her fork down for a second. "Put all those thoughts out of your mind. And remember, we may suspect that the reason Rebecca Scott left Newton for Cambridge with her two daughters was because her husband, David Warner, abused her. But we don't know that. We have no proof. And, of course, until you identify Rebecca Scott, we have no proof that she's the woman who gunned down Charles Devir. So one step at a time, and whatever happens, no contact with this woman at all." She picked up her fork again and took a stab at her linguine.

Abby finished her salad. "OK, but what about this? As I told you the day we met, I've had a great deal of success with a variety of investments. What if I set up a college fund, possibly in some sort of trust, for this woman's children? Of course, I have no idea what her financial situation is. I know Newton's a pretty upscale town, but my guess is that with the road she's taken, her husband will probably not be of much assistance. When I was at Cisco, I headed up a project that funneled money into scholarships for kids in San Jose. I'm thinking of something similar here with myself acting as a personal trustee."

"That's very generous of you, Abby. But again, it puts you in a personal relationship with Rebecca Scott."

"Let me work on that with my lawyer. There are ways trusts can be established that may disguise the benefactor."

"Well, trusts and wills are not my bailiwick, but you want to be very, very careful about how you do that. An enterprising Cambridge cop with an enterprising Middlesex County district attorney can get subpoenas that will pierce that device—unless, of course, your pal on State Street is really good, and I mean really good."

Abby smiled. "He's good, all right. Whether he's in Ursula McGuire's league or not is another question."

Ursula laughed and shook her head. "That's very nice of you to say, Abby, but there are a lot of things that can go wrong with any investigation, believe me. Maybe you better wait to see how things turn out before you get too complimentary."

CHAPTER 9

Robert Rosario and Rebecca Scott had parted on a mutually beneficial basis. Cold words, he thought, but they accurately captured the nature of their separation that evening on Chauncy Street. Rosario detested the language of psychology, especially as it reared its ugly head in his own field, and one of the words he hated the most was *closure*. Yet he supposed it was something similar they both wanted when they said goodbye.

Tonight, back to his routine, he moved swiftly through his weight workout at Mike's Gym. It was a far cry from what he used to lift as a young man, and now, all around him, guys half his age pressed, curled and rowed their way through poundage that would have sent him staggering into the emergency room of Mt. Auburn Hospital. One of them, with the agility of an orangutan, swung off the chinning bar and landed next to his buddy. "You check out that babe in the kickboxing class?"

"The one in the red tights? Fuckin' A. I've seen her in here before. She's gotta be what? Thirty-five? But she's so fine!"

"Yeah, but I mean you should see her fight. It's a little fuckin' scary for a chick. Come on."

The two of them, nicknamed Cro and Magnon by one of the women at the gym, crossed the floor, and when Rosario finished his last set of rows, he joined them. Outside the glass partition, a crowd of onlookers stared into the big room reserved for classes. Inside, Yukio Hosogai, the gym's aikido and karate instructor, was putting his class through its paces, and among the men and women moving rapidly through a series of fighting positions, was Rebecca Scott. Dressed in her red leggings and black sweatshirt, her blonde hair pulled back behind a red headband, she cut a striking contrast to all the other women in the group.

Rosario had seen Yukio conduct this drill before. He would pick one of the more promising students to go on the attack, while he held a padded shield of leather-bound rubber in front of his chest to absorb the blows. Tonight, he was demonstrating what could be done with a fast, hard, alternating assault with both fists and feet aimed at the defender's upper body. This required not only strength and determination on the part of the attacker, but agility as well, for the kicks had to strike high over the belt to be effective. Now was Rebecca's turn, and she moved in on Yukio quickly, ramming his shield with high driving kicks and solid punches and slamming powerful blows into his chest and mid-section until she had pushed him back across the floor. Usually self-contained and effortless in his defense, Yukio was sweating profusely, and the muscles in his arms clenched and jumped as she went after him with savage enthusiasm. Finally, she jammed him against the wall and he shouted at her to stop. She fell back for a moment, waiting in the attacker's pose while Yukio pushed himself away from the wall. Vanquished, he dropped his shield.

No one in the crowd heard what was said in the room. But they could see Yukio saying something to Rebecca and laughing, and then the students began to clap their hands.

Reluctantly, the crowd broke up and one of the guys he had followed punched his friend lightly on the arm. "Remind me never to hit on her. Whoa!"

Rosario walked over to the far side of the gym and worked on his chest and his shoulders and then called it a night. He was out the door and almost home free when he heard her voice behind him in the parking lot. "Hey, Robert Rosario."

He turned around. "Ms. Scott. How are you?"

"Fine, fine. A little tired after my workout."

"Well, if I had a workout like that, I'd be tired too. You put on quite a show."

"I didn't mean to. I had no idea people were watching. I mean outside of the students in the class."

He smiled. "I think you scared the hell out of all the guys in the gym."

She looked at him. "Well, no harm in that, is there?"

"I guess not. Remind me never to tick you off."

"I don't think you would. You're not that kind of guy."

"What kind of guy is that?"

She remained silent for a few seconds, as if she were thinking carefully about her reply. "Bad guys, I guess you'd call them. Is that too simple a phrase?"

"Not for me."

"Good. It's interesting how much language is spent these days explaining away the existence of evil, isn't it? But the fact of the matter is that there are some bad people out there, even though they seem perfectly respectable to their friends and neighbors. But I'll classify you with the good guys. How's that?"

Rosario looked at her. Her face was flushed from her battle with Yukio, and strands of her blonde hair curled slightly around the sides of her face. "Well, I'm glad I'm in with the right crowd." Then he changed his tone. "If you're worried about any bad guys tonight, I can follow you home until you lock your car and get inside your place."

"Oh, thanks. But the bad guy I'm thinking of will be damn sorry if he runs into me tonight. He's nothing I can't handle. Not anymore."

"So I see."

"Don't worry. I've got all my aggression out for the evening."

"Yukio looked whipped."

"He's a wonderful teacher."

"He'll be a wonderful ex-teacher if he gets any more students like you."

She smiled and started to turn away. "It's been nice seeing you again. I have to go back inside to call Lizzie to come and pick me up. I lent her the car tonight."

"Don't bother. I'll drive you home."

"You don't have to do that. The thing is I wanted to stop in the Square to pick up a copy of *Scientific American* at Nini's. I don't want to hold you up."

"Nonsense. It'll take all of five minutes. Unless you're worried about getting in a car with a complete and utter stranger."

She laughed. "Well, I guess you're not complete and utter any longer."

A few minutes later, as he turned out of Appian Way onto Brattle Street, he spotted a space in front of the Loeb Theater and went for it. As they got out of the car, a massive sports utility vehicle pulled up alongside of them, and a middle-aged man stuck his head out the window. His large bald head shone like a polished egg, and he wore a pair of expensive looking glasses with blue-tinted lenses. "I had my eye on that space."

Rosario stared at him. "Sorry, I was in front of you."

He frowned. "I'm afraid I saw that space first."

Rosario nodded. "Look, it's getting late. I'm not in the mood for a debate about a parking space. Have a nice night."

Rebecca Scott stepped between them. "I can't believe how polite you're being to this pretentious yuppie bastard."

Rosario, a little taken aback, looked into her eyes. "Relax. We're just having a little disagreement, that's all." He glanced back at the man in the SUV. "Isn't that right?"

He expected the guy to be angry, but he wasn't. Evidently, like Rosario, he had reached the stage in life where temper tantrums had become counterproductive. "That's right." He glanced at Rebecca. "Thus your use of the term *bastard* to refer to me, madam, is both unwarranted and noisome."

Rebecca Scott glared at the man and then turned and looked at Rosario. "How typical of Harvard Square. Anywhere else, people would be screaming at each other. Instead, we have to be subjected to a vocabulary lesson." She looked back at the driver. "You are really an annoying person." Suddenly, she thrust her fists through the open window of the SUV and pressed her thumbs on both his lenses, leaving a large imprint on each one. "There. Now you'll be able to find even fewer parking spaces."

The driver cursed and roared away down Brattle, and Rosario burst into laughter. "I knew somewhere buried in all that ferocity was a sense of humor."

"Do you see me laughing?"

"No, but I am. Did you see the expression on his face?"

They walked into the Square in silence. Only as they approached Nini's did she finally speak. "I suppose you think I overreacted."

Rosario stopped in front of the newspaper stand. "Oh, no. Not at all. In fact, I'm surprised you didn't kickbox him to death."

He had meant to be funny, but then he remembered who he was talking to, and as he looked at her he wondered if he would have spent an iota of time with this difficult woman if she hadn't been so beautiful. He felt a bit of shame, having to admit this about himself, but there it was. It was only their third encounter, and already he could feel a certain weariness creeping into his heart. The irony of it all was that he enjoyed women who could dish it out as well as take it. Ursula, of course, being a prime example. He found it hard to connect with passive women, women who always looked to him to take the lead, to set the ground rules, to define the relationship. Women who always gave way when conflict arose. But it was one thing for a woman to be strong and independent and willing to stand up for herself. One thing, for that matter, to be argumentative and contentious. It was something else again to carry around a smoldering belligerence that threatened to explode at any moment.

Yet, according to Ursula McGuire, this was a woman who had been abused by her husband; someone, he assumed, she must have loved and trusted at one point in her life, so it was perfectly natural for her to carry around a certain active hostility to men who seemed aggressive and unreasonable. To him, of course, the guy in the SUV had simply been an irritant. But to her, well...

Unexpectedly, she smiled at him. "I'm sorry. You've been very nice to me, and all I've done is subject you to a couple of angry outbursts."

"That's all right. Forget about it."

"No, it's not all right. I apologize."

"Apology accepted."

Her apology softened him, and then it turned his mind in another direction. What, after all, now that he thought about it...what exactly had Ursula McGuire discovered? She had told him on the phone about the fiasco at the doctor's office. But what was it that she actually knew? Nothing, really. She knew that Rebecca and her daughters had lived in Newton. She knew that she was or had been married to a guy named David Warner. She knew that Warner—not Rebecca Scott, he emphasized to himself—was a registered gun owner. But what else did she actually know? Certainly not that Rebecca had been abused. And certainly not that she had shot and killed Charles Devir. The fact of the matter was that there was no actual evidence for either one of these charges.

She turned toward the magazines, and as he looked at her it seemed inconceivable that she could have done such a thing. There was no question that she had a hair-trigger temper, but, Rosario reflected, so had he for most of his life. It was only after he had reached his thirties that he had learned how to control it, and who was he, with such a glaring lack of evidence, to judge this woman?

He glanced down the street and noticed a man in black rounding the corner of Mass Ave and heading away from the Square. Then he saw the white crew cut and the side of the man's face. It was the priest from the other night. Rebecca had the magazine in her hands. She touched his arm. "Give me a second. I'm looking for something."

He turned back. The priest was gone. "Take your time. I think I just saw an old friend of mine." He walked rapidly around the bend, passed the Coop, and caught up with him near the entrance to the subway. "Good evening, Father. We seem to keep running into each other."

The priest tilted his head and the ice-blue eyes bore into his. "Not this time, my friend. You seem to be running after me."

"Well, seeing you twice in such a short period of time worries me. I just wanted to make sure the Church wasn't after me for anything."

"Like what?"

"Oh, I don't know. Absent without leave, maybe."

"How long has it been?"

"Not long. About thirty years."

The man laughed. Not a friendly laugh either. "I'm sure they've forgotten all about you."

"Good. Well, maybe I'll see you around."

The priest turned and hurried down the steps to the subway. When Rosario got back to Nini's, Rebecca gave him a puzzled look. "So how's your friend?"

"He's not my friend. He's a priest. I keep running into him around the Square. It's a little strange."

She smiled. "Maybe he's after you for some great sin. Maybe I shouldn't have classified you with the good guys after all."

Someone grabbed his elbow. "Hi, Mr. Rosario."

He turned. "Gretchen, how are you?"

She grinned. "Fine. I thought that was you. I wasn't sure, though." She took his arm and turned him around and pointed across the street at the Curious George store. "Look." Three more of his ex-students were standing at the corner of Kennedy Street waving at him. He smiled and waved back and Gretchen squeezed his arm. "Come, on. We want to buy you a beer."

"You don't have to do that. Besides, I don't want to horn in on your party."

"Are you kidding? The minute we saw you we all thought of it at once. We owe you big time."

"You don't owe me anything, Gretch."

"But we do. I still have my Rosario notes. They got me through my first two years at UCLA." She was tugging his arm now. "Come on. No excuses."

"OK, OK. But I'm with someone. Gretchen, this is Rebecca Scott, a friend of mine."

"Hi, Rebecca. I'm Mr. Rosario's favorite ex-student. In fact, I'm the best student he ever had. Right, Mr. Rosario?"

"And the shyest."

Gretchen just reached right over and put her arm through Rebecca's and began leading them away from Nini's. "You have to help us get Mr. Rosario into Grendel's Den before he can think of another reason not to join us."

He expected Rebecca to spurn the invitation, to respond haughtily to Gretchen's aggressive spontaneity. But she surprised him with the gentle friendliness of her demurral. "I'd like to help you out, Gretchen, but it's probably more appropriate for you kids to have some time alone with your old teacher."

Gretchen grinned at him again and then turned quickly back to Rebecca. "He *is* kind of old, isn't he? All the more reason for you to come with us. He might keel over after his first beer, and we'll need someone responsible to take care of him."

Rebecca smiled and shook her head. "Actually, I've just finished working out. I think I should be drinking water rather than beer."

"Nonsense. Beer is great after a workout."

Suddenly, Rebecca just gave up, surrendering to Gretchen's charm. "OK, Gretchen. You win."

Gretchen laughed, genuinely pleased. "Hey, that's great. So how long have you known Mr. Rosario?"

The light changed and they walked across the street. "A very short time."

"Thank God! You still have time to break off the relationship before it's too late."

Rosario groaned. "Gretchen, give it a rest. Rebecca and I are acquaintances. We hardly know each other. Don't embarrass her."

"I think you're the one who's embarrassed, Mr. Rosario. Don't you think so, Rebecca?"

Rebecca laughed, surprising him again. "I think you might be right on that one, Gretchen. But what he says is true. We're just friends."

"Uh, oh. I get it. Stop prying, right?"

They reached the corner and the rest of the group came up to him. Michelle, Gretchen's best friend in high school, gave him a hug and the two guys, Nate and Sully, shook his hand and clapped him on the back. Once inside Grendel's, they found a table against the wall near the fireplace and Nate ordered a round of Bass Ales. For the next hour, they exchanged stories of their times together at Liberty High, and once, after Sully told a hilarious story about Gretchen frightening off a potential boyfriend with her hyperactive personality, Rosario turned and Rebecca smiled at him. There was nothing particularly meaningful about the smile. But it told him something. It told him that she was capable of sitting around with a group of strangers and interacting with them as if she were a normal human being. She even seemed to be having a good time. How then, could this woman..."Hey, Mr. Rosario! Tell the one about Cindy Miller!"

"Gretch, come on! Now that *is* embarrassing."

"No, it's not. You handled that fairly well for a male teacher."

Michelle looked across the table at Rebecca. "Mr. Rosario has this rule that nobody goes to the bathroom during one of his tests."

Rebecca raised an eyebrow. "Nobody? What if there's an emergency?"

Nate stood up and imitated him. "There'll be no emergencies during my tests!"

Everybody roared and then Sully leaned over to Rebecca. "Actually, it's a good rule. Kids go out to the lav where they've hidden copies of chapters or articles Mr. Rosario assigns so they can cheat." He shrugged. "I mean everybody knows why the rule is there."

Michelle laughed. "Well, yeah, but this one time, we're about ten minutes into the test when suddenly Cindy Miller, who sat in the first seat in the middle row, raises her hand and says, 'Mr. Rosario, I gotta go to the girls' room,' and of course, he says, 'Cindy, you know the rules. You know you can go before the test but not during the test,' and Cindy says, 'Yeah, but Mr. Rosario,' and he says, 'Not now.' Meanwhile, everybody goes back to working on the test, so only the two kids to the right and left of Cindy see what happens next, one of whom happens to be me. So, get this. Cindy very quietly reaches into her purse and pulls out a tampon. Then she says in this really sarcastic voice, 'Oh, Mr. Rosario?' He looks up and sighs and says, 'Yes, Cindy?' and she looks him right in the eye, and without a word, she shakes the tampon at him as if she's threatening him with it. Hah! Do you believe it? Mr. Rosario just rolls his eyes and waves her out. Irina and I were dying laughing."

Later in the evening, when they reached Chauncy Street, she looked up at him. "Those young people said some very nice things about you tonight. About the impact you made on their lives. How you taught them how to write and how to do research and how to survive in college. Your career really gives your life meaning, doesn't it?"

"Yes, it does."

"Most people's careers are just jobs. I'm good at what I do, but I don't have the chance to interact with people like that. I don't affect their lives the way you do."

"You affect the lives of your daughters. It seems to me you've done a damn good job with them. I meet quite a few kids who are worse off for having the parents they do. But yours are better off for having you as their mother."

She stared at him. "Well...thank you."

They looked at each other for a moment without speaking, and somewhere inside him a voice of both wisdom and experience whispered its warning. Time to go, Rosario. Time to go. He smiled and extended his hand. "Goodnight, Ms. Scott."

She took his hand. "Goodnight, Mr. Rosario...Rob."

He let go of her hand and said goodbye and walked away.

CHAPTER 10

When Ursula McGuire returned to her office on Beacon Street, she found her secretary hissing through clenched teeth at a tall handsome stranger. Brandishing her steaming mug of Murchie's Irish Breakfast Tea, Lily O'Donnell leaned forward over her desk like a cobra ready to strike. "You will only see Ms. McGuire, sir, by appointment. That is the way this office works. Do you understand?"

Lily was an ex-nun, and not one of those kindly, benevolent ones from the eighties or nineties either. At sixty-four, she was old enough to have taught Ursula McGuire or Robert Rosario while they were still in grammar school and to have slapped them around with the ruler-wielding terror common to the sisterhood of that era.

Although Ursula had never seen Lily O'Donnell until the day she interviewed for the job, after one glance at those iron eyes and furrowed brow, Ursula recognized the type. At first, she was put off by Lily's manner, but having been disappointed by a string of warm, charming, and completely unreliable younger women, she started to have second thoughts. Mark, as she expected, argued for giving her a chance. He gently urged her to put her eternal resentment of the Catholic Church aside and consider the woman as an individual. Rosario, surprisingly, echoed this sentiment, for it was about this time that he had started to mellow. There were the occasional outbursts, of course. But by and large, he seemed to be coming to the conclusion that the incendiary anger he carried around with him had to go, and somehow, agreeing with Mark on hiring Lily O'Donnell appeared to be part of that process. So Ursula gave her a shot at the job and never regretted it. Tough, efficient, and loyal to the core, Lily had been her right-hand woman for over thirteen years.

Ursula closed the door behind her, and Lily straightened up and put her free hand on her hip. "This finely attired hooligan stormed into the office demanding to see you. The word *appointment* does not appear to be a part of his vocabulary."

The man's hair and eyes were jet black and his face almost gaunt, though there was a kind of ruthless good looks about him. He was dressed in an expensive charcoal gray suit, and when he turned to look at her, she noticed immediately there was a stiffness to the movement, and that right below his left shirt cuff, the tip of something like a cast or a brace was clearly visible. She stepped over to Lily's desk and looked into his eyes. "What exactly seems to be the problem?"

"I'm afraid, Ms. McGuire, that you seem to be the problem."

"Is that so?"

"Indeed it is. My name is David Warner. My family physician, Dr. John Crust, informs me that you paid him a visit at Newton-Wellesley Hospital, and that you asked him what both he and I consider to be extremely intrusive questions. Are you in the habit of violating people's privacy like this?"

"It depends on the situation, Mr. Warner. In the case of Dr. Crust, I had a very good reason for my visit. Would you like to discuss it out here or in my office?"

She turned back to her secretary who stood indignantly by her chair. "Thank you, Lily. I'll take Mr. Warner off your hands. Now don't forget your Murchie's." She patted Lily's arm and ushered David Warner into the office.

One of her cardinal rules was to never, no matter what the circumstances, show surprise or a lack of certainty. Yet now she felt both. The very fact that he would dare to show up in her office like this, the very fact that he would demand to know the reason for her visit to his doctor, and to do both in the presence of a witness...well, this did take her by surprise. And for one fleeting moment, an ounce of self-doubt did indeed creep into her mind. A man guilty of abusing his wife, and having been told by his physician the reason a lawyer had come to his office, knew full well what the lawyer would say to him when he posed such a question. A calculating person would not have asked that question in front of a third party. Unless, of course, he was simply a careless man. The trouble was he didn't look like a careless man.

Once in the office, he seemed a little less angry, a bit more subdued, and this was because, Ursula knew, she had shown neither her surprise nor that momentary feeling of self-doubt. She acted as if she were a hundred percent sure of everything she said, and she could already see that it was having its intended effect. At first, it looked as if he were going to remain standing and deliver his accusation right there on the rug, but when she gestured to the chair across from hers, he took it. Then he sat back and stared at her. "Now would you please tell me the reason for your visit to my physician? I have every right to know."

She sat down in her chair and studied him. "But surely you already know why I visited Dr. Crust. He called you and told you and you came storming over here."

"I demand to know why you are doing this. Listen to me, Ms. McGuire. I own and run the most successful accounting firm west of Boston. I am a community businessman with a community reputation. I have *never* laid a hand on my wife in anger. Do you have any idea what even a rumor to this effect can do to me?" He glanced around her office for a moment and gestured at the photographs on the wall behind her, at the paintings and the furniture, and then looked back at her. "Surely, Ms. McGuire, having attained all this, you can appreciate what's at stake here for me. I've worked very hard for what I have accomplished as I'm sure you have. For you to go to my doctor and ask him to review our medical records for proof of a vague suspicion that I might have ever hurt my wife is about as unprofessional a thing as I have ever seen."

She kept her eyes on his the whole time, but despite herself, that little ounce of self-doubt began slinking back again. "Yet your wife and your daughters have left you and have moved to another town. A rather radical decision, wouldn't you say?"

"Families break up all the time in this country, Ms. McGuire, and you know it. After all, you're a lawyer, aren't you? Speaking of which, perhaps it's time for me to contact my lawyer. I believe your actions may not have been only unprofessional, but may have indeed skirted the edge of what might be considered illegal."

She decided to call his bluff. "If you had been contemplating legal action, Mr. Warner, I would have heard from your attorney, not you. You decided to come over here in person. Actually, I'm perfectly comfortable dealing with your attorney. Then it will become a lawyer-to-lawyer relationship, and you know how those things can work out. Before you know it, you may discover that what I have done is in fact perfectly legal, and if we push the matter further—legally, that is—we may enter the realm of the courts, and if that happens, certain information could see the light of day. Once that occurs, the information goes public, rumors fly, and people get hurt. So you decide."

"Look here. You're invading my life. I'm not invading yours. Furthermore, I've done a little checking on you. From what I can see, you're primarily a political investigator. One of those hired guns that goes around gathering information on a politician's opponent." Here he paused and pointed his finger at her accusingly. "A friend of mine who's quite active in Republican politics here in the Commonwealth referred to you as the scourge of his party. He claims you are involved in giving information about those workers in Indiana to the *Globe*. That you are spearheading the effort to discredit Mitt Romney's labor record and trying to save Kennedy's ass."

Ursula laughed. "I'm quite sure the Senator can take care of himself."

"Not this time. He's running scared and you know it. You're a pretty powerful woman, Ms. McGuire. You've got some friends in high places. So the question is, why are you coming after me? What is it you want?"

"You know what I want. I went to your physician to find out if you have at any time abused your wife."

"But why? You're not a law enforcement officer. You're not seeking my arrest. Why do you want to find out something like that? You can't possibly be representing my wife. In the first place, she knows I've never hit her, so why would she have you come after me? Secondly, I'm willingly providing support for my two girls. And finally, I'm not harassing her. So why would she hire you?"

"She hasn't. I have no connection to your wife whatsoever."

"Well, you're not doing this for fun, are you? Who is it that you're representing?"

"I'm not at liberty to say."

"Oh, really. You're not at liberty to say. You want to turn my life upside down, but you're not at liberty to tell me why. Typical lawyer behavior."

"And you're more than welcome to bring your own typical lawyer into the matter."

"Which you know I'm not going to do."

"But surely if you're innocent, Mr. Warner, you have no…"

He slammed his good hand down on her desk. "I *am* innocent! You know damn well why I don't want to bring another lawyer in on this. You just said so yourself. I cannot afford even the appearance of such a charge. I'm not some hotshot attorney like you. I'm not some public employee with a powerful union behind him. I'm an independent businessman whose whole world will come crashing down around him because of some baseless, scurrilous charge. What on earth motivates someone like you to do something like this? It's political, isn't it?"

"Absolutely not."

"Of course, it is. We have your boy on the ropes with our ads on welfare and crime. You're flailing around for issues, so you're taking the low road and going after the people in his campaign. Right?"

"Wrong. It has nothing to do with the campaign."

"Nonsense! Everything you do is connected to politics. This is opposition research run amuck. If you can bring me down, you can undermine the clean record of the Republican candidate for the United States Senate. You can tar a good man through guilt by association. *Romney's Major Fundraiser*

Abuses Wife. That will look great, won't it? Well, I'm afraid it won't work. And it won't work because it's not true."

She held his gaze, watching for signs of duplicity. The glance away. The forced passion. The feel of insincerity in the voice. But he was steady as a rock. At last, she answered him. "The only thing that would make me do what I have done is the fairly certain knowledge that a woman has been abused, and that it is important to discover the identity of that abuser."

"What if that fairly certain knowledge is based on false suppositions, and what appears to be fairly certain is fairly uncertain?"

Ursula smiled. "Don't play word games with me, Mr. Warner."

"Then don't play mind games with me, Ms. McGuire. What would it take to make you go away and leave me alone? I can't have this sword of Damocles hanging over me and my reputation."

"Prove to me that you've never subjected your wife to physical abuse."

"How can I do that?"

"Think about it. You're an intelligent man. And a clever one, too. I liked that little classical allusion just then. That reference to Greek mythology."

For the first time, he smiled. He had very even, white teeth and his black eyes almost sparkled, and she wondered if he had used his looks to have his way with women over the years. He looked capable of it. But he was also presenting himself in a damn convincing way, and not in that trumped up, overly rehearsed manner so common to the corrupt politicians and cornered criminals she had dealt with over the years. His defense came across as compelling and genuine, and she didn't like it one bit. This was not the way she had expected things to be working out. She had a lot on her plate, and she didn't need to get dragged into some hideously complex marital battle. She thought of Rosario's jumping ship and wished for a moment that she had jumped with him. This was what happened when you went into a case with your heart instead of your head.

He stood up and walked over to the window, and she noticed again the stiff way he held his left arm and shoulder. "You have a magnificent view." He turned and looked at her. "All right, then. Try this. I give you permission to examine all my medical records. I waive my right to privacy. How's that?"

She was completely taken aback and paused for a second before answering. "That would certainly be very helpful, Mr. Warner, but I can't guarantee, of course, that I won't seek evidence elsewhere."

"Fine. Go wherever you like. But it should at least count as a gesture of good faith on my part, don't you think?"

She stared at him and nodded. "Yes, Mr. Warner. On first glance, it does appear that what you're offering me is a gesture of good faith."

He smiled at her. "How carefully you choose your words, Ms. McGuire. How lawyerly of you."

"Lawyers can't help being lawyerly, Mr. Warner. It's in our nature."

He turned back and looked out again. "And you go right ahead seeking evidence elsewhere. You won't find it, because it doesn't exist. Whoever your client is, and whatever that person has told you has no basis in fact. It simply isn't true."

———

Later that evening at dinner, Mark frowned at his wife. "So suddenly you don't seem so sure."

"I'm still fairly certain."

"I warned you about visiting that doctor."

"Indeed you did. But since in this marriage we never indulge in even mild recriminations, we certainly don't have to get into that."

He laughed and reached across the table and took her hand. "I'm sorry. I certainly didn't mean to imply that you've blundered into this one. All I'm saying is that Warner is proving to be a worthy opponent. You've faced worthy opponents before. So the question arises, what if he's telling the truth?"

"Good question. If he is, then we've got a real problem on our hands."

"We?"

She leaned forward and smiled. "That's right, buddy. *We.* After all, you're the one who got me into this. Abby Whitman is your student, remember, and wasn't it you who volunteered that *your* wife just might be happy to help out?"

"Ah, yes. Now it's coming back to me."

"Good. I thought you might begin to see things my way."

He took a sip of his wine and leaned back in his chair. "One more thing."

"Uh, huh."

"What do you make of the stiff arm and shoulder? And the cast or whatever you saw by his wrist?"

"He's been hurt, obviously."

"Well, obviously, my dear. The question is how he was hurt."

She shrugged. "I didn't ask him. He could have fallen down the stairs in his house or slipped on the street on a rainy day."

"Possibly."

"Or like Max when he tripped and fell and ripped off a layer of skin on that tennis court in Brookline."

"Also a possibility. Or…"

"Or what?"

"Or somebody could have hurt him."

She nodded and then smiled again. "Somebody like whom?"

He drained his wine glass and then placed it down firmly in the center of the table. "You're the investigator, counselor. Why don't you tell me?"

CHAPTER 11

On Friday night, Rosario joined some friends for dinner in the North End. The evening was cool and clear with a strong salty breeze blowing in from the harbor, and they walked through the narrow streets for over an hour until they were tired and hungry. At L'Osteria Ristorante they ate veal and pasta and shared a hearty Tuscan red while watching the Friday night crowds stream up and down Salem Street.

Later, when he returned to Cambridge, relaxed and content, two message lights blinked at him from the darkness of his study. The first one took him by surprise, and for a second or two, he couldn't place the voice. "Hey, Mr. Rosario. How are you doing? My English teacher just sprang this project on us today with no warning at all. It's really unfair and like...ridiculous. I think she's mad at us or something. Oh, this is Emily Warner...I guess I should have said that in the first place. My mom told me not to bother you with this since it's the weekend, so she doesn't know about this phone call. I apologize and everything and I wouldn't have done it but I remembered that night we got the

Thai take-out and you said if I ever needed any help with school to call you. Mom has to work Saturday morning so if you call me then, I'll be home. Thanks. I really appreciate this."

The second message was from Ursula McGuire. "Rosie. Called on the spur of the moment to see if you wanted to join us for a late dinner at The Blue Room, but I see you're nowhere to be found. I'll bet you went to the North End. Am I right?" Rosario shook his head and smiled. "Call me when you get in. We'll be up late. I hope you're not out with anyone…anyone dangerous. Take care, Rob. Be sure to call."

He brought the phone over to his Morris chair and punched in her number. "Hi."

"Was I right? Did you go to the North End?"

"Yes, Ursula. That's where I was. Good guess."

She laughed softly. "I knew it. You're such a creature of habit. Look, I've been feeling guilty about dragging you into the Rebecca Scott thing, and I want to apologize. You had every right to drop out."

"Well, I'm afraid I haven't quite dropped out altogether."

There was a pause. "What do you mean?"

"When I signed off on the case, I signed off on Rebecca Scott. It was as simple as that. Then one night I was out for my walk and she spotted me. She pulled over and thanked me for helping her out that night, and then she asked me to come over for dinner."

"And you accepted."

"Yeah, I did. Why I did, I'm not sure."

"God, Rosie. You broke training for her. That's impressive. Did…did you have a nice time?"

"I had a very nice time, although not the kind of time I'm used to. In a way, I felt like an intruder. The odd man out in what was really just an informal, family dinner."

Ursula groaned. "So I guess we've got a problem, then. I mean because of this...this relationship."

"Not really. We parted on friendly terms, and we both agreed that there should not be a relationship."

"You've seen her two times and you're already at the stage where you both agree there should be no relationship?"

He decided not to mention the third time. "Ms. Scott is very direct."

She sighed. "And I got you into this, didn't I?"

"That's right, Ursie. You did."

"So, how does it stand?"

"The way it stands is that two people have decided to steer clear of each other but somehow keep bumping into each other due to their close geographic proximity. That's about all I can tell you. None of this, however, need interfere with your investigation."

"Well, then it's a damn good thing nothing has happened between the two of you. Now, forgive me for asking, but how will you prevent this relationship from growing if you keep running into her like this?"

"I've been doing OK so far."

"Uh, huh...but you slammed that kid around when he threatened her daughter. That must have put you in the mother's good graces."

He laughed. "This is not a woman who seems to possess good graces, Ursula."

"But you know what I mean. If she warms up to you, it will make it more difficult for you to keep your distance."

"I wouldn't worry about that. I'm pretty good at keeping my distance."

"That you are, Robert. That you are."

E mily Warner stiffened a bit. "What's so funny? I don't think it's a funny topic to choose."

Rosario shrugged. "I don't think it's funny, Emily. I just think it's interesting, that's all. My parents read Longfellow in school back in the thirties, and my father used to love to recite lines from *Hiawatha* while he was shaving. *By the shore of Gitche Gumee...By the shining Big-Sea-Water.* I can't remember the rest, I'm afraid. I'm just amazed someone your age and in this era would choose him."

She looked at him suspiciously. "Amazed good or amazed bad?"

"Amazed good. How's that?"

She smiled. "That's OK."

He took her down Mt. Auburn Street rather than Brattle, so that her first view of Longfellow's mansion would be through the park and the trees. They paused at the stone pillars with the wrought iron gates that led into the poet's former grounds and she stopped and stared. "Wow. God, it's beautiful. We've lived here since April and I've never even noticed it. Typical dumb teenager, huh?"

"I don't think you quite fit into that category, Emily."

"How did a poet afford a place like that?"

"He married a rich girl. Her father gave them all these grounds and that mansion as a wedding present."

Emily looked at him. "I guess that beats all that gift registry stuff at Crate and Barrel."

Rosario laughed. "Definitely. The yuppies would turn green with envy."

They walked between the pillars to the pathway that circled the lawn, inhaling the fragrant scent of freshly cut grass. He pointed across the park at the big yellow house shining in the sunlight. "Way before Longfellow lived there the house served as General Washington's headquarters during the early stages of the Revolution. Does your teacher want background like that, or is she looking for something else?"

"Well, this is for English and she's really into poetry big time. She wants us to find things that reflect a sense of place."

"What have you read?"

"So far, *Evangeline, The Song of Hiawatha*—that was pretty corny, I gotta admit—*Tales of a Wayside Inn*. That one I really liked. You're laughing again."

"I'm not laughing. I'm just smiling. Most of my kids won't read anything unless they know I'm going to test them on it."

"You must give lots of tests."

"I do indeed. And essays. If your teacher's looking for a poem that reflects a sense of place locally, however, you won't find it in those. *The Village Blacksmith* might work."

"The one about the spreading chestnut tree?"

"That's it. The city cut the tree down when they widened Brattle Street back in the 1870's, but the blacksmith's house is still there."

They approached Daniel Chester French's bronze bust of the poet and the white wall with the carved figures of Longfellow's literary creations. Emily pointed at one of them. "That's Evangeline."

"Right."

"And that's obviously Hiawatha and there's the blacksmith. I don't know the others."

"Step closer and you can read the names."

After a while, she turned and looked at him. "I think I'm going to write about the blacksmith. I've decided. My English teacher tried to discourage me from doing my research on Longfellow. She says no one reads him anymore because he's just a sentimental storyteller."

Rosario frowned. "Well, that's certainly true, but I think it's perfectly OK for fourteen-year-olds to still have some room in their lives for stories and even a dose of sentimentality if they see fit. You have the rest of your life to get old and cynical. Who did she want you to choose?"

"She said I was an advanced enough student to try someone like T.S. Eliot."

This stopped Rosario in his tracks. "What!"

"Yeah, I know. I tried him but I couldn't understand anything."

"Don't worry about it. Most adults can't understand him either. They just won't admit it."

"One of the poems she recommended even had footnotes after it. Footnotes after a poem! Didn't he trust his readers?"

Rosario chuckled. "Actually, Eliot once lived a couple blocks from here. I can show you the place after we see Longfellow's."

"Is Eliot's house open to the public?"

"God, no. You have to have footnotes to get in."

She laughed and they walked away from the wall and strolled through the rest of the park and across Brattle Street. He opened the wooden gate for her, and they moved toward the mansion slowly, as he explained some of the architectural detail and pointed out the floor where Longfellow did his writing. Then they passed around the right side of the house near the long porch and went into the garden, where she stopped to gaze at the red and white and purple flowers gleaming in the morning sunshine. She began to poke around among the plants and stooped to examine the old sundial, so he decided to let her explore on her own a while. When she was finished, she joined him by the porch, and he took her down Brattle Street to the white clapboard house where the village blacksmith had lived.

She turned and smiled at him. "In this very house?"

"In this very house."

"That's great, isn't it? I mean that it's still here?"

"It sure is."

"Lizzie would never be interested in anything like this."

"Most kids wouldn't be. So what's Lizzie up to today?"

"She's going to spend time with my dad. He's picking her up and they're going shopping at the Chestnut Hill Mall."

"Do you usually stay home when Lizzie sees your father?"

"Sometimes. Mom treats us both the same, but my dad favors Lizzie. They have more in common."

"Like what?"

"They're into things. They buy things. He's a big spender. He sort of buys her love."

Rosario was silent for a moment. "And you?"

"I'm not for sale." She shook her head and opened her hands. "Well, I guess I'm being overdramatic like my mom always says. What I mean is that he tries harder with Lizzie."

"Why is that?"

She waved her hand. "Oh...well, that's a long story."

There was no anger or bitterness in her voice. She had simply made the statement as a matter of fact. How was it, he asked himself, that a man who abused his wife had a younger daughter who was only mildly resentful of him and another who seemed to be his pal? At last he broke the silence. "Did you have a big breakfast?"

"I didn't feel like much of anything."

"Well, I'm hungry. How about a muffin or something?"

She smiled. "OK. Thanks."

They went into the bakery in the Blacksmith House where he bought two big blueberry muffins and two cups of steaming hot coffee, and they brought them outside to one of the tables near the sidewalk. Emily watched the people walking along Brattle Street toward the Square and then turned and grinned at him over her coffee. "Boy, this sure beats Newton. My mom and I really like it here but Lizzie just sort of tolerates it."

"Well, given that jerk who's been bothering her..."

"It's not just that. She misses all her boring, stupid, mall-hopping friends, but I like Cambridge. There are definitely fewer snobs. People are more accepting here and there's more kinds of people too." She glanced at the corner of Farwell Street where a tall thin man with a white ponytail was dancing all by himself. "What's with that guy?"

"He's just groovin' along to some music that the rest of us will never hear. He's been hanging around Harvard Square for as long as I can remember."

"One too many acid trips back in the sixties, huh? What is that move he's making? What kind of a dance is that?"

Rosario sipped his coffee. "It appears, if I'm not mistaken, to be a somewhat inaccurate rendition of the Mashed Potato."

"The Mashed Potato! What's that?"

"You don't want to know, Emily. Believe me."

She laughed and mumbled through a big mouthful of blueberry muffin. "By the look of him, that guy must have lived the sixties to the limit."

"I'm sure he did. That's why he missed the seventies and the eighties."

She choked on her muffin. "You're a funny guy, you know that? Oh, my God!"

"What?"

She looked at her watch. "It's almost 10:30. My dad's picking Lizzie up at 10:45, and Lizzie told me to bring you by to meet him after we were through with the Longfellow stuff. She told him about how you helped her out with the creep and he wants to thank you."

"That's very nice of him, Em, but I don't feel quite right about showing up outside your place in the middle of a family occasion."

She interrupted him. "Believe me, it's not a family thing, really. My mom makes sure she's never there when he comes to pick us up. I told Lizzie it was a dumb idea, anyway."

He sipped his coffee again. "Well, it's not that it's a dumb idea. I just don't feel comfortable about it."

"I figured you'd say something like that."

"And you figured right." He stood up and tossed their coffee cups and muffin wrappers into a trash bin. "Come on. I'll walk you back to the corner of Chauncy Street, and then I'll be on my way."

"OK." They walked down Appian Way past the Gutman Library and then along Garden Street by the Cambridge Common. "I really appreciate all your help, Mr. Rosario. I know you gave up your Saturday morning."

He laughed. "Nonsense. I didn't give up a thing. What we did this morning is pretty much what I do every Saturday morning, and it was nice to have some company. And outside of showing you a few sights, I haven't really helped you much at all. If you need any real help on the research or the paper itself, call me again."

He stopped at the corner of Chauncy and they shook hands. She looked up at him and smiled. "Thanks."

"No problem."

But suddenly there was a problem. They could hear Lizzie's voice calling to them and when they turned to look, she was leaning against the side of a shiny black Mercedes and waving at them to come over. Emily waved back and sighed. "Uh, oh. Now what?"

"I guess it's time to meet the old man, isn't it?"

She cast him a guilty smile and shrugged. "I didn't mean to get you into this, you know."

"I know. Come on. Let's get it over with."

They walked down the street together and a man with black hair stepped out of the car. He was dressed casually in a navy polo shirt and khakis, and despite the unusual warmth of the morning, he wore a lightweight sport coat. Then Rosario realized why. There was something wrong with the way he held his left arm, and he carried himself with a certain restraint as if he had been injured. He walked up to the two of them and gave Emily a hug. Then he turned to Rosario. "I'm David Warner. I want to thank you for defending Lizzie. She told me all about it."

Rosario shook hands with him and noticed him wince a little as he reached forward. "Are you OK?"

"I'm fine. I had a humiliating and stupid accident, that's all. All my own fault. Got a little too aggressive on the handball court, crashed into the wall, smashed the hell out of my rotator cuff and sprained my wrist to boot. I'll live. Sometimes I forget I'm forty-seven and think I'm twenty-two. Anyway, I owe you a debt of gratitude. I guess I'm not always there when my kids need me." David Warner glanced at his daughters and they smiled up at him. Emily a little less so than Lizzie, but nevertheless she did smile. It was obvious from what she had said before that there were problems between the two of them, but unlike her mother, she was there. She didn't particularly want to go with her father today, but she was willing to speak to him, willing to let him put his arm around her for a second or two.

Suddenly, Emily stared at her sister. "Hey, that's my shirt!"

120

Lizzie sighed and rolled her eyes. "Come on, Em. I just borrowed it."

"You didn't ask me and furthermore…"

David Warner raised his good hand in the air. "Girls. Stop. Go inside and settle it." They walked quickly toward the house, squabbling all the way. When the door slammed shut, Warner looked back at him. "What you did was above and beyond the call of duty. Apparently, he hasn't bothered Lizzie since."

"Let's hope it stays that way."

"Absolutely. Look, I'm not sure what you know about our situation."

"Not much, really. But it's none of my business. You don't need to say anything."

He glanced toward the house for a second and then looked back. "I know I don't need to say anything, but I will anyway. And the reason is that I want to return the favor you've done for me. But I need to choose my words carefully, because I don't want you to misunderstand me. Lizzie told me that you've been over to dinner once, and she told me how you were helping Emily today. My relationship with my wife is over. So please do not confuse what I am going to say with anger or jealousy or any other emotion that a husband in this situation is supposed to feel. I feel none of them. What I want to do is warn you. Be careful. Be very careful of Rebecca. She's not the kind of woman any man wants to get involved with. No matter what she's told you about me…"

"She's told me nothing."

"Good. That means you're not in too deep yet. Take care not to get too involved with this woman, Mr. Rosario."

The door to the house flew open and Lizzie came bounding out wearing a new outfit. "Ready, Dad! See ya, Mr. Rosario."

"See ya, Lizzie. Have fun."

He turned and looked back at David Warner and they shook hands again.

"Take care of yourself, Mr. Rosario."

Rosario nodded, released Warner's hand, and walked back toward the Square.

CHAPTER 12

This time, the pink-faced Dr. Crust was nowhere to be seen, but his secretary could not have been more accommodating. So far, David Warner had proven true to his word. But once Ursula reviewed the records, his readiness to come clean became apparent. David and Rebecca Warner's charts contained nothing even remotely related to any signs of abuse. Rebecca Warner had never complained to Dr. Crust, at least, of anything out of the ordinary and had never been treated for bruises, contusions, or broken bones. But Ursula had half expected that. Abused women, once they summoned up the courage to act, often sought out physicians other than their family doctor.

What surprised Ursula, however, was the lack of any record that David Warner had sought treatment for an injured arm or shoulder. There was no question that Warner had been hurt. So why not go right to the local hospital?

She went back into the office to return the file and speak to the secretary. "Thank you. You've been very helpful. One more question, if you don't mind. If someone is treated in the emergency room here at Newton-Wellesley, aren't copies of the records sent to the patient's primary care physician?"

"Certainly."

"Well, that's what I thought. Thank you, again."

———

S he met Mark for lunch at a little sandwich shop in Kendall Square. "So you see where I'm going with this?"

"Uh, huh. You're thinking a community businessman doesn't go to his community hospital, because his injury is something he doesn't want to report."

"Correct. And why would he be ashamed to report a fall or some other kind of accident?"

"He wouldn't."

"Exactly. David Warner didn't have an accident. Someone deliberately injured David Warner. If a stranger had injured him, if he had been mugged or attacked, he would have gone to the Newton police and to Newton-Wellesley Hospital. He did neither. He wanted to keep the cause of this injury quiet. Now, why?"

"Because, if I follow the train of that unassailable logic of yours, his abused wife had reached the end of the line and struck or stabbed or shot him out of desperation or hatred or vengeance."

"Or all of the above. Now all I have to do is figure out which emergency room he did go to."

A girl with spiky orange hair called their number from the counter and Mark bounded up to get their food. He brought the sandwiches back to the table and took a sip of his ice tea.

"There's only a zillion hospitals in the metropolitan Boston area. That should be fun."

She took a bite of her sandwich and thought for a moment. "Actually, it might not be as difficult as you think. Let's assume for a second that Rebecca Scott shot her husband."

"Just as she shot Charles Devir."

"Well, of course, although certainly less severely than she shot Charles Devir. But let's assume she did. Where does he go if he doesn't want the locals to find out?"

"I don't know. Mass General? Beth Israel?"

"What hospital treats gunshot wounds on a regular basis? What hospital is least likely to make a big deal out of someone walking into the emergency room with a gunshot wound?"

He put down his sandwich. "Boston City, of course. But I'm having a hard time picturing this accountant from Newton making his way through that neighborhood, especially if it was after dark. Besides, where do you come up with that kind of presence of mind after being shot? Don't you just go to the goddamn hospital? You think this guy sat around with blood pouring out of his shoulder or arm and a bullet inside of him deciding where he should go? Come on, Ursie!"

He was cornering her, and with no reply readily available, she simply shrugged. "You underestimate, my dear, the workings of the criminal mind."

"Criminal mind! You have no proof of anything other than the fact that this man was or is married to Rebecca Scott, runs a successful accounting firm, and had the balls to confront you in your office and thus incur your ire. Just the other night, this man was stirring doubts in your mind, but now, in the face of increasing medical evidence to the contrary, he has suddenly achieved the exalted rank of *criminal*. How do you figure that?"

"This man subjected his wife to violence, and in my book that makes him a criminal."

He leaned toward her, both index fingers placed against his temples. "What book is that? *The No Proof Book? The Lack of Evidence Book? The Star Chamber Book?*"

She laughed. "Don't start getting historical on me."

He shook his head and picked up his sandwich again. "Yes, well it seems to me that the medical history you just looked at this morning gives you exactly zero data for your assumptions about this man's guilt. Thank God for the founding fathers."

"What the hell do those old guys have to do with it?"

"They gave us a Constitution to protect us all from the likes of you."

Mark was right when he had informed Rosario that Bob LeClerc had inadvertently given Ursula the idea of walking into a major Boston health facility wearing a white coat back in the Barbara Upton case. Furthermore, Bob's assistance continued over the years, and on a number of occasions he had testified for Ursula in court as a medical expert. But as Bob grew older and more successful in his field of pediatric medicine at Massachusetts General Hospital, the less desire he had to get involved in some of Ursula's more questionable activities. The problem was that he owed her. And he owed her big time.

A few years back the hospital hired a consultant to create "efficiencies" in the Department of Pediatrics. Armed with his newly minted Harvard M.B.A. and backed by two hospital administrators who had clashed repeatedly with LeClerc, the consultant embarked upon a strategy of challenging Bob's authority and questioning his expertise. Bob parried the young man's every move, but eventually tiring of the sniping and badgering, he ordered in the heavy artillery.

Delighted to take on what she viewed as an arrogant, ivy league post-adolescent out to discredit one of the city's finest physicians, Ursula leapt into the case with relish and quickly struck gold, discovering, but allowing Bob to reveal in a triumphant performance before the hospital's review board, that the consultant had been accused of serious conflict of interest on a previous contract. By the end of the week, the consultant was no longer consulting at Massachusetts General Hospital.

Now Ursula knew that in addition to his duties at MGH, Bob LeClerc taught medical students at Boston City and also had staff privileges there. So it was time to call in her chips. As she expected, Bob was resistant at first, but once she explained it was an abuse case, his moral scruples quickly eroded. Bob had treated enough children of abusive parents to feel few qualms about invading the privacy of these kinds of people.

The following evening they met at the Hatch Shell and walked along the Charles River. "Did you have any trouble?"

"When a physician has medical staff privileges, he has access to medical records. I must admit, however, that I was a bit nervous just the same. Had someone called me on it, I would have had to come up with a pretty fancy explanation. You're sure this guy is an abuser, right?"

"Pretty sure."

Bob stopped abruptly. "What do you mean, *pretty* sure?"

"Did I ask you if you were one hundred percent sure that consultant would wreck the Department of Pediatrics?"

They started walking again. "If I had known I would have to do something like this later in life, I would never have tried to pick you up that night in college."

"I was very flattered that you asked. But I was in love with Mark by that time. Had you run into me before Mark and I had met, I would have gone out with you."

He shook his head. "There's been a lot of water under the bridge since then and you two are still together."

"Yup. The old boring married couple. So how's the trophy wife?"

He laughed out loud. "No one but you would phrase the question that way. She's fine, Ursula. We're both fine."

"Has she started teething yet? That can be painful."

He laughed again. "Knock it off. After twenty years with Connie, I deserved a second chance."

"No argument there. I could never stand that woman, but did you have to take up with a teenager?"

"Keane is twenty-nine, not sixteen. Enough."

"And where did she come up with that name? Keane? Are you sure it's not her last name? Have you checked her birth certificate? Maybe her first name is Peachy."

"All right, Ursula. Stop. Let's get to the business at hand. It turns out you were quite correct. A Mr. David Warner was treated in the ER for a gunshot wound to the left shoulder on the night of April 14th. Attending physician was Dr. Rupesh Chandra. The interesting thing is that Dr. Chandra noted that there was no police report. This guy did not call the cops."

"I expected that."

"Really?" He paused. "Tell me something. I inferred from the little you told me that you suspect that this abuser was shot by his abused wife. Am I correct?"

"Not bad for an elderly physician who marries young women with strange names."

He smiled. "OK. The thing is Warner told Chandra he was shot on Columbus Avenue. That he was mugged."

"Uh, huh. A man is mugged and does not report the crime to the police? Again, while I hadn't foreseen the exact form his excuse would take, that also makes sense. If the abuser says his wife shot him, then the cops interview the wife and the wife fingers the abuser. If he says he was mugged and he says it at Boston City Hospital, well, so what else is new? Warner's just another statistic. And that's just the way he wanted it."

"Yes, but there's just one problem with that."

"What?"

"Would his wife have accompanied him to the hospital?"

She stopped and stared at him. "Not the wife I'm thinking of."

"The bullet missed this man's heart by inches. Warner was lucky as hell. Yet David Warner was accompanied by a woman. Dr. Chandra's notes are mostly of a medical nature, as they should be. But he did write down that a man and a woman came to the emergency room at 11:20 the night of April 14th. That the man reported being shot on Columbus Avenue by an assailant who demanded money from him and his companion. But that's all he said. It was not like a police report, of course. No information about what they were doing in that area at that time of night or whether the couple was married."

"Or what kind of a bullet Dr. Chandra extracted from David Warner's shoulder."

"Correct. I hadn't thought of that, of course."

"Mmm...I guess I need to have a little chat with Dr. Chandra."

"And just how are you going to pull that off, Ursie babe? No more white coat routines, I hope. We're all a little too old for crazy shit like that. Right?"

"Relax. My white coat days are over."

"And you can't pretend you're a cop, right? My God, Ursula. You wouldn't do anything like that, would you?"

She laughed. "Don't worry, Bob. We mature ladies don't employ those kinds of tricks. Maybe I'll just play it straight and tell him who I am."

"Fine. Just make sure you don't tell him who I am."

"Don't worry, Doctor. I never betray a source. Especially one who's married to a girl named Keane."

———

D r. Rupesh Chandra proved overly cooperative, but for all the wrong reasons. "You have lovely skin, Ms. McGuire. You are what...still in your thirties? I am a very good judge of age. Especially of beautiful women. Am I close?"

"I'm afraid not, Doctor. You're off by over a decade. I'll be fifty in December. But thanks for the compliment."

"It is hard to believe that you are approaching fifty. I am fifty-five, myself. So that gives us something in common. That and our cultural affinities."

"Cultural affinities?"

"Indeed. Both our peoples have been victims of British imperialism."

She pulled away from the emergency room entrance and took a right on Harrison Avenue. "Well, Dr. Chandra..."

"Please. Call me Rupesh."

"All right, Rupesh...But you see, I was born here in Boston. Not in Ireland."

"Still, your people suffered a great deal here." He put his hand on hers. "I've read about the upper-class English Americans, and how they treated you when you were immigrants. I had to laugh when I learned they were known as

Boston Brahmins. You can imagine how pleased I was to hear a phrase like that here in your country."

She pulled her hand away and let it rest on top of the steering wheel. "Don't get the wrong idea, Doc…Rupesh. My invitation for a drink is purely business."

"Well, I know you said it was purely business, but still, when a woman as beautiful as you meets a man as lonely as I…"

"I thought you said you were happily married."

"That is true, but as I'm sure you know, being happily married and being lonely are not incompatible states of consciousness."

"Don't go getting metaphysical on me, Doctor."

He looked over at her and placed his hand on her right knee. "My thoughts were running more along the physical rather than the metaphysical." She was about to push his hand away when she realized where she was and pulled over and stopped the car. The lust drained from Dr. Chandra's face, instantly replaced by astonishment and panic. "What is this? What is this? This is not necessary at all. I apologize. Please accept my apologies and my promise to put an end to all unwanted advances." They were parked at the corner of Plympton Street and Harrison Avenue, smack dab in front of the new Boston Police building. Three cruisers with their engines running formed a menacing line five feet from Ursula's bumper. Dr. Chandra recoiled into full body cringe and began nervously rubbing his palms together. "You told me you were not with the police, Ms. McGuire."

"I'm not." She nodded toward the building. "But I've got some friends inside."

He held his hands up. "OK, OK. Point well taken." She drove away and took her next available turn toward Washington Street. "Well, well. You can't blame a man for trying."

"No, but I can blame a man for persisting."

"Yes, yes. Point well taken. Here is your cathedral, Ms. McGuire."

She glared at him. "*My* cathedral?"

"Yes, yes. This is your archbishop's headquarters, no?"

"That is his headquarters, but I'm not exactly on a first-name basis with him. Let's just say I'm not a fan."

"That is good. With friends in the police department, that would give you too much power in both the secular and spiritual centers of this great city. Ah, here we are. Right across the street. If you are hungry, they have wonderful soups and hors d'oeuvres to go with our drinks. Do not worry. I will pay for those."

"Nonsense, Rupesh."

"Ah, we are back to Rupesh. That is good."

"And if Rupesh keeps his hands to himself that will also be good. I'm buying."

She drove across Washington Street and parked in front of the Vietnamese restaurant Dr. Chandra had suggested. Pho Republique did indeed have wonderful hors d'oeuvres, and as they ate and sipped glasses of cool Chardonnay, he began to answer her questions. "The wife? I would say she was in her forties. Short brown hair. Brown eyes. Attractive. Nothing like you, of course."

"OK, Rupesh. Give it a rest."

He smiled and shrugged. "And very smart. She asked very intelligent questions while I was debriding the wound. By *debriding*, I mean…"

"I know what debriding a wound means, Rupesh."

He raised his hands again as he had done in the car. "Sorry. I'm surrounded, it appears, by attractive women who know as much as I do."

"What do you mean?"

"Well, she was quite acquainted with medical terms, health insurance matters, and even the kind of physical therapy that Mr. Warner would need."

"Did you get the feeling she was a doctor or a nurse?"

"I did indeed and even asked her. She said no on both accounts but did not offer to tell me what she did for a living, or how she came to know so much about medicine."

"How did they act together?"

"Fine. She was very sympathetic to him. She seemed to know a great deal about him psychologically. Like how well he was dealing with the gunshot wound. How he was the kind of man who would follow a physical therapist's regimen, how..."

"What about how their children would react to all this?"

He put down his wine. "No. No mention of children at all. In fact, while there was a certain intimacy between them, he never referred to her as his wife, nor did she call him her husband." He paused and stared at her for a moment. "Ah, I see where this is going. This is an adultery case, is that it? These two are not married. Is that what you're saying?"

She shook her head and smiled into her wine glass. "I said nothing of the sort. You made that inference."

"Well, you know. It's interesting. I assumed that they were married because I had no reason not to, and then there was her familiarity with his character. But that is no necessary sign of marriage, is it? My wife certainly does not understand me in many ways."

"She certainly doesn't. Especially the way you come on to other women."

"Now, now, Ms. McGuire. No need to bring my wife into this. She has no need to learn of this evening anymore than Mr. David Warner does."

"Right you are, Rupesh. I'm glad to see we have an under-standing. Now one more thing. I realize you are a physician and not a policeman. But is there anything you can tell me about the bullet you removed from David Warner's shoulder?"

"Indeed I can. I may not, as you say, be a policeman, but I've removed enough bullets from enough patients in the past two years here at Boston City Hospital to qualify as a ballistics expert."

"And?"

"And, Ms. McGuire, the bullet that entered David Warner's shoulder was fired from a semi-automatic weapon. It was a .380 caliber bullet." He drained his wine and stared at her intently. "I see that answer was very satisfactory to you, Ms. McGuire."

She laughed. "You're a very perceptive man, Dr. Chandra. Very perceptive indeed."

CHAPTER 13

Rosario walked straight down Cambridge Street into the old industrial heartland of the city. It was here where Ursula's great-great-grandfather, Delano McGuire, a refugee from the Great Famine, staked out his claim to the American Dream. And it was here, all around him, where his own relatives, newly arrived in the North End a generation later, came to work in the factories making glass, candles, soap, pottery, bricks, beer, glass, and furniture. He took a left on Fourth and then a right on Gore Street and glanced at one of the old workers' cottages and smiled. Delano. Ursula's grandmother, Nora, told him once that if he ever had a son, he could call him Delano Rosario just for the sound of it.

He swung around to the right on Second, crossed Cambridge Street, and took another right on Thorndike. Several blocks later, he stopped for a moment in front of Delano's home, still there after a hundred and fifty years and five generations of McGuires. A red Volvo station wagon pulled up to the curb, and two little kids jumped out and ran along the brick walkway to the front door. A young couple stepped out of the car and the man walked up to him, a wary look on his face. "Can I help you?"

"Nope. I was just admiring your house. I'm not sure Nora McGuire would have gone for the bright yellow paint job but I think it's great. This street needs some color."

"Ah, so you knew the previous owners?"

"Very well. Half the research for one of my college papers was done in your dining room and upon completion of that paper, several pints were consumed in your kitchen. Eamon and Nora knew more about the commercial history of East Cambridge than any of my professors."

He seemed to relax a bit, relieved, Rosario figured, that the grubby, middle-aged man in the hooded sweatshirt was not contemplating breaking and entering. "Well, of course, we never met them. We met the two sons and the daughter at the closing after the mother died. The men were eager to sell, but the daughter seemed sad about letting the old homestead go. As did their granddaughter—that lawyer."

The wife turned on her way down the walk toward her children and smiled. "Did you hear that? *That* lawyer? My husband was very taken by the family lawyer. He could hardly keep his attention focused on the real estate transaction. Luckily, he has a very astute wife."

The husband laughed. "And a very beautiful wife."

She called over her shoulder. "Not in the same league as *that lawyer*, I'm afraid."

"That was ten years ago. She's probably turned into an old hag by now." He looked at Rosario and grinned conspiratorially. "Help me out here, pal."

Rosario called back to the wife. "Worse than a hag. Children run screaming when they see her on the street. She's a big hit at Halloween." The kids glanced up apprehensively and the wife gave him a strange look. Rosario turned to the husband. "The place looks great. Keep up the good work."

They shook hands and he walked away and took a right on Sixth Street in front of the library. He was halfway past the grim Gothic pile of St. Joseph's Church when a priest emerged from the last door on the left. Rosario stopped and stared. It was him again, but this time Rosario decided to remain silent. He let the man get a block away and then followed him eastward down Cambridge Street to Sciarappa. For a moment, it looked as if he were headed for the rectory of St. Francis of Assisi Church, but instead, he kept to the sidewalk across the street and disappeared into an old green building.

The second time he had seen him, that night outside Nini's, he began to wonder if Rebecca's jest about the priest being after him might just have some validity. But it was clear that this time the priest was oblivious to Rosario's presence. He waited at the corner for a few minutes and then started back toward the Square.

At home, on top of the mail, he noticed a small envelope with unfamiliar handwriting. He dropped into his chair and opened it.

Rob:

Emily received an A on her Longfellow paper. I did not know about her calling you like that and I certainly hope it was not a terrible inconvenience. I owe you one. Why don't you let me take you to dinner this weekend if you're not out painting the town with Eve Taylor?

Rebecca

He sat back and stared at the wall for a second. There was an odd friendliness to the note that somehow didn't fit with the personality of its author, and he couldn't quite picture Rebecca

Scott using a term like *painting the town*. But he had to smile at the mention of Eve Taylor. There was something so naturally feminine about that touch. It was something only they two would understand because of the strange nature of their meeting, and it created, he felt, a note of intimacy between them. And that, of course, was the problem. He put the note aside, and as he rose from the chair, he remembered David Warner's parting words: "Take care of yourself, Mr. Rosario."

———

She was dressed in a black silk blouse and black slacks and looked devastating. There was simply no other way to describe her. He started the engine and pulled away from the curb. "So where are you taking me?"

"Have you been to Duckworth Lane?"

"Sure. Love their appetizers. Good choice."

The light at the corner of Chauncy Street turned green and he took a left on Mass Ave. She stiffened a bit and then looked over at him. "Aren't we going the wrong way?"

"Duckworth Lane is in Arlington, right?"

"They closed that one. It's in Brookline now." They were gliding through the light at Wendell Street, but it was too late to turn. Off to his left across Mass Ave the big wooden windows of the dining room at Chez Henri were thrown open to Shepard Street, and coming up on their right was Abby Whitman's bar and the alley where Charles Devir had been gunned down. He couldn't help but glance at her. She stared straight ahead. Not a curve in her face was disturbed. Not a muscle moved. Not a sound came from her lips. He turned right on Sacramento Street, right on Oxford, and then down Wendell until he came back to Mass Ave, but she didn't speak another word until they were in the Square and heading down Kennedy Street toward Brighton.

"Sorry."

"For what?"

"For not being much of a conversationalist. That kid was giving Lizzie some mean looks Friday in school, and I'm starting to worry about him again."

"Looks are nothing to worry about. If it gets beyond that, let me know."

"If it gets beyond that, I'll take care of it. Believe me."

He was quiet for a while. They crossed the Lars Anderson Bridge, and as they passed the stadium she looked over at him. "Now you're not speaking."

"Just thinking."

"About your boring date?"

He laughed. "No, of course not. Look, put that kid out of your mind. Lizzie will tell you if he goes beyond the evil eye bit, and you can have the school step on him. The new assistant principal is an old friend of mine, and he's a pretty tough customer. In any event, try to put it out of your mind for tonight. Let's try to have a good time."

The good time started immediately when the hostess informed them they would have to wait twenty minutes for a table. Rebecca shot her a glance that forced the young woman to retreat a good six feet and mumble apologetically about two seats at the bar. Rosario put his hand on Rebecca's shoulder and smiled. "The bar will be fine, thank you."

She hissed in his ear. "If we go to the bar, we'll have to be around *people*."

"Oh, my God. We can't have that, can we? Come on. Sometimes sitting at the bar can be fun. We'll order some apps and a glass of wine and if you don't like it, we'll go somewhere else. How's that?"

"Fine, fine."

"I knew you'd take that reasonable approach, and the humorous, lighthearted manner in which you just agreed with my suggestion bodes well for a real fun evening."

A reluctant smile crossed her lips as he steered her over to the far side of the bar, where a cheery faced boy of a bartender bounced over to them. "What can I get for you folks?"

Rebecca ordered a Merlot from Sonoma and when he chose a glass of Vouvray, she glanced at him and raised an eyebrow. "Going with a French wine, huh?"

"That's right. Anything wrong with that?"

"Not really. I just have little use for the French."

He laughed and shook his head. "OK. Dare I ask why?"

"Well, they don't like us very much despite the fact that we saved their asses in two world wars, they're rude and self-centered, and their women spend their whole lives trying to please men."

He smiled at her. "Well, that about covers it, I guess. I better send the wine back the moment it arrives. For argument's sake, however, since I have the feeling this might be a contentious night, consider this. First of all, while some Parisians may at times be rude to Americans, you can find a hell of a lot of Bostonians and New Yorkers who are rude to everyone regardless of race, color, creed or nationality. Secondly, while the French elites and the French media may be anti-American, the majority of French people are certainly not. And finally, any nation that can produce Isabelle Huppert can't be all bad."

The waiter returned with their glasses of wine and placed them on the bar, but before he could turn away to fill another order, Rebecca grabbed his sleeve. "I'm sorry, but for six dollars a glass, I think we need a little bit more wine." The young man sighed deeply and looked around. She patted his hand. "You seem like a good kid, and I'm sure the owner here has told you the exact amount of wine he wants you to pour. But frankly, this is a rip-off. So how about another inch?" He glanced around again to see if anyone was watching and hurriedly topped off their glasses. Rebecca smiled at him. "Thank you." Then he rushed off to the other side of the bar where a waitress was signaling him impatiently. "Don't you hate that?"

"I do. But frankly, I've grown tired of fighting with people all the time. It's not worth it. What did that one less inch of wine cost you? Fifty cents? A buck? Am I going to blow a fuse over a buck? Not anymore."

She sipped her wine and then looked back at him. "Sometimes you convey a certain kind of weariness with the ways of the world. I don't mean passivity or boredom. That's not what I'm getting at. You're very much alive. Very much interested in things and so involved with your work. I guess it's just what you said a minute ago. You're tired of fighting all the time."

"Right."

"Yeah, well, I've just begun to fight. Now who said that one?"

"John Paul Jones."

She nodded and sipped at her glass again, the red wine licking her soft red lips. He had finished over half of his Vouvray already and he was beginning to get a little buzz on, just enough to anesthetize his annoyance at her behavior. And then of course there was her beauty. That was helping a lot.

She put her glass down and leaned a little closer to him. "I don't know what it is, but I sense that once upon a time you had more fire in you."

He swirled the cold white wine around his glass. "I did. But you can't spend your whole life on fire, you know. Eventually, you'll burn out. I guess I've got the burner on low for a while."

"For a while?"

"Sure. Why not? But don't worry. I have no intentions of turning up the heat on you."

"Good. That's what I like about you. I like the fact that we understand each other."

Four jabbering young women were sitting along the center section of the bar perpendicular to Rebecca, and suddenly, like a flock of flapping magpies, they rose in unison and flew off, instantly replaced by two middle-aged couples. The men sat together next to Rebecca, and after eyeing her appreciatively several times, fell into a conversation about sports. Next to them the wives talked about their children, and how well they were all doing at their respective high schools and colleges. Rebecca turned her back on them, and finishing her wine, leaned toward him again and lowered her voice. "What insufferable bores, especially the women. God, how I hate it when they brag about their offspring. Listen to them." She turned and glanced over her shoulder at them and then looked back at Rosario. "Look at how the big blonde one with the mammoth breasts is doing all the talking. The other one with the short hair can't get a word in edgewise. Ugh. There was one like that in Newton. A real professional *Mom*, if you know what I mean. That was another reason I was glad to get out of there."

"Another?"

"Uh, huh. I'll fill you in on all the other ones sometime when I'm in a really foul mood."

He couldn't help but smile. "What do you call the mood you're in tonight?"

She smiled back at him. "The somewhat mildly annoyed mood."

"I think you need to drop those two adverbs."

Before she could respond, the bartender interrupted them. "Two more?"

They nodded and Rosario picked up the menu from the bar. They looked at it together and ordered the Thai dumplings, the chicken pesto pasta, and the grilled squid with spicy red pepper salsa, and when the food arrived—along with their glasses of wine filled to the proper level—they attacked it with relish.

Rebecca's mood seemed to improve as they ate and talked quietly together. But then the big-breasted blonde mom began holding forth in a much louder voice. "And I told that teacher a thing or two. That was an A paper if I ever saw one. A solid A. Yet this woman gave him a B. Can you imagine such a thing?"

Rebecca put her fork down, looked over her shoulder, and then turned back again. "What I can't imagine is bragging about my children in public. Do you run into parents like that at Liberty?"

"Some of them are like that. A friend of mine was at the local market one evening and heard two of the moms bragging about their kids' SAT scores. But most of them are good people who want the best for their sons and daughters. They're reasonable folks." He couldn't resist. "You know. Like the French. Only *some* of them are rude and obnoxious."

The woman's voice boomed over the bar. "And when I was through, the assistant principal apologized and the principal himself apologized!"

Rosario watched the woman. She prattled on and on about her son and the school, and every time her companion opened her mouth to talk, the big blonde rode roughshod over her. Rebecca turned and glared at her and then looked back again at Rosario. "I'd be the first person to go to the school principal if I thought my daughters were being bullied or threatened— Jackson Foster being a case in point. But to interfere in the daily education of my children seems so intrusive. Who is she really doing it for? Herself or her son? I don't remember my parents being involved in their kids' lives to that extent, do you?"

"Hell, no. I would have been embarrassed beyond belief if either one of them had shown up at school. Are you kidding?"

"I wonder which one of those poor bastards behind me is married to that hideous creature. Do you see the one right in back of me? He's got a ponytail. How pretentious. He's obviously a well-heeled businessman of some sort. What's with the goddamn ponytail? Look at him. He's reveling in his own unattractiveness."

Rosario laughed out loud and looked over at the wives again. The little dark-haired woman had actually managed to get in a whole sentence. But she had no sooner uttered the term *college* than the blonde seized upon the word like a loose football and ran with it. "And did I tell you what Kirk did this year at Amherst?"

Rebecca whirled around in her chair. "No, you didn't! But please share it with the whole restaurant. We're all so fascinated with your *Oh So Important* life that we can hardly wait for the next chapter."

The entire bar was stunned into silence. Finally, the big blonde responded. "No one was addressing you, madam."

"Really? I thought you were addressing the entire establishment. Certainly everyone can hear you. And your poor friend hasn't had a chance to say a thing." Rebecca gestured sympathetically toward the little woman. "You know, you've shown great patience this evening. I don't know how you've been able to stand it. But I've just thought of something for you to say. Try this. Turn to your friend and say, 'Hey! I'm talking now! I had to listen to your boring stories about your boring children, and now you have to listen to mine!' Give it a shot."

A young couple at the other end of the bar began to laugh and next to Rosario on his right, an elderly man chuckled and poked Rosario in the side. "Touché! That's quite a gal you have there."

Then the boasting blonde counterattacked. "Maybe we'll just have to give you first prize for rudeness."

Rebecca fired back instantly. "And we'll give you a big blue ribbon for *Most Productive Uterus* and plant it on your ample bosom." Everyone at the bar howled, and across from them, a furtive look of immense satisfaction settled over the face of the blonde's beleaguered little companion. Rosario drained his wine and turned to the old man. "Time to beat a retreat."

He smiled. "Seems more like a victory to me, young man."

Rosario signaled the waiter, paid the bill, and hustled Rebecca out to Beacon Street. She pulled away from him. "Hey! Talk about the bum's rush."

"I just thought we ought to leave on a high note."

She laughed. "That was fun, Rosario. Who else can we do battle with?"

"Well, now that we've invaded Brookline, we can attack Boston or regroup in Cambridge."

"Let's go back to the Square. I don't like the way you paid the bill in there. I was supposed to buy. Remember?"

"Next time."

"We'll have a nightcap at Casablanca on me."

The nightcap turned into two and later, as they walked up the stairs to Brattle Street into the cool night air, he realized he was a little drunk. They strolled along the brick sidewalk together past the corner where they had met, past the Loeb Drama Center and the old Greenleaf mansion, until he realized they were getting too close to his place. He knew now, in his current state, that if they got any closer he wouldn't be able to resist asking her in. He took her elbow and guided her across Brattle toward James Street.

She put her arm through his. "Good move, Rosario."

He laughed with relief. It was as if she had divined his thoughts. "Yeah, well. You know. Don't want to push things on the first date."

"Good. Another thing I like about you. You're not pushy." As they turned the corner by the Schlesinger Library, a group of college kids came flying down the sidewalk, and in stepping aside to let them go by, they were thrown closer together. He looked at her and felt a tremendous urge to take her in his arms and kiss her. But once again he mastered his impulses, and they moved on silently though the Cambridge streets.

As they passed the Hotel Commander, she glanced at him curiously. "You weren't always this controlled, were you?"

"Oh, no. This is strictly an old guy thing."

"So age has some advantages, huh?"

"So I hear. But I don't believe it."

"I like your cynicism. It matches mine."

They were almost at Chauncy Street. "Well, Rebecca, the thing about cynicism is that it's kind of like cholesterol. There's good cynicism and there's bad cynicism."

They turned down her street and stopped in front of her house. The lights were all ablaze and music blared from the front room. She looked up at him. "The girls are home."

"Good."

She smiled, and putting her hands on his chest, she leaned up and kissed him quickly on the lips. "Thanks for the nice evening, Rob. Next time, I'm paying. I mean it."

She slipped away and he turned and walked toward the Square. It wasn't until he reached the end of her street that he realized he was trembling with desire.

CHAPTER 14

The best view of David Warner's office was from the third floor of Lindh's Used Book Store, and it had taken Ursula McGuire two early evening visits and a lot of schmoozing with Sophie Lindh, the ninety-year-old proprietor, before she struck pay dirt. Now, as she sat beside her carping husband, Ursula hoped that her third trip would be the last.

"I'm getting a little tired of dropping you off in Newton Centre. The traffic on Beacon Street at this hour is murder. Isn't this woman a little curious about all the bogus research you're doing on the North Shore?"

"She hasn't said anything about it yet. She seems more interested in gossiping about all her neighbors than in what I'm doing."

"Including David Warner."

"Including David Warner."

"A fortuitous development, my dear. So I take it that the North Shore section is closest to her big picture window?"

"You got it."

"So what happens if she loses interest in gossip and begins to interrogate you about the rise and fall of the shoe industry in Lynn or whether Beverly or Marblehead is the birthplace of the American Navy?"

She smiled. "In that case I shall punt. Either that or say something insulting about my increasingly irritated husband."

"Well, it *is* taking a hell of a lot of time. I thought you were almost done casing this joint."

"I am, I am. Don't be so impatient. You're Mr. Calm. You're Mr. Zen. Put your philosophical money where your mouth is and let me handle all those base emotions you think so little of. I didn't choose this week for my car to break down. Besides, all you have to do is turn around and drive back to BC and do your run around the reservoir just like the past two times. What's the big deal?"

Mark sighed. "The deal is that I'm getting tired of running the Res. I miss my city run. I'm a creature of habit."

"You're a creature, all right. Don't you think I miss my city walks? Don't you think I'm getting tired of marching around Newton Centre in my shorts and T-shirt?"

He put his hand on her bare thigh. "I like your shorts."

"Hands off, buster, until you can be nicer to your wife."

"Nicer? I've driven you over here three times!"

"The car will be done tomorrow. Besides, I work for a living, remember? This is the only time I have. And as it turns out, by the time I finish my walk, it's just about closing time at Warner and Associates."

He laughed. "It'll be closing time for *you* if he recognizes Counselor McGuire in her T-shirt and walking shorts wiggling around town."

"I don't wiggle!"

He grinned. "Actually, from behind you do, and I'm all for it."

"Shut up."

"Unfortunately, you're recognizable behind those sunglasses and that Red Sox hat. *My* Red Sox hat, I might add."

"Uh, huh. Well, I needed something a bit on the large side, and anyway the only reason you recognize me is because you know me so well. He's only met me once." She pointed toward Dewar's Meat Market. "Let me out here."

He pulled into a space and she got out of the car. "I plan to be a while tonight, so I'll take the T home. Thanks for the lift." She closed the door and waved goodbye and started to walk away when she heard him call after her. She turned and put her hands on her hips. "What?"

He was still in the parking space, leaning out of the window and watching her. "You're wiggling."

"Keep your eyes on the road, you old horn!" She crossed Beacon and walked around to the right and passed the row of shops opposite the MBTA station. Then she looked at her watch before she headed out of the center of town. It was almost 6:00.

When she returned, hot and re-energized, it was 7:10. A good workout for an old gal, she thought, and then it occurred to her that she was thinking like Rosario. But it *was* a good workout and she felt damn proud of herself. She strolled around the block once more to cool down, grabbed a bottle of water at the local variety store, and then paused in front of the bookstore. To her left, a few shops away, an elderly man was slowly making his way past a pay phone. Impulsively, Ursula walked down to the corner and punched in a number. "Hi, Rosie. I miss our old guy walks."

He laughed. "*Our* old guy walks?"

"Well, *your* old guy walks. I keep getting younger and younger."

"Well, you certainly look it. I'll grant you that. But it seems to me that you're the one who has had to cancel recently."

"So have you. We're walking past each other, I guess."

"I guess."

She glanced around and leaned against the booth. "I met the husband. Involuntarily, I might add. He stormed into my office after being notified by the family physician that I was prying into his medical history."

"Imagine that. I told you that kind of thing was risky."

"Your exact words, I believe, were that it was a little ballsy."

"Well, it was, and I believe your exact words were that you were acting for the greater moral good. So it looks as if the greater moral good came back to bite you in the ass."

"Not necessarily. It's just a temporary setback."

"Mmm." There was a pause. "I've met him too."

"Really!" She wanted to ask him under what circumstances but sensed that this might be the wrong question. "Did you notice the arm?"

"Uh, huh."

"What do you make of it?"

"I don't know. He told me it was a handball injury."

There was a lot to fill him in on, she thought. But not now. There wasn't enough time. "What about the wife?"

"What about her?"

"Still running into her?"

"Occasionally. You know how it is in the Square."

"So...how does it stand?"

"There's that question again. So how does it stand? Like I told you before." There was another pause. "I'd say the way it stands is that we're relative strangers."

"Relative strangers? What the hell is that?"

He laughed. "That, my friend, is none of your business. Where are you, anyway? You've got a rotten connection."

"Newton Centre."

"Newton, huh? Sounds like you're hot on the trail."

"You got it, Rob. And I better get going before the trail runs cold. I'll call you back sometime when you feel like talking more about your relative stranger."

"I'm off the case, remember?"

She looked back down Beacon Street and smiled. "Oh, that's right! Damn, I forgot. Good night, Rosie."

"Good night, Ursie. Behave yourself."

Ursula hung up the phone, walked down to Lindh's bookstore, and climbed the stairs to the third floor. "Hello, Sophie."

The proprietor was seated at her massive mahogany desk in the center of the room thumbing through a file box of index cards. "Back again, young lady? I've never seen anyone so interested in Boston's North Shore. Are you a sailor?"

Ursula shook her head. "No, no. My husband is interested in colonial history and drags me up to Salem and Marblehead with him on occasion."

The little old lady frowned. "I, for one, would never have to be dragged to a lovely place like Marblehead."

"You might be if you had to analyze the architectural details of every other house in Old Town. After about an hour of that I'm ready to analyze the bar at Flynnie's."

Sophie chuckled. "So is that what you're doing? Looking up the bars of the North Shore? I'm afraid I don't have anything like that in stock."

Ursula laughed and edged over by the shelves to the right of the window. "Actually, we're going up there for a weekend soon, so I thought I'd familiarize myself with some of the hiking trails. At least I can get some exercise while he's poking around all those nooks and crannies he loves so much."

"Is that you're hiking outfit, my dear?"

"Uh, yes. Yes, it is." Something in Sophie's tone reminded her of her mother's complaints back in Ursula's miniskirt days, and she wondered if Mark were right. Maybe these shorts were a bit much, especially for someone her age.

"You should have said something to me before. Look under D. Debbie Driscoll's book on hiking north of Boston is a good one, although it's ten years old. I know a lot of these towns are developing trails out of the old railroad beds, so they might not be in there. But try it."

Ursula found the book on the second shelf and sat down in one of the ancient, cracked leather chairs by the big picture window. Holding the small volume in her left hand, she swung around so she had her back to Sophie and her eyes trained directly on the line of shops across the street. On Monday night, with a little artful prodding, Sophie Lindh had drifted from a wistful tale of the founding of her family bookshop to a history of Newton Centre that might have kept Mark rapt with attention, but had nudged Ursula close to the edge of deep slumber. But when Sophie turned to the present, and began a scathing account of what the modern age had done to her beloved town, and what businesses had replaced all the old shops below her third floor perch, Ursula perked up. And she perked up even more when the venerable bookseller began to name names. David Warner was just one of those many names, so Ursula was careful to ask questions about several of the characters in Sophie's narrative. She learned a bit too much about the nice Chinese family that ran the restaurant on the corner and way too much about the promiscuous hairdresser next to the bank who wore those terribly revealing outfits, but not quite enough about the handsome accountant who was so active in town government.

By Wednesday, however, through patient inquiry and her own third floor observation, Ursula had learned what she needed. David Warner left his office every night between 7:00 and 7:30. He was followed shortly thereafter by his secretary who closed up shop. On one of those evenings, David Warner was accompanied by a woman not his wife. Now, of course, Sophie had stressed, it was possible that the woman in question was a client or a political associate, so she didn't want to impugn the character of a fellow Republican with a history of fine service to the town. And in her favor, mind you, were the woman's sensible, tasteful clothes, a welcome contrast to the indecent costumes of that cigarette-smoking, gum-chewing hairdresser strutting up and down the streets like some common harlot.

Now, Thursday evening, Ursula found what she had come for. Across the street, David Warner and a slim attractive woman with short brown hair were crossing the municipal parking lot. Ursula stood up and smiled. "Well, Sophie. I've got to meet my husband. But I'd like to buy this book. It's enthralling."

"You did look rather engaged."

"Indeed I was."

Five minutes later, Ursula McGuire was engaging with David Warner's secretary. "Hi. Have I missed Mr. Warner? We were supposed to touch base around 7:15. I'm afraid I'm a bit late. The traffic around Cleveland Circle was just awful."

"Oh, I'm sorry. Are you with the Romney campaign?"

"Why, yes," Ursula replied, smiling brightly at the very idea of it. She tried to think of a proper Republican name for herself, but the woman was obviously in a hurry to leave.

"We're just closing up for the night. We always run late during campaigns, as I'm sure you know. But if you want to catch him, he and Ms. Robinson went over to the Union Grille. I'm sure he'll want to touch base with you if you're with Mr. Romney."

Ursula felt as if her smile had been pasted on her face, and her cheeks began to ache. She had never impersonated a Republican before and it was starting to hurt. "Ms. Robinson? You mean Ms. Robinson, the nurse?"

The secretary laughed. "Oh, Brenda's not a nurse. She's a physical therapist."

"Ah, that makes sense. One of my colleagues at Romney headquarters met her once and was so impressed with her knowledge of medicine that she thought Brenda was a nurse. So she must work at Newton-Wellesley Hospital."

The secretary looked puzzled. "Well...not that I know of. She works at the Spaulding."

"Oh yes, the Spaulding. My brother was there after a hockey injury years ago. They did a great job. Well, thanks so much."

Ursula waved and headed out the door and made straight for the T. It was time for a shower and a late supper and some serious thought as to how she would approach Ms. Brenda Robinson of the Spaulding Rehabilitation Hospital. It was clear she had been rehabilitating Mr. David Warner. The only question was why.

CHAPTER 15

Five minutes into his walk, he ran into Emily Warner and two other girls. "Hey, Mr. Rosario."

"Hey, Em. How's it going?"

"Pretty good. This is Lindsay and this is Keisha."

"Hi, ladies."

"Hi."

They were standing on the corner of Waterhouse and Garden across from The Hotel Commander. Emily looked up at him. You got a second?"

"Sure."

"I'll see you guys tonight, OK?" She waited until the two girls walked away into the Cambridge Common. "Am I interrupting your run?"

He laughed. "I wish you were interrupting my run. Unfortunately, it's my walk."

"Still…"

"It's OK. What's up?"

"First of all, thanks again for all your help with the paper."

"You're quite welcome. So...second of all?"

"Well, it's my mom. That kid is starting to hassle Lizzie again and she's getting really mad. I don't know if you've ever noticed but she can get kind of..."

"Fierce."

Emily laughed. "Yeah, fierce. I mean not to us but to anyone who threatens us. Sometimes if my mom thinks we're being pushed around or treated unfairly, she can get right in someone's face. Or if anyone does anything to her."

Rosario looked into her eyes. "Like what?"

Emily glanced away. "Oh, I don't know. I mean I don't want to give you the wrong idea or anything. It's not like she's angry all the time. So anyway, Lizzie came home yesterday and said that Jackson Foster was making some comments about getting her back for breaking up with him, and Mom was on the phone in like six seconds from her office telling the principal that if he didn't take care of the situation, she would."

Rosario shook his head. "Whoa."

"Yeah, whoa. The thing is I'm afraid she might actually go into school and do something to him."

"I don't think she'd actually go that far."

"Yeah, well I do. She's done stuff like that before. In Newton there was this cute guy at the high school who was Lizzie's guidance counselor. The word was he used to flirt with some of the girls, and when Lizzie was a freshman he told her she was a babe. Lizzie thought he was just kidding around, but she made the mistake of telling the story at dinner and Mom flew into a rage. Dad tried to calm her down but it didn't do any good. The next day she went into school and practically destroyed the guy's office."

"Emily, come on. *Destroyed* his office?"

"Well, OK, not destroyed, but she screamed at him and pushed all the papers off his desk and grabbed him by the tie and threatened to strangle him with it if he so much as looked at Lizzie again. Boy! Lizzie was really embarrassed, let me tell you."

Rosario tried to stop himself, but finally he had to laugh. "Remind me never to run afoul of your mother."

"Yeah, but that's what I wanted to talk to you about. The thing is you kind of defuse her. Know what I mean? She seems to calm down when she's around you. You even make her laugh once in a while, and that's a big deal, believe me." She held up her hands. "Hey, look, don't get me wrong. I'm not trying to start anything between you and my mom. I just...I just wondered if you could maybe stop by and sort of..."

"Defuse her?"

Emily sighed and then wrinkled her nose. "Yeah. Yeah, that's what I mean."

"She still at work?"

"Uh, huh. I was going to go over and meet her."

"All right. I'll go over there now."

Emily turned to go. "Thanks—and good luck.".

Rosario smiled. "Yeah. Thanks a lot, kid. It's a good thing I don't have a necktie on."

He watched her laugh and wave as she headed down Garden Street. Then he crossed the Common and walked down Appian Way past the Gutman Library. Rebecca Scott was standing at the corner of Brattle and Story Streets, and when she saw him, she smiled slightly in surprise. "I was expecting my daughter, not Rocky Balboa."

He smiled back. "Don't like my sweatshirt, huh?"

"I thought the Liberty High version was a bit more stylish."

"Well, this is one of my old ones."

"So I see."

"Mmm...for a while there, I thought you were different than other women. But that was a quintessentially female remark."

"Well, you wouldn't want me to be completely without female characteristics, would you?" She took a step toward him and tugged at his sweatshirt. "Hey, if you want to get along with me don't throw around Harvard Square words like *quintessential*. You didn't see Emily along Brattle Street, did you? She's never late."

"Don't worry. I ran into her and two of her friends over on the Common. That's why I'm here. She sent me over to intercept you. Actually, to *defuse* you."

Rebecca glanced across Story Street for a second and then looked back. "Oh, I see. She told you Jackson Foster is bothering Lizzie again, didn't she? I'm not going to put up with it."

"I don't blame you. It's the manner in which you're not going to put up with it that's got Emily worried. I can talk to my friend. We can try to work within the system first." He touched her arm. "Is today your gym day?"

"Uh, huh."

"What do you do for your warm-up?"

"The elliptical and the treadmill. Enough to work up a sweat."

"Good. Well, I have an idea. Why don't we sweat together? Why don't you go home and change, and I'll meet you at the corner of Garden and Chauncy. We can walk to Fresh Pond, go around for a couple miles and then you can cut right across Concord Avenue to Mike's Gym. That should defuse you for a while. What do you say?"

She looked back at him. "OK. I'll see you there in twenty minutes."

Twenty minutes later they moved quickly together toward Huron Avenue and finally across the Parkway and down through the trees to the trail bordering the reservoir. She kept right alongside him, walking smoothly with swift athletic strides and maintaining absolute silence. He touched her arm again. "Did you give my proposal any consideration?"

She nodded. "I did. It was quite thoughtful of you, but you've done enough for us already."

He smiled. "I could always call Uncle Rosario back into action again. Bang the kid around a little."

"Uncle Rosario doesn't need to risk his reputation at Liberty High by doing anything like that. I'm afraid you don't have an excuse. I do."

"The aggrieved mother."

"Correct." She was quiet for a moment or two as they passed the last visible area of the golf course. Then she glanced over at him and that fierce look came into her eyes. "I'll take care of Jackson Foster."

They kept up their pace, moving rapidly side by side and following the gradual curve of the ground until they came to the grove of trees that cut the path in two. Suddenly, a large hairy dog leapt out of the bushes, cutting in front of them and almost tripping Rebecca. A young woman in a tracksuit ran past them and tried to grab the animal's collar, but it jumped away and bounded down the path. "Ollie! Ollie! Come back here! Come back here now, Ollie!"

As they caught up with her, Rebecca stopped and put her hands on her hips. "What the hell is wrong with you, anyway?"

"Pardon me?"

"Your dog almost crashed into us. Don't you read the signs? *Control Your Dog.* Get it?" She pointed toward the furry black blur galumphing along in the distance. "You call that *control?*"

"Well, after all, look at the size of him. He's a little bit difficult for me to manage."

"Then buy one of those annoying little yapping dogs you *can* control."

Rosario grabbed her arm and pulled her away. "Come on. You're going to ruin your workout."

They started walking again and she pulled out into the lead. She reached back and put her hair up in a ponytail and called back over her shoulder. "I've got to keep moving or I'm liable to go back and strangle that dumb girl!"

Rosario increased his speed and caught up to her. "You have to love all these environmentally conscious Cambridge residents who let their dogs run rampant around here. I got sideswiped once by a giant poodle the size of a calf."

"Let me guess. Another young woman?"

"I'm afraid so."

"What did you do?"

"You mean after I beheaded the dog and stuck its head on the fence?"

A slight smile crept across her face. "Yes. After that."

"If memory serves me right, I adopted the Rebecca Scott method and strangled the owner."

A hundred yards behind them they could still hear the girl calling the dog, although her voice was muffled by the trees and the water. "Ollie! Ollie! Come back!"

Rebecca tightened her ponytail. "You know, sometimes I'm afraid I can't stand my own sex. So many of us can't control things. Whether it's something as simple as controlling a pet or balancing a checkbook or something as complicated as disciplining our kids or dealing with the people who hurt us, too many women simply can't seem to take charge of their lives. It's pathetic."

"There are plenty of pathetic men in the world too."

"Sure. But the problem is that when women are young, they're attracted far too often by strong-willed men with forceful personalities. Men who don't compromise at work and figure they don't have to compromise at home either. A lot of these guys may not be bad guys at first, but they get bad as they get older. Or maybe they're bad in the first place, but women don't recognize the bad traits until it's too late. And the killer is that women are so often each other's enemy. My mother-in-law, for example. She must have had some insight into her son's character, yet she never warned me. Of course, she never liked me from the beginning. I wasn't quite good enough for her son. So why would she? Nice, huh?"

"No. Not nice."

"Have you ever been married?"

"Nope. My mother kept warning my girlfriends about what a terrible person I was."

She looked over at him and laughed. "Always slipping in that humor, aren't you?"

"Yup. Sorry. I can't help myself."

"That's OK. Actually, it's better than OK, but…"

"But you were talking about something serious, and you think I'm treating it too lightly. I'm not. I was treating my own life lightly. Not yours."

"I know."

As they came around a bend, they saw Ollie standing next to a tree staring up longingly at a squirrel. They stopped and Rebecca called him over. "Here, Ollie. Your irresponsible moron of an owner is looking for you. Ineffectually, I might add." Ollie ambled over and stood in front of them, and Rebecca leaned down and patted his head.

Rosario smiled at her. "For a moment back there I thought you were anti-dog too."

"I'm not anti-dog. It's not Ollie's fault. Right, Ollie? It's the irresponsible owners that I can't stand. Come on, I'm beginning to sweat. Let's keep going."

They said goodbye to Ollie and moved on, passing the Cambridge Water Authority on their left and approaching another grove of trees. Rosario caught the smell of pine in the wind and stopped and breathed deeply and looked across the water. In the distance, the setting sun warmed the western sky with a soft golden hue, and just above the tree line purple clouds drifted along the horizon. A few lone gulls, stragglers on their way home to the sea, glided through the vanishing light. Sensing her impatience, he started up again. "Sorry. Didn't mean to break your stride."

"It's OK. Look, I'm sorry I brought this whole thing up. We should be out here enjoying the exercise and this beautiful weather and not getting into the grubby details of my life. Yet somehow I feel a need to explain to you that I'm not this negative, horrible person that I must seem."

"You don't have to explain anything to me."

"No, you don't understand. I *do* need to explain." She stopped and stared at him. "Look, I'm not going to indulge in a lot of psychobabble and hand wringing. That's not my style. I don't sit around with a bunch of girlfriends and *share* all my feelings. I keep them to myself. In fact, I've kept everything to myself." She laughed and shook her head. "In fact, I don't really have any girlfriends. I'm just a very private person. I've never really fit in with the suburban mom scene. I just always felt like an alien out there. You see, the thing is…" She turned and looked out across the water. "Let's just say that I've been kicked around some in my life and that lately I'm kicking back."

She looked at him as if she were throwing down a challenge. "So is that good enough?"

"Good enough for me. I'm a great believer in kicking back. And as I said, you don't have to explain anything to me." He could see that she was struggling with something, and that she wanted to tell him more, but to do so she had to overcome some great inner reluctance. He could see it because he knew the feeling himself, knew it as deeply and as intimately as he knew anything. "Come on. There's a breeze blowing in from that big pond out there. You need to stay warm if you're going to pump iron tonight."

"You're right, Rosario. You're right. Let's move." They were off again, rounding the spot where they had first come in. Two teenage boys wearing Belmont High track team jerseys raced past them, and a small woman with a look of intense determination marched by with two leashed dachshunds. Rebecca nodded approvingly. "There's a lady with things well in hand."

He smiled. "My kind of woman." They picked up the speed, moving as fast as they could without breaking into a run. "That path leads up to the bus stop on Concord Ave across from Smith Street. You know your way from there. I'll go up with you." They slowed down and walked into a shaded area, and just as she turned to say something, two Dalmatians charged down the path in front of her. She stepped aside and losing her footing, she fell into his arms. She pulled back, her hands against his chest, his arms around her waist, her eyes searching the landscape for the offending owner. He put his hands on her hips and shook her lightly. "Stop."

"Huh?"

"Stop. Save your anger for the stuff that counts. Calm down. If you go into that gym all riled up you'll have a lousy workout. Calm down."

"OK, OK." She stopped and looked into his eyes. "Trying to defuse me again, Rosario?"

"Might not be a bad idea." They kept looking at each other. He liked the way her hips felt under his hands, and he was struck once again by the cold beauty in her light gray eyes. He could feel his heart beating under the warmth of her hand. It was hard to resist her. But resist he did.

She smiled. "No move, huh?"

He smiled back. "No move."

"Are you like this with all women or just me?"

"Just you." They both laughed in each other's arms. "I'm just kidding."

The smile disappeared. "It doesn't matter if you're kidding or not, really. I'm dead to men."

"Dead to men? You feel pretty alive to me. Where did you get that phrase? The bad guy?"

"Yes, as a matter of fact. He told me that many times. That was part of his routine. Part of his pattern. Part of the way he kicked me around."

"I thought you had learned to kick back."

The fire returned to her eyes but she kept her hands on his chest. "I have."

"Then don't absorb such abusive language."

She kept looking at him. "OK, Rosario...Rob. OK." She sighed. "I...appreciate your friendship. I do. And actually, I have to say, I appreciate the fact that you did not take this opportunity to make a move."

He nodded. "Look, you appreciate my friendship and I appreciate yours. What could be simpler? Besides, as far as women go..."

"I know. You told me at the bar in Brookline that your burner was on low for a while. But I can tell you're not dead to women."

"Dead to women? There's that phrase again. No, I'm very much alive to women. I'm just hibernating, that's all."

"Hibernating?"

"Yeah. It's just a stage."

"A stage? Aren't you too old for a stage?"

"It's an old guy stage. But be careful. You never know when I might come out of the woods."

She smiled. "Like Ollie?"

He laughed and let her go. "That's right. Just like Ollie."

CHAPTER 16

Ursula leaned against the door of Mark's study and sighed. The very qualities that attracted her so many years ago were often the very same qualities that made him so exasperating when it came to her work. His honesty, his straightforwardness, and his empathy for his fellow human beings proved absolutely maddening when it came to sharing her thoughts about a case. It wasn't simply that he didn't understand the need for secrecy and duplicity in the pursuit of just goals, but he possessed a kind of naiveté about the real nature of bureaucratic organizations. Rosario, who might not like some of the methods she used, usually understood why she used them. But then again, since Rob was half-Italian, he operated with a natural cynicism totally absent from Mark's upright Anglo-Saxon sense of morality.

She shifted her weight. "I know exactly what I'm doing."

"I didn't say that. Obviously, your little ruse at Warner's office with the secretary got you what you wanted. What I'm trying to tell you is that your usual bull in a China shop routine may not work with this woman."

She folded her arms. "What do you mean, bull in a..."

He looked up from his computer. "You just barged right into Dr. Crust's office, for one, and you strolled right into Boston City to ask that physician for a drink as if he had nothing better to do."

"He was just getting off duty."

"But you didn't know that. Look, what I'm trying to say is that it might not be a great idea to confront Warner's girlfriend at her place of employment. This is a woman who probably works with severely injured people. That's what Spaulding is all about. Whatever you uncover about Warner, this woman, by the very nature of what she does for people, deserves some consideration and respect."

She pursed her lips and thought for a moment. "All right, Mr. Nice Guy. Maybe you've got something there. Maybe this calls for a little subtlety."

He pressed his fingers lightly against his eyelids. "You're such a politician, Ursie. I didn't mean for you to adopt a technique. Just do it on the assumption that she might very well be a decent person."

"I'm a lawyer, remember? An investigator. If I operated your way, I'd never accomplish anything."

He pushed his chair back and swung around to face her. "I'm not trying to impede your investigation. You know that. But you asked for my reaction. So here it is. The fact that you have located Brenda Robinson and the manner in which you've done so is, as usual, impressive. But the fact that you've caught them together doesn't mean they're sleeping together, and even if they are, it doesn't mean David Warner abused his wife."

B renda Robinson emerged from the last streetcar arm in arm with an elderly woman. They made their way slowly through the crowd of students and commuters and stopped a few feet away from the front door of O'Leary's Pub. Ursula stepped forward to greet them. "Ms. Robinson?"

Brenda nodded and the two women shook hands. "I'm sorry I'm late, but there was a delay at Kenmore Square. This is Margaret Franklin. Margaret's had a little trouble with her knee and I'm going to walk her home. So I'm afraid I'll be a few more minutes."

The old woman raised her cane a few inches and shook her head. "No, no, no. You've done enough for me today, Brenda, please. I'm only one block down from here. Really."

Ursula linked her arm through Margaret's and looked into Brenda Robinson's brown eyes. "We'll both walk you home, Margaret."

Margaret looked up at them. 'Well, you're both dears. Thank you so much."

On the way back to O'Leary's, Brenda explained that Margaret's son refused to deal with the rush hour traffic between Boston and Brookline and had informed his eighty-seven-year old mother that she would be perfectly fine on the T. Ursula opened the door to the pub and they grabbed the table closest to the window. Brenda slung her purse over the back of her chair. "Perfectly fine with a cane and fractured knee from her latest fall!"

Ursula pulled up a chair and looked across the table. She liked the anger in Brenda Robinson's voice and her obvious contempt for the son. And she especially liked the fact that she had taken so much time at the end of the workday to see her elderly patient home safely. What Ursula didn't like was having to admit to herself that her husband had been right. "I'm surprised you agreed to see me so readily."

The woman leaned forward. "David has told me all about you and what you're trying to do to him. It seemed to me that you might understand his side of things if you and I had a woman-to-woman conversation rather than my avoiding you. Although having a mutual friend made it easier for me."

The waitress arrived and they each ordered a glass of white wine. "Mutual friend? Who's that?"

"Ruth Bernstein."

Ursula sat back. "Ruth Bernstein! How do you know Ruth?"

"We worked together on a number of public health issues for Dukakis in the mid-eighties."

"You and Ruth?" Ursula couldn't help but laugh. "So what are you doing hanging out with a Republican activist like David Warner?"

Brenda raised her eyebrows. "What are you talking about? Ruth tells me you're *married* to a Republican!"

Ursula chuckled. "Touché. I was out of line. But still. Somehow he doesn't strike me as your kind of man."

"Maybe that's because you know so little about him and absolutely nothing about me. But before we go any further, how did you find out about me? About who I was and where I worked?"

The waitress returned with the wine and Ursula took a sip. "Sorry. I don't want to get anyone in trouble."

The door opened and Ursula heard the MBTA cars rumbling up out of the tunnel to the stop at St. Mary's. "Ms. McGuire, let's cut to the chase. Exactly what is it you want from me?"

"I believe that Rebecca Scott was an abused wife. I believe that she was hurt by her husband, David Warner."

"But you don't know that. You only believe it, and apparently, you want me to confirm that belief."

"That's correct."

"Well, I've known David Warner for a long time, and I can assure you that he is not an abuser. David tells me you haven't been hired by his wife, but by some mysterious third party that you won't name. It appears to me that you don't really know anything whatsoever about David. You believe this outrageous notion, but you do not know it."

Ursula decided to stop wasting time. "All right, Ms. Robinson. Let me tell you what I *do* know. I know that your friend Mr. Warner has a severely injured shoulder."

"Anyone can see that."

"Yes, but not anyone can see why." Ursula swept her wine glass aside and leaned forward. "I'm not sure what David Warner tells his friends and colleagues about that injury, Ms. Robinson, but you and I know the truth, don't we? You and I know that David Warner was shot." Ursula saw, instantaneously, the shock in Brenda Robinson's eyes. "We know that he was shot with a .380 caliber bullet fired from a gun owned by Mr. Warner. We know that you accompanied him to Boston City Hospital where you both gave a false statement to the physician in charge, because you did not want to seek medical attention at a local hospital where word of the shooting would quickly become public. And finally, Ms. Robinson, we know who shot him, don't we?" Brenda leaned back, almost pushing herself away from the table. Ursula pressed her advantage. "It was David Warner's wife who shot him, and she shot him after years of physical abuse."

Brenda held up her hands. "All right! Stop it!" Several customers turned and looked at them. Brenda ran her hand slowly through her hair and glanced away toward the interior of the pub. She was fighting for time to think and Ursula decided to give it to her. She had pushed her far enough. Brenda turned back and lowered her voice to an indignant whisper. "Evidently, you know a great deal more than I had imagined. Everything you just said is true except for the abuse. He did not physically abuse her for years."

"Oh, he only abused her recently, is that it?"

"That is *not* it. Now you listen to me. The only reason I agreed to meet you tonight was to convince you to stop this harassment. David's career and his position in the Republican Party would be irrevocably damaged if the community believed he abused his wife, and that is precisely why we went to Boston City and not a local hospital. But his wife did not shoot him because he abused her. She shot him because she is subject to bouts of rage that go way beyond normal anger. I have personally witnessed these eruptions and believe me, they are extreme."

"Extreme in what…"

"Hear me out! When Lizzie, the older girl, was a freshman in high school, her guidance counselor made some flirtatious remark, and Rebecca went right onto campus while school was in session and wreaked havoc in the guy's office. David had already spoken to the young man by phone, but that wasn't good enough for Rebecca. And this kind of thing goes back a long way. A *long* way. My husband and I have been divorced for years, but as a couple we knew the Warners when all of our children were small. One time—I'll never forget this—Rebecca and I took our toddlers on the T to a mutual friend's house here in Brookline. As the trolley pulled into Coolidge Corner, we had to wait to get off because a waif of a girl, probably no more than twelve or thirteen, was fumbling through her purse for the correct change, and the driver was berating her, humiliating her

in front of all the passengers. Rebecca was in front of me holding her daughter's hand, and she turned around and looked
in my eyes with an expression so furious that it frightened me.
She took my wrist and placed Lizzie's hand in mine and then
stepped between the trolley driver and the trembling teenager.
She took the girl gently by the shoulders and told her that she
would take care of things.

"She turned back, faced the driver, and reached into her
purse. 'You want exact change? Well, I've got the *exact* change
for you.' Then she hurled a handful of pennies and nickels at
him with such force that it knocked the man's glasses right off
his face. We grabbed the kids and jumped off the streetcar
and raced down Harvard Street. The children thought it was
some kind of a game and were shrieking with laughter, and
Rebecca was laughing right along with them, her long blonde
hair whipping in the wind and her face flushed with what I can
only describe as triumph or victory."

Ursula exhaled. "Wow."

"Extreme enough for you?"

"Yes, but…"

"Hold on. I can go on and on with these stories. Imagine
yourself married to someone like that who pushes you into
an emotional corner all the time. Who is subject to this kind
of fury. And that's exactly how she was the night she shot
him. In a fury. A towering rage. She was leaving that night
for Cambridge. She and the girls had moved the previous
weekend, and that evening the girls were at their new place
unpacking. Rebecca came back for the gun. He tried to stop
her. As they were struggling over the weapon, it went off and
she almost killed him."

Ursula nodded slowly. "So you see David Warner as blameless in this matter?"

"Blameless in the slow disintegration of their marriage? No, I don't. Blameless in this shooting? Absolutely. I've watched this man over the years and I've watched her. I've seen the integrity he brings to his work. I've seen his kindness toward my children after their father walked out on us. I've seen the kind of father he is. By the way, Ms. McGuire, have you ever asked yourself why his children still connect with him? Still like him?"

Ursula was silent. She hadn't expected this kind of spirited defense, and it set her back a moment. Outside on Beacon Street, the T rumbled up out of the ground again, and the image of Rebecca Scott throwing a pocketbook full of change in the driver's face rose powerfully in her mind. "Do you think that Rebecca Scott is a bad mother?"

Brenda leaned forward again. "Absolutely not. On the contrary, she loves her daughters with a fierce intensity and protectiveness. That guidance counselor is a case in point. But I've often thought about what would have happened if she had taken that gun with her to the school. I've thought about that a lot. She was like a mother tiger defending her cub. I'd hate to think of what might happen now if she thinks either one of her girls is threatened. And that's why David tried to talk her out of bringing the gun to the city with her. As he saw it, just the idea of a perceived threat might be enough to set her off. But she wouldn't listen. She insisted that she had to have it with her."

Ursula finished her wine. Then she glanced out the window at the traffic on Beacon Street and thought for a while. There had been that conversation with Rob on the phone. It was late in the evening back on the day he had first met Rebecca Scott. A meeting, she contemplated ruefully, that she had set in motion. That she was responsible for. Some kid had harassed one of her daughters, and Rebecca Scott had shoved him into the street.

"Ms. McGuire?"

"I'm sorry. I was just thinking about what you've said. I have to ask you…how…how did she react to what she had done? I mean it was you who brought him to Boston City Hospital. Did she simply abandon him and return to Cambridge?"

"Of course not. Rebecca's not a monster. She was horrified at what she had done and wanted to take him to Newton-Wellesley right away. At his urging, she called me and I came over immediately. Rightly or wrongly, David decided on our course of action and sent Rebecca home to their daughters."

"Why call you?"

"Because everyone regards me as the neighborhood medical expert. I could see that the bullet had missed any vital organ or major artery, but we had to deal with the bleeding pronto. David wanted to avoid going to Newton-Wellesley Hospital and tipping off the local authorities, so he came up with the Boston City idea."

"Actually, it was a pretty good plan considering the circumstances."

"Well, the way he saw it his business and his political work were at stake. He had to think fast. Look, David Warner is no saint. He's a man with all the faults that men have. Things were not good between him and Rebecca on a number of levels. But you need to free yourself of the image you have of him. It's not who he is. Believe me."

Ursula placed her hands on the table. "You said that Rebecca did not shoot her husband because he abused her. You said she shot him because she is subject to bouts of rage. But in both cases you've cited, the guidance counselor and the MBTA driver, her rage was a reaction to an injustice. A wrong. The rage didn't just erupt without reason. In this instance, according to you, her husband is trying to talk sense into her. Was there no reason, no cause, for her rage at David Warner?"

Brenda stared at her. "There was a reason. But the question for you is whether that reason warranted the extremity of her response. David purchased that gun for Rebecca quite early in their relationship. He purchased it for her protection and took her to a shooting range to show her how to use it. Even though David had bought the gun and registered it in his name, both of them thought of the weapon as Rebecca's. Rebecca wanted what she felt belonged to her. David resisted."

"Purchased it for her protection…protection from what?"

Brenda shook her head and smiled. "You seem to have amassed a great deal of information in a very short time about David Warner, haven't you? And from that information you've made some assumptions. Granted, those assumptions were well reasoned. The problem is that you've left one out."

"And what would that be?"

"That would be, Ms. McGuire, that Rebecca Scott was indeed a victim of abuse. It's just that you've got the wrong man."

"The wrong man?"

"That's right. The wrong man. But not just the wrong man. You've got the wrong husband."

CHAPTER 17

The article was buried toward the end of the first section of the *Cambridge Chronicle*, so even the editors didn't give it much credence. But there it was. The reporter assigned to the Devir murder, doggedly pursuing any angle she could, had combed over the police reports and found the account of a beautiful blonde in a silver dress. She included the decision by the police that the source, a homeless drunk who hung around at the corner of Wendell Street and Mass Ave, was intoxicated on the night of the murder and incapable of any accurate description of the events of that evening. Nevertheless, she pursued the source, only to discover that he had been treated repeatedly at Cambridge Hospital for alcoholism and hebephrenic schizophrenia, conditions which cause, among other symptoms, vivid hallucinations. She concluded the article validating Abby and Jeannie's description of a young brunette in a red dress.

Rosario threw the paper down on his desk and yelled out loud. "So why the hell write the article in the first place?" Still it was disturbing. Karl Hamilton, the bartender at Chez Henri, had seen a woman in a silver dress, but Ursie had elicited that information on the pretense of a missing persons investigation. Mrs. Tang had seen a woman in a silver dress but as far as he could remember, the police had never talked to her. So the Cambridge reporter was on to something—only she didn't know it. The local television stations and the *Globe* and the *Herald* had lost interest in the story, but what if one of their reporters came across this article and pursued it? And so what if they did? The whole notion that the blonde in the silver dress could be Rebecca Scott was ludicrous. It just wasn't possible.

The phone rang and he jumped. "She's on the warpath again. Better be careful today."

He laughed. "Thanks for the heads-up, Em. Same problem?"

"Same problem."

"A problem in need of an imminent solution, I'm afraid."

"Boy, I'll say. Lizzie and I are seeing my dad today, so maybe he'll try to come up with something. Something legal that is."

"I'm sure your mother isn't going to do anything illegal."

"Assault and battery's illegal."

"Emily, come on."

"I know, I know. I'm exaggerating. But look, this Wellesley idea is horrible. We can't let her get away with it."

"We?"

"Can't you kind of subvert this whole operation?"

"I'm a teacher, Em. Not a CIA agent."

He heard her laugh. "You know what I mean."

"So first I'm supposed to defuse her, and now I'm supposed to subvert her."

"But Wellesley? That's even more boring than Newton! And it's even further from the city."

"I'm sure she's not serious, Em. Relax. So where are you going today?"

"Walden Pond. My grandfather lives in a condo in Concord and he loves to hike in the woods, especially around Walden. You'd like my grandfather. He's really into history."

Rosario remembered the bitterness in Rebecca's voice when she talked about her mother-in-law. "Is your grandmother going too?"

"Oh, no. She died a long time ago."

"I'm sorry."

"Well, I never knew her. She died when my dad was a child."

"When he was a child?"

"Yeah, he was only five or six at the time. Why? You seem surprised."

"I don't know. Somehow I had the impression...well, never mind. Wrong impression, I guess. Hey, gotta run. I see your mom's car out front."

As they approached Watertown Square, Rebecca Scott slowed down. "I appreciate your coming with me, especially on a Saturday."

Emily's words came back to him. "Well, if it prevents you from committing assault and battery, then it's worth it."

"I don't know why the hell I'm even bothering with this. Lizzie wouldn't mind leaving Cambridge, but Emily would go through the roof. There's no reason I should even be considering this except for that little bastard Jackson Foster."

"Then turn around and we'll go back. We can take care of the kid next week, the way I suggested in the first place. Use the authorities in the school, and if that fails, use the authority of the Cambridge Police Department."

"We've already discussed that."

He decided to change the subject. "You know, speaking of Cambridge, in another hour they'll be serving lunch at Siam Garden. A little Chicken Satay and Tom Yum soup with shrimp, lime juice, and lemon grass. That sure beats house hunting in Wellesley."

The light turned green and she crossed over to Route 16. "Don't tempt me. I have to go through with this. A colleague at work was kind enough to make the appointment and I have to keep it." Rosario laughed and she glanced over at him. "What?"

"I don't know. It just seems so unlike you to think you need to bring a man along."

"Well, some of these suburban brokers, especially the older ones, don't really put themselves out for single women. Especially single women with children. They want to make sure there won't be any trouble getting the mortgage and closing the deal."

He laughed again. "So who am I supposed to be exactly? Mr. Rebecca Scott?"

She allowed herself a smile. "Just be with me, that's all. Let the brokers figure it out. What's important is that they're dealing with a couple. That way they'll be less tempted to show us all their crummy properties. Just play along...although there is one problem."

"What's that?"

"Our initial appointment is with Jean Bellingham. It's her agency. Nicole claims the woman knows Wellesley like the back of her hand, but as she was telling me this, she laughed out loud and warned me under no circumstances to stare at her hair."

"What do you mean, don't stare at her hair?"

"I don't know."

Rosario smiled. "Well, this sounds like fun."

"Don't say anything funny, OK?"

"Sure."

Jean Bellingham was a jolly woman in her late sixties with sparkling green eyes and an enormous white coiffure that rose from the top her head like a mountain of glistening cotton candy. Rosario couldn't take his eyes off the thing and didn't dare glance at Rebecca. He knew that if their eyes came into any kind of contact—even fleetingly—it would be all over. He inhaled deeply and then bit his lip as he listened to Rebecca and the realtor discuss home prices in various neighborhoods. At one point, just as he was gaining full control of himself, Jean Bellingham lifted her right hand and softly patted the side of her hair as if it were about to slide off her head onto the floor. Quickly, before it was too late, he began to stroke his chin, pushing the pressure of his smile downward, and risking rudeness, he shifted in his chair and stared out the window, using every power at his command to stifle the rising tide of hysteria. For there was no question about it. The hair was simply beyond the pale. Had he been with Ursula, he would have broken by now. She would be shrieking with laughter, hanging out of her chair, and he would be doubled up on the floor gasping for breath.

He heard the realtor mention something about the current state of the housing market in Wellesley, and feeling his sense of composure returning, he turned back and tried to focus on the bright green eyes instead of the hair. Abruptly, Jean Bellingham changed the subject. "So how is Nicole? I haven't seen her for a year or so. She's such a doll. A lovely girl. Too bad about her husband, though." She touched the side of her hair again. Rosario slid his palms down his thighs, grabbed his kneecaps and held on.

Rebecca's voice took on a sympathetic tone. "I...I didn't know anything was the matter."

"Well...no, I meant his size. He's so overweight, don't you think?"

"I've never met the man."

"Oh, let me tell you. He's as big as a house. Why if he were my husband, I'd put him on the market!"

Suddenly, Jean Bellingham jerked back in her chair and barked out a series of high-pitched cackles ending in an explosion of wheezing laughter. For a split second, Rosario stared at the woman in disbelief, and then, whether it was a release from the previous effort of holding himself back, or the sight of this quaking, spluttering real estate broker with a head of hair like Mt. Rainier, he leaned forward and howled. It was several minutes before either one of them could regain control, and by then his face was wet with tears.

Finally, Jean Bellingham handed him a tissue and took a deep breath. "My, my! Oh, dear! Well, I must say, I didn't think my little joke was all *that* funny, but you are a wonderful audience, Mr. Scott. I haven't had this much fun in months. Now where were we?"

Rebecca looked at her. "You were mentioning the open houses today."

"Oh, yes. Yes, of course. We usually run our open houses on Sundays, but there are several properties on the market that the owners are quite eager to sell. So I agreed to some limited Saturday morning showings. I think you should start with those homes. They're in areas I think you'd find desirable. I have agency business to attend to this morning, but there will be a broker at each house, and if you would like to see something else later on, just call me."

The first open house was a long brown ranch with a garage door that had been gnawed at and partially pulverized
by carpenter ants. The broker, an older woman in a bright red
pants suit and a voice ravaged by smoking, assured them that
the house had been treated and that the door was no problem.
The wet basement was no problem either as the owners were
planning on installing a sump pump before they left. While
Rebecca examined the kitchen, Rosario went out on the deck
in the back yard to get some fresh air. But there wasn't any. The
house was only a hundred yards from Route 9, and the sound
of the traffic was deafening. When he turned around, the broker was right behind him. "Lovely deck, don't you think?"

"Lovely? Maybe, but it's pretty damn close to the highway."

She lit a cigarette and waved it around. "Oh, that's not really a problem. It dies down at night."

Rosario noticed several pools of standing water to the left
of the deck. "Right about the time the mosquitoes come out?"

She laughed. "Every town has mosquitoes. It's…"

"No problem?"

"That's right. No problem."

Back in the car, Rebecca slammed her door shut and
looked over at him. "That wasn't too great."

"You're right, but then again, it's…*no problem.*"

The second property was a Victorian cottage high on
a hill off Crest Road. This time the broker was a plainly
dressed, dour-looking woman in her forties who took an
instant dislike to Rebecca. Rebecca had been polite, so it
was certainly nothing she had said. But as they moved from
room to room, Rosario could see that it was Rebecca's beauty
that angered her. While she explained the features of the
house thoroughly, her attention kept returning to Rebecca's

face and her figure and her clothes. Suddenly, she asked if Rebecca had children.

"Yes, two girls. They're both in high school."

"Ah, that's such a tough age. They really need supervising."

Rebecca glanced over at Rosario. "You're not kidding."

"Do you work, Mrs. Scott?"

"Yes, I work for a contract research organization in Cambridge."

The broker nodded. "That's a lovely skirt. Do you mind if I ask where you bought it?"

"Not at all. The Studio in Brookline."

"That's a pretty high-end clothes store, isn't it?"

Rosario saw the element of suspicion come into Rebecca's eyes as she turned and faced the woman. "I guess you could say that. Sure."

"I made the decision not to work full time. I thought it was important to be there for my children."

Rosario waited for the withering counterattack, but it didn't come. Instead, Rebecca spoke quietly, almost as if she were thinking aloud. "Well, I had to work my way through college, and I guess I just couldn't stop once I got the hang of it. But you know, sometimes things happen to people. Some women have to work, especially when their children are little. That doesn't make them bad mothers."

"I didn't mean to imply that you..."

Rebecca looked at Rosario with steel in her eyes. "I think I've seen enough. Ready?"

He smiled at her. "No problem." Rebecca laughed. Her first real laugh of the day. He took her arm, and they walked away from the now-silent broker and stopped at the sign in sheet. With Rebecca standing next to him he wrote, "What's your *problem?*" He was going to write more, but Rebecca tugged his arm and they walked away.

As they drove to the next open house, he sat and watched her profile. "You were pretty calm, cool and collected in there. She was kind of a bitch."

"Yeah, well I'm trying to practice a little self-control."

"Good job."

"Thanks. I was going to make some comment about how Wellesley was a pretty *high-end* town, and maybe that had something to do with all the time she had to be such a great fucking parent."

"Uh, oh. There goes the self-control. Watch the language, *Mrs.* Scott. They don't allow that kind of talk here in Wellesley, you know."

"Sorry. One more and I think I've had it. This one is over near the Weston line." Ten minutes later she pulled up in front of a Dutch colonial with an overgrown lawn and children's toys scattered all over the driveway. "Brother. What a mess. This is depressing, you know that?"

"No comment."

"Let's just look at the inside and get the hell out of here."

"Now you're talking."

This realtor was friendlier than the first two, but exuded a kind of fanatical perkiness so intense that Rosario decided to stay outside and pretend to examine the yard. In the driveway, he discovered a basketball behind a large trash can and began shooting hoops and thinking about Emily's phone call. Rebecca had said quite clearly during their hike around Fresh Pond that her mother-in-law had never liked her. Yet according to her own daughter, she couldn't possibly have known the woman.

A second later, the hyperactive realtor came fluttering out the front door vibrating with anticipation and holding her hands together in mock prayer. "Your wife seems really interested."

Rosario rolled the ball back behind the trash can. "No kidding."

"She's upstairs looking at the bedrooms. Frankly, I think it's the perfect house for you two." He resisted the urge to make her explain, slowly and carefully, how she could possibly know such a thing having only just met them. She took a step closer to him and grinned conspiratorially. "Go for it!"

Rosario laughed out loud. "Go for it? Just like that? You must run into some pretty impulsive buyers."

She nodded enthusiastically. "All the time."

"Mmm...well, we usually like to think things through—strange as that might seem."

A faraway look came into her eyes and she began to fiddle nervously with her fingers. Suddenly, Rebecca appeared at the front door. "Can we take a look at the basement?" The broker bustled back inside and Rosario decided to follow. In the kitchen the woman was struggling with a large, old-fashioned brass key. "I can never seem to get this door open." Rebecca glanced at him and rolled her eyes. The broker tried again, rattling the key and pulling at the door like a lunatic trying to break out of a cell. Finally, she threw her hands into the air. "Oh, well. It's just a basement! If your husband wants to look at it, I can take him around the back. We can see if the bulkhead is unlocked."

Rebecca looked at her. "Well, that's all right. I have a pretty good idea of the house now. I'll let you know if we're interested."

As Rebecca shook her hand, the realtor seemed to deflate like a child's balloon. Then she turned quickly to Rosario, and with a look of desperation, began yammering wildly. "Why... why don't you check out that bulkhead and the rest of the property, and perhaps your wife and I can talk girl to girl. We can have a little chat."

Rebecca stared at the woman. "Chat?" She spat out the word like an obscenity.

The woman backed away but held on bravely to a chipper little smile. "Yes. I mean, you know, perhaps a cup of coffee and a little small talk."

Rebecca frowned. "Small talk? I don't do small talk. I only do big talk. So if there's not going to be any big talk, then there's no talk."

Back in the car, she gripped the steering wheel. "You know what really got me?"

"About the house?"

"No. The house was a dump. About her."

"I would imagine the frenetic personality."

"Well, that for sure. And the interminable chatter. But the killer was that comment about the cellar. 'Oh, well. It's just a basement!' As if that wouldn't interest a woman in the least. I hate it when mindless women try to get me down on their level like that. How unprofessional." She sneered. "A real kitchen broker."

Rosario put his hand under her elbow. "Do me a favor."

She stared at him in surprise. "Of course. I certainly owe you big time for this morning."

"You don't owe me anything, but I think you were a little rough on that woman with the small-talk big-talk comment. She wasn't a bored automaton like the first one or a witch like the second. She was just trying to do her job. I think if you went back in and apologized, you would be doing yourself a favor."

She looked away for a moment. Then she turned back to him. "You're right, Rob. You're absolutely right. I was taking out my anger at that odious woman on Crest Road against a person who didn't deserve it." She opened the door and stepped out. "I'll be right back."

When she returned, she started the car and drove toward the center of town. "Thanks."

"For what?"

"For putting up with me."

"Nonsense."

"And thanks for being my fake husband."

He laughed. "Hey, that's the best kind."

"You still interested in lunch?"

"You bet."

"Good. Let's get back to the Square before I get any more dumb ideas. I've already run away from one problem. No point in running away from another, right?"

"Right."

When he glanced over at her again, she was staring straight ahead. She took a deep breath and then exhaled slowly. "I can't go back to this way of life, especially as a single woman. I'm not going to let a creep like Jackson Foster harass my daughter and drive me back into this."

CHAPTER 18

U rsula McGuire was analyzing the latest polls when shouts from the outer office broke her concentration. She jumped up from her desk and flung open the door. Lily O'Donnell, leaning over her desk, pointed accusingly at David Warner. "Your man fired those workers. It's just another case of Republicans caring only about big business and the rich and the rest of us be damned!"

Warner seemed calmer this time, more in control. "I'm not going to scream at you, madam."

Lily pushed herself away from her desk and folded her arms. "I should certainly hope not."

Warner sighed. "Let's try it again. Mr. Romney left the company before they let those workers go."

"And then had the unmitigated gall to offer to hire them back part time and without any benefits!"

"That was no longer Mr. Romney's company. This is guilt by association at its worst."

"It's guilt by association because he was associated with the company. Therefore, he's guilty."

"Clearly, you don't understand how businesses are structured these days. Mr. Romney's company was Bain Capital. It was a subsidiary of Bain in Indiana that closed that plant and then reopened it. And when that decision was made, Mr. Romney was no longer there."

"No longer by how much time? Weeks? Besides, don't give me that subsidiary garbage. That's how all you businessmen cover up your shady dealings."

Ursula decided that it had gone on long enough. "OK, Lily. I think we've shown Mr. Warner how politically unbiased we are here at McGuire, Witherspoon, and Key. Now Mr. Warner and I have an appointment."

Lily plopped down at her desk. "I'm sorry, Ursula, but I just can't help it when I'm dealing with these right-wing Republicans. What's happening to this state? Whatever happened to all those nice, moderate Republicans like Governor Sargent and Senator Brooke?"

Warner smiled. "They were driven out of office by liberal Democrats. That's what happened to them."

Ursula ushered him into her office. "Congratulations, Mr. Warner. Not too many people get the last word in with Lily."

He collapsed into the chair opposite Ursula's desk. "Brother! Isn't it enough for me to come into the lion's den in the first place without having to put up with an armed sentry? She's a real piece of work, isn't she?"

"That she is, Mr. Warner. And it was unprofessional, I grant you. I apologize."

He looked as if he were about to speak but then turned and glanced across the room. "Those prints. That's a Benson on the left and a Paxton next to it. You've put them in some pretty expensive frames, I see." He swung around and looked at the wall next to the door. "And that, if I am not mistaken, is no print. That's an oil painting by Edmund Tarbell. Is that an original?"

"Very good, Mr. Warner. You're quite the observer. Quite the connoisseur."

"I'm no connoisseur. I just like beautiful paintings. But I sure don't have anything that valuable. You've come a long way for a girl from East Cambridge. I learned a little more about your background from your pit bull out there. She's got the class warfare scenario all sketched out in her head like most Democrats. Working-class gal vs. the evil Republican rich guy from the suburbs. Too bad she's not more of a connoisseur. Tarbell's painting alone would shatter that myth. To say nothing about a political consultant with an office on Beacon Street. Married to a Harvard professor and published author. Home on Beacon Hill. I'm afraid I'm…well…outclassed."

She laughed. "Don't take it personally."

He smiled and pointed over her shoulder. "And those photographs! When I was here the first time I couldn't really absorb what I was seeing."

"Well, you were upset."

"Look at that! With the crown prince of Camelot himself. How old were you? Sixteen? Seventeen?"

"Fifteen. That's my grandfather, Eamon McGuire, on the right. He was a typesetter at Ginn and Company. That was taken out in front of The Athenaeum Building at the beginning of the 1960 campaign. He knew Jack was coming through Cambridge that day and got me out of school."

She watched his eyes travel over the wall of photographs. He stopped at the picture of Bobby Kennedy and a crowd of young women. "Look at you in the miniskirt and the shoulder length hair. Was that the '68 campaign?"

"No, that was '67. I was still in college and had an internship with the Middlesex District Attorney's office. Bobby had come up from New York to speak at a law enforcement seminar, and the assistant D.A. got me and some of the younger staffers in."

Warner looked over at the one of her and Teddy and Joan outside the office during the 1980 primary fight against Carter and then grimaced as his eyes moved from right to left. Humphrey. Muskie. Mondale. Dukakis. Cuomo. The Clintons. The senators. The congressmen. The mayors.

As he studied the pictures, she studied him. It was easy to see how Rebecca Scott had been attracted to him. He was extremely good looking, certainly one of the more handsome men she had seen in quite a while, but his attractiveness, she thought, resided purely in his physical appearance. His high, almost feminine cheekbones, his fine clothes, his jet-black hair and dark eyes. For some reason, she couldn't picture him dealing patiently with a troublesome wife the way Mark dealt with her, and she had certainly caused Mark enough trouble to try that patience sorely. She also couldn't picture him making a woman laugh the way Rosario did. Yet Rosario, for all his humor and warmth, had never committed himself to a woman, and this man had. David Warner had become a family man, a husband and a father. A man whose daughters still felt connected to him.

He shook his head. "You've got a regular rogue's gallery up there, Ms. McGuire. I wonder if we added it all up, we could possibly arrive at a recognizable number for the amount of money that crew has lifted from the wallets of the American taxpayer." Then he spotted another one high up on the wall next to her diploma from Simmons. "My God, is that Curley? There's the greatest rogue of them all. Why, my grandfather would have regarded a photograph like that as evidence of collusion with the devil."

"Yes, well it's probably because of people like your grandfather that the people of this city needed a devil like that."

"Look at him. Look at that wink and that crooked smile. He was as corrupt as they come. And there you are with your hair in braids! You're just a little girl."

She turned around and looked up at the old black and white print. "That was the 1951 mayoral race against John Hynes. Curley lost."

"The last hurrah."

"Not really. There would be two more campaigns after that. Curley would lose those too. Time, I'm afraid, had passed him by. If you look carefully, you can see I'm standing on a fruit crate from The Upham's Corner Market. I'm wearing my navy blue coat and matching beret, and the arm holding me up belongs to my grandfather. One of his pals was a Curley aide, and they were helping the old man campaign in Dorchester all day. When my grandfather told his buddy it would be my seventh birthday in a few weeks, he told Curley, so James Michael himself took me over to Brigham's for an ice cream cone with two reporters and a photographer in tow, and then we crossed back over Columbia Road for the photograph in front of the market."

"So there's the cone in your right hand, and your left hand is on the devil's shoulder. Age six. It looks like an old newspaper photo."

"It is. The old *Boston Post*."

He stared at her. "Were you baptized in politics?"

"Just about."

"But now you work behind the scenes. No more photo ops in Upham's Corner."

"You could say that."

"And here's what else I have to say. Working from behind the scenes, you've chased down Brenda Robinson. I'm not going into how I feel about you acting like some prosecuting attorney firing fusillades of accusations at her until she…"

Ursula leaned forward. "They were not accusations, Mr. Warner. They were facts. The visit to the emergency room. The name and location of the hospital. The false statement to the attending physician. The caliber of the bullet. The identity of the person who shot you. All indisputable facts. You know it and I know it."

"And I think I can guess what you're going to do with that knowledge."

"Really?"

"Yes. As I mentioned to you before, my sources tell me that you are involved up to your eyeballs in this Indiana worker business. That you are one of the attack dogs behind these new television ads that are trying to paint my candidate as an unfeeling oligarch totally out of touch with the working class. This is an act of desperation on your part because for the first time ever, a Republican challenger is running neck and neck with the senior Senator from Massachusetts. Your ads are designed to sway independents away from Mr. Romney and to get out your Democratic base. And if you can paint Mr. Romney's major fundraiser as a wife beater, then it's the icing on the cake. Wouldn't the *Globe* love to run with that story?"

He looked away for a moment and then got up from his chair and walked to the big window overlooking the Common and the Beacon Street entrance to the Public Garden. Ursula gave him time to think. Slowly, he turned back to her and folded his arms.

She smiled. "Your arm is much better. You couldn't do that the last time you were here."

He nodded. "Brenda asked me to see you. If it were not for her, I wouldn't be here."

"Brenda speaks very highly of you. How helpful you were to her during a trying period of her life."

"Brenda gives me too much credit. Her husband was an alcoholic who walked out on his wife and kids. Many of the husbands and wives in our neighborhood helped her out over the years, especially with the children. We made sure they were always involved in family trips and sports events and other things that kids need growing up."

"Did your wife involve herself in those things?"

"No comment." She thought of Rosario again and frowned. He paused for a moment. "For some odd reason, Brenda tells me that you might be willing to listen to me this time."

"I'm always willing to listen."

He laughed grudgingly. "Yes, if one is a liberal Democrat or what your secretary calls a *moderate* Republican."

"Not at all. One of my best friends was a Goldwater girl back in 1964."

"So was Hillary Rodham Clinton."

Ursula laughed. "This one, I'm afraid, is still a rock-ribbed conservative who has no use for moderates. *Moderation in the pursuit of justice is no virtue.* Remember that line? It continues to be her credo."

He turned away again and looked out over the city. "Brenda tells me your husband is a Republican."

"Ah, but he's easy to get along with. He's one of those Yankee Republicans with good sense and moderation in his bloodline. His grandfather was an aide to Henry Cabot Lodge, Sr."

"Really? Well, you two must have a great deal in common. Until I became involved with Brenda, I had no idea what that was like."

"Yet you were married for quite a while. Two children…"

"Stop. You know better than that. You may have been lucky enough to have found the right mate but about fifty percent of us haven't. With Rebecca, it was simply foolishness on my part. She was the most beautiful woman I had ever met, and so impressive, successfully balancing her career along with being a single mother..."

"A single mother?"

"That's right. She had escaped an abusive husband in New York and took her little girl with her. Lizzie was three years old when I met her. I thought Brenda told you."

"She told me there was an abusive husband. She probably thought any other details were none of my business." She smiled. "She felt none of this was any of my business. Why didn't you just tell me all this the first time you were here?"

"Because I didn't trust you, that's why. The whole abuse issue aside, all I could think of was the damage you could do if you discovered that I had been shot by my wife. And frankly, because it was..."

"None of my goddamn business, right?"

"Right. I was so angry at you and I couldn't imagine what you wanted from me."

"That's because you can't imagine the circumstances that have given rise to my involvement in your life. But let me put your mind at ease on one score. Despite all political appearances, I'm not out to destroy your professional life or use what your wife did to you to damage Mr. Romney's campaign. You have my word on that. Senator Kennedy will defeat Mr. Romney on the issues, as it should be. This has nothing to do with politics."

He gestured at the wall of photographs. "But everything you do is political!"

She stood up and came out from behind her desk and extended her hand. "Good luck in your campaign, Mr. Warner. I think our business has ended."

He reached out tentatively, took her hand, and frowned slightly. "I'm a little puzzled. Our business has ended...how exactly?"

"Exactly as I said. You won't hear from me again. Now, if I may, one final question. About the gun. It's a .380 caliber. That's a semi-automatic weapon. Not what you'd expect from your average accountant. Is it registered in your name or your wife's?"

He smiled. "Why do I think you've already discovered that?"

She smiled back. "Humor me."

"It's my gun. I've owned it for years. I believe a man still has a right to own a gun to protect his home and family."

"It didn't protect you from your wife."

"No, it did not. But it might very well have protected the young woman I fell in love with back in 1979. The young woman whose angry husband knew where she had escaped. I asked Rebecca to marry me only months into our relationship, but she kept putting me off saying how disastrous her first marriage had been. How she just couldn't do it. We started living together and even after she became pregnant with Emily she refused. Finally, shortly after Emily's second birthday, she agreed. During this time I taught her how to handle that weapon." A slight smile crossed his face. "She became an ace at the shooting range, believe me."

"I believe you."

"I know what you're getting at. I have to admit that as time went on and I got to know Rebecca better, I did come to regret buying that gun, especially when we never heard from the man, and as the girls grew older its presence in the house worried me more and more." He sighed. "The point of arming Rebecca was for defense, but at times, when she would speak of him, I began to feel that she might take the thing and seek him out."

"So he never called? Never tried to contact her in any way?"

"Not until this year."

She stared at him. "So sixteen years later he suddenly…"

"That's right. Sixteen years later. According to Rebecca, he called and begged her for forgiveness. He seemed, after all this time, as if he were consumed with guilt and self-recrimination."

"Why now?"

"Lizzie. He wants to meet his daughter. You see, Lizzie turned eighteen this year. Eighteen-year-olds have certain rights, you know, and this man—like you, Ms. McGuire—is a lawyer."

She looked into his eyes. "I'll ignore the invidious comparison. Did he say or intimate in any way that he would use the law to seek out his daughter?"

"No."

"But she still sees him as a threat, and that's why she came back for the gun the night she moved to Cambridge. The night you were shot."

He nodded. "The thing about Rebecca is how…how difficult she is. You can explain the behavior of someone you've loved. You can explain it, excuse it, forgive it, but over time, if the behavior never lets up, you get to a point where you can't take it any longer. After a while, it just kills whatever it was that drew you together in the first place. Frankly, I don't know what to believe about this man, but I do believe that whatever danger he poses, it pales in the face of any perceived danger on Rebecca's part. Lately, a kid at school has been hassling Lizzie. I worry about what Rebecca might do to him. And who knows, really, about this ex-husband of hers? What if he wasn't as bad as she says he was? What if he insists on seeing Lizzie and she flies into a rage?"

"Well, at least there's one thing you won't have to worry about."

"And what's that?"

"Me. Come on. I'll show you out so Lily doesn't take a bite out of you. You've been banged up enough lately."

CHAPTER 19

Late in the afternoon, they crossed Brattle Street and walked into the grounds of the Episcopal Divinity School, stopping in front of St. John's Memorial Chapel. The waning rays of the sun slanted through the trees onto the wall of the church, and for a moment, Rosario watched the stone absorbing the light in a pale fading glow. They strolled past the big tree in the center of the quad where a trio of squirrels, sitting up straight like vigilant vergers, munched on acorns and flicked their tails. In the distance, high up on the roof of the First Church of Cambridge, the golden rooster gleamed in a dark blue sky. "Lots of religion hereabouts, Brother Rosario. Maybe we'll run into your pal."

"My pal?"

"The priest you keep seeing around the Square."

"Oh, *that* pal! I'm afraid by the looks of him, he wouldn't fit in around here. This place is all about tolerance and acceptance. Very ecumenical. This guy's from the dark side. Believe me."

Rebecca glanced up, her eyes taking him in. "Emily mentioned something to me the other night, and I feel as if I owe you an explanation. She told me she called you the day we went to Wellesley and mentioned that David's mother died when he was a child. She said you seemed puzzled and then I realized what it was. My comments about the bad guy were vague, because I didn't really want to talk about him, and I see now that you assumed that David Warner was the bad guy. He isn't. The bad guy is my first husband, and he's a real bad guy. The mother-in-law I talked about that day at Fresh Pond was *his* mother."

"I never doubted your word, Rebecca."

"But you certainly must have wondered. It's only natural. I would have. She was, I'm afraid, a presence. An affliction. The Wicked Witch of Westchester."

He smiled. "That's quite a title."

"A title she richly deserves."

"It's so hard for me to imagine you, of all people, in a situation like that. You as a victim."

"Well, I was young. And he was not a bad guy at first. In fact, he was quite charming. Attentive. Polite. Charismatic. That was the key for me. His personal dynamism. The boys I knew in high school and the guys I met in college all seemed to blend into a single superficial character, devoid of substance, intellect, or interest. They had nothing to say and weren't in the slightest bit interested in what a girl had to say." She paused a moment and looked back toward Brattle Street. "It's funny… my family was like that too. My parents have always been kind of…well, bland. Quiet. Even-tempered. Calm."

"Like you."

She laughed, her gray eyes shining silver in the autumn light. "What I mean is they had little to say about ideas of any kind. They had no strong opinions on anything. And this was in the sixties! They just did their jobs, came home, and watched TV. That was it." She stopped and looked into his eyes. "You grew up Catholic."

"How did we get off on that?"

"Because it's at the heart of the matter. I grew up Protestant. Episcopalian. Typically Protestant, I suppose. Church rarely. Religious doctrine non-existent, and all of this, I believe, all of this non-commitment, non-engagement, left me unprepared for the appearance of a powerful personality."

"That's a pretty blanket judgment of Protestants. The Pilgrims were pretty committed. The founding fathers were pretty engaged. Even in our own era there were Protestant ministers in the vanguard of the civil rights and anti-war movements."

"OK, sure. But religion was taken seriously in the seventeenth and eighteenth centuries, and those people you refer to from the sixties and early seventies…what percentage of the broad Protestant middle class and working class were they? A measly fraction of the intellectual elite. Those weren't the people you met in everyday life."

"Those southern Baptists are pretty feisty."

"But they're from the South. I'm talking about our place. The Northeast. Protestants don't speak in tongues up here. They don't yell out in church."

"African Americans do. I attended a wedding of one of my former students at the Peoples Baptist Church in Roxbury last month, and there was plenty of noise. Everyone was swaying and clapping and singing and having a great time."

She sighed. "Will you stop it? I'm trying to make a point. My background and the background of millions of people like me didn't put an emphasis on engaging one's religion or one's politics. I know I'm overgeneralizing, but I had a friend in high school named Rachel Brownstein. Whenever I was at her house for dinner it was like something out of a Woody Allen movie. It was wild. Same with the Catholics I knew. Arguments, discussions, debates. Then home to Snoozeville."

He laughed. "Well, all those arguments are because of all the guilt and repression that Jews and Catholics go through. If I had it to do over again, I'd be an Episcopalian. A nice, calm, vanilla Anglican."

She smiled slightly and then glanced back at the chapel. "You say you can't imagine me as a victim. Let me tell you how victimization begins. It starts when you meet a charismatic figure. Someone larger than life. Someone with depth after all the shallow men you've met. Someone substantial after all the lightweights. That's the opening act.

"For me it was at The Palm in New York, a popular bar on Second Avenue. I was working at Pfizer at the time on 42nd Street, and a colleague and I went out for a drink after work. Amy was a bright girl and we got on well, but once we left the job, our conversations seemed to run out of gas. This was late 1973 and Watergate was dominating everything in the news. Ford had just become vice president, and now the big controversy was the Rosemary Woods catastrophe."

"The mystery of the eighteen-and-a-half-minute gap on the tapes."

"Right. I used to come home every night after work to my apartment on East 84th and devour the news. Unfortunately, I had two vapid roommates who could care less. They were complete birdbrains. Totally disconnected from the world beyond their hairstyles and their clothes. Amy, on the other hand, had a good mind, but once she left work, she just shut it down. So we're at this bar and I'm trying to gin up a little discussion of Nixon and the tapes, and she's totally focused on whether her boyfriend is going to take her to a Knicks game that weekend. The talk was becoming tedious, almost claustrophobic. I tried to feign interest but after a while the conversation began taking on the same deadening, vacuous tone that permeated my apartment. I thought I was going to scream.

"Then behind us, I heard someone mention the tapes and an argument broke out with three or four voices rising above the general din of the bar. I remember turning my head and looking over at the table. There was a crowd of men, all in suits, and one of the youngest among them swept his hand above the others and laughed. 'Do you believe what Haig said? Here he is, the President's chief of staff, and he says that some sinister force created the gap on the tape!'

"A man at the center of the table, clearly older than the rest of the group, lifted his drink and smiled. 'Yes. A sinister force named Richard Nixon.' Everyone laughed, and at that very moment he noticed me. When I say older, don't misunderstand me. I was twenty-six at the time and everyone at his table was obviously my general age. But he was more conservatively dressed than the others. His hair shorter. His general demeanor more mature. I guessed him to be in his early or mid-thirties. He kept staring at me and then he waved us over, inviting us to join their debate. Was Nixon guilty of covering up impeachable offenses? Was all this, instead, a liberal conspiracy to bring down a man they couldn't defeat at the polls? What did we think? And when I told him what I thought he listened to me. Really listened. This was not a trait I had encountered in men before.

"As it turned out, they were lawyers, all from the same firm. It was obvious that the man who had extended the invitation was in a more senior position, and despite the boisterous camaraderie at the table, the younger men all treated him with a certain element of deference. As lawyers, much of their talk focused on the legal aspects of the Nixon presidency, and soon the invasion of Cambodia came up. But by this time we were all feeling slightly drunk, and the Cambodia discussion degenerated into a spate of stories about who was in what college during the student protests against the invasion. Three of them were Ivy Leaguers and another three from big name state universities. The younger guy, the one who had been so worked up about Al Haig, pointed at me to get my attention. 'And where were you in the spring of 1970?'

'I was in my senior year at Connecticut College for Women.'

"I expected a snide remark since he was a Princeton boy, but I saw his boss cast him a look which must have stifled any patrician impulse. So when he spoke his tone contained only a minimum of condescension. 'And did the women at Connecticut College for Women go out on strike in protest like the rest of us?'

'Many of them did. I did not.'

'Oh, really! So you approved of Nixon's actions?'

'No, I didn't. But unlike many of my classmates, and most assuredly unlike you and your friends here at this table, I had to work my way through college. Some of us, especially in the sciences, didn't have the luxury of missing our education. I paid for those classes and I wanted my money's worth. I expected my professors to be educating me, not making some easy political statement. Anyway, from what I could see, the professors who went out in solidarity with their students were the ones who didn't do much work anyway.' That shut the little creep up for a while."

Rosario smiled at her. "Well done, Ms. Scott. Nice job. Perhaps Connecticut College gave you a better political education than the Ivy League."

"Perhaps it did. But no one gave me enough education to deal with Ryan O'Connor."

She was quiet for a moment, a distant, lost look crossing her face like a shadow. "He liked me that night. Liked me right away because I wasn't afraid to take on his snooty colleagues. He called me the next evening and took me out to dinner and we talked for hours. Hours. The first thing I liked about him was that after he asked me what I did for a living, he actually listened to me and then asked questions that showed he was listening. He didn't spend the night talking about himself. He didn't brag. And he had a kind of mordant wit that appealed to me. He was intense, and I needed that intensity. He had strong views, clear opinions. I was parched for companionship, for communication, for some kind of connection beyond the ordinary and the mundane. And for a man who was aggressive in his career, an aggressive lawyer in an aggressive law firm, a man who emanated self-confidence, he never tried to seduce me. Never pushed himself on me. Our relationship progressed gradually, and bit by bit it turned into an old-fashioned court-ship, certainly a strange turn of events for the 1970's."

"How old was he?"

"Thirty-four. An eight-year age difference. It didn't seem so important at the time."

"And during this courtship...no warning signs?"

"Not that I could see at the time. Except one. It took him a long time to take me home to meet his parents. A real long time. And when he finally did, I realized why. We drove out of the city one Saturday to New Rochelle and into a neighbor-hood a million miles from the kind of place I grew up. He could sense my nervousness and held my hand and told me that whatever happened to remember that he loved me."

"Whatever happened? That was a bit of a signal."

"Yes, but I didn't pick up on it. Or rather I didn't want to pick up on it. The father was civil. A placid, friendly man but the mother—I don't know where to begin."

"Let me see if I can make a stab at it: Stiff. Uptight. Proper. Cold."

She stared at him. "All of the above and much more."

"I know the type. There are several of them on my mother's side of the family. The Irish Catholic side."

"And your mother?"

"At the time, she was all of those things but not too much more. What saved her was that she had a sense of humor, four sons who rebelled against her sense of propriety, and a tolerant, but strong husband. In other words, we didn't let her get away with it. You see, Rebecca, you're in my territory here. I'm quite familiar with the native species."

She smiled for a moment, distracted. "But given your Italian side, it's only half your territory."

"Don't get me wrong. I loved my Irish grandparents, and I loved all the Irish lore I heard whenever I stayed with them in Dorchester. There's a great deal about my Irish heritage I feel quite proud of. But there's a type of Irish, usually referred to as *lace curtain*, who are better off than the working-class Irish and feel compelled to look down on them. My uncle Pat Walsh from West Fourth Street in Southie used to call them the *two terlet Irish*. That's the type I mean."

She paused. "Then that's what my mother-in-law was. Lace curtain. Except that she looked down on everyone less fortunate than herself, not just her fellow Irish. In any event, there was no rebellion in the O'Connor family, either from Ryan or his sister Mary Margaret. The father gave his wife whatever she wanted and she ruled the roost. When we entered her perfect house filled with white furniture and white rugs and religious pictures on the wall, she was a model of politeness and decorum. But there was that forced smile, that cold cordiality. Without ever saying anything, she made it clear that I didn't fit the bill. Didn't quite make the grade. A Protestant, blue-collar girl from Norwalk wasn't part of the game plan. When Ryan announced after lunch that he had asked me to marry him, his father seemed immobilized by the news but managed a feeble little smile in an attempt to mask his sense of disappointment. His mother, sitting ramrod straight, quietly folded her napkin, left the table, and went upstairs to her room. She never returned."

Rebecca Scott didn't speak for a moment. She looked back at the chapel and then turned to face him. "I remember the drive back perfectly. The sun was setting as we crossed the Triborough Bridge, and the city was burning and glowing with reflected light. Scarlet clouds hovered over the skyscrapers, and the whole scene was like a massive shining force welcoming me back to the place I belonged. This was the place I had chosen to work and to live. This was the place I had found this wonderful man, but now some omen, some specter had arisen to threaten our happiness. I felt such desolation, such laceration in my heart. I remember I had this thought, this fleeting insight that this was not going to work, that I was headed for some disaster and that I should break it off then and there. But he was so full of affection that day, so apologetic for his mother's rejection, so reassuring that what we had would overcome anything life threw our way. I had never seen him so emotional, so loving, so caring and so persuasive. So persuasive that my fleeting insight simply evaporated. When we got back to his apartment and shared a drink and talked out the afternoon, I had this feeling he was going to abandon the restraints of his self-imposed courtship and make love to me. Take me into his

heart and tie me to him in an act of intimacy that would prove
he was committed to me and not to those people back in that
cold house in New Rochelle. But he didn't. He said he wanted
to but that it was more important for us to wait until we were
married. That it was more important for him to remain true to
his values and his beliefs. His faith.

"During the weeks that followed, his mother told him repeatedly, in no uncertain terms, that I was unacceptable. But
he resisted and stood by me. Apparently not used to resistance,
she flew into a fury. Unable to budge him and finally realizing
that he meant to marry me, she put on a show of reasonability
and floated the idea of my converting to Catholicism. Had she
been a woman who accepted me with kindness and affection, I
might have even considered it simply as a gesture, a signal that
I valued becoming a member of her family. But this family,
headed by this vile woman, wanted nothing to do with me. I
rejected the notion out of hand, and he stood by me again.

"We married in the Episcopal church in Norwalk and the
ceremony itself was lovely. The church was filled with people
I knew. My family, friends from high school and college and
work, and the kindly old minister carried off the occasion
without a hitch. But of course, there was a hitch. Not one member of Ryan's family showed up. Not his mother. Not his father.
Not even his sister Mary Margaret, who on the surface at least,
had always been kind to me.

"Ryan and I did well at first. We were both happy. We loved
living in New York and enjoying the city together. The muse-
ums. The walks in Central Park. The restaurants. Just talking
together in the evenings. Out of consideration for me, he kept
our visits to the ice palace in New Rochelle to a minimum.
Kept me away from the atmosphere of stifling sobriety that
hung over the household. Away from this finicky, fastidious

woman who had dismissed me out of hand. This implacable enemy. Then I got pregnant."

"Pregnant?"

"Yes, those things do occur, you know."

He laughed. "No, no. What I mean is I assumed all along that Lizzie…"

"Oh, I'm sorry. You assumed she was David's child. Of course you would. No, I'm afraid not."

"That explains Emily's comment that Saturday outside the Blacksmith House. She said that he tries harder with Lizzie than he does with her."

Rebecca smiled. "She said that, did she? She's a funny kid. Well, she's right. David always felt he had to because of what happened to us in New York. The trouble started when Ryan's mother began her campaign to ensure that Lizzie be brought up a Catholic, and Ryan, to my astonishment, fell right in with her plans. Up to then we discussed things. If we disagreed on something, we talked it out. But now it was simply decided ahead of time. I wasn't even consulted. As if being the mother of the child were somehow irrelevant. The funny thing was that I really had no strong objection to the idea itself. If Ryan had brought me into the discussion, if his mother had been someone else, well…maybe I would have agreed.

"Up to this point, as long as Ryan was in my corner, I could ignore the maliciousness of this woman. But now, as my resentment began to build, I began to see my husband in a different light. Now he was suddenly the dutiful son who began speaking in terms of *we*. '*We* believe, after much reflection'—as if there were an iota of reflection! '*We* think'—as if there were an iota of thinking! It was just the party line. That word *faith* made its appearance again just as it did the night after my first visit to his family. The faith was reasserting its power. Lizzie was to be a Catholic. It was, after all, an article of faith. That was the end of it.

"After Lizzie was born, my mother came down from Connecticut to help for a few weeks. Shortly after she left, without a word to me, Ryan and his mother took Lizzie to a church and had her baptized. He told me that night and I was so stunned at his betrayal, so incensed at his treachery, that I just sat on the bed and stared at him. My initial reaction was to stand up and confront him, but I didn't want to do anything to disturb my baby. So I just sat there quietly. As I looked into his eyes, I saw that his face had become distorted with pride and ideological purity, and I had this sensation he had removed a mask, and that I was in the presence of a stranger. The man I met at The Palm that night, the man who had courted and comforted and married me, had vanished.

"Then, instead of sitting down on the bed next to me and trying to win me over to what they had done, he began pacing the floor and issuing demands. I would not go back to work. I would stay home and take care of our child. Ironically, I had already decided to do just that, but he announced that I was *never* going back. That he expected me to be the mother of his children and that was to be my *only* role. Soon, after we had saved some more money, we would give up our apartment and move to the suburbs. To New Rochelle, in fact, where Lizzie could be close to her grandparents. No mention of my parents, of course. And to the *parish*—not the town—the *parish* he had grown up in. Point by point, in the most lawyerly fashion, he mapped out the rest of my life right in front of my eyes. He was, of course, expecting a response, a rhetorical counterattack, no doubt. He knew what kind of a woman I was. He knew this would not sit well with me. So when he finished, he stepped over and looked down at me, his hands on his hips, waiting for my reaction.

"I looked up at him in dismay. 'What's happened to you? I feel I don't know you at all. How did you go from being my partner to being my boss in one day? This is beyond my comprehension. I can't express to you how I feel about this, Ryan. There is such a void in my heart.'

"For a split second, it looked as if my words were affecting him, but then he snapped to and stood straight, steeling his spine against me. Some force held him in its grip. 'We've had a wonderful time, Rebecca. But the birth of our child requires us to open our eyes to the kind of life we want our daughter to lead. It requires a clear path toward the future.'

'But this is a path that we decide upon together, don't you think? A path we travel where we don't do things behind each other's backs.'

"He turned away and looked at the sleeping child. 'Sometimes it is necessary to act alone when the salvation of a soul is at stake.'

'The salvation of a soul! This is a marriage, not a theology seminar.'

"He turned away again. 'I need to go out for a walk. I need to think.'

"I glared at him. 'When you return, bring the old Ryan back. I don't like this new guy.' He slammed the door behind him."

Rosario stared at her. "And when he came back?"

"The old Ryan never came back. The new guy was here to stay."

CHAPTER 20

Across the still blue water, above the trees with their leaves gleaming red and gold in the morning sun, the gothic towers rose up on the heights of Chestnut Hill. It was a damn good thing they were out in the open and walking, for Ursula could barely control herself. She had promised not to interrupt him, but her temper flared with every incident as the whole story reverberated with a toxic familiarity.

"Rebecca's natural inclination, of course, was to fight back, but she had read about the effects of parental strife on infants, and she wanted at all costs to protect her child. So she repressed her instincts. She decided to go along with things for as long as she could. She quit Pfizer and stayed home with the baby as she had intended to do. She even went along with the move to New Rochelle. She hid her contempt for her mother-in-law, masked her disgust at the weakness of Ryan's father and concealed, as best she could, her bitterness at this harrowing shell of a marriage. So she became the compliant wife, the dutiful daughter-in-law, a hostage, as she called it, to the impenetrable rectitude all around her."

"Impenetrable rectitude. I like that. It's a perfect…"

"No interruptions, remember?"

"Sorry, Rosie."

"Her only escape was Sunday when they bundled the baby off to Mass, and she drove to Norwalk to see her parents. But even there she found no solace. Her father was a distant man, usually off with his buddies on the golf course, and her mother, while seemingly sympathetic, felt that wives needed to make the best of things in order for a family to work. Her mother's way of dealing with Rebecca was to take her out to shop, not to talk. Month after month went by like this—a vast, forlorn time when her only joy was her child. At night, over dinner, Ryan would talk to her about his work, tell her stories that he thought were amusing or insightful, trying with a kind of willful ignorance to reignite what they once had.

"Then, shortly after Lizzie's second birthday, Ryan proposed a Saturday in the city. Just the two of them. A walk though their old neighborhood and Central Park. A visit to the Metropolitan Museum and maybe dinner at The Palm. It had been so long since he had suggested anything remotely like this that her suspicions were immediately aroused. What was he after? To torture her over everything they had left behind? He seemed, after all, to have no understanding of what their early days had meant to her. No conception of the nature of this suburban prison he had locked her up in. So what was the point?

"She learned soon enough. After the museum, they passed by Cleopatra's Needle, and he stopped under a tree and took her by the shoulder. 'I know, Rebecca, you have not been happy recently. I know you can't, as much as you seem to try, abide my mother's meddlesome nature.' The use of the term *meddlesome*, such a weak euphemism for her rapacious interference, simply demonstrated to Rebecca, once again, that he hadn't a clue about the power this woman wielded over him. 'But I've also seen, and I want you to know how much I appreciate, what a wonderful and loving mother you've been to Lizzie. And it's this love, this maternal side to your otherwise somewhat combative nature, which holds the key, I think, to your happiness. I've decided that it's time for us to have another child.'

'*You've* decided!'

'Yes, Rebecca. I've decided, and I hope that you will agree with me so that there will be no more unpleasantness between us.'

'No more unpleasantness! These past two years, except for Lizzie, have been nothing but unpleasantness! Are you blind to the way you treat me? The way you relegate me to your worn-out notion of a wife as second-class citizen. If you think you're going to turn me into one of these baby machines your religion seems so intent on producing, you've got another thing coming. You don't really believe this nonsensical rhythm method has prevented another pregnancy, do you? I went on the pill one month after Lizzie was born.'

'You what!'

'You heard me.'

'This is…this is unbearable. This is utter defiance of a husband's will. This is simply intolerable.'

'No! You are intolerable, Ryan O'Connor! This marriage is intolerable. I'll never have another child with you. Ever!' His eyes narrowed in anger, and glancing around quickly to see if anyone was watching, he slapped her across the face with such force that she stumbled and fell to the ground. He grabbed her by the arm, yanked her to her feet and pulled her away from the park toward Fifth Avenue."

Ursula flung out her hand. "Birth control! Of course! How fitting! I should have guessed that would be the issue upon which this so-called marriage would founder. That's what this guy is all about. Control. Power. Authority. But when a woman wants a measure of control, well, that's another matter entirely."

"I could swear that was an interruption. Maybe even an outburst."

"Well, I couldn't help it! Just like Rebecca's outburst in Central Park. He wasn't ready for the revolt when it finally came. Just like any tyrant. That's why he hit her. Did she try to break free and run away?"

"No. No, she didn't. She made up her mind then and there to play her assigned role a little longer, until she could figure out her escape. She let him think that the slap had cowed her, and she lapsed into a remote passivity that unnerved him. He found her pills and seeing the name of her gynecologist, called and told him Rebecca was switching to a different doctor. Then he threw the pills away. Rebecca found another physician and acquired a new prescription which she kept well hidden."

"How could she possibly have sex with a man like that again?"

"She didn't want to talk about that, Ursula, and I didn't ask her. All she said was that whenever she tried to disengage he slapped her again. He never punched her. Never left any bruises. And whenever he struck her he would quote Church doctrine on a wife's duty to her husband."

"Church doctrine! Sounds like a form of rape to me!"

"During the course of their marriage, Rebecca came to learn the full extent of her husband's ties to New York. His position in his Manhattan law firm, his ongoing relationship with Fordham where he had attended undergraduate and law school, his active membership in his parish church. These ties nailed him down to New York. If she could break free, get out of his reach, he couldn't really come after her in any permanent way. At thirty-eight, he couldn't just drop everything and chase after his wife. He could find her, but he couldn't stay for long, and if he tried to drag her back, she would accuse him of abuse and endanger his position in the community. For Ryan O'Connor and his family, disgrace was not an option.

"Then one day, with the excuse that they were visiting the other grandparents in Norwalk, Rebecca and her little girl escaped to Boston. She had already lined up a job at Peter Bent Brigham and an apartment and a day care center in Brookline, and for one month she lived in absolute freedom. Then he found her. Shortly after 9:00 on a Friday night, there was a sharp knock on her door. Assuming it to be her landlord, who had promised to fix a leaky kitchen faucet, she opened the door. The look in Ryan O'Connor's eyes was so accusing, so damning, so overwhelmingly violent, that she instinctively backed away, enabling him to enter the apartment.

"He raised his hand and she flinched. 'Don't worry. I'm not going to strike you. I'll never hit you again. I promise. I can see now that you were a victim of forces beyond your control.'

'Forces beyond my control? What are you talking about? *You* were the force beyond my control. Now I'm out of your control. And if you don't get out of here immediately, I'm calling the police.'

'Hear me out. Pay attention. You were a victim of the women's movement. You were a victim of this so-called liberation propaganda that captured the attention of the media and did so much to undermine the traditional role of women in society. I think if we could erase the late sixties and early seventies we'd all be the better for it. You and I would still...'

'Are you so blind that you can't see who's at fault here? Are you so contemptuous of me as a person that you can't grant me the ability to make my own decision? You know I'm an intelligent person. You know I was trained as a scientist. But when it comes to decisions about *my* life, *my* body, *my* rights, you think it was all due to the women's movement? As if I could not come up with the concept of freedom by myself? You think this decision was made by an outside force? *The Women's Movement?* I'd say that's pretty ironic since everything wrong with you and your mother is the result of a movement called *The Church.*'

"His skin flushed and as he took a step toward her, she backed into the kitchen. In desperation, she reached behind her, yanked open a drawer and pulled out the biggest, sharpest knife she owned. She could feel, she told me, the glad fullness of the wooden handle and the sharp edge of the blade against her thumb. 'Touch me ever again and I'll kill you!'

"He staggered back, catching his balance against the door. 'The look in your eyes is…mutinous. I never, *never* realized the intensity of your hatred.'

'Now you know.'

"He stood staring at her. 'I want to see my daughter. You know I would never harm her.'

'No, you never did. You reserved that honor for me. She's asleep in her bedroom. Go see her.'

'You know that she's safe with me.'

'But I wonder for how long. I wonder how safe she'd be when she becomes a teenager and gets into that rebellious stage and doesn't tow the party line.'

"He looked at her oddly, as if the thought itself were incomprehensible. Then he backed away, turned, and opened the door to the child's room, standing quietly at the entrance and gazing at his daughter for quite some time. Rebecca thought he might sit on the bed and touch Lizzie's face or her hair or kiss her. But he never moved, and when he finally turned around he seemed lost for words. 'I…I don't quite know what to do. After all, you know how we feel about divorce.'

'Uh, huh. Well, luckily we live in a constitutional democracy and not in medieval Europe.' She gripped the knife tightly in her hand. 'I'm divorcing you and that's that. Don't even try to fight me. You're a lawyer. You know who ends up with custody of the child—even if I never said a word about the abuse.'

"He looked at her for a while. Looked at her holding that knife and glaring at him. A strange, malevolent look came into his eyes and he shrugged. 'Well, you both have chosen your beds, and now you must lie in them.'

'A two-year-old child does not deserve that kind of dismissal. She's your daughter. I won't stand in your way if you want to see her. Is that some perverted way to get back at me? To punish me? Is that your version of Original Sin, Ryan?'

"He turned away from her, left the apartment, and she never heard from him again."

Ursula stopped walking and crossed her arms. "Until now."

"Until now."

"When did you find out?"

"She told me at the end of her story…and you?"

"Warner told me. In my office after I had learned of this first husband's existence." This seemed to be the time to tell him about the gun. The struggle with Warner and the shooting. The fact that the gun was the same type used against Devir. But something held her back. After all, she didn't know it was the same gun. She didn't know for sure that Rebecca Scott was the killer. Everything pointed in that direction, but still… "What did she tell you? I mean about his manner. Warner seems to think the man has undergone some kind of change."

Rosario nodded. "Rebecca says that in his calls, his voice is different. It seems to have lost its edge. It has an eerie calm, a sense of exhaustion. He seems consumed with remorse. Overwhelmed with guilt."

"Well, he's a Catholic. Welcome to the club."

"She doesn't believe him, of course. She refers to him as the *bad guy*. A man beyond redemption."

"And how do you feel about him?"

He glanced away. "How do I feel about him? I feel that if he threatens Rebecca in any way, he will regret it. I will hurt him." He curled his fingers into a menacing fist and looked back at her with anger in his eyes. "That's how I feel."

It had been a long time since she had seen him like this. Anger had been his great fault, and he had fought hard over the years to purge himself of it. As far as Ursula was concerned, he had every right to his anger, for it was brought on by all the same forces that had produced a Ryan O'Connor and legions like him. Yet at the same time it was her fault that he was involved with this woman. Her fault that he was coming under the sway of his old emotional nemesis. She knew she should say something to calm him down, but she fell right in with his fury. She couldn't help herself. "He sees himself, no doubt, as the good Catholic layman. You know the type. Lots of sexual repression masquerading as virtue. Lots of talk about the sacredness of marriage, but deep down they hate women. I don't doubt that he fell for Rebecca in the beginning. What man wouldn't? But they got to him. The stiff, cold, Irish Catholic mother. The weakling father. The Church with all its psychological power. Sure, he strayed a little. Wandered away from the flock when he found Rebecca. But they roped him back in pretty quickly, didn't they? It's like what you and your friends had to put up with in high school. The Christian Brothers. Christian! They kicked the faith right out of you."

She stopped and tried to shake herself free of all the old resentments. "We've ploughed this ground too many times in the past." She glanced back at the long path around the reservoir. "We've only done a couple miles today, Rosie."

"Hey, it's Saturday. We can give ourselves a break. Come on."

They crossed over to Beacon Street and walked through the campus until they came to a bench near the Bapst Library. Rosario laughed. "Did I tell you my mother asked me to forgive her for sending me to the Christian Brothers?"

Ursula smiled and shook her head. "What brought that on?"

"Apparently, one of the priests in her church has gotten himself in a little hot water with some of the altar boys and the parishioners are fed up. Not like the old days when the clergy could do no wrong."

They sat down and watched the leaves blow across the campus lawns. She glanced up at the BC Eagle, a golden predator, perched threateningly on its column. "So did you forgive her?"

"Of course. She's seventy-four years old. What was I supposed to do? Drag up the past all over again? Forgive us our trespasses, Ursie. Remember?"

"As we forgive those who trespass against us. You see, they still have their clutches in us."

"No, they don't. That's not the organization talking. That's the spirit talking. Those are good words."

"Just remember them if you run into Ryan O'Connor. I don't want to be defending you in court for assault."

Two Jesuits strolled past them, heading toward Commonwealth Avenue. Rosario laughed again. "That reminds me.
There's something else I forgot to tell you. I've got this priest
following me around Harvard Square."

"What!"

"Well, maybe it just seems that way. I've run into him three
times. Twice while I was with Rebecca and then once again
when I was walking through your old neighborhood."

"What was he doing there?"

"I don't know. I had just passed your grandparents' old house
and spotted him on Sixth Street coming out of St. Joseph's. I
followed him around the corner and down Cambridge Street
to Sciarappa. It looked as if he might be headed for St. Francis
of Assisi's, but he kept to the left side of the street and went
into an old green house."

"Did you talk to him?"

"Not this time. But I did the other two times."

"What did you talk about?"

"Catholicism. But it was nothing serious. We weren't having a theological debate or anything. It was banter."

"So you hit it off?"

"Not really. I was kidding him, actually. But he took it
gracefully."

She stared into his eyes. "So you were with Rebecca on
both these occasions?"

"Not exactly."

"But you said you were."

"Uh, oh. I feel an Ursula McGuire interrogation coming
on here. Any particular reason?"

"Yes. Yes there is. Tell me about the first time."

"The first time was the day I met her."

"The day you had the run-in with the kid who was hassling the daughter."

"Right. When we said goodbye it was getting dark, and I ran into him down the street at the corner of Chauncy and Garden."

"And the second time?"

"We were at Nini's and she was buying a magazine, and I spotted him a few yards away walking around the corner past the Coop. I followed him and teased him about how we kept running into each other. I told him I was worried the Church might be after me for something."

She glanced away and stared into space. "What's this guy look like?"

"My height. But thinner. Wiry. Gaunt. He has a white crew cut, military style. If priests were soldiers, he'd be an officer. A true believer. What's the look for, Ursie?"

She shook her head. "You know...I've just decided that it's a good thing you dropped out of this case after all. You would have been no use to me. Clearly, the approach of your fiftieth birthday has had a profoundly negative effect on what's left of your brain. You don't see it, do you?"

"See what?"

"This priest *is* following you. And he's following you when you have just left or are in the company of Rebecca Scott. And this is happening to you at the same time that Ryan O'Connor has come out of nowhere to beg forgiveness of his former wife. Get the picture?"

He stood up and walked slowly down the path toward Bapst Library. When he came back, he stood in front of her. His voice was smoldering. "Well, counselor. It appears that Father O'Connor and I need to have a little talk."

"Calm down. This guy's no fool. He's discovered that she is living apart from her husband. He has come to stay or to live in East Cambridge. He wants Rebecca to forgive him, and he wants to meet his daughter. He just can't figure out who the hell you are and how you fit into the picture. This man, for some reason, has abandoned his legal career and has taken Holy Orders. That means he has undergone some great change. Some transformation."

Rosario laughed in derision. "Transformation! You've certainly changed your tune all of a sudden. Less than two hours around Boston College and you're using terms like *Holy Orders.* What happened to the great cynic?"

"Stop. My cynicism is alive and well. Obviously, this man has a great deal to answer for. Listening to Rebecca's story, I felt as if I could kill him. But frankly, given the fact that this man is now a priest, and that sixteen years have passed, I don't think this guy presents any danger to Rebecca Scott at all. In fact Rob, I think it's just the opposite. To say nothing of the trouble Rebecca Scott presents for you."

"For me?"

"Yes. For you. And it's all my fault for getting you involved with her in the first place."

"Come on, Ursie. You don't know this woman at all."

She hesitated a moment, feeling an overwhelming surge of remorse and anxiety. She tried to choose her words carefully. "I feel I've come to know her a little more through this story you've told me today and also through my investigation of David Warner. What she has been through, I think, has damaged her. Warner was sparing in the details of their marriage, but there seems to be enough instability here to worry about what that means for your own happiness. This woman seems so...so ferocious."

"I've seen you be pretty ferocious, and I'll be pretty ferocious with this bastard if..."

"No. Stay away from this guy. You're too involved with his ex-wife. You'll go after him as her protector. Wrong strategy, my friend. Let me handle him. Any interference on your part will just create more instability. More emotions. More anger. That's what you've been trying to get away from all these years, remember?" She stood up and grabbed him by the shoulders and shook him. "Besides," she laughed, "we always used to joke about how some day you might need a lawyer. Maybe this is it. Think of it as if you are turning him over to your lawyer."

He smiled, despite himself. "Yes, but you're such a ferocious lawyer."

She let go of him but did not return the smile. "A lot less ferocious than your friend will be if she gets a hold of him. Think about it."

CHAPTER 21

Will Pearson placed two ice-cold Cosmopolitans on the bar at The Blue Room and pushed them slowly forward. He tried valiantly to keep his eyes off Rebecca Scott but without much success. "There you go, Robert. For you and your lady. On the house."

"Will, come on. You don't have to do that."

The bartender laughed and waved his hand. "Hey. For old times' sake."

They watched as he turned and went to the other side of the bar to take an order from one of the waitresses. Rebecca raised the glass to her lips. "Mmm. Wow. This guy makes a mean Cosmo. This is delicious."

"I told you."

She smiled. "You look very impressive with a pink drink in your hand. I like it. It brings out your feminine nature."

"Thanks."

"So how do you know Will?"

"He was the bartender at Casablanca in the old days before they ripped it apart and glamorized it."

Rosario glanced over at the table nearest the bar. Two couples, probably in their mid-thirties, were finishing their meals. The two men and one of the women, deep in conversation, lingered over their drinks, but the other woman was turned to the side, talking on her cell phone. Rebecca nudged him. "Look at her. Wanna bet she's on the phone to her kids? The development of the cell phone has been such a boon to these uber-moms, hasn't it? The wireless umbilical cord. God forbid she should join in with the others and enjoy a night out in the city." The woman put her phone away and sat staring out at nothing, totally disengaged from the animated discussion taking place around her. Rosario could hear their voices clearly. They were arguing about the election, the men both Romney supporters and the other woman defending Kennedy's record.

One of the men leaned across the table and his voice rose. "It's not just Kennedy. It's the whole liberal wing of the party and all their liberal supporters here in this state and in our own town, for Christ's sake. Permissive on crime, permissive on welfare, permissive on taxes, permissive on education, permissive culturally. My grandparents voted Democrat. Four times for FDR. For Truman. For JFK. They'd never vote for this crew. The party has completely lost touch with the working and middle class who they always claimed to represent. We have to vote for Romney for no other reason than to balance the scales. The same reason we voted for Weld. And let me remind you, my dear, Massachusetts voted for Reagan. Twice."

His wife pointed at him. "And you somehow see Romney as a tribune of the people? After what his company did to those Ampad workers in Indiana? It just proves Teddy is right. Romney's all about profits, not people. The absolute ruthlessness of those firings. Those men and women have families, and now their families have no health insurance. How would you like it if we had no health insurance? How would you like it if there were no Medicare, and we had to pay your mother's hospital bills? We sure as hell wouldn't be eating dinner here at The Blue Room. Helping working people and health care is what this whole election is going to turn on, and your pal Romney is going to get his ass kicked."

Rosario half expected the husband to turn up the volume; but instead, the man laughed and the three of them lowered their voices and gestured and drank as they talked, all in good spirits. Behind Rebecca, waiting for some bar seats to open up, a group of young people in their twenties jostled and buzzed with conversation about Boston and Cambridge and their jobs and who was going out with whom. In front of him Will concocted magic cocktails that resembled raspberry sodas for two sleekly groomed elderly women.

He looked at Rebecca and followed her glance back at the two couples. The woman was still staring, but now she was drumming her fingers on the table. The bill had been paid, the tip had been left, and finally, the other three rose to go. Immediately, with the signal that it was time to leave, the woman came alive. Jumping up from the table, her face alight with relief and joy, she left her companions behind and marched out of the restaurant. Rebecca sank her elbow into his arm. "That takes care of that. Back to the suburbs."

He laughed softly. As he listened to her words and looked at her beautiful profile, he felt a sudden closeness to her, as if he had known her for a long, long time, or as if they were old friends who had been separated by a lifetime and were coming together at last. He felt an overwhelming urge to put his arm around her and tell her. But something stopped him.

He wasn't sure if it was Ursula's warning earlier that day, or whether it might be something else.

She tapped him on the hand. "Hey."

"Hmm?"

"You look lost in thought."

He looked into her eyes. "I was thinking…" He paused but the words rushed out of him before he could stop himself. "I was thinking how beautiful you look tonight."

She blushed and looked away. "You're not supposed to say things like that."

He laughed. "I know. Sorry. I forgot the rules of engagement here."

She turned back and smiled. "You mean for the abnormal and the alienated?"

"Those are the ones. Actually, I wasn't thinking how beautiful you are at all. I was thinking how hungry I am."

"Now that's better. That I can deal with."

"But not with compliments, I see. You're as pink as your drink."

"I am not."

Will came over with a basket of Iggy's Francese bread and a dish of olive oil, and they dipped the bread in the oil and sunk their teeth into the soft warm crust and sipped their martinis. She breathed deeply and looked at him. "My God, this is good. What's in the olive oil besides herbs and spices?"

He drained his Cosmopolitan. "I think there's a little chili pepper going on there too. You want to do some apps or a meal?"

"Let's start with the appetizers." He handed her a menu but she shook her head. "You pick them."

He nodded to Will. "Will, we're going with the pasta of the day with the garlic and Asiago cheese, the tuna sashimi, and the sautéed scallops in the ginger and soy sauce."

Will grinned. "Pretty eclectic, Robert."

"Well, I'm in a pretty eclectic mood."

When he turned back she was finishing her drink. He watched her profile again, trying not to stare at her. The Cosmopolitan had gone to his head. He knew if he had another one, he'd put his hands on her. That he wouldn't be able to help it. He wanted to grab the bar chair and just pull her into him. He wanted to slip his left hand behind her lovely neck and put his right hand on her hip or her waist or her thigh and kiss her as long as he could. He managed to glance away just as she put her empty glass on the bar and turned to him. "Hey, Robert."

He looked into her eyes. "Hey, Rebecca."

"You're getting kind of pink yourself."

He smiled. "It's these damn Cosmos. They surge right through your bloodstream."

"Shall we have another?"

He laughed. "If I do, you'll have to carry me out of here."

"You're no fun." She waved at Will. "Will, can I have another Cosmo? That was fabulous."

"Coming right up. Rob?"

"I'll have a glass of the Sauvignon Blanc."

Will grinned and looked back at Rebecca. "Real men don't drink Cosmos and order glasses of Sauvignon Blanc. What are you doing with this wimp, anyway?"

She laughed. "You got me."

"What were you thinking?"

"God only knows."

JOE KELLEY

Will laughed out loud. "I knew this guy when he drank nothing but beer and didn't even know what the hell Sauvignon Blanc was."

Still looking at the bartender, Rebecca leaned toward Rosario and put her hand on his left shoulder. It was a simple gesture, almost comradely in nature, but it pulsed right through him. "I think I like this version better," she said to Will. "I think maybe he's improved with age."

Will sidled over to the other side of the bar to mix her drink. "Nah. He's just a shadow of his former self."

A young waitress appeared behind them. "Tuna sashimi and scallops with ginger and soy sauce." He felt Rebecca's hand slip off his shoulder as he took the plates from the waitress and put them on the bar. Will returned with her second Cosmopolitan and poured him a glass of the cold white wine and they dug in.

She cut a slice of the tuna and put it in her mouth. "Mmm... am I supposed to dip it in that green paste?"

"Yeah, but just a little. That's Wasabi. It's hotter than hell."

"Whoa, that *is* hot."

Rosario inhaled the aroma of the ginger and soy as he chewed the soft, meaty scallop and sipped the cold, tangy wine. Then the waitress came back with the pasta and placed it between them. They twirled it around their forks and devoured it, the garlic and the Asiago hot and sweet together. She waved her hand in front of her mouth and took a drink of water. "Whew."

He laughed. "You'll knock your kids over tonight with that. But at least it will keep the werewolves away."

She placed her water glass down on the bar and took a sip of the Cosmo. Then she looked at him. "They won't be home tonight. They're in Newton with their father."

He looked into her eyes and they stared at each other for a moment. Then she shook her head and plunged back into the meal. When they were done, she sat back and sighed. "That was some of the best food I've ever had. They should call this The Fat Room instead of The Blue Room."

"Nothing very fattening in what you ate. It's all good for you. Want to split an entree?"

She put her hand on her stomach. "No, are you kidding? I'll explode."

Will was busy at the other side of the bar as they finished their drinks and paid the bill. They left him a big tip and waved goodbye as they went out the door. Then they walked up the stairs and out into the cool October night, and as they strolled along silently, passing other couples and groups of young people out for Saturday night, he took her hand for the first time. She glanced at him and smiled but neither one of them could think of anything to say. They crossed the street to the parking garage next to the Kendall Square Cinema, and he paid the woman behind the glass window. Rebecca stopped him at the stairwell to the second floor. "Let me split that with you."

"Don't worry about it. You can buy me a beer in the Square."

They walked up the flight of stairs to the second floor and headed toward his car. Rebecca stopped abruptly and glared at a brand new silver Porsche, parked at a forty-five degree angle and taking up two spaces. "I hate it when these bastards do this. You and I had to drive around this place for five minutes to get a space, and this jerk just takes two so his precious toy doesn't get scratched. What should we do about it?"

He looked at her incredulously. "I have a howitzer in the trunk. We could blow it to smithereens."

"No, look. I'm really serious."

"I can see that you are. But it's probably a good idea to avoid arrest, especially on a Saturday night."

"They can't arrest us if they can't see us, now can they? Do you have a tire gauge?"

"Sure. But you're not really going to…"

"Yeah, I am."

He walked over to his car and unlocked it and removed the gauge from his glove compartment. When he turned, she was leaning against the hood of the Porsche with her arms crossed as if she owned the thing. She smiled at him and waved. He shook his head and came over and handed her the gauge. "Good evening, ma'am. Having car trouble?"

"Oh, how kind of you to ask. Actually, there *will* be some trouble in just a few minutes. Would you mind standing guard for me?"

"Not at all."

She bent down in front of the Porsche, and he watched the perimeter of the parking garage. Suddenly, a blast of air escaped from the right front tire. Thirty seconds later, a flash of headlights bounced off the walls and a jeep careened around the corner of their lane. He reached down and grabbed her arm. "Come on!"

She jumped up and put her arm through his and they started to walk away toward the exit. The jeep circled around, unable to find a space, and then rumbled up the ramp to the third floor. She pulled away and returned to work, this time rocking back on her high heels, her skirt sliding up high along her beautiful legs. She glanced up at him, a feline, almost savage look of delight in her silver eyes. The air shot out again, this time even louder than before and getting louder every second. Finally, it stopped, leaving a dead silence. She stood up and backed away to admire her work. "Flat as a pancake, Mr. Rosario. What do you think?"

"I think we better get the hell out of here."

They jumped into his car and as he took off, she laughed with exhilaration. "You know, sometimes you just have to let off a little steam."

He smiled. "Sometimes? You're at it constantly."

"That was fun. What other damage can we do? I know. Let's pay a little visit to Jackson Foster."

He stepped on the brakes, stopping the car a few feet from the ramp leading down to the first floor. "Jackson Foster?"

"You know. The kid."

"I know, but you must be joking."

"Of course, I'm joking. I would never involve you in anything crazy like that."

"Look, Rebecca..."

"What?"

A horn sounded behind them and the driver flashed his high beams through their rear window. She turned and looked back. "I guess I'll have to let the air out of their tires too."

"No, you don't."

She laughed. "Can I just give them the finger?"

"No. Let's go get that beer instead."

He drove out of the garage and took a right past the cinema and then a left on Cardinal Medeiros and stopped at the red light near Tommy Doyle's Pub. She looked over at him. "Is Donnelly Field around here?"

"Donnelly Field? Why?"

"Mr. Foster seems to spend a lot of his free time over there."

"Yeah. It's around here." The light turned green and he took a right on Cambridge Street. "Look, Rebecca. I don't know what you have in mind for this kid, but..."

"Don't worry. It won't be tonight."

"Or any other night, I hope. The Donnelly Field area, even though it's pretty safe during the daytime, is still not a place a woman should be going to at night."

"All right."

"All right, what? That didn't sound very convincing."

"All right, I won't go there at night. How's that?"

"That's good—if you mean it. But I'm serious. Cambridge Street is fine. There are bars and restaurants and people milling around, but all you have to do is go in two or three blocks, and you can hit some places where there's trouble. Coming down here after dark looking for where Jackson Foster lives is a bad idea."

"Oh, you misunderstood me. He doesn't live in this area. He just hangs out here. I pumped one of Lizzie's girlfriends for some information on this guy. He comes down here to pretend he's a street kid. He lives over on Irving Street in the same neighborhood as Julia Child and John Kenneth Galbraith. The old man's a psychologist and the mother's an architect. Just think. All those genes and they get a kid like that."

They stopped at the red light at Willow Street. All they had to do was take a left and Donnelly Field was right down the end of the road. But he was damned if he was going to say anything about it. She glanced over at him again. "It's funny how so many suburban women fear the city, isn't it? They fear for their children. None of the tough working-class kids from these streets bothered my girls. It was this spoiled bastard. You don't mind if I walk around Julia Child's neighborhood at night, do you?"

He laughed. "It all depends what you're going to do there. If you're going to whip up some chocolate soufflés with Julia, that's fine. But I get the feeling that's not quite your thing, is it?"

"No, I'm afraid not."

"Well, unless you're going to discuss economics with Mr. Galbraith or take up residence at the Harvard Divinity School, I'd recommend that you stay out of there too."

"You certainly are limiting my access to the city, Mr. Rosario."

"It's not the city I'm worried about."

They drove through Inman Square and crossed Hampshire Street. From here, it was a straight shot into the heart of Harvard Square, and he stepped on the gas. As they approached Irving Street, she stared out her window intently and then looked back at him. "Wrong end."

"Hmm?"

"Wrong end of Irving Street. He lives down the other end."

"Well, sure. That's the section beyond Kirkland Street near Francis Avenue. What your realtor pal from Wellesley would refer to as a *high-end* area." They were coming up to the light at Quincy Street. "But what do you say we forget about Irving Street for a while and concentrate on that beer."

"There you go again trying to defuse me, Robert." The light turned red and he came to a stop. They looked at each other and she reached over and touched his right wrist. Then she slid her hand up his forearm and grasped his bicep. He felt her grip around the muscle like a talon. "OK. You win. A beer it is."

CHAPTER 22

Mark Stevenson leaned back from his writing and looked at his wife. "And just what do you plan to do when you track him down? Descend upon him like a banshee and defrock him?"

"As a matter of fact, I've decided to give the guy a chance to explain himself."

"Explain himself! He doesn't owe you any explanations. If Rebecca Scott had hired you as counsel, then this line of attack just might be plausible but..." He stared at her suspiciously. "Hold on a second. You're not going to represent yourself as her lawyer, are you?"

"Not exactly."

He groaned. "You've never met the woman. What's the purpose of this exercise, anyway?"

"The purpose is to prevent him from confronting his ex-wife. If he does that, something terrible might happen, and that something might draw Rob into a situation which I will ultimately be responsible for."

He stood up, pushed his chair into his desk, and walked over to the doorway, almost as if he were blocking her path. "Look, Ursula. I understand what you're trying to do. I know you feel guilty about involving Rob with this woman. But between your rabid anti-Catholicism and your Irish temper, you'll completely undermine any rational dialogue between you and this man. You said yourself that he seems to have changed. Let him keep changing on his own. Stay out of it."

She folded her arms. "He *appears* to have changed. But I'll soon find out what the man's game is one way or the other."

"Nonsense. You'll take one look at his priestly collar and flip out. Everything you've got against your religion will erupt into a pointless tirade. You carry with you an insatiable thirst for vengeance against the Church. Even Rob has managed to put his aside. The things you've said over the years about Catholicism and the clergy form an insurmountable indictment. You're incapable of dealing rationally with this man."

She put her hands on her hips. "You're incapable of understanding the damage the Church has done, because you haven't lived through it."

"Maybe so. But I've known enough Catholic priests and brothers who are decent men. The Xaverian Brothers at St. John's, for example, who turned my brother around when no prep school or public school could do the job. That sure put an end to my father's anti-Catholic prejudice."

"OK, fine. But you've heard Rob's tales of the Irish Christian Brothers."

"Yes, I have. But I'm sure they can't all be like that, and that was thirty years ago! What about Father Moynihan in the philosophy department here at Harvard? A true scholar and a fine human being."

"That well-fed, bouncy cleric? That paragon of ecumenical idealism? He's an academic Catholic. Not a real Catholic."

"What do you mean, not a *real* Catholic?"

"I'm talking about down-to-earth, guilt-ridden, woman-hating, sexually repressed Irish Catholic men who bought the whole package. The whole false bill of goods. They bought it hook, line, and sinker. And that's what this guy is. He's the real thing. He's a real piece of work."

"You should hear yourself. You should taste the venom in your mouth. And this is precisely why you're the wrong woman for this job. Give it up."

———

U sing the time and the day of Rosario's last East Cambridge walk, Ursula drove down Thorndike Street toward Sixth. But she stopped for a moment and pulled over in front of her grandparents' house. Selling the place had torn her heart out, but that was what her parents and her uncle had wanted. She could still see her grandfather, Eamon McGuire, sitting in his chair in the living room reading the paper and sipping his stout from his old pewter mug, and her grandmother Nora correcting papers at the dining room table. Eamon took her to Fenway for her first Red Sox game in 1950 when she was five years old and taught her how to do the scorecard. Williams, Pesky, Doerr, Dropo, Stephens, Dom DiMaggio. She remembered them all, and every game after that he trusted her to do the scoring right. Nora, the only one in the family to go to college before Ursula, showed her there was a world beyond East Cambridge. The Museum of Fine Arts. The Gardner. The Public Garden and the Boston Common. The long beautiful stretch of architecture down Commonwealth Avenue in the

Back Bay. Other than her great-grandfather, they were the only people in her family who paid any attention to her. The only people to take her anywhere and show her anything. The only people who really loved her. She felt a terrible sadness rise up in her heart, and gripping the steering wheel, she drove slowly away, turning right on Sixth Street and parking in front of the library.

Ten minutes later, a priest with a white crew cut marched out of St. Joseph's Church and headed toward Cambridge Street. *Church Militant*, she thought, eyeing his stride with a grim smile. She started the car and pulled up alongside him. "Can I give you a lift, Father?"

He gazed down at her, a startled look in his blue eyes. "No thank you, madam."

"I insist."

"And I insist not."

"I know why you're here."

He stared at her. "What are you talking about?"

"I know why you're here—Rebecca Scott."

He came to a halt. "I don't have to talk to you."

She took a gamble. "Actually, eventually you will."

"I assume you are my wife's attorney."

"Assume what you will. But let's forget the drive. Let's walk. It's a beautiful evening."

She parked across from the church and got out of the car and joined him on the sidewalk. She extended her hand and he took it reluctantly. She expected an iron grip, but he held her hand softly and looked guardedly into her eyes. "Who are you, exactly?"

"My name is Ursula McGuire and yes, I am an attorney. Like you."

"May I ask where your training was?"

"Sure. Undergraduate degree at Simmons College. Law School at BU."

"Really? I would have thought a good Irish girl like you would have attended Emmanuel and BC."

"Well, I wanted to get away from good Catholic boys like you."

"Well done, Ms. McGuire. But I am no longer an attorney, as you can see. Am I being served with anything?"

She shook her head. "Not exactly. At least not yet. I think if we can clear matters up between us, it might not come to that." She nodded toward Thorndike Street and they walked past the library. She pointed at the small brick building. "The William Cardinal O'Connell Branch Library. Spellman was your cardinal in New York, wasn't he?"

"That's right. Down into the sixties."

"A big advocate of the Vietnam War, as I recall. Urging Catholic boys to go off and fight the communist enemy while he hid in his cathedral at home. I've always wondered at the Church's hostility to communism when it operates in exactly the same manner. A tight hierarchical organization, a dictator at the top, mind control for the masses, and purges for the dissidents. Men in skirts, Father. Never trust them."

She had pushed him too far already and waited for the response. But he wasn't biting. "Well, I'm glad I didn't wear my cassock."

She smiled. "Somehow I hadn't expected a sense of humor."

"Because of what my wife has said?" Ursula remained silent. "Well, everything she has told you about me is true. I have no excuse for my behavior. It's not necessary, however, for you to attack the Church to get at me. Just go straight for the jugular. I can take it."

"But I think the Church explains you."

"Is that so?"

They stopped in front of Nora and Eamon's old home. There was a red car in the driveway now and two children— two little strangers—played and shouted with glee in the yard to the side of the house. "New life."

"Pardon?"

"New life. Those kids. I spent many happy hours in that house with my grandparents when I was their age and many happy hours later. Houses like these were known as workers' cottages, most of them built in the 1830's and 1840's. My great-great-grandfather, Delano McGuire, escaped the famine in County Louth in 1846 and worked as a glassblower at The New England Glass factory near where the Lechmere station is today. He saved every cent he made and bought this place in 1860. His son, Christopher, inherited it from him and his son, Eamon, my grandfather, from him. After my grandparents died, my parents and the rest of the family decided to sell it. You know, you can see the side of the house from the steps of St. Joseph's Church, which was always a great comfort to me. I found that mass of gray stone frightening, both inside and out, and I was always afraid of the priests. I thought they were going to grab me and drag me into the confessionals and hurt me. The fact that I could always see a part of this house from those steps meant that my grandfather was in there to come and save me, and my great-grandfather too when he was still alive back in the fifties, a fierce old man who had little use for the clergy." She nodded toward the gamboling children. "So new life, Father. New life in the old homestead."

She led him down Thorndike toward the courthouses. He raked his hand through his coarse white hair. "Was your whole family like you? Filled with this kind of bitterness?"

"God, no. My mother's side of the family was as devout and submissive as sheep. True believers. Rattling their rosary beads and genuflecting their lives away. A good part of my father's side too. But my father's parents, my grandparents, while Catholics, were a very independent sort. They went to church every Sunday, but they weren't slaves to the faith."

"And your parents?"

"My father went through the motions. My mother remains, I'm sorry to say, a religious fanatic."

"So if the Church explains me, then it explains you too, doesn't it?"

"In some ways...yes, it does. Let me tell you a story, and perhaps the bitterness you've observed will become more understandable. My father was a lineman for Boston Edison. When he came home at night, he drank beer and watched sports on television with his two older sons. He wasn't a bad guy. He didn't desert his wife or spend all night in the bars on Cambridge Street or gamble away his salary. But all he cared about were his two boys and sports. That was it. His daughter and his youngest son didn't count. Me because I was a girl and Denny because he wasn't like the others. Denny was quiet, thoughtful, artistic. He liked to read. He wasn't a jock, so he didn't rate.

"There was a priest who would come to visit. He wasn't a local priest from St. Joseph's or St. Francis of Assisi. He was a friend of my mother's family from some parish in Dorchester, and he always managed to show up when my father and my two older brothers were at a Celtics game or out shooting hoops somewhere. It would be the four of us at dinner. My mother and me and Denny and this priest, Father Gerald. He was a small man, a comfortable, plump little prelate full of stories and jokes. A real charmer. When it was time for us to go to bed, he would tell my mother that before he left he would be sure to go upstairs and give little Denny his blessing, and my mother would nod and smile like a fool. But instead of blessing my little brother, Father Gerald would touch him. Father Gerald sensed, before anyone else, that Denny was gay, even at such an early age, and took quick advantage of his discovery. He was a predator, Father Gerald, a pervert who insinuated himself into our house because of my mother's naiveté and colossal ignorance. Denny never told anyone because he knew no one would have believed him. After all, this was the fifties. Things like that didn't happen back then. Priests were apostles of Christ, not criminals. Denny kept it to himself—at God knows what emotional cost—until he told me one night when the two of us were in college. Despite growing doubts about my faith, I was still attending Mass at that time. But the molestation of my brother was the beginning of the end for the Church and me. You people are the messengers of Christ. With messengers like that, the message gets lost. In short, Father O'Connor, the Church has lost its moral authority."

Ryan O'Connor's eyes burned with shame, and his skin flared as if she had struck him a blow across the face. "I am as disgusted and as angry as any Catholic at such unmitigated cruelty to innocent children, and I am truly sorry that such horrors deprived you of your faith. But Ms. McGuire, I cannot answer for the sins of the Church. I can only answer for my own."

Halfway between Fifth Street and Sciarappa, as they emerged from the shade of the trees that lined the sidewalk, the ugly concrete pile of the Middlesex County Courthouse loomed above them. Ursula pointed at it. "Hideous enough for you?"

"Hideous indeed. Is this why we're walking here? To assault me with such a brutish image of justice? I suppose you'd like me up there on one of the top floors."

"In the jail?" She smiled sardonically. "It's a thought, I suppose. But I'm afraid the statute of limitations on your offenses has passed long ago." They turned left on Third Street in front of The Registry of Deeds and walked down one block to Otis Street and then into the shade of the little courtyard near Bulfinch Square. She nodded toward the second bench on the left and they sat down together. In front of them stood the brick wall of the original courthouse and then higher up the cupola with its gilded scales of justice.

"You have a flair for setting, Ms. McGuire. Perhaps you should have gone into the theater instead of the law."

"Well, there's a lot of interaction between those two fields, isn't there? And now here you are a priest. Yet another field. I remember a comment P.D. James made in one of her novels. Something like how theology isn't so different from criminal law. Both rest on a complicated system of philosophical thought which hasn't much to do with reality."

He glanced down and away from the scales of justice and stared at her. "Very good, Ms. McGuire. But I'm no theologian, and I'm through with complicated systems. Believe me."

"But you're part of a complicated system, one of the most authoritative, dictatorial, totalitarian systems the world has ever seen."

"The Church has a lot to answer for. Just as I and those who believed in its doctrines have a lot to answer for. Systems are the problem. Doctrines are the problem. Jesus Christ, in his message of love and forgiveness, had nothing to do with systems and doctrines—something it took me many years to learn."

She thought for a moment of his comment about the theater and wondered if this was all some penitent pose, some kind of perverse act he had worked out for himself. Rebecca

Scott, according to Rosario, didn't believe a thing he had said to her in his phone calls. So why should she?

An evening breeze started to blow in from the harbor and across the river and brought the smell of the sea into the court-yard. It tossed the leaves back and forth high up in the trees and softened everything around them. Several young women in suits and brightly colored dresses strode out of Bulfinch Square, their hair flying behind them, their voices filling the air. Life was stirring all around them, everything in motion. Only this solitary man, dressed in black, his head bowed, re-mained still, his only movement a clenched, tightly-gripped rubbing of his hands like a prisoner in the dock.

"You've told me a story to help explain your bitterness. Now allow me to tell you one that may help you know what I am."

He touched the side of his head near the temple as if to ward off some sudden pain. "Because of my work in our lo-cal parish, because of my profession and the fact that I taught a course at Fordham Law School, I would be asked for legal advice by certain influential officials of the Church in my area of New York. About ten years ago a case arose in a neighboring town involving allegations of child abuse at a parish elemen-tary school. The case, as it was presented to me by the school principal, was a matter of slander. A false accusation had been made against a revered member of the faculty, and would I be interested in joining a committee of community members which had risen to his defense? After contacting some people I knew in that town, I was assured that the man in question was undoubtedly innocent and the victim of a vendetta by a small group of disgruntled parents who objected to the strict manner in which he ran his classroom.

"I agreed. But after several meetings, it became clear to me that these so-called disgruntled parents had a very convincing case, and that my role was to join with the clerics and the other Catholic lawyers on the committee to discredit the parents and to set in motion a cover-up. These lawyers, I realized, were front men for a Church bureaucracy that was more interested in circling the wagons around one of their own rather than getting at the truth. But the parents wouldn't give up, and one of them threatened to go to the local paper with their accusations. The pressure worked and the committee decided the only way out was to settle the case with the parents. I was chosen to negotiate.

"When I met with the parents the first time, I had already decided that the committee was morally bankrupt and that instead of being a negotiator, I would be a listener, and what I heard shook me to the core. I remember to this day the simplicity of their language, the honesty of their sorrow, and especially their anger and their cries for justice—and these were deeply religious people, none of whom wanted to be at war with their Church. As they spoke, I kept remembering, in committee meeting after committee meeting, the unconvincing propaganda of both the priests and the laymen as they defended what was clearly a predator. Face after face appeared before me. Hard-eyed Pharisees out to protect one of their own. The cynical refusal to act on behalf of innocent children. The deliberate choice made between victimizer and victim. The way they mixed pompous moralizing and absolute certitude with self-serving rhetoric was appalling, but even more appalling was that the more they spoke, the more I began to see myself in their eyes, in their expressions, and in their very words. Not that I would have ever condoned such a crime or made it easy for such a criminal to prey again, but they made me see the kind of man I had become. I was one of those Catholic purists who haunt Church affairs. Straight-laced puritans who want to aid the clergy in laying down the law. A man mired so deeply in religious ideology that he would drive away the woman he loved and never attempt to see his own child. The crimes weren't the same, of course, but the mindset was. It was profoundly inhumane. And I was profoundly inhumane. A man unable to be a loving husband or a caring father. Unable, above all, to be a Christian.

"When the parents were through, when they had described each and every crime perpetrated on each and every child, children who would have been my own daughter's age at the time—a child I had abandoned in a fit of pique and anger and resentment at my wife—the road ahead was clear. I offered my services as their legal representative and together we drove that man out of town and out of New York…"

Ursula sighed. "Where the Church transferred him far away and unsupervised."

"No doubt, Ms. McGuire. No doubt. When it was over, I felt as if I had let these people down. That he should have been arrested and tried and punished. Not transferred. But the parents were unwilling to put their children through the trauma of testifying in court, and there was nothing else I could do. When it was over, I felt this great need to go to Confession. To cleanse my soul. To beg God for forgiveness for what I had done years ago to Rebecca."

"You never had that urge before?"

"No, I hadn't. In my mind, it was all her fault. All her doing. I was right. I was the righteous one. I went to Church on Sundays. I prayed. I donated time to the parish. I was in the right."

"All those years."

"All those years. Until I was called to that committee." He straightened up and looked into her eyes. "So one Saturday afternoon I drove into the Bronx to Fordham, hoping to confess to some stern, intellectually superior Jesuit who would bring hell and damnation down upon my soul. Who would preach to me, excoriate me, punish me, make me suffer for my sins before there was any hope of absolution."

"Did you find him?"

For the first time, Ryan O'Connor laughed. He raised his hands and shook his head in frustration. "No. Instead I found a priest sitting outside his confessional in a pew, reading the sports section of the *New York Times.*"

Ursula laughed too. "Hey. My kind of priest."

"Not entirely, Ms. McGuire. He was a rabid Yankees fan, I'm afraid. He tucked the paper under his arm and waved me into the confessional in the most cavalier fashion possible. Once inside, I knelt down and began, 'Bless me, Father, for I have sinned. Forgive me, Father.' I kept repeating the phrase like some guilt-wracked automaton. 'Forgive me, Father. Forgive me, Father.' The incantation kept rushing out of my soul, escaping from my lips. And that, Ms. McGuire, was as far as I got. Suddenly, amazingly, I began to cry, something I had not done since childhood. I was overwhelmed with grief, with loss, with desperation. I couldn't stop. I sobbed and sobbed until finally the poor man had to come out of his confessional box and help me stand up and walk me out of the chapel. It was all a bit much for him, I'm afraid. He was winding up his Saturday afternoon confessional duties, looking forward, I imagine, to a snack and a cup of tea and the tail end of the Yankees game, when suddenly this creature from a Dostoevskian nightmare stumbled into his chapel to torment him with a litany of sins he was not quite prepared to listen to. So he patted me on the back and told me to return when I could articulate more clearly what it was that was troubling me."

Ursula sat back and looked at him. "So no help from the Jesuits."

He laughed ruefully. "Well, not that night I'm afraid."

"That must have been a very bad night for you."

"It was. It caused me, for the first time in my life, to doubt my faith. Not my faith in Jesus Christ. Not my faith in His message, as you called it. But my faith in the organization that had sprung up in the name of His message. And as far as bad nights go, no night could compare to the nights I put my wife through." He stopped for a moment and stared at her, his cold hard blue eyes glowing like sapphires in the waning sunlight. Two deep creases, running from his cheekbones to his chin, looked almost like scars. She knew, from Rosario's account, that he was eight years older than Rebecca Scott. So that made him fifty-four. Yet his stiff white hair, brushed back almost violently, and his timeworn face, ravaged by years of shame and regret, made him look a great deal older. He glanced away and bowed his head again. "For it was that night, denied the comfort of the sacrament of Confession, that I was forced to face the incontrovertible truth that I had turned a woman's heart into an instrument of hate. And having done that, having committed such an unpardonable sin, I have paid and I am paying with a degree of guilt and self-loathing the magnitude of which you cannot comprehend."

CHAPTER 23

Together, they drifted along Brattle Street through the Saturday night crowds. On their left, a group of middle-aged couples stood in a semi-circle on the sidewalk listening dreamily to a street singer whispering Edith Piaf songs into a microphone. He sang slowly in a kind of mellow hush, his melancholy voice echoing all around them. She smiled and shook her head and Rosario laughed. "What?"

"I see that guy here every weekend. I always wonder if that's a real French accent or if he's just faking it."

"He's been around for years, but if we find out he's from France, well, we'll just have to deport him, won't we?" His arm was around her waist, his hand on her hip. The wall of resistance he had built up against her was beginning to crumble. They had looked at each other too many times tonight. Touched too often. They passed Crate and Barrel and then stopped at the corner of Story Street to let a young couple get by. The husband, looking strained and debilitated, pushed a double stroller with two whining children strapped in like inmates from an insane asylum. Rebecca looked at her watch. "10:30. A little late for toddlers, isn't it?"

The young man nodded toward his wife. "It's her idea. We have to do everything together. The whole family. *All* the time."

His wife glared at Rebecca. "I don't see how it's any of *your* business!" Then she turned on her husband. "You don't owe her or anyone else an explanation about anything!"

The couple pushed by them with the husband in full rejoinder. "Maybe you owe *me* an explanation. Why do we never get a baby sitter? Why is it…"

His voice trailed away behind them and Rosario pulled her closer. "Nice one, Ms. Scott. Sowing a little marital discord on Saturday night."

"Oh, I'm sure that wife was capable of creating plenty of marital discord all on her own. Imagine having little kids out this late. Come on. What's the matter with these young couples today, anyway?"

They passed Café of India and stepped around a mob of chocoholics lined up outside Burdick's. She stopped for a moment and peered inside. "Lizzie absolutely loves this place. She says it's like Candyland for adults." He looked over her shoulder. All the tables were full, the waitresses dashing back and forth serving brownies and cake and huge steaming cups of hot chocolate. Then she turned and glanced back at the corner of Story Street. "That's where we met."

"Where you accosted another couple, as I recall."

"As I recall, that couple accosted me. Actually, they crashed into me."

"Crashed? Didn't they just bump into you?"

She turned back and came closer to him and looked up into his eyes. "Oh, that's right. You were the one who crashed into me."

"Hardly."

She paused for a moment. "You're right. You were very nice and I was cold and distant, wasn't I"

"Just a tad."

"Well, I've warmed up a little, haven't I?"

He smiled. "A little." He looked into the courtyard by the Blacksmith House. "Come here for a second."

"Where?"

"Right here."

He took her by the hand and walked her into the courtyard away from the street and the sounds of the city. There were vines growing up the brick wall and yellow leaves along the vines and other leaves falling slowly all around them. He pushed her gently against the brick wall and encircled her waist with his right arm and placed his hand on the small of her back underneath her black top. Her skin was warm to the touch. He pulled her close and kissed her. She pressed against him and wound her arms around his neck and kissed him back. Then they broke apart and stared at each other, and in another moment she smiled. "So, you finally made your move. What was it?"

He took her by the shoulders. "I think it was the sight of all that chocolate."

She laughed. "No, really."

"Really? Really...well, it was you. You wore me down. You broke my will to resist."

"I didn't do anything to wear you down."

"You didn't have to."

She looked away for a second and then glanced at him, almost shyly. "Thanks." She took his hand and led him away from the brick wall, and then she put her arm around his waist and they walked down Brattle Street past The Loeb. A party was in progress on the dark lawn of the Greenleaf mansion, and the sound of a band wafted through the air. As they got closer, he recognized the melody of a Doors song from the late sixties, one of the more spellbinding, romantic ones, but he couldn't place the title. Despite the youth of the musicians, they were doing a pretty decent job of it, and as he and Rebecca strolled away from the Square toward Ash Street Place and his home, the music faded into the softness of the autumn night.

Once inside, they attacked each other. She kissed him fiercely, wildly, wrapping herself around him. He was all over her, pressing her against one wall and then another until they stumbled into his study and fell on the couch, and in his frenzy to possess this woman, he abandoned every last vestige of restraint. He pulled her on top of him, and the scent of her perfume and the touch of her lips made him want to devour her. They broke apart and stood up and started tearing each other's clothes off until they were naked and gasping for air. He was surprised at the intensity of her passion, but forced himself not to push too quickly. He sat her down gently on the edge of the couch and then slipped behind her and held her breasts lightly in his hands and kissed her on the back of the neck until she began moaning softly. Then he turned her around and took her in his arms and kissed her on the lips and let her lie on her back. He knelt in front of her, moving her thighs apart and then bending down to kiss her throat and her breasts and her stomach and then moving back up to her ears and her neck. He paused a moment and looked into her silvery eyes and kissed her mouth for a long time.

Then he knelt back, and placing his hands under her hips, he drew her close and pushed gently but deeply inside her. She moaned again, louder this time, and he began to move back and forth slowly and then at a more measured pace, relying on the sounds she made to make sure he wasn't hurting her. They made love this way for several minutes until he began to realize that her response, which at the beginning seemed real enough, was beginning to fade. He stopped. "Are you all right?"

"Sure."

He smiled and touched her face. "That wasn't very convincing. Am I hurting you at all?"

"Not really. It's just...it's just that's it's been a long time."

"Me too."

"I'm sorry if I wasn't communicating with you. I never talk too much during sex."

"That's OK."

"I suppose you've had women who yell and scream."

He laughed. "Oh, all the time. Some of them in high-pitched Brazilian accents." She laughed and looked away and then held her forearm over her eyes. Her took her wrist and pulled her arm away. "Stop hiding from me."

"I'm not hiding."

"Sure you are." He swung their bodies around so she was on top of him, and she sat up and began to move her hips in a slow, circular motion, her breasts swaying and her hair falling over her eyes. He put his hands on her hips and rocked along with her until she began to respond once again. He thrust harder, deeper until he was on the verge of climax. "Stop for a second. I'm getting close."

"That's OK. I want you to come."

"No. You first."

She smiled down at him and then leaned forward and put her palms on his chest. "Well, that's a bit of a problem, I'm afraid. I don't come that often. It seems to take an awful lot of time and effort, and that's not something men like to do while they're having sex. Too much intimacy, I guess."

He placed his hands over hers. Then he smiled and shook his head. "God save us from intimacy."

She laughed softly. "That's right, Mr. Rosario. God save us from intimacy."

He looked into her eyes. "I want you to sit up again but turn around." She moved back and lifting up her left knee, she pivoted slowly on top of him so that he was still inside her. "Now lie back." As she came down on top of him, her back against his chest, her soft buttocks pressed against his groin, the back of her legs against the front of his, he took her breasts in his hands and pushed deep inside her again. He kissed the back of her neck and whispered into her ear. "Lie quietly for a while."

She turned and gazed into his eyes. "This is kind of a strange position, isn't it?"

"It's Brazilian."

She laughed out loud. "Brazilian! There you go again with that comic sensibility of yours."

"Hey, when you come up with a metaphor ya gotta run with it."

He reached down between her thighs and touched her, running his finger along the warm, wet ridge of flesh, but all the while staying hard and still and deep. She opened her thighs wider and raised her hips higher and her breathing grew faster and hotter against his neck. Then, very slowly and very gently, he moved back and forth inside her, pulling out as far as he could without pulling out of her and then pushing back in until he was up to the hilt, all the while running his finger up and down and then around in little circles until the flesh under his touch seemed to swell and tremble.

Suddenly, her hips leapt and she arched her back. "Oh, my God! Oh!" He took her left breast in his free hand and kissed her again and again behind her ear. She threw her head back and shut her eyes, and her bared teeth began to sink into her lower lip. Then she opened her mouth and cried out, and he prayed that he could hold off long enough. But her lurching, tossing body was unleashing his own climax and her cries in his ear were sending him over the edge. Her voice rose in pitch and her hips began to shake and she arched her back once again, her stomach muscles tightening above the grip of his hand, her whole body churning and vibrating beneath his touch. She opened her mouth wide as if she were going to scream. "Oh, my God! Oh, I'm coming! I'm coming!" Then her whole body plunged into a series of violent spasms, and the last one, a rocking tremor like an electric current, ignited his own orgasm until they were caught together in one final jolting convulsion.

He tried, with this beautiful woman lying on top of him, her breasts rising and falling and her lovely features flushed with color, to think if he had ever experienced anything better. But he couldn't.

After a few minutes, she turned around and lay her head on his chest. "Wow. Hope I didn't disturb your neighbors. I've never shouted out like that before."

"Are you sure you don't have any Brazilian relatives?"

She raised her head and looked into his eyes and smiled. "Not that I know of. So…what was that position, anyway?"

"Well, you've heard of 69…"

"You think I'm sexually repressed, don't you? Of course I've heard of 69!"

"Good. That was 66."

She burst into laughter and slapped him on the arm. "66! What are you talking about?"

"I met a girl in 1966 and she showed it to me."

She raised an eyebrow and pursed her lips. "Oh, really."

"Really." He smiled. "She informed me it was a real crowd pleaser."

She slapped him again and then nestled into his arms. "Well, you sure pleased this crowd." Suddenly, she sat up. "Hey! I never bought you that beer."

"Thirsty?"

"After that? What do you think?"

"Back in a flash." He jumped off the couch and walked into the kitchen for two cold Stella Artois. When he returned, she was standing by his desk looking up at the photograph of Fort Sewall. He stared at her. "Wow."

She turned, her blonde hair grazing her shoulder. "What?"

"You. I didn't get the full view from the back before. You're gorgeous."

"No, I'm not. I'm forty-six years old."

"So. I'm forty-nine. That makes you a younger woman."

"Relatively speaking. This photograph is beautiful. Where is it?"

"Marblehead. I'll take you there sometime."

"Is that a promise?"

"That's a promise."

He handed her a beer and they both took a long drink. She ran her hand through her hair. "God, that's good." She walked around, examining the pictures on the wall of his family and his friends. He couldn't keep his eyes off her. She stopped in front of a photo taken in 1962. "Who on earth are these guys? Frankie Valli and The Four Seasons? Dion and the Belmonts? Wait...that's you with the combed-back hair. Hah! You look like a bunch of hoods."

"My best friends from high school."

"This one below it? Is that the PT boat in Vietnam?"

"Yup. That's the Mekong in the background. The guy with the walrus moustache is Captain Harry Shapiro. Lieutenant Commander, actually, but everyone called him Captain Harry."

She took another step. "This one is definitely late seventies, right? Check out your moustache and long hair." She turned and ran her finger along his upper lip and kissed him, her lips cold from the beer. "I like you better without the moustache." She turned again. "Now this one is more up to date. You and your kids from Liberty High. Is this your classroom?"

"Uh, huh. That's our end of the year party. The last day. Post-exams. Post-thesis papers. They deserve it."

She wandered back to his desk and lay her hand on the stack of essays he was working on. "You're so dedicated. I wish my girls could have you as a teacher." She glanced to the left and inspected a smaller stack and picked up the top sheet. "Look at this. A history teacher who gives vocabulary tests. This guy got a 90% since he got one wrong out of ten, but then you took two points off for a misspelling. Isn't that 88%?"

"When they have no idea what the answer is, and they try to bullshit their way though it, if they make me laugh they get two bonus points. Read #6."

She took another drink of the beer and cleared her throat. "*Catalyst*—an analyst for cattle and other troubled livestock." She leaned back and laughed. "That's really clever."

"I have a file folder full of them. One of my favorites was for the word *caucus*. The kid wrote that it was the last name of a politician whose first two names are Michael Du."

She laughed again and then stopped abruptly before a photograph of him and Eve Taylor with Ursula and Mark on Singing Beach in Manchester-by-the-Sea. The girls were wearing bikinis, Ursula, a black one that matched her hair, and Eve, a sexy zebra pattern. It occurred to him that it might not be a good idea for Rebecca to know what Ursula looked like, but it was too late now. They were in their late twenties in the picture, and he tried to tell himself that the passage of time probably made any recognition unlikely. But since both women had aged so beautifully, he knew he was grasping at straws.

Rebecca pointed at Eve. "My God. She could be my sister."

"I told you."

"I know. And I thought it was just a pick-up line." She looked closer. "Amazing." She turned and put her free hand on his hip, and he felt himself begin to stir again. "Tell me how you met her."

"Ah, we're too old to discuss stuff like that, aren't we? Old girlfriends?"

"No, we're not. Fess up."

"I'm not sure you want to hear about this."

"Try me."

They left their beers on his desk and he took her hand and led her back to the couch, and they lay down together side by side. "Before they modernized the Harvard Square T station, there was an old, rickety, wooden escalator, that was so long and rose up at such a steep angle that when girls started wearing miniskirts, you could watch a parade of asses making their way above ground. Around this time, most young women had finally stopped wearing those old-fashioned white cotton underpants and replaced them with colorful bikini panties that clung to their buttocks—a major technological advance in the textile industry, by the way."

"Is that why you have your hand on my buttocks? Because you're telling me a story about a parade of asses?"

"You mean outside of their perfect shape and sculpted circumference?"

She laughed. "Yes, outside of that."

He smiled and kissed her and leaned up on his elbow. "So anyway, I've got my eyes on this incredible blonde about twenty steps ahead of me, and as the escalator rises I see she's wearing navy blue polka-dot bikini underpants and filling them quite nicely. Suddenly, some moron in a big rush plows past me and a bunch of other people and flies up the clacking wooden steps toward the exit. As he muscles his way past the blonde, she loses her balance and comes tripping back through the passengers in front of me. She was all legs and blonde hair flying, and I caught her in my arms and held on to her and looked into her big blue eyes, and this great line just came to me out of nowhere."

"Just pure inspiration."

"Just pure inspiration. I loosened my grip a bit and said, 'I've heard of sexually aggressive women, but this is ridiculous.'"

"You're making this up."

"Nope. I never lie when I'm holding a woman's bottom. Especially one as nice as this."

"Did she laugh?"

"She did. We almost tripped over ourselves when the escalator spewed us into the Square. She insisted on buying me a beer for saving her and off we went to Grendel's Den. That's how it started."

"And unlike me, she actually bought you a beer."

"Well, you were going to buy me one tonight. Your intentions were good. We just got waylaid."

"I'll say. So it was a nice beginning, you and Eve. How did it end?"

"We got involved very quickly and within weeks we were living together. We found a great apartment up on Mason Terrace off Beacon Street in Brookline and stayed together for several years. It was my job that ruined everything. Young couples need time together, and I was too absorbed in my work."

"But certainly she understood the commitment that teaching involves."

"No, no, no. I was a reporter back then and I was gone day and night."

She put her hand on his shoulder. "Oh, that's right. You wrote for *Stars and Stripes* in Korea. You had that month in Vietnam. Of course, it makes sense you'd go into journalism."

"I landed a job with the *Globe* covering The Office of Public Service, which my boss thought was an insignificant enough story for a young reporter. No one else wanted it. But that office turned into Mayor White's Little City Hall program which did become a big story, and that led to covering some of White's political campaigns, such as his ill-fated run for governor against Sargent in 1970 and his successful re-election contest against Louise Day Hicks in '71. Covering that race was important for me, because I had missed their first battle in '67 when I was in the army, and those two campaigns were enough to give any reporter a firsthand education for the busing crisis that was to come in 1973 and 1974. I covered that catastrophe non-stop, and Eve just felt as if the job were more important than she was."

"Was it?"

"I don't like to think of it that way. We loved each other. But she wanted to get married and have a family and I just wasn't ready. I thought Vietnam was history. But this was history I participated in. Forced busing in the Boston Public Schools and the violence in Charlestown and Southie and the political ramifications on all levels of government was history on steroids. I was consumed with it. So we agreed to split up and I think it was for the best. She's married now with two kids and she's happy. It's what she always wanted."

"So Eve got married and you ended up in teaching. How did that happen?"

"Covering the busing fiasco and getting inside the schools and watching what a well-intentioned, supposedly progressive policy did to destroy the education of Boston's children—both black and white. That got me in. That got me in big time. A group of idealistic adults wreaked havoc on the lives of children. They forced children to take on the moral challenge that adults should have taken on themselves."

"Was Teddy a part of that?"

"Part of it? He didn't design the plan. The judge did that. But he supported it. I never held it against him. He acted out of principle unlike a lot of other pols. I just found myself disagreeing with his policy."

"You're voting for Romney, aren't you?"

"Yup."

She smiled. "How ironic, because I think I'm going to vote for the big guy."

"I thought you said he was too liberal?"

"Ah, you just caught me on a bad day. You know—the day we met?" She punched him lightly on the shoulder. "My whole career has involved health care, and on that score he's been a great senator." She pressed against him pushing him into the couch. "Maybe by applying a little pressure, I can influence your vote."

"I don't think so, Ms. Scott." He pressed back and without meaning to, pushed a little too hard, and she rolled off the couch onto the rug.

She lay there for a second leaning back on her elbows, her hair tossed to one side and her silver eyes smiling at him. Then up she sprang and pounced on him like a panther. "It sounds to me, Mr. Rosario, as if you were an investigative reporter."

"I was."

She grabbed both his shoulders and pinned him down and wrapped her legs around him. Then she leaned down and stared into his eyes. "Well, just don't go investigating me."

CHAPTER 24

T hey stood, the two of them, on the highest of the steep
stone steps of the courthouse. He had lowered his hand,
heavy as a bear's paw, and rested it lightly on her shoulder,
a hand she had seen wield hammers and awls and blocks of
firewood despite his age and his stoop and his legs laced with
arthritis. Her father and her grandfather had told him to stop
climbing those steps and try to confine his tours of the past to
level ground. But he never listened.

Ursula knew the old man had no use for his grandchildren
or his other great-grandchildren, for they never listened to him
when he tried to wake them up and shake them out of the present and take them back in time. "I know you're only nine years
old, Ursie. But you are my hope. You will carry with you our history, our struggle. It's only you, Ursie. You're the only one who
pays attention, and because you do pay attention and because
you question things, you will leave the rest of them in the dust."

He lifted his hand from her shoulder and pointed once
again over the streets of East Cambridge. "It was over there.

Across the O'Brien Highway where that long rectangular building is now. The smokestack rose over two hundred and thirty
feet into the sky, higher than anything around, higher Ursie,
than even the Bunker Hill Monument, and when they blew the
pipes at the end of the day, a cloud of dark foul fumes would
blanket the town and settle over us like a shroud. Sometimes,
if we were lucky, the wind would blow it across the river to
Boston and then out to sea. Other times, we weren't so lucky,
and it came after us like the plague and stuck in our lungs so
we had to breathe the filthy stuff. Inside the factory, it was all
burning heat and glowing metal, the molten glass pouring into
the molds and the furnaces roaring like hellfire. I started at fifteen in 1880. Ah God, Ursie! Think of that. Fifteen and there
I was on a factory floor, dashing through the smoke and the
lead dust like a little devil, fetching and carrying for the glass
blowers and cursed at by the gaffers if I wasn't fast enough."

Often, as her great-grandfather took her with him through
the town, he would talk of the Irish—their *race*, as he called
them—a word not used by her grandfather or father. Their
race. Their people. The need for Ursula to carry with her their
story. But when he spoke of his work, both at New England Glass
and then later as a carpenter at A.H. Davenport, he spoke for
all the immigrants he labored with. The Italians, the Poles, the
Portuguese and all the others. The brutal working conditions
they faced. The low wages that barely kept a family alive. The
deaths of their children and the short, hard lives of their parents.

His voice was raspy with age and his blue eyes would stare
into hers as he spoke. Eyes surrounded by great white bushy
brows and below them, on his face, the scars and the burn
marks from the blast of the furnaces—still with him after
all this time. After a fierce argument in her early teens, her
mother had turned on her with a look of penetrating hostility.

"You have his eyes," she had said, waving her long forefinger at her as if a genetic trait were a crime. "You have those deep blue eyes and all the stubbornness and questioning of things that go with them. Stop all the arguing, Ursula, and accept things for what they are. Stop questioning everything. And while we're at it, stop spending all your time with the men in the family. Your great-grandfather. Your grandfather and his politics. The only woman you listen to is Nora, and it's only because she has an education, isn't it now Ursula? You're a bit of a snob I think. Last Thanksgiving you spent the whole day in the living room listening to the men. Not a word for the other girls in the house or your cousins or your aunts. Try being a normal girl for a change. It might do you some good."

Christopher McGuire would stare at her and hold her by the shoulders and their deep blue eyes would interlock. "Carry it all with you, Ursula. Your grandfather Eamon and his good wife Nora carry it with them. But your father and mother never listened and your older brothers, those numskulls..." Here he rolled his eyes and shook his head. "They are, I'm sorry to say, next to useless. Idjits." Ursula had laughed, for her brothers, with their bored, inattentive looks, never had any use for her either. "It's the glance away I can't stand, Ursie. The shift of the eyes as they ignore both me and their own heritage. Your younger brother, well, from what I can see he lives in his own little world, and he's too young to know what I'm talking about. So it's up to you, Ursie. It's up to you."

Now, forty years later, she stood at the top of the same steep stone steps with this strange, guilt-wracked man, the two of them gazing over the roof of the brick firehouse. It had been a brilliant blue day with her great-grandfather, a Saturday, she remembered. A day of sunlight reflecting off glass and steel and brick. But now, here with this man, the light was dying all around them. Despite herself, she smiled. She could almost feel the weight of her great-grandfather's hand on her shoulder and hear his tender, ragged voice. "That was in 1954. I was nine and he was eighty-nine. No generation gap there despite that great span of time." She laughed. "You see the firehouse in front of us? The Sealtest factory used to be there. On Fridays, after school, we'd run down and watch the trucks unload, and every once in a while the driver or a warehouseman unloading the truck would toss us a pint of ice cream."

He pointed across the O'Brien Highway. "So the place where they all worked. New England Glass. There."

"That's right. You and I can only see it in our imagination. But to Delano and to Christopher McGuire it was right there in front of them every day. Delano started work at New England Glass at age twenty and labored there for his whole life. For Christopher, it was all over in 1888 when the plant closed and the business moved to Ohio. But in its heyday it dominated the landscape, squatting over the town like a behemoth. At one point, it was the biggest glass firm in the world."

"So this man Christopher. Your great-grandfather. He was, I assume, a Democrat, a union man."

"All the way. As I'm sure you would have been had you been in his position. American Federation of Labor. Delano had been with The American Flint Glass Workers Union. *The Flints*, they called them. There was a strike against New England Glass in the early 1880's and Christopher, even though he was only eighteen at the time, was elected a strike captain. But in 1888, at twenty-three, he tried to get the union to moderate their wage demands as a second strike loomed, and he tried to get management not to push too hard. He realized the owners were serious about moving to Ohio, which, unfortunately, was what they did."

"Well, perhaps the union pushed too hard. Yet Christopher seems to have been a reasonable young man for the time. He was a negotiator, in other words."

"You could say that."

"And having inherited his deep blue eyes, have you also inherited his propensity for negotiation?"

"Sometimes."

"I only ask because you seem to be pushing pretty hard today yourself."

"Not in the last hour or so. Seems to me I've been fairly benign since we left Bulfinch Square."

"So you have, Ms. McGuire. So you have. And I've enjoyed the history lesson. I've learned quite a bit about my new surroundings."

"Which brings me back to the original purpose of our meeting."

"You mean *your* original purpose."

"That's right. It was my original purpose, wasn't it?"

He began to descend the long stone stairway as if to avoid the topic. "Tell me something, Ms. McGuire. Do your parents and any of your family still live here?"

"Nope. My parents moved to Florida in the seventies. The numskulls live in New Hampshire and Pennsylvania, and Denny lives in California with his partner. Five generations of McGuires and there's no one left. History evaporates."

They stopped at the foot of the steps and he looked at her. "I take it you don't live here either."

"I live in Boston."

"Any children?"

"No. Why do you ask?"

"I just wondered if you had others to carry it on. But that's all right, for actually history doesn't evaporate now, does it?

We both know you don't really mean that. It leaves its tracks behind for us to follow, and here in Cambridge and Boston it leaves whole chunks of it. Thanks to your great-grandfather, you've carried it on, just as he asked you, and you've given it to me. I've learned more about my people and my heritage, and I've learned a little more about my country. Thank you."

"You're welcome. Needless to say, I've left a little bit of our history out—for your sake, of course."

"Let me guess—the role of the Church."

"That's right. How at every step of the way, they've kept us down. Kept us back."

They started to walk down Cambridge Street in the gathering dusk. "Was that what you were arguing with your mother about when she said you had your great-grandfather's eyes? The Church?"

"That's right. How perceptive of you."

He laughed. "In your case an easy perception. What was the issue, if I may ask?"

"Whether the Church would ever allow women to become priests. I was in ninth grade and a girl picked up some radical tract in Harvard Square on the subject and brought it to class and the nun went ballistic. Called the girl a heretic. A heretic! Can you imagine? That girl was something else. So I asked my mother why we couldn't become priests if we wanted, and she went as nuts as the nun."

"So it wasn't just the abuse of your brother that started to turn you away."

"No. The nuns did their part for sure. The way they participated in the male domination of women and the endless innuendoes about the dangers and the horrors of sexuality. That whole notion of the Immaculate Conception. Why not have Jesus born of man and woman? Nope! No deal. No can do. It has to be immaculate. Normal sexuality is not immaculate. So somehow, it's dirty. Get it?"

He sighed as they crossed the street. "Yes, Ms. McGuire. I get it. I get it more than you think. We were all, men and women, victims of that line of thought."

They stopped near the corner of Sciarappa Street in front of St. Francis of Assisi, and Ursula placed her hand on the door to the little chapel. "Locked. Too bad. I was going to show it to you. I used to pray in here as a child and even as a teenager when I was still holding on to my faith. It was very quiet and the Franciscans were kind men. When you went to confession here they forgave you unconditionally. No lectures and light on the penance. See? If I had been an Italian I might still be a Catholic."

"I've prayed in here. But my work is with the other church, the one you found so frightening when you were a little girl, and I think you'd find it a much different place now."

She stared at him. "So…what is your work?"

He looked at her for a second. "Come with me for a moment and I'll try to explain it to you." They walked up to Sixth and crossed Cambridge Street again. As they approached St. Joseph's, a young priest and a middle-aged couple stood by the steps to the church deep in conversation. The priest waved to Ryan O'Connor, and the man and woman glanced away as if they had been caught in an act of some shameful transgression. When the man turned back, Ursula recognized the watery eyes and the red face, stained with alcohol and suppressed rage, the hunted, haunted look she had seen in so many police stations and courtrooms. Ryan O'Connor took the man and the woman by the arm, and as he turned back toward Cambridge Street, he peered over his shoulder at her. "Perhaps, Ms. McGuire, we can finish our conversation at a later time."

She watched them go and turned to the young priest and introduced herself. He smiled. "So how do you know Father O'Connor?"

"We have a mutual friend. And you, Father?"

"He came here two months ago from a parish in New York City. He works primarily counseling families who have been the victims of abuse with one, I would say, rather unique qualification."

"And what is that?"

"He seems to have a very high success rate with the abusers themselves. Why, I don't know. I've never met anyone quite like him in that regard. But our church can only do so much to help his work financially. He operates out of a little storefront office on Cambridge Street with a social worker and a psychologist, but it's touch and go in terms of funding. There's been a state grant here and there, but you know how hard it is getting support for community programs like that."

She nodded and they shook hands, and she turned and walked down Otis Street until she reached the old Davenport furniture building. It was here where her great-grandfather had learned and practiced his trade as a carpenter after New England Glass left town, and she wandered into the courtyard and gazed up at the four stories of brick walls and the dark green window frames. It was being refurbished now, renovated and retooled for the new century. Six years away now. What struck her was the lack of sound. Forty years ago he had taken her to this very spot and pointed to the corner window of the second floor to show her where he had worked at the turn of the twentieth century. Even then, in the 1950's, years after he had retired, they were still making furniture, and the two of them listened to the slamming of the hammers and the high pitched whines of the buzz saws and the clanging of tools being dropped on the floors. Now everything was hushed, the office workers moving swiftly and quietly out of their law firms and venture capital offices and design shops. She wondered what the old man would think of it all. And then she had an idea.

She walked back through the old neighborhood and found Ryan O'Connor's storefront office between Seventh and Eighth Streets where an auto supply store had been when she was in high school. She looked through the window and saw him sitting alone at a desk with his head in his hands. She knocked on the glass and he waved her in. "Ms. McGuire. Somehow I thought we were through for the night."

"Not quite. I talked to your colleague from St. Joseph's. He thinks very highly of you."

"Mmm...well, it's nice to be appreciated."

"No hope for that couple?"

"There's hope. It's just going to be a long journey for them. That's all."

"As long as yours?"

"Hopefully not."

She folded her arms and stared at him. "Why are you here, Ryan O'Connor? What is it, exactly, that you want of your wife?"

"I want to see her. I want to ask for her forgiveness in person, and I want to meet my daughter. I want to see how she's turned out."

"But Rebecca does not want to see you. Not ever. And she will never allow you to meet with her daughter. It's not going to happen. Period."

"Possibly. But that's no concern of yours, and there's nothing you can do to stop me."

She pulled up a chair and sat across from him at the table. "Unless, of course, we make a deal."

"A deal?"

"Yes, a deal. While you were helping this couple, I took a walk around the courtyard of the old Davenport building, and while I walked I thought of my great-grandfather, and then I remembered your comment about him having a propensity for negotiation. So in honor of Christopher McGuire, let's negotiate. Your young colleague tells me your ministry is in great financial danger. That, in fact, you may not be able to continue the work you are doing. So here's my deal, Ryan O'Connor. Give up your wife and daughter—after all, you've already done it, haven't you? Promise me you will give up this quest, and I will make it possible for you to continue with your penance."

"My penance?"

"That's right. Your penance. That's what this is all about, isn't it? You are saving souls. You are giving back for what you have taken away."

"And just how will you make that possible?"

"I have a client with deep pockets who is dedicated to helping victims of domestic violence. Deal with me, Ryan O'Connor, and I guarantee that your good work will continue."

He glanced away and stared at the wall for what seemed a long time. Then he turned back and looked into her eyes. "Tell me something. If by any chance I agree to this offer, would you consider something that is as hard for you as this would be for me?"

"Try me."

"Would you consider meditating upon the virulence of your anti-Catholicism? After all, perhaps we can both become a little more human." He leaned back in his chair and folded his arms. "Your steadfastness in protecting my former wife is admirable."

"Maybe you've got it wrong."

"How so?"

"Well, who knows? Maybe I'm trying to protect you."

CHAPTER 25

They wound their way through Haymarket, moving slowly through the swarming crowds and the fruit and vegetable vendors. In front of them, a tall man loomed up like a giant sentinel, standing guard in front of his lettuce cart and yelling above the catcalls of his competitors. "Three for a dollah! Three for a dollah!" They passed a group of old men squeezing lemons on oysters and slurping them from their shells. The old men glanced at Rebecca and elbowed each other, and Rosario smiled and took her by the arm. "You have some fans."

"No thanks. They're even older than you—if that's possible."

He laughed and they crossed Blackstone Street and walked through the little pedestrian tunnel under the expressway. On the other side of Cross Street, customers ducked into Martignetti's to pick up wine, cheese, and pasta, and in front of them traffic emerging from the Sumner Tunnel clogged the road with a fleet of honking cars and taxis. The light turned and they crossed the street and walked down Hanover past

Mother Anna's and Ida's and Caffé Paradiso. They stopped at Richmond Street, and he pointed over at a convenience store at the corner of Hanover and Parmenter. "There was once a beautiful old drugstore on that spot called Macaluso's. When I was little and we would visit our relatives in Boston, my grandfather would take me there and buy me a cone of colored ice, and I used to stare at the old wooden counter and the tiled floor and the black and white marble and the gleaming soda fountains. Macaluso's is gone now. The beautiful old wood and the tiles and the marble have all been taken away and sold."

She squeezed his hand and they crossed Hanover and walked past Caffe Vittoria and Mike's Pastry and Caffe Dello Sport, the men and the boys all along the way staring at her as they strolled by. At the corner of Prince Street they paused outside of St. Leonard's. "Did you attend Mass here when you visited your relatives?"

"Yes, I did. I still go in once in a while to light a candle for my grandparents."

He took her into St. Leonard's Peace Garden. The statues of the Virgin and the children of Fatima stood off to their left surrounded by flowers, and to their right, overlooking row upon row of yellow, white and purple mums, were the statues of St. Francis of Assisi and St. Anthony. She turned slightly and nodded toward the entrance to the church. "Is that gentleman over there in the robes a monk?"

He smiled. "Well, first of all, he's not a gentleman. He's a Franciscan. Uh, oh. He's coming our way. Behave yourself."

"Stop it."

The priest came over and smiled and welcomed them to the garden. He appeared to be a man in his late sixties, and he spoke with a soft, gentle voice as if he had just spent hours in meditation. He asked them if there were anything they would care to know about St. Leonard's. He hadn't, he said, noticed them around before. She smiled and thanked him for his interest and asked him about the statues and about the history of the Franciscan order. He seemed very pleased to be asked such a question, and as he talked to her, Rosario drifted off a bit and looked at the flowers and the buildings and the passersby on Hanover Street. When he had told her to behave herself, he hadn't imagined she would take him so seriously. He turned and looked back, thinking what an odd couple they made— this very modern, stylish woman and the priest with his brown robes and his beads, for all practical purposes a man who had just stepped out of the thirteenth century.

When he rejoined them, the priest looked up at him and smiled. "Your friend tells me you used to come to our church."

"When we were children, my little brother and I used to go to Mass here with our grandparents, Rafael and Mary Rosario. My mother's parents were from Dorchester. St. Peter's parish."

The priest nodded thoughtfully. "Did you attend Catholic schools?"

"Sometimes. It depended upon what state we were living in at the time. I ended up in New Jersey for high school. A regional Catholic high school."

He smiled hopefully. "The Franciscans?"

Rosario shook his head. "I'm afraid not, Father. I would have liked it very much if your order had been in charge. No, I'm afraid it was the Irish Christian Brothers."

He nodded sympathetically and looked into Rosario's eyes. "Whew. The ICB's. They're tough. Well, I hope your faith survived." Rosario couldn't think of an appropriate answer for this kind and gentle man and an awkward silence ensued. The priest glanced over at the statue of St. Francis for a moment, and when he looked back he smiled conspiratorially and bent toward them, lowering his voice. "St. Francis may have loved the birds, but I'd like to shoot them. All they do is flock in here and eat up the seeds we plant for our flowers." Then he winked at them and turned and walked out of the garden to Hanover Street.

Rebecca laughed. "He's not exactly in the Franciscan spirit, is he? Shooting the birds!"

"Maybe he's a right-wing Franciscan. Maybe he'll vote for Romney and help us independents get rid of Teddy. Listen, I'm going in for a moment to light a candle for my grandparents. I'll only be a minute if you'd rather stay here in the garden."

"No, I'll come in with you. I can see things are different here."

It was cool and quiet and dark inside, and they were the only ones in the church. Ahead of them was a statue of St. Anthony holding the Christ child, flanked by two huge gold candlesticks and rows of glowing red votive lights. She looked all around and stared at the brightly colored stained glass windows. Then she leaned toward him and whispered, "You Catholics are certainly into gold and stained glass." She gazed up at the ceiling over the altar. "I was always so struck whenever I went into a Catholic church. All the imagery."

"We can't help ourselves."

Suddenly, the aroma of tomatoes and garlic wafted into the church and she inhaled deeply. "No church I ever attended smelled like this. Wow. Where's that coming from?"

"Assaggio. It's right around the corner on Prince Street."

He left her for a moment and went over and pressed a button to illuminate one of the red candles and knelt down and said a prayer for Raphael and Mary Rosario. As he rose from the kneeler, he heard a burst of noise behind him, an invasion of discordant voices disturbing the soothing silence of the church. He turned in time to see Rebecca hold up her hand in front of a group of tourists loaded down with guide books and festooned with cameras. "Quiet, please."

One of them, an eager intruder who had failed to remove his hat, spoke back to her. "You don't appear to be a member of the clergy. Who are you to talk to us like that?"

She pointed at him. "Appearances can be deceiving. This is a house of worship. Show a little respect or the Lord will smote you with his great sword." She paused for a moment and took a few steps toward the group. "And if the Lord does not, *I will*." Intimidated, they scurried out the door.

Rosario took her hand. "I liked the smote part."

She laughed. "Me too."

He slipped his arm into hers and they walked out of the church into the fading light. As they turned left on Hanover, they saw the Franciscan deep in conversation with a family, but he noticed them and waved. They waved back and walked down the street past Emilio's and stopped in front of the statue of Paul Revere. Down the Prado the tall white steeple of The Old North Church rose up into the evening sky.

Over to their left several groups of old men sat at little stone tables next to the brick wall that ran the length of the Prado. They were playing checkers and drinking beer. One of them waved to him. "Hey, Roberto!"

He touched her elbow. "I'll be back in a second." He walked over to the table and they shook hands. "How are you, Mr. Solari?"

"Bene grazie, Roberto. And you? How are your parents? Still living in that town in New Jersey with the crazy name?" Mr. Solari chuckled. "What was it? Ho-Ho-Ka-Mug?"

Rosario laughed out loud. "Ho-Ho-Kus. They're still there."

"Say hello to your father for me. And what about you? Where are you living these days?"

"In Cambridge."

"In Cambridge! With all those crazy intellectuals? How do you stand it?"

"I do my best."

Mr. Solari glanced over at Rebecca Scott. She was standing by the brick wall opposite them, examining the war memorial plaque. "Who is the beautiful lady?"

"A friend."

"We should all have such friends."

They smiled and said goodbye and he walked over to her. She looked up at him. "There's a Rosario here on this memorial."

"My grandfather's brother Calagero. He was killed in World War I. What a waste of human life that catastrophe was. For what?"

She took his arm and they walked down the Prado to the Old North Church. Inside, they stared up at the bright white ceiling and walls and the white piers that extended to the second story landing. The plain, stark, rational nature of the architecture and the inner décor was a striking contrast to St. Leonard's. There were no stained glass windows or ruby red candles glowing in the darkness. No passionate appeals to the soul. No sensual symbols. When she turned to him, it was if she had read his mind. "Not enough imagery here for you?"

"Actually, I'm very attracted to this aspect of Protestantism."

"And what aspect is that?"

"The idea that the beauty of the physical world distracts men's minds from spiritual truth." He looked into her eyes. "The notion that man's absorption with physical beauty is dangerous—for his soul, that is." He wasn't quite sure why he had added that last part. It was almost as if Ursula McGuire had crept up behind him and whispered a warning into his ear.

Later, he took her to L'Osteria for dinner where they ordered the Veal Braciolettine served over linguine. They ate slowly, savoring the veal stuffed with prosciutto and mozzarella and mushrooms and drank Dolcetta D'Alba between forkfuls of the pasta. When the meal was over, she sighed with satisfaction. "You weren't kidding about this place. That was absolutely fantastic."

"Room for dessert?"

She laughed. "I didn't know you were a dessert guy."

"Only in the North End. Come on. I'll show you why."

They split the bill and walked up Parmenter to Hanover and then into Caffe Vittoria. Like all Saturday nights it was packed, but Rosario spotted a couple rising from a table near the jukebox and grabbed it. As soon as they sat down, he felt the warmth of a hand on the back of his neck and turned around. "Alessia Cavalla! Where you been?"

Holding a tray of cappuccinos against her hip, her long black curls falling all around her shoulders and her saucy, almond eyes flashing, she looked like a gypsy princess. "You're never here when I am. My kids are teenagers now so they're running me ragged." She looked at Rebecca. "And you! It's been years since I've seen you here with him. You look different somehow. Is it your hair?"

Rebecca took the case of mistaken identity in stride. "That's probably it. I wore it longer in those days. Or maybe it's just the aging process."

Alessia shook her head. "Are you kidding? You look better than ever. I used to be jealous of you, you know. I was sixteen when I started here and I used to flirt with this guy. You know...the attractive older man thing. You were what, Rosario? Late twenties?" She laughed. "A real codger. He never paid me much attention. Always buried in his newspaper. I mean he was polite and everything."

Rebecca nodded. "Well, at sixteen you were jailbait. Mr. Rosario is a very cautious man, especially when it comes to women."

Alessia pointed at her. "I remember the first day you came in here with him. People stopped eating their pastries and drinking their coffee and just stared at you. I knew then I didn't have a chance."

Rebecca waved her hand. "Nonsense. I'm sure with those exotic looks of yours, you knocked all the boys dead."

"And you were always arguing politics. I remember one time you walked out on him. You were yelling at each other about Kevin White. I remember thinking to myself, 'Holy shit! This great couple is going to break up over the mayor of Boston. Can you imagine such a thing?' You still argue like that?"

Rebecca smiled. "No. That's all over. He's mellowed in his old age."

Alessia grinned and put her hand on Rosario's shoulder. "He's not so old. At least he still looks good." She ran her purple fingernails through the side of his hair. "A little grayer maybe. Hey! Gotta run. Those guys in front will not be happy if they get cold cappuccinos."

She slipped around their chairs and ran up to the tables near the window. Rebecca looked at him. "She's pretty forward, isn't she? Running her fingers through your hair like that."

"Just a gesture of affection for the near elderly. After all, as she said…" Rosario smiled at her. "She knew the first time she saw you, she didn't stand a chance."

"The first time she saw Eve Taylor, you mean." She leaned forward. "Is it possible we look that much alike?"

"You saw the photograph."

"Yes, but to have this woman think I was actually her. It's a little unnerving."

"Don't worry about it. The two of you are quite different." He signaled another waitress, and a few minutes later they were savoring the sweet powdery taste of the cannolis with their cold smooth ricotta and crisp pastry shell, and sipping Vittoria's cappuccinos, silky to the tongue with their swirl of chocolate-sprinkled foam. For good measure, he ordered a Sambuca and they shared it, licking the strong licorice flavor and feeling the slight burn as it trickled down their throats.

On the way out, Alessia waved to them. "Say hi to Kevin White for me!"

Rosario laughed. "He's retired. We have nothing left to argue about."

"What about Teddy? You can argue about him!"

He looked over his shoulder. "We'll give it a try."

They walked slowly along Hanover Street, breathing in the ocean air and mingling with the crowds. They stopped in the Prado again where it was dark and stood in the shadow of Revere's statue. For a moment, they looked up at the man on the horse and then moved close to one another. The wind blew in off the harbor and the sights and smells and sounds of the city played all around them like spirits in the night. She slid her hands along his forearms and raised her face to him, and he kissed her for what seemed an eternity. She locked her body into his, pushing her hips against him and winding her arms around his neck. The urgency of her kiss took him by storm and he yielded to her, pulling her closer and tighter until finally their breath escaped in a sudden rush. She leaned back in his arms and smiled. "Guess what?"

"What?"

"That was the best kiss I've ever had."

As he hung their jackets in his front closet, she wandered into his study. "Hey! I didn't notice this one before."

"Which one?"

"You and this pretty girl at an amusement park."

He smiled. "That's no amusement park. That was the World's Fair in New York. 1964. I was nineteen and she was seventeen. We asked a stranger to take the picture. I remember that later I took her into the Village to a bar called The Ninth Circle on West 10th Street, and we drank beer and ate peanuts from big barrels. You were supposed to throw the peanut shells on the floor, as I recall, so the place was littered with them. I barely got her home in time."

"She's lovely. She must have been pretty special. Outside of Eve Taylor, I don't see any other photographs of you with women."

"She was."

"Were you in love with her?"

"We never got to the love stage."

"What happened?"

He looked at her. She had turned on an antique chimney lamp near the photograph, and the soft glow brought out the silver in her gray eyes. "Well, let's just say I'm not quite sure it's an appropriate story for you." He had tried to make this a lighthearted remark, but it hadn't come out that way.

"And why is that?"

He held her by the shoulders and kissed her forehead. Then he leaned back, watching her face. "Because of your occasional, shall we say, tendency toward anger. Toward rage. Toward revenge."

He thought for a moment she was going to argue with him, but instead she laughed. "Ah, hah! So this is a revenge story. Fill me in, Rosario. Fill me in."

"Not tonight. It's not just that it's inappropriate for you as a person. It's inappropriate for tonight. We've had a nice day together. Let's not drape a cloud over it."

"OK. But you will tell me sometime, right? You know. Like at an *appropriate* time."

He laughed and took her hand. "Next time. I promise."

He led her upstairs. "Is that the guest bedroom?"

"Uh, huh. Want to be my guest?"

"Only if I can sleep with you."

He took her into his bedroom and undressed her. Almost as if by mutually silent consent, there was no furious animal rush this time, but a slow kiss-fueled passion, a deep, longing desire, a holding off as long as they could until their nerves were trembling and they couldn't stand it anymore. She lay on the bed and watched him take off his clothes. "You have a great body, Rob."

He shook his head. "You're the one with the great body."

She smiled. "So are we going to try that crazy position again?"

Naked, he approached the bed and sat down next to her. "Oh, no! No way! That's only once every ten years."

She sat up and laughed and put her arms around his neck. "And why is that?"

"It's in the Constitution. Article I. Section 2. But I think I know a way around it."

"You do, huh?"

He took her in his arms and kissed her, and she fell back on the bed and opened her legs and gasped as he slipped inside her. They made love this way for a long time, slowly, steadily, until suddenly she raised her legs higher and urged him on, revolving her hips in a rolling, voluptuous movement, as he drove himself in and out, faster and harder. He slowed his pace and then stopped, and still inside her, he turned her over, and started moving once again, their bodies slapping wetly together and her breathing quickening and her cries filling the room. Gently, he reached underneath her and slipped his hand between her thighs, her perfect, sculptured buttocks twisting and shaking beneath him. Then she cried out again and buried her face in the pillow until her orgasm had spent its force.

She lay still for a while, breathing deeply, and then she turned around and looked at him, her face and her neck and her breasts flushed pink from their lovemaking. He didn't even have to move. The very sight of her, the very power of her beauty released in him a surging rush of ecstasy, a moment of bliss he could almost see racing around a corner somewhere deep inside him, until, like a series of shock waves, each leaping spurt and shudder lifted him out of the world into a dimension of feeling so intense he thought he would lose consciousness. And then he did. In the deep, warm web of her embrace.

CHAPTER 26

Ursula McGuire paced back and forth in front of Savenor's Market and waited for Rosario's train to come rumbling over the Longfellow Bridge from Cambridge. Tonight he was a little late, so she went inside and stood in front of the meat counter and watched the butcher at work. She liked to do this because it reminded her of when she was a little girl, and her grandmother Nora would take her to Dorchester to visit her friend Mame who lived in a big three decker at the top of the hill on Rosseter Street. They would sit in Mame's kitchen and play cards and have tea, and then in the late afternoon the three of them would walk down the hill to Saul's Market on Washington Street to buy dinner.

Saul would slice the blood red steaks with his long sharp knife and slam his butcher's hatchet into big yellow chickens and then wrap the fresh cuts of meat in long swaths of brown paper that spun off a big metal spool on the wall. Savenor's was a far cry from Saul's. Here they served everything from beef, chicken and lamb to buffalo meat, ostrich steaks, and ox tails. In the fifties, Saul's customers had been primarily Jews and Irish Catholics from the surrounding neighborhood, but today, here at the edge of Beacon Hill, Savenor's served every race, color, and creed known to man, and Ursula, just as she had so many years ago, would stand off to the side and stare with fascination.

She went outside again and saw him coming down the stairs to Charles Street with a newspaper tucked under his arm. He hugged her and smiled. "How goes the battle?"

"The battle is nearly won, my friend."

"Don't be so sure. There's always time for a Hail Mary pass."

"Uh, huh. Well, Teddy's running against Romney, not Flutie." She saw he was in a good mood so she dropped the politics. They could always get into that at dinner. "So how are things with your...your lady friend?"

"Things are just fine."

"Not getting in too deep?"

"You know me."

"I thought I did. But you never know what can happen to a man as he approaches the crucial half-century mark."

He laughed and took her arm. "You're right behind me, kid."

As they walked past Hanrahan's, the clamor of youthful voices and the musty, stale smell of spilled beer drifted into the street. They breathed it in, a wave of nostalgia washing over them. She stopped and struck a masculine pose, her shoulders hunched and her hands pushed out in front of her. "Yo, Rosie. Wanna toss down a beeyah? Yah know...like the old days."

He laughed again. "I haven't been in there for years."

"Remember the time you punched out that obnoxious dolt?"

He looked away. "Well, that was long ago and far away."

"He tried to move in on Eve, as I recall."

"It was the way he did it. If he had just talked to her, I would have let it go. But he manhandled her. So he deserved everything he got."

Suddenly, she realized what she had done. At first, flushed with guilt, she tried to shrug it off with a flip comment. "Uh, oh. The old Rosario is back." But he didn't smile or say anything. "Rosie, I'm sorry. I don't know why I dredged that up."

Then he took her arm again. "Don't worry about it. Like I said, he got what he deserved. He was a bully. Then he wasn't a bully anymore. Simple."

"Still, I shouldn't have…"

"Nonsense. You walked by Hanrahan's and the memory just popped into your head. Perfectly natural. Relax."

But now she couldn't relax. The point of the evening was to tell him what she had discovered about Ryan O'Connor. That the man had changed radically and was no longer a threat. She needed Rob to listen and to listen calmly to what she had to say. Instead, with a thoughtless comment, she had resurrected the old anger he had taken such pains to put behind him. And the old anger, the anger from way back, was frightening.

That night at Hanrahan's the four of them had found a table near the wall and were drinking Lowenbrau and talking about the McGovern campaign. She was on Rosario's case over an article he had written about how Teddy had screwed Kevin White out of the vice-presidential nomination, and Eve was trying to calm the two of them down. As usual, Eve was the best looking woman in the bar. She could still see her dressed in those tight faded jeans and Rob's old black and red checked woolen shirt, her long blonde hair falling down to her waist. Rob stood up and stepped over to the bar for another round when a big beefy guy grabbed his chair and put his arm around Eve's shoulder.

Eve slipped from his grasp. "I'm with someone else. Take your arm off me."

He laughed and put it back and grabbed a handful of her hair. "You're something else, babe. All this gorgeous hair."

Mark leaned forward. "Why don't you be a good boy and take your hands off her?"

"Maybe I don't feel like it."

Rob turned and looked and the anger just swept him away. In an instant, he fell upon the intruder like a beast of prey, grabbing him by his ears and yanking him to his feet. "Feel like it now?" Then he spun him around and punched him so hard the guy flew backwards and smashed against the wall, collapsing like a rag doll.

As if anticipating her fears, Rosario squeezed her arm lightly. "So what did you find out about our priest? Do I have to punch him out too? At this age? I might break my hand. How will I correct all those papers?"

At this last sentence, she breathed a little easier, for his voice had lost its rancor and had taken on a softer tone as if he were trying to soothe her. "Let's put the priest talk off until after dinner, Rosie."

"OK with me. What's Chef Mark coming up with tonight?"

"Beef tenderloin."

"The one with the thyme and red wine sauce?"

"You got it."

"Oh, my God."

As they started walking again, she pointed across Charles Street at the Eugene Galleries. "I was with Eve in there the time she bought you the Currier and Ives print of Boston in the 1870's. She was so excited that she found it. She knew you'd love it."

"I still do."

"She bought it for your thirtieth birthday, Rosie. It seems like yesterday."

"Really? Somehow it feels like a million years ago." He smiled. "You're really pushing the age bit tonight, pal."

"I know, I know. I just can't believe we're all going to be fifty."

He laughed. "Yup. It's all downhill from here."

They turned left on Chestnut Street and walked up the hill to the townhouse. Ursula opened the door to the smell of sizzling beef and the sweet, melancholy sound of Ray Bryant's piano playing "I'm a Fool to Want You." She glanced at Rob and saw that he was struck by the music and wondered if he was thinking of Rebecca Scott. She had always assumed, somehow, even long after the affair with Eve was over, that at this time in their lives it would still be the four of them together. She had always thought that somehow, sometime, Eve and Rob would reunite and things would be as they were. But now Rebecca Scott was in the picture. And it was all her fault.

In the kitchen, Mark was carefully moving the meat from the oven to a carving board and covering it with foil. Then he turned and presented them both with big round glasses of rich Merlot. Ursula took a long delicious sip and tried to take her mind off the music and what she had done to her friend. She smiled. Maybe a good political argument would do the trick.

She leaned against the doorway of her dining room and stared at Rosario. "So? Have you made up your mind yet?"

Rosario took a drink of the Merlot. "You mean about your inevitable return to the Church as you glide seamlessly into old age?"

She shook her head. "You know perfectly well what I mean. The election is right around the corner."

He looked her in the eyes. "I'm voting for Mr. Romney."

Mark lifted his wine high in the air and the two men clinked glasses.

She glared at him and then looked back at Rosario. "What's happening to you? After all these years you're turning into a Republican?"

Mark almost choked on his wine. "Good Lord! We can't have that! A fate worse than death."

Rosario spoke with exasperation. "Just because I won't vote for your pal Teddy, I'm a Republican?"

"Well, you voted for Weld for governor in 1990 and you're voting for him again. Weld for governor and Romney for senator. That sounds pretty Republican to me."

"Nonsense. You're upset because I'm not towing the Ursula McGuire liberal line. You don't like it when your friends turn independent on you. I've voted for Teddy in the past. I voted for Kerry over Rappaport last time."

Ursula scowled. "Rappaport! That real estate developer."

Mark shook his head. "Uh, oh. Real estate developer. Bad. Bad. Can't vote for anyone like that."

Rosario leaned against the refrigerator. "And I voted for Clinton two years ago. That doesn't sound too Republican to me. Unlike you and Teddy, he had the good sense to see what the left wing of the party was doing to the Democrats. To his credit, he tried to move the party to the center, but this health care fiasco he's got himself embroiled in flies in the face of what independent voters believe in. Here he is flailing leftward and gift-wrapping the House of Representatives for Gingrich. He's handing him the anti-big government issue on a platter."

She took a step into the kitchen and confronted him. "Hillary's plan is the culmination of the Democratic party's health policy since Harry Truman first proposed it in 1945."

"I doubt very much that a Missouri populist like Harry would have worked up a program in secret, excluded doctors, nurses, and health professionals from its formulation, and left Congress out of the process. No way. If Hillary had served as a senator like Harry, she might have come up with something that could actually have passed. Clinton earned a lot of respect with independent voters on his budget bill and his trade policy. He showed us that he was serious about the deficit and the economy, and that he was not another free-spending Democrat—like you! And now he's blown it with this health care disaster. And none of this, by the way, is helping Democratic politicians running for re-election, including Teddy."

"You've completely lost your principles."

"No, I haven't. I believe the federal government has a strong role to play in health care. I support Medicare. I believe industry needs to be regulated. I support the EPA and pollution controls. While I do believe in the second amendment, I support the Brady Bill and the ban on assault weapons, as does Mr. Romney, I might add."

She grunted. "For now."

"He doesn't support Newt's Contract With America."

"For now."

"He supports a woman's right to choose."

"For now."

Rosario turned to Mark. "This is quite a cynic you're married to."

Mark shook his head. "Now we're seeing Romney fall behind because of these ads Ursie's pals have been running about the fired Indiana workers—ads based on *her* opposition research."

Rosario smiled and wagged his finger at her. "Bad wife. Bad. Even worse than those awful old real estate developers.

But speaking of opposition research, Ms. McGuire, let's return to the subject at hand. What, exactly, have you learned about Ryan O'Connor?"

"Trying to change the topic, huh?"

"I thought that was the topic for tonight."

She leaned back again and sighed. "It is, Rosie. It is."

"So you believe that this man has changed. Changed fundamentally. That he has finally escaped the weight of the Church and his family, and that he is dedicating his life to doing good."

Ursula put her free hand on her hip. "I'm as acutely aware of the weight of the Church as you are, my friend, and I remain as adamantly opposed to its undemocratic and dictatorial..."

Mark groaned as he sliced into the beef tenderloin. "Uh, oh! Here we go again. The Catholic Church under attack! Bang! Biff! Boom! I think I'll buy you a sexy Cat Woman outfit like the one Michelle Pfeiffer wore in *Batman Returns,* only this time there will be a symbol of an exploding cathedral on the front. How come I never hear of the good things the Church has done? In 1862 while your people were rioting in the streets of New York against Abraham Lincoln's draft, burning block after block and murdering innocent blacks left and right, it was the Catholic priests who came out into the streets to try to stop the mob and help the police restore law and order. Hundreds of those nuns and priests you so execrate went from house to house here in Boston during the influenza epidemic of 1918, feeding people, caring for the sick, and ministering to widows and children who had lost their parents. My grandmother, as you well know, was a nurse at that time and deeply involved in the relief efforts. She was brought to tears by the dedication of these men and women. And what about now? What about the work the Church is doing for inner-city children while the public schools are a disgrace?"

Ursula stared at him. "I am not talking about individual acts of good. Acts of heroism. I'm talking about the weight of the Church, especially the Irish Catholic Church, on the souls and hearts of the people. There's no doubt that heroic acts exist side by side with the mind control and totalitarian leadership of the Church. I'll wager it wasn't the cardinals and the bishops that were out there stopping the draft riots and helping the victims of influenza. You can bet on it, Mr. Historian."

Rosario laughed. "It looks to me as if Mr. Historian has prepared us quite a dinner, here, Ursula McGuire. Why don't you ease up so we can eat?"

She smiled at her husband. "Why can't you be one of those bigoted Wasps like those cranky old Brahmins my ancestors had to fight? You're so...so fair minded."

"I thought you liked that about me."

She laughed. "I do. I do. It's just that sometimes it gets a little annoying."

"You mean like now?"

"Yes! Precisely. Like now."

Mark spooned helpings of the fragrant basmati rice next to the beef, and they brought their plates into the dining room and sat down. She looked across the table at Rosario, his features softened in the candlelight. "In answer to your question, Robert. I do. I do believe that this man has fundamentally changed."

Rosario glanced over at Mark. "Is this the woman I just called a cynic?"

Ursula smiled. "As you did at BC that day. But my time with Ryan O'Connor has only reinforced what I felt then. This man presents no danger to Rebecca Scott. Quite the opposite, I'm afraid. I know you don't want to hear that."

"No. No, I don't want to hear that. At least not without any proof against her. Any proof, that is, as to how dangerous you think she really might be."

She looked up at him through the flickering flame of the big red candle in the center of the table. "I wonder, my friend, what you would do if you actually found that proof."

CHAPTER 27

I t was the first time in her place, in her bedroom, and she came at him in a rush, springing on top of him, sitting upright, her head flung back in a kind of unhinged ecstasy, her hair flying and her breasts swaying, her eyes half closed and her moaning bringing him closer and closer. She rode him hard, up and down, pushing and pulling her hips in a thrusting, grinding fury, and he gave himself up to her completely, letting her urgent, driving rhythm and the cadence of her tremulous cries take him away until he burst into a shattering, explosive orgasm so powerful he thought for a moment it might never stop.

She waited until his last shudder and then laughed softly. "Happy birthday, old guy."

He reached up and ran his hands through her hair. "That was some birthday present."

She rolled off and cuddled up to him and whispered in his ear. "Brazilian enough for you?"

He laughed out loud. "I'll say. Worthy of all of Latin America."

"So I guess there's still some hope left for us Episcopalians." She put her hand over his beating heart. "And speaking of hope, I hope you haven't forgotten your promise. You know— the story. The pretty girl at The World's Fair in 1964. The story you promised to tell me at an *appropriate* time. The next time, you said. Well, Mr. Rosario, that time is now. Fill me in."

He smiled and closed his eyes. "You know, that Episcopalian sex was really strenuous for an old guy. I think I'll take a little nap."

She sat up and slapped both palms on his chest and laughed. "Come on."

He opened his eyes. "Hey, I forgot to tell you. I've got a new vocabulary word from my kids."

"Don't avoid the topic."

"No, no. You'll like this one. One of the words I put on the test was *ephemeral*. So this kid has no idea and informs me that it's a general in the feminist army."

"Very good. I like that. Did he get his two points?"

"You bet he did."

"Why are you so reluctant to tell me about this girl?"

"I'm not. It's what happened that caused our breakup."

"That's the part you think is inappropriate for me to hear, isn't it? Try me, Robert. I'm a big girl." She paused. "But before you begin, one quick question. 1964 was thirty years ago. That's a long time to keep that photograph. If you and she never fell in love, why keep it?"

"I keep it to remind myself that there are good people in the world that I should listen to. Pay heed to. I keep it especially to remind myself of the unintended consequences of anger. Even justifiable anger."

She stared into his eyes and was silent for a moment. "Go on."

"Well, there were these three guys in high school. Brauer, Hayden, and Reilly…"

"Wow," she whispered.

"Wow…what?"

"The anger that just came into your eyes when you spoke those names. The fire!"

"Sorry about that. I guess you bring out the best in me. But don't worry. It was all a long time ago. I'm a real pussycat now."

She looked at him very seriously. "You misunderstand me. It's good to see the anger in your eyes. You're always so reasonable. So calm. The only time you catch fire is when we make love." She glanced away and then looked back again. "I interrupted you. I'm sorry. Go on."

"These three guys were bigger, tougher, and meaner than the rest of us, so we all steered clear of them. They would rough people up, pick on defenseless kids on the bus, and generally wreak havoc."

"Didn't the teachers do anything about it?"

"Actually, a few of them did. Several of the brothers were decent men, but they couldn't control what went on outside of school. So anyway, there was a group of us who hated the place and didn't fit in."

She smiled. "That would be the guys in the picture. Dion and the Belmonts."

He laughed. "Those would be the guys. So one Friday afternoon in our senior year we drove up Route 17 and crossed the border into Suffern in New York State where you could buy alcohol at eighteen. We got a case of beer and drove back to Ho-Ho-Kus and hiked up into the woods behind the railroad station to a spot along the brook across from the old bleachery."

She shook her head. "I can't get over that name. *Ho-Ho-Kus!*"

"It's from the language of a native American tribe called the Lenni-Lenape."

"Oh, really?"

"Yes. He ran his hand along her thigh. "It means *time for squaw's orgasm.*"

She laughed and pushed his hand away. "No you don't. Back to the woods, pal."

"When we got there we ran into some friends of mine from Ridgewood High School and it turned into a party. I can still remember to this day the sound of the place. It had rained a lot that spring and the brook was swollen so that it rushed past us like a river, and the wind was blowing hard, bending the trees and tearing some of the new leaves off the branches and driving them into the water where they flew downstream over the rocks and boulders. It was an odd pairing, actually. The Catholic school kids with our sideburns and Elvis haircuts and tight black pants and the preppies from Ridgewood High with their clean-cut looks and chinos and varsity sweaters. But we all got along. Everything was fine until the bad guys arrived."

"I know all about bad guys."

"I know you do. But these were really bad guys. From what you've told me, your guy didn't really enjoy being bad. They did. They started by trying to goad a couple of the Ridgewood jocks into a fight. But Brauer was so big and had such a reputation that the jocks backed down. They knew what they were in for. When that didn't work the three of them turned their attention to us and began mocking Ronnie Torris. We didn't know at the time that Ronnie was gay, and I'm not so sure he did either. We had our suspicions but we didn't care. He was our friend and that's all that mattered. For sure, he did have some effeminate mannerisms, but he was on the basketball team and had a cute girlfriend named Jane so how gay could he be, right? Of course, the word *gay* wasn't around back then. It was all *fag* and *queer* and *pervert*. We hadn't a clue what kind of private hell Ronnie and other gay kids went through in those days. Not a clue.

"So they went after Ronnie, grabbing him and pushing him back and forth among the three of them, and then suddenly Reilly slapped Ronnie across the face. For no reason at all. Just for the hell of it. That's when the rest of us jumped in. They beat the crap out of us in two or three minutes. All five of us were on the ground, the three of them standing over us and laughing. We didn't stand a chance, of course, which was what the Ridgewood guys knew all along. I was lying on my stomach, and I remember looking over at my buddy Al from Glen Rock who was on his side holding his ribs and grimacing in pain. The two of us had been lifting weights together in his basement since junior year and we were putting on muscle, but we were no match for these guys. Al could see what I was thinking, or maybe all he saw was the rage in my eyes, and he shook his head in warning. But the rage took hold of me and I jumped up and went for Reilly. I went for Reilly because he had started the slapping. I went for him blindly, roaring out loud like a madman and tackled him, driving him into a tree and punching him hard in the face until he went down. The next thing I knew Brauer and Hayden had me pinioned on my back, and Reilly was kneeling over me with a beer can opener."

She touched his face. "*They* did this to you, didn't they?" He nodded but didn't speak. In the telling, the old rage had returned, and it was beginning to burn through his body. She ran her finger along his cheekbone.

He turned and faced her and kissed her lips. "Don't look so sad. Besides, in the end justice was done. They paid for what they did. Big time."

She gripped his shoulder. "Now *that's* the part I want to hear about." She shook her head. "To do what they did requires malevolence. Those guys were evil. People simply beyond redemption." She ran her finger along his scar again and then kissed his cheek. "It's not really a very big scar, Mr. Rosario. It doesn't mar your beauty."

"Thank God for that."

"When you came home so wounded, what did your parents do?"

"They took me to Valley Hospital where I was cleaned up and given a Tetanus shot and stitches. That was it."

"No legal action?"

"This was 1962, Rebecca. Boys got into fights. Boys got hurt. Life goes on."

"But this was a little bit more than getting hurt, wouldn't you say?"

"I would say. But they didn't. It was very clear to me that my parents were not going to seek justice. In fact, there would be no justice at all—that is, unless I provided it. Two days after I graduated from high school, I packed a suitcase and headed for Boston. I stayed with my Irish grandparents on East Cottage Street for the summer and worked in a warehouse in Dorchester. In the fall, I got a better job unloading trucks in the North End and moved in with my Italian grandparents up on Hull Street. All my high school buddies from Jersey went on to college except me. I just wasn't ready. I was too immature. Too unfocused."

"You were focused on something else."

"That's right. That's exactly right. Between all the meat and potatoes in Dorchester and all the pasta in the North End, I put on fifteen pounds in one year. I worked out like a bandit so every pound was muscle. But I still didn't know how to fight.

Then I lucked out. The boss took me off the loading dock for two weeks and assigned me to be a trucker's helper. This was a great job because we drove all over the whole city making deliveries, and the day was over before you knew it. But the trucker was the best part. Nico Travato. Nico was a boxer. Not a pro, but an amateur boxer who actually got in the ring and fought other guys for money." He stopped and looked at her. "Is this getting boring? Most women hate fight stories."

She stared at him. "Not this one."

He laughed. "Now that was a dumb question, wasn't it?"

"Yes it was, Mr. Rosario. It just goes to show that you don't know me all that well yet, do you?"

He paused for a moment and then brushed aside some wayward thoughts that were infiltrating his mind. Thoughts that sounded too much like Ursula McGuire's voice. "Nico was pretty good as an amateur and he used to get me into some of his fights so I could watch, and then as he got to know me better, he let me come to his gym and actually spar with him."

"How was that?"

"It hurt."

She laughed. "Did he really hurt you?"

"Not really. He was easy on me. And he was a great teacher. Very patient and very thorough."

"So how did you go from all this working and training and fighting to college?"

"Nico and I used to make deliveries to all the local schools and I really liked the BC campus, and whenever we ran into any Jesuits, they seemed like good guys. They used to joke with us when we unloaded the truck. Nico always had to sign off on a delivery at the business office, which was run by a Jesuit named Father Solvetti from Arthur Avenue in the Bronx. Every time we came in he'd say, 'Here come the Muscle Brothers from the North End.' When I filled out my application I went to him for a letter of recommendation, and he actually gave me one. I often wonder if that's how I got in."

"So that means you started BC in the fall of 1963, right? Still working out? Still finding time to spar with Nico?"

"You got it."

"Still planning. Getting ready to strike. Picking the right time. Not going back to New Jersey until you're ready. By my count you've been gone well over a year. In all this time, did you see your parents?"

"They came up a few times to visit family in Boston. We saw each other."

"But you hadn't forgiven them yet for not seeking justice."

"That's right."

"So when's game time?"

"Game time is Christmas vacation."

"You finally come home. Now comes the part I've been waiting for."

"Well, not quite yet."

"What!"

"Hold on. There was a problem. I met this girl."

"And this girl, I take it, postponed game time."

"She did. But at first it wasn't just her. Two of those guys didn't come home for Christmas. They were at Notre Dame and went skiing in Utah with some guy they met in South Bend. The other one was home but every time I tried to set something up, the occasion slipped through my hands."

"How so?"

"I couldn't just find this guy and kick the shit out of him. His father was a lawyer, and unlike my parents, he *would* seek justice. I had to set it up so it looked like self-defense. It had to happen at a bar or a party or a situation like that. And I needed witnesses. It took time and I was spending so much of it with this girl."

"She must have been something else."

"She was. She was beautiful and smart and funny, and for the first time in my life I found a girl I could really talk with. That had never happened before."

She frowned. "So I take it that part of all this talk was trying to talk you out of your plan."

"Part of it, sure."

"So things got postponed. She wanted to stop you from taking vengeance. She didn't want you to do it. But you did."

"Yes, I did."

"Good for you."

"Yes, but not good for us, I'm afraid. You see, the amazing thing about this girl was..." He could see her attention span waning. He marveled, though he shouldn't have at this point, at her lack of interest in the girl. Other women would have wanted details about the romantic side of the relationship. What was this girl like? What made her so different than all the others he had met? What was her name? Where was she from? And the odd thing was that he felt a need to tell Rebecca what had happened between the two of them, because in the long run, the loss of this girl was so much more important than the vengeance he had wreaked upon his enemies. Now, thirty years later, he rarely thought of what he had done to them, but he often caught himself remembering her face, her laugh, her kiss...the developing bond between them, the emotional intimacy just beyond reach. She had come so close to talking him out of it. But the anger in his soul had been too strong. Had he simply beaten them up, she might have understood. But the ferocity of the beating frightened her. Convinced her, even at such a young age, that they couldn't go on together.

Rebecca squeezed his arm, pulling him out of his reverie. "So...if not Christmas, when?"

"That summer. The summer of 1964. Late in August right before I went back to BC. Brauer was first. He was the biggest. The enforcer. The guy who intimidated everyone. So he needed to be knocked down first. There was a bar right over the Jersey line in New York where we all used to go when we hit eighteen, and I found out through a high school buddy when he could be found there. I had four friends from Boston with me: two from BC, one from Harvard and a girl from Simmons who was dating the Harvard guy. The girl, like the rest of us, had just finished her freshman year, but she already knew she wanted to be a lawyer and had signed up for a couple summer law courses at Suffolk."

"Your witnesses."

"Exactly. In addition to which this girl knew exactly what I could get away with as far as avoiding any assault charges."

"So she was part of the plan."

"Right."

"Totally the opposite from your New Jersey heartthrob."

He smiled. "Well, yes, if you put it that way. She was a tough Irish girl from East Cambridge. When someone hit you, you hit back."

"Not one of us suburban softies."

He laughed. "Yeah. You're a real softie. So we went to the place, and sure enough, there he was at the bar, regaling a herd of morons about his latest exploits in South Fucking Bend, Indiana."

She touched his lips. "You're getting angry again."

"Mmm...so my four friends got a table near the bar, and I stood up and leaned on the counter and ordered a beer and waited until he turned around. 'Rosario! You look a little bigger than I remember. But not big enough, I'm afraid. You want to take up where we left off?'

'Not me, James. I'm just here for a beer. Just like everyone else.'

'The hell you are. I know why you're back. I heard you were looking for us. So now you found me.' He turned to the morons. 'Watch this. You're gonna learn something.' Then he spun around on the stool and came at me like a bull. The trick with a guy like this is never to let him near you or it's over, so I sidestepped him at the last second and punched him in the ear as hard as I could. It's a great shot if you do it hard enough, because it disorients your opponent by producing a kind of pulsation and ringing in the ear. Brauer staggered and fell over the barstool, so I grabbed his hair and twisted his head to the side and poured my mug of beer right into his ear. He went down like a ton of bricks screaming bloody murder. That's how you know when you've punctured someone's eardrum. If you ever get smacked in the ear, never get any water in it."

She leaned up on her elbow and stared into his eyes. "So you actually set out to rupture his eardrum?"

"Sure. I had a long time to brood over this moment, Rebecca. I wanted to come as close to killing him without killing him."

"Jesus, Rob." She drew back, almost as if she were recoiling from the violence of his story.

"I thought you wanted details. Want me to stop?"

"No, of course not. Go ahead."

"Rebecca, this is the way you deal with a guy this size. You have to disable him right away or you're dead meat. And he was tough. Let me tell you. He got up and came back for more, but he was weaving. I could have hit him in the jaw and ended it right there. The fight was essentially over. I could have walked away and made my point. But I couldn't let it go. I wanted to *damage* him."

"Bursting his eardrum wasn't enough?"

"Nope. I let him come at me and then hit him with a direct shot to the throat, and he started gagging, desperate for air. Then I just used him as a punching bag, jabbing and hooking and crossing until I had damaged every part of his body. When he fell, the whole floor shook. Then I asked the morons if they thought they had learned anything. No one said a fucking word."

She took a deep breath and let it out slowly. "I guess I can see why."

"Hayden was next. I tracked him down at a party in Waldwick. I won't bore you with the details."

"That was hardly boring."

"It was essentially the same treatment I gave Brauer."

"You punctured his eardrum too?"

"No, I broke his nose. There was blood all over the floor of this girl's rec room. Now for Reilly."

"The one who cut you."

"That's right. Saving the best for last. You would think, having heard what happened to his pals, that he'd try to avoid me. But just the opposite. He sent his little brother over to my house to tell me to meet him up by the bleachery in the woods."

"The scene of the crime. What confidence he had."

"Reilly knew how to fight. The other two guys were essentially bruisers. Bums. How they ever got into Notre Dame was a mystery to me."

She drew closer and nudged his shoulder with her nose. "Well, you got into BC."

He laughed as she coiled herself around him. "Another mystery. So my friends and I show up in the woods by the brook, and Reilly's there with three guys I don't know. College buddies, it turns out. All four of them baseball players at the University of Maine. Reilly had been a star pitcher on our high school team and a real ace for Maine that year. Maine was a baseball powerhouse back then. That's why he went there. He was going all the way, he used to tell everybody on the bus back in high school. He was going to take that vaunted arm through college and then to the majors. It was his dream.

"Luckily for me—legally, that is—he puts on a real show in front of everybody, standing up on a rock and challenging me, throwing every insult he can imagine, jumping around and pumping his fists in the air and psyching himself up for battle. They'll be no question as to who started this one. Then he leaps off the rock and runs right at me. By this time, I'm bigger than Reilly both in height and weight, so I don't have to sidestep him like I did with Brauer. I just wait and stiff arm him in the nose and let his own momentum bring him down. But he gets right up, wipes the blood off his face with his sleeve, and comes at me again. He's pretty fast but he doesn't have anything Nico hadn't taught me to block or duck, so I let him take shot after shot until he starts getting tired and frustrated that he can't land anything. So instead of punching him, I start to slap him. Just like he did to Ronnie. Big loud slaps against both sides of his face that everyone can hear and he can't do anything about. Humiliating slaps. Over and over. Echoing in the woods all around us. This is deliberate. If I punch him out, the fight's over and I don't get to inflict the damage. He doesn't get the payback for the scar. But the shame he's undergoing, the total inability to defend himself against slap after slap is going to make him do something desperate. So desperate it will play right into my hands. And then, sure enough, staggering under the weight of the blows, his face scarlet from the slapping, he throws a right cross, but I see it coming from a mile away. I catch his right hand in mine, grab his precious arm right under the elbow with my left, and then wrench it as hard as I can. There's a crack. Louder than hell, and a kind of communal groan rises up from everyone there. Reilly collapses on the ground, holding his arm and screaming in pain. So there he was. Mr. Tough Guy. Mr. Baseball. Defeated and broken and sobbing. I think he knew right then that the dream was over. But those are the breaks. You cut someone's face open, you pay the price. A scar for a sports career. I think I got the best of the bargain."

She was silent for a while. Then she knelt up in front of him. "Kneel up and show me."

"Show you?"

"Show me how you broke his arm."

He knelt up and faced her. "Try to punch me. But do it in slow motion so I can show you correctly." Her fist came toward him in a slow arc and he grabbed it, lifting her arm slightly with his free hand. She winced. "Get it?"

"I get it. Thanks for not twisting."

"Well, I didn't want to hurt you. And I don't want you hurting anyone else. It's a good defensive move if you're ever attacked. Defense, not offense. Agreed?"

She smiled. "Maybe. Although I kind of like it as an offensive one."

"Gee, there's a surprise."

"You know what else I get? I get why that girl had to end things between you. You were too much for her. Too dangerous. What you were back then, I mean. But I like you for what you've become." She threw her arms around his neck and kissed him, and he slid his hands down her back and pulled her close. In seconds he was inside her and they thrust themselves against each other, grappling and moaning until they collapsed together on the bed.

When he awoke in her arms, coming slowly to consciousness in that pleasant, sensual numbness that obliterates all sense of judgment, he began to wonder what it would have been like if he had met her long, long ago, before Ryan O'Connor, before David Warner, before the anger had taken hold of her as it had taken hold of him. He pulled her closer, basking in the heat of her body. How vastly different his life would have been.

The room, he noticed for the first time, was bathed in a soft pink glow from a small lamp on her bureau. From the window behind the bed three thin rays of white light emanated from a street lamp outside the house next door. They gleamed like moonbeams through the nearly closed wooden shutters and shone on her closet door. She stirred and sat up and put her hand on his chest and smiled at him. "I'm going to take a shower."

"Keep the water running and give me a holler when you're done."

She bent down and kissed him. "OK." Then she stood up and opened the closet, and the three rays of light flickered and fell on a rack of clothes behind her. There was something blue and something violet and something behind the two that glittered in the background. She pulled out a long white robe and wrapped herself in it. "Don't let any Brazilian girls in while I'm gone."

"I wouldn't dream of it."

She walked out of the bedroom and down the hall to the bathroom. He sat up on the edge of the bed. He didn't give himself time to think about what he was going to do, because then he knew he wouldn't do it. So he stood up quickly. Behind a blue dress and a long violet sweater, hanging on a second rack in the back of the closet, was what he hoped he hadn't seen. It was a silver skirt and a silver top and slung across them both from a hook on the wall, a silver purse shimmering in a shaft of light.

CHAPTER 28

Abby Whitman was flushed with excitement as they left the Kennedy School. "God, that was so great! She was terrific. Even if she is a Republican. Thanks so much for bringing me along."

Ursula laughed. "I love these forums. Anytime you want to come with me just call."

"I will, I will. Although I imagine Peggy Noonan is going to be hard to beat. I loved the opening line. 'So here I am in the belly of the beast.' That brought the house down."

"Well, it's true. Except for Mark and a handful of other conservatives around here she's in alien territory. Yet she got a standing ovation at the end. Not bad for one of Ronald Reagan's favorite speechwriters."

They stopped at the corner of Eliot Street and waited for the red light. "So Professor Stevenson will be with her at dinner?"

Ursula nodded. "Sure. They're taking her to Bombay Club for a night of Indian cuisine and political strategy. Two of the guys are Romney people. They'll be hitting Noonan up for all kinds of speechwriting ideas."

"I was surprised your friend Rosario wasn't there tonight. You know, for someone who teaches history and politics."

The light changed and they hurried across. "He usually is. But I haven't seen too much of Rob recently. He's been involved in some...some educational projects that have been taking a lot of his time."

"You must be pretty happy with Teddy's big lead. That debate really sunk Romney, in my opinion. Once they got on to federal financing of social and economic programs and current legislation in Congress, he just seemed over his head."

"He is."

They walked down Eliot and then over to Brattle Street and down the stairs to Casablanca. Ursula waited until they were settled in their booth and had started their first glass of wine. "You ready?"

"Uh, huh." Abby raised her glass. "This will help. But why tonight?"

"I think it's time. I'm pretty damn sure about who this woman is, but you haven't actually identified her yet."

"I've been ready from the start."

"I know you have. But I had to make sure she was what we thought she was."

"And?"

"And you were right. Rebecca Scott was abused both psychologically and physically by her husband. But unlike what I suspected when we talked during lunch at Toscano, David Warner is not the guilty party. Their marriage has come to an end and they have separated. But it was not abuse that caused it. The abuse occurred many years earlier with her first husband, a man she escaped from and a man she hasn't seen in sixteen years."

Abby's eyes widened. "Sixteen years! That's such a long time to keep…" She shook her head. "I don't mean a long time to be angry, a long time to hold onto resentment…but to explode like that so suddenly. To be carrying a weapon."

"Well, in her defense, there is a reason. That is, a reason to be carrying a weapon. Not necessarily a reason for gunning down Charles Devir in cold blood. After an absence of sixteen years, in fact while she was still living with Warner in Newton, this man began to contact her again. He begged her for forgiveness and asked if it were possible to meet their daughter. This is the older girl who has just turned eighteen. Rebecca believes this is a ruse. That he hasn't changed at all and that he presents a real and present danger."

"And what do you think?"

"Without going into a lot of detail, I believe the man has indeed changed. That he does not present any danger whatsoever."

"So you think that this woman is…possibly disturbed in some way? Disturbed enough to gun a man down? Even though she saved two lives by doing it?"

Ursula was quiet for a moment. "Assume for a second that your woman was an off-duty police officer or a transit cop or an NRA gal coming home from shooting practice. How would they have handled the situation?"

"Differently, I'm sure. They might not have taken Devir's verbal assault so personally."

"Exactly. They would have used their weapon to warn him off and probably only fired if he had threatened them physically. Yet your woman fired three shots into him with a deliberate coolness that boggles the mind."

A look of ambivalence crossed Abby's face. "Don't think I haven't thought of that. The coolness, I mean. The lack of anger. The lack of passion. One thinks of justifiable crimes of passion, but…"

"But this wasn't one of them."

Abby responded with a tone of conviction bordering almost on righteousness. "Well, it was justifiable, all right. That abusive, ignorant bastard got what he deserved. Everything he did was a crime and he never got any punishment. Not until that night when she arrived on the scene. But yes, Ursula, you're right. Not a crime of passion. At least not that night. But the act itself may have been driven by her fear that her first husband would find her, and that she and her daughter would be in danger. So that fear and anger must have been present the night of the shooting. But I do know one thing. The actual act itself, no matter how coolly performed, saved Jeannie Devir's life. For me, it was just one night. But for her, it was going to be forever. It was only a matter of time before he killed her. You know that, Ursula."

Ursula nodded. "I know, Abby. I know." She paused for a moment and glanced at her watch. "We still have some time, so we need to talk about your plan to help Rebecca's children. The last time we met, you were talking about setting up some kind of a trust for Rebecca's kids. Where, exactly, is all that at?"

Abby leaned forward. "That, I'm afraid, is a lot more complicated than I thought. Not financially. That's the easy part. But the legal issue is going to take some time. My lawyer says that…"

Ursula held up her hand. "I want you to listen very carefully to what I have to say. I hope you've thought about what I told you that afternoon at Toscano. A smart cop in the

Cambridge Police Department could get a district attorney to subpoena whatever legal device your lawyer comes up with should this woman ever come under suspicion. Don't entertain any fantasies to the contrary. And your lawyer is probably asking you some pretty intrusive questions as to what this is all about, right?"

Abby laughed. "Right. That's what's holding things up."

Ursula stared into her eyes. "I'm afraid you're going to have to hold things up permanently. You have to quash this thing now. David Warner loves his children and they love him. He is a man with ample financial resources who will provide for his children's needs. There is, however, a way you can pay your debt to Rebecca Scott. Mark and I are about to contribute to an organization that counsels and aids women who are victims of abuse, and which also focuses on families in trouble. Families for whom it is still possible to prevent abuse, where angry, confused, bitter men can get help before they turn into Charles Devirs. In a real sense—I don't mean to sound religious—this group seems to be in the business of saving souls. But this organization is in desperate need of financial support. Is that something that interests you?"

"Yes, absolutely."

"You will not have to set up a trust, and I can handle the details for you. Are you comfortable with that?"

"Of course, Ursula. Of course."

Ursula glanced once more at her watch. "Good. One more thing before we go. Please listen to me. You need to back away from this woman now. Do not in any way do anything that will link you to her. I know she saved Jeannie Devir's life. I know she may have saved you from a severe beating. But she is not your guardian angel. She did not come to your rescue for any personal reasons, so therefore you must have no personal connection to her. One thing remains to be done. We need to be sure that the woman we are talking about really is Rebecca Scott. You need to identify her, and then you need to cut the cord. Got it?"

Abby stared back and then nodded her head. "Got it."

"Hungry?"

"Not really."

"Then let's get it done. Rebecca Scott is a clinical data manager at Pharmaceutical Data Research here in Harvard Square. Are you familiar with that line of work?"

"Sure. One of my college roommates who worked at Amgen left to become a clinical data manager at Excel Data in San Francisco. PDR is a competitor."

"OK. So here's the deal and here's why tonight's the night." Ursula pulled an event sheet out of her purse and slid it across the table. "Rebecca Scott from PDR, Diane Perry from Excel Data, and Michael Randall from the FDA will be the main presenters this evening at a clinical data quality conference at The Charles Hotel. The conference ends at 9:00. As it breaks up, all you have to do is get close enough to look at her. You'll be surrounded by conference attendees, so there's none of the pressure or discomfort of a one-on-one situation. Ready?"

"Ready." Abby finished her wine and laughed nervously. "Ready and feeling lots of pressure and discomfort."

Ursula smiled and paid the tab and they walked outside and up the stairs. Abby took a deep breath. Ursula put her arm through hers, and they walked up Brattle and then over toward the hotel. "Relax. All you have to do is look."

Abby stopped in front of Charlie's Kitchen. "Whew! I'm a wreck. Let's duck in here and get the double cheeseburger and a beer instead."

Ursula laughed and they crossed the street, walked over
to the hotel, went into the lobby and took the elevator to the
third floor. The conference was just ending and groups of
people, talking loudly and animatedly, brushed past them on
all sides and streamed out into the corridor. Ursula felt Abby
grip her arm and turned to her left. Rebecca Scott, dressed
in black and carrying a briefcase, emerged from the crowd
like a phantom. Ursula stared at the woman, astonished once
again by her beauty, and as Rebecca passed by, she glanced
at Ursula quickly, enigmatically, as if she were searching for
something just beyond her grasp. It was a look that almost
verged on recognition.

Ursula turned back to Abby and found her pale and trembling. "I need some air. Let's get out of here. Right now." She
grabbed Ursula's arm again and they rushed out of the hotel
in silence, back to Brattle Street, and still without speaking,
moved rapidly away from the Square until they were standing
in front of St. John's Chapel. Then Abby looked around and
pulled Ursula into the shadows of the trees. "It's her, Ursula.
It's her! My God. Did you see her face? She didn't recognize me
at all. I can't believe it."

Ursula gazed at her. "On that night, Abby, she wasn't looking at you. She was looking at Devir. All you and Jeannie got
was a passing glance. That was enough. Her eyes were trained
on Devir like a laser. You can be sure of it. And you can be sure
of something else. This is a very dangerous woman to be associated with. Do you understand?" Ursula turned for a moment
and stared through the darkness across Brattle and down Ash
Street toward where Rosario lived.

Abby sighed. "I know that, Ursula. I'm not a fool. But I'm
glad I saw her. Isn't she stunning? I'm so glad I saw her again."

Ursula turned back. "Just let that be the last you see of her."

"It will be."

Ursula shook her lightly by the shoulders. "You've got to keep clear of her."

"I will. I promise."

Ursula led her out of the dark grounds and back along Brattle Street. "Speaking of promises, I have a vague memory of promising you dinner. Hungry? I certainly am."

"I could use another glass of wine. That's for sure."

———

After dinner, they walked through the Square and said good night at the corner of Church Street. Ursula waited until Abby had crossed Massachusetts Avenue and disappeared into Harvard Yard. Then she turned quickly and headed toward Brattle and over to Ash Street and Ash Street Place. She knocked on the door and waited. No luck. She rang the bell. Still no luck. She sat down on his steps. It was Thursday. Sometimes he did his old guy walk at night. She'd wait. Ten minutes later, a hooded figure rounded the corner, his breath visible in the cold evening air. "Hey, sweaty guy! I didn't see you at The Forum tonight. Peggy Noonan was speaking."

"What! I didn't know that. Shit! Why didn't you call me?"

"You usually call me on these events. You're the Harvard Square guy. Something must be distracting you, my friend."

"There you go being nosy again, counselor." He sat down beside her on the step. He was still breathing heavily from the exercise.

She put her arm around his shoulder. "Happy birthday, Rob."

"Thanks, Ursie. But the least said about this one the better."

"Remember when we used to celebrate our birthdays?"

"Well, we had something to celebrate. Now we're officially codgers."

She laughed. "I'm still unofficial."

"Not for long. Mark in November and you in December. Like ducks in a row. We'll have a party for the three of us in December. How's that?"

"It sounds good, Rosie. Sounds like fun."

He looked at her from under the hood like some medieval monk peering out of his cowl. "The Forum's usually over by eight o'clock, Ursie. What have you been up to?"

"I took Abby with me to see Peggy Noonan. Afterwards, we went out for a drink." She paused. "Then we went over to the Charles Hotel to what is known as a clinical data quality conference." The hood was far enough over his eyes so she couldn't read his expression. "I thought it was time for Abby Whitman to meet Rebecca Scott."

He pulled the hood back and stared at her. "And?"

"It's her, Rob. She's the one. There's no doubt about it."

He was very quiet for a moment and then he nodded. "I know."

"Jesus! How long have you known?"

"Since Saturday night. Five days. So I guess you and I have to have a talk, don't we? Come on. Walk with me."

"Seeing Rebecca Scott up close, I now see the difference between her and Eve. It's mostly in the eyes. Eve's eyes are blue. Eve's eyes have a soft loveliness. Rebecca's eyes are gray, tigerish, suspicious, and she glanced at me almost as if she recognized me from somewhere. Has she seen that photograph in your study? The one of the four of us at Singing Beach?"

"Uh, huh. But she was concentrating on Eve. On how much they looked alike. I wouldn't worry about it."

"She is, of course, devastatingly beautiful." He nodded again. She tried not to say anything else, but she couldn't help herself. "Just make sure she's not too devastating."

He rose and gave her his hand and pulled her up. They moved away from the stairs and down the street and headed toward the river.

CHAPTER 29

L inda Friedman, the history department secretary, grabbed his sleeve as he headed into the meeting. "Rob! I think one of your kids is on the phone. Slightly hysterical, if you ask me. Don't you ever ease up on the homework?"

He smiled at her. "It's good for them, Linda. Besides, they may whine and complain, but they don't go hysterical."

"This one has."

He ducked into her office and took the call. "Mr. Rosario? It's Emily Warner. You gotta help me. I'm sorry to call you at work and everything but I figured classes were over by now or otherwise I wouldn't have bothered you. The thing is I think Mom's going to do something crazy."

"Crazy? Slow down, Em. Take a deep breath. What do you mean?"

"Jackson Foster grabbed Lizzie in the hall today, and she kicked him and he knocked her books all over the floor and then some kids broke it up and then Foster said he'd get her af- ter school and Lizzie yelled at him to go ahead and try, so after school a couple of her guy friends walked us home so she'd be OK and then she called Dad and he came and got us and took us back to Newton for the night. So meanwhile, without telling Dad, Mom called school and raised hell, and they've set up an appointment for her with Foster and his parents and the assistant principal for 3:30."

"That's pretty unusual for a school to respond that quickly. She must have been pretty convincing."

"*Convincing* isn't the word. I don't know exactly what she said, but she really put the pressure on. So what I was thinking is if there is any way you could get there in time to go with her..."

"Your mother might not be too pleased to see me just waltz into a meeting I haven't been invited to. I work for Liberty, not Cambridge. What's my ticket in?"

"I've already taken care of that. I persuaded her that since you saw Foster's fight with Lizzie on Chauncy Street and you had to intervene, that you're a witness to the way he harasses her."

"And your mother agreed?"

"After a while, yeah."

"After a while, huh?"

"Yup."

"OK, Em. I'm on my way."

"Thanks so much for everything, Mr. Rosario. I mean it."

Route 2 was jammed all the way to Fresh Pond, so he took his alternate route through Belmont Center and then over to Huron Avenue and down to Cambridge Street to the high school. When he reached the front door he could see Rebecca in the lobby with Jerome Johnson, the assistant principal. He pulled it open and walked in and Jerome hooted at him. "Robert Rosario! You're not the witness Ms. Scott has been talking about, I hope."

Rosario laughed. "Guilty as charged, brother."

Jerome grabbed him in a bear hug and turned to Rebecca. "Pretty unreliable witness you got here, Ms. Scott. Nah, just kidding. We go back to the seventies, me and Rob. I was teaching at Roxbury High, and he interviewed me for the *Globe* about the busing plan that was to go into effect the following year. We were the black school and Southie was the white school, and the idea was to mix us all up and things would be just hunky-dory. Didn't quite work out that way. Did it, Robert?"

"I'm afraid not."

Jerome smiled. "On the other hand, it turned this guy into a teacher. So that was something."

Rebecca nodded but her eyes were steeled for battle. "Yes, Mr. Johnson. That was something. He's helped my younger daughter with a couple of her assignments. I've seen what he can do."

Jerome's expression grew serious. "I'm on your side on this issue. I will do everything in my power to help you, and as I think you will soon discover, this boy is going to be punished. But a word of warning, Ms. Scott. I know you're angry. You have every right to be. But be careful what you say to Jackson Foster's father. He can get quite litigious."

Rebecca crossed her arms and glowered. "The reality is his son is a bully. He can't sue his way out of that. In any event, maybe Mr. Foster deserves a blinding, stinging blow that will make him forget he ever heard the word *litigious* in the first place."

She looked away toward the office, and Jerome glanced at Rosario and rolled his eyes. "Well, be that as it may, it's time for us to go in."

The three of them walked down the hall and entered the office. Jerome sat down and Rebecca and Rosario took the last two chairs in a semi-circle that surrounded the assistant principal's desk. Jerome opened the meeting. "This is Rebecca Scott, Lizzie's mother, and this is Mr. Rosario from Liberty High School, a witness to a previous incident involving Jackson."

Rosario looked over at Foster's parents who seemed taken aback by the mention of any previous incident. The boy glanced at Rosario uneasily and looked at the floor, and the father, clearly worried, raised his hand like a confused student. "I was under the impression that this meeting would take place in the guidance office as our previous ones have."

Jerome stared at him. "This meeting is taking place here because we're done with guidance. Your son's behavior hasn't changed at all. This is the fourth young woman he has bullied and harassed. Three of those cases, handled by my predecessor and Mrs. Wilton of the guidance department, resulted in your son being suspended. I took this job because the principal and the superintendent assured me that this school system meant business about creating an educational atmosphere where students feel safe and where they can learn. I have consulted with both the principal and the superintendent, and they have given me their complete support for the action I am about to take. I regret to inform you, Mr. and Mrs. Foster, that I am expelling Jackson from Cambridge High School as of today."

The Fosters flinched, stunned into abject silence. The father, impeccably groomed and fashionably attired, cast a glazed look past Jerome to some invisible point on the wall. Rosario stared at him, hoping for some kind of reaction. Then he realized what he was looking for. He was looking for shame. But there was no shame in this man's bland, expressionless eyes, and it occurred to him that shame seemed to have disappeared as a public emotion. Shame wasn't in style anymore.

The boy looked as if he had been hit by a sledgehammer. As if he couldn't believe he had heard the word *expel*. As if the word *suspend* were going to fall automatically from the assistant principal's lips as it had so often in the past. The mother too seemed immobilized, but Rosario could see a mounting anger taking control of her features. Slowly, she rose to her feet, the color rushing to her face. She shook a long bony finger at Jerome. "My son is an honors student! A Merit Scholar! You can't expel a *Merit Scholar!*"

Rosario glanced at Jerome. Professionally, the two of them had been baptized in the racial politics of Boston and had often heard the white complaint that blacks possessed a sense of entitlement. But in Rosario's experience, nothing could match the sense of entitlement harbored by affluent white parents who thought their children more gifted than others.

Foster rose and moved his wife aside. "Calm down, Eliza. I'll handle this. I'm not quite sure, Mr. Johnson, if you or your superiors are quite prepared for the legal challenge I intend to mount."

Jerome smiled. "Oh, I think we are, Mr. Foster."

The man lifted his chin in a supercilious, smug little pose. "*Doctor* Foster."

Rebecca had been unusually quiet, temporarily mollified, no doubt, by Jerome's swift and devastating dispensation of justice. But Foster's smirking, pompous insistence on his professional designation loosened her tongue. "Are you a physician, Mr. Foster?"

"No, I am a psychologist. I happen to hold a doctorate..."

"Well, well! Aren't we impressive? A doctorate of all things! Who would have guessed? And speaking of guessing...guess what, *Mister* Foster. Doctorates are a dime a dozen these days. You're in Cambridge, remember? There's a Ph.D. on every street corner. If you can't deliver babies or cure diseases, you're out of luck in the title business."

Foster began spluttering with rage. "Nobody speaks to me that way! Now all of you listen to me. I have tested my son thoroughly, and I can tell you as a trained psychologist that he suffers from Attention Deficit Disorder."

Rosario and Jerome groaned in unison and Rebecca went after him. "If you think you're going to excuse your son's bullying behavior with a quack diagnosis like that you're dreaming."

"Quack diagnosis!"

"That's right. It's a designer disease."

"What the hell is that supposed to mean?"

"What it means is that it only seems to afflict upper-middle-class children whose parents can't seem to discipline them. You psychologists ought to be ashamed of yourselves. You dig up phony diseases, list every possible human frailty as a symptom, and then start pumping drugs into kids. At least give your son a diagnosis that fits his personality. You know, like *psychopath*?"

Now the boy was on his feet too. Rage flashed in his eyes and seeing it at once, his father held up his hand. "Let us see if we can understand what's going on here. Let us see if we can approach this situation reasonably and calmly like intelligent people."

Rosario watched him. The man, no doubt, had talked his way out of situations like this before. Rosario could only guess at the number of times, but it was clear from his practiced delivery and the smooth flow of his voice and the way he spun his web of words through a fog of jargon, that he was a nimble rhetorician with a well-stocked repertoire of tricks and devices. There was a sleekness about him, an aura of the performing seal who spins and balances unctuous phrases instead of brightly colored balls. As he neared the end of his speech, he began marching out a procession of educational and psychological clichés, all lined up like little foot soldiers to do their part in the battle for Jackson Foster, a misunderstood youth deserving both special care and deep sympathy. Rosario couldn't deny the man his due. It was a masterful performance. Then, turning sad and sentimental, Foster looked pleadingly at Jerome Johnson and whispered with a theatrical flourish, "Well...I guess I don't know what else to say."

Jerome stared at him. "Well...then why don't you say, *Goodbye?*"

The utter finality in Jerome's deep, rumbling voice left the man dumbstruck, and he staggered back toward his chair. Suddenly, his son took a step toward Rebecca, and Rosario got ready to move. "This is all your fault, you fucking bitch!"

The father jumped forward and grabbed his son's arm. "Calm down, Jackson! You're playing right into their hands using language like that. Calm down."

"Fuck you, Dad! I won't calm down. I'll say whatever I like." He stared at Rebecca, a lascivious, demonic grin replacing the anger. "I'll say this for you, Mrs. Warner. You're a real looker, all right. You're even sexier than your daughter. Hell, you're a real piece of ass."

Rosario waited, holding back his own anger, resisting the urge to deliver that blinding, stinging blow Rebecca had mentioned outside the office, and he could sense Rebecca doing the same. Together with Jerome, they were letting the kid do just what his father had warned him not to do. Play right into their hands.

The kid shook himself free of his father's grip. "You know what I'd like to do to you, Mrs. Warner? I'd like to fuck the hell out of you." Then a rabid, vicious look came into his eyes and the lust was gone. "But here's what I think I'll do instead."

In a split second, before Rosario could move, Jackson Foster threw a ferocious roundhouse at Rebecca. Instantly, she leapt out of her seat, grabbed his right wrist with her right hand, and gripped his elbow with her left. Rosario, transfixed by her speed and agility, anticipated in a flash the wrenching twist that would break the boy's arm. But she took him by surprise, and holding Jackson Foster at bay, she reared back and kicked him in the groin so hard that the boy crouched forward grasping his genitals, his mouth a circle of soundless pain. She waited a moment, stepping back like an artist ready to finish a masterpiece. Then her fist shot forward and landed just below his jawbone, sending him sprawling to the floor. She stood over him in triumph. "Looks like our *Merit Scholar* won't be fucking anybody tonight."

B ack at Chauncy Street, the fire in her eyes was almost searing. But the only visible signs of what she had done were a bruised right knuckle and a flush in her complexion. "What did Mr. Johnson say to you after I stormed out? That I had ignored his warning and made his life more difficult?"

He looked at her across the table and smiled. "Not at all. After the Fosters dragged their wounded from the battlefield, he shook his head and laughed out loud. 'What a woman!' he cried. 'Where'd you find her, Rosario? You got any soul sisters like that for me?'"

"Stop it."

"I'm not kidding. Those were his exact words. You made quite an impression in there, Ms. Scott. Especially on the Foster family."

She folded her arms. "I really don't care about the impression I made on the family. It's the impression on Jackson Foster that counts. And he better get the message, or the next time he'll be sorry he ever saw the light of day."

"From what I saw there isn't much more you can do to him without getting yourself into a great deal of trouble."

"Maybe it would be worth it." Anger suffused her face, honing her already sharpened features into an ominous fury. "If this beating doesn't work, I'm perfectly capable of taking things a step further."

"I believe you."

"And I have the means to do so."

They stared at each other. He knew then that it was time to tell her the truth. To tell her that he knew what she had done. It was the only way he could convince himself that she wouldn't take that further step, and it had to be done now, for there was a wildness in her eyes, a look of incipient panic that told him she realized she had gone too far. That she had let her anger betray herself into telling him too much.

He leaned close to her. "You have the means to do so?" She looked away. "I certainly hope the means is not a weapon. Especially not a gun. Because if it is, it puts you in danger of not just losing your liberty, but your family. Your girls."

She looked back at him, the anger momentarily eclipsed by an expression of great sorrow. "Don't you think I haven't thought of that?"

"Well, keep thinking. That's what you have to do. Keep thinking long and hard until the thinking overcomes the emotion. Don't be a fool. You need to get rid of that gun." Suddenly, they had passed beyond any discussion as to the existence of the weapon. It was simply a fact. "It has to go. It's what we Catholics call the near occasion of sin. Without the gun, you won't do it."

A vague, almost amused expression lightened her eyes. "I thought you were an ex-Catholic."

"Well, when it comes to sin, once a Catholic, always a Catholic. But listen to me, Rebecca. You have to get control of yourself right now before it's too late. Give me the weapon." She looked away again. "You're going to have to trust me on this, Rebecca."

Her hands were trembling. "I'm still shaking with anger."

"Another reason for you to give up the means." He put his hands over hers. "You know, it's a strange thing."

"What is?"

"Something we've never discussed."

"What's that?"

"The case of Charles Devir."

Quickly, she pulled her hands away, but he took them back. "Here's a violent crime that took place in our general neighborhood. Just a few blocks from here. An unexplained killing that's been all over the media, yet it's never come up between us. I bring it up now because imagine, Rebecca, if the weapon you have happens to be a .380 caliber handgun. Imagine, should you decide to take things a step further with Jackson Foster—or Ryan O'Connor, should he show up—that an enterprising Cambridge police officer discovers that both Charles Devir and the new victim were shot with the same caliber gun. All the officer has to do is approach the case from a different angle. Imagine further that despite the witnesses' description of the killer as a brunette in a red dress, he begins to wonder if perhaps—just perhaps—those two young women, out of some misguided sense of gratitude, had the presence of mind to give the police a false description of the woman who shot Devir. Imagine then that this same officer decides to revisit the stores, restaurants and bars in the vicinity of the crime to dig deeper than the investigators did on the night of the murder. It might not take him long to connect the prime suspect in the new shooting to the unidentified suspect in the killing of Charles Devir."

She removed her hands from his and hugged her arms close to her chest as if she were suddenly very cold. A look of desperation came into her eyes. "Why are you bringing this up?"

"Because I'm worried about what you might do, and I'm worried about how the police might respond. So let's remove the means before it's too late."

She placed both hands on the table and pushed herself up slowly and stood looking down at him. "I guess you're right. I guess I am going to have to trust you." She came to his side and put her right arm around his shoulder and looked down into his eyes. Then she put her left hand on the side of his face. "But you know, Rob. I don't *have* to trust you. I already do."

She walked into the bedroom. He could still feel the touch of her hand on his face. Then she came back and handed him the weapon and he took it, and he remembered the .45 he had with him on that crazy trip to Vietnam so many years ago. Plenty of people on both sides got away with murder in that place. Why should this place be any different? And sometimes murder was the right thing to do. It certainly was in the case of Charles Devir. He leaned over and put the gun into his briefcase behind his folders and papers and books and then zipped it tightly.

She sat down again and held his hand. "What are you going to do with it?"

"Get it out of here first. Then you and I will go somewhere and get rid of it for good."

"You seem so sure of yourself. As if there will never be any repercussions."

"Well, you never know, do you? So all you can do is either act or not act."

The doorbell rang and they both jumped. She stood up and looked out the window near the door. "Looks like the repercussions have arrived."

She walked to the entry hall and opened the door. Rosario heard a man's voice. "Ms. Scott?"

"That's right."

"I'm Officer Curran. I think you know why I'm here."

"I think so. Please come in."

They walked into the room and Rosario stood up and shook his hand. He was a young cop, probably in his late twenties. Rebecca gestured to one of the empty chairs, and Officer Curran perched on its edge, alert and attentive. Rosario sat down again and felt the bulk of his briefcase against his knee. Rebecca stood behind her chair with her hands resting on its back. "Mr. Rosario is an old friend of the family."

The young cop smiled. "So, Mr. Rosario, what do you make of Ms. Scott's performance this afternoon at Cambridge High School?"

It was an unexpected question, so he paused a moment. "What do I make of it? I guess I'll be very careful about making Ms. Scott angry."

The cop laughed and then looked up at Rebecca. "I'm not here because I want to be, Ms. Scott. The eyewitness account by Assistant Principal Johnson acquits you in my eyes, and we've seen Jackson Foster before on a number of juvenile offenses. His credibility is zero. But the deal is that the kid's parents want to press assault charges against you, so here I am. I need you to stop by the station tomorrow."

"Should I bring a lawyer?"

"You can if you want, but I don't think his parents will persist once we make clear the number of other aggrieved mothers and fathers who will be in your corner. As far as the assault charge goes, it appears you were simply defending yourself." He shook his head. "Although according to Mr. Johnson, that was some defense. The Celtics could use a defense like that."

Rebecca stood back and folded her arms. "Do you have any children, officer?"

"Two. A five-year-old boy and a three-year-old girl."

"I have two also. Both girls. And I don't want the likes of Jackson Foster harassing my daughter."

The cop stood up. "I'll see to it that he doesn't, Ms. Scott. But if he tries, leave it to me. Based on what I heard, next time you might just kill the little bastard."

She nodded. "I hear you, officer."

"See you tomorrow. Ten o'clock all right?"

"I'll clear it with my boss."

"You don't have to tell him what it's for. If you like, we can be arguing about a traffic violation. I'm pretty sure we can wrap things up fairly quickly."

"Thank you so much, officer."

"Nice meeting you, Mr. Rosario." They stood and shook hands again. "Looks to me like you better behave yourself with this lady."

Rosario laughed. "I always have. After all, I don't want to end up like Jackson Foster."

When the door closed behind Officer Curran, Rebecca collapsed in her chair. "My heart is pounding."

"Mine too."

"All I could think of was your enterprising Cambridge police officer."

"Well, I think for now you're in the clear. But Officer Curran strikes me as a young man who given the right circumstances might prove to be just the enterprising kind. The day we went house hunting in Wellesley, there was an article in the *Cambridge Chronicle* by a reporter who was obviously searching for a story, pursuing a new angle on the Devir case. She reviewed all the police reports and found an account of another witness, who claimed to have seen a beautiful blonde woman in a silver dress with a silver purse slung over her shoulder leaving the area shortly after the shooting."

He stopped and waited for a reaction. But she remained silent, her gaze fixed on his like a woman in a trance. "Luckily— for this beautiful blonde woman—the witness is a local street person who was drunk the night of the murder, and who also suffers from a form of schizophrenia that causes vivid hallucinations. So the reporter discarded the witness as not credible. But let's say for a moment that other people saw this woman. People who didn't see this article, buried as it was at the end of the first section of the paper. People who saw her but didn't connect her in any way with the crime, because they believed the reports in the media. They had one image in their minds. A brunette in a red dress." He reached across the table and took her hand. "You said you trusted me. Now you're going to have to trust me some more."

"About what?"

"About Charles Devir." He paused and looked into her eyes. "I know, Rebecca. I *know.*"

She stared back at him for a long time, a wary, watchful look about her. He expected her to pull her hand away, but instead she tightened her grip. "How? The gun?"

"Not just the gun. Last Saturday night you left the door to your closet open after you put on your robe and went to take a shower. The light from the street lamp outside your house shone right onto your clothes. Right onto the silver dress and the silver purse hanging across it."

She loosened her hold but left her hand in his. "That's sort of an invasion of privacy, don't you think?"

"No, I don't think. You left the door open and I saw what I saw. In any event, let's not quibble about invasions of privacy when we have a murder on our hands."

"*Our* hands?"

"That's right. We're going to have to get rid of the silver dress and the purse too. I know an old pub in Salem with a couple of dumpsters in back that will do just fine."

Gradually, the apprehension faded from her eyes. "Why Salem? You know some other witches besides me?"

He laughed. "Because Salem is on the way to the place where we're going to get rid of the gun."

She ran the fingers of her free hand through his hair. "You seem to be just accepting what you know. It's so hard for me to believe."

He kissed her softly and leaned back and shook his head. "All these black kids killing each other every week in Roxbury and Dorchester. If white kids had access to weapons and drugs when we were young, there would have been plenty of killings like that. If I had gotten my hands on a gun, I would have killed those three bastards the day after they beat us up and cut my face open. Not a doubt in my mind. Lucky for me, I didn't. Lucky I didn't have the means."

She was quiet for some time, and then she leaned forward and stared at him. "Can I ask you a question?"

"Sure."

"Why, given what you know, are you taking a chance on me?"

He smiled. "I don't know. I guess there's no accounting for some people's tastes."

A brief smile passed her lips. "I guess I was looking for a more convincing answer."

"OK. I confess. It's your sweet, complacent nature, your fervent commitment to non-violence, and especially, your ability, soon to be put into action, to use your thinking to overcome your feelings. How's that?"

She laughed. Actually laughed given everything that had happened and everything he had said to her. "That's better. I guess I'll have to live up to that image, won't I?"

"Yes, you will. Well, maybe not the sweet and compliant stuff, but everything else, yes. Absolutely. Otherwise, you can't expect me to take that chance, can you?"

"No. No, I can't, Rob."

"All right, then. We have to move fast. Right now. I need to use your phone to call an old friend and then we're out of here."

She frowned. "A friend?"

"That's right. A friend so close that I can completely rely on his discretion and his loyalty. But above all, a friend we can *both* trust." He took her beautiful face in his hands and pressed his forehead to hers. "Grab your broomstick. We're heading north."

CHAPTER 30

Together, they looked down at the great expanse of the harbor. The water glittered in the setting sunlight and splashed in small waves against the few remaining sailboats. Overhead, orange clouds drifted through a swath of dark blue sky. She put her arm through his and they breathed in the cool, salty smell of the sea. "This is so intoxicating. I can't believe I've never been here before." She held him tighter. "The first night we made love you promised to take me here and now you have. I guess that makes you a man of your word, Robert Rosario."

"Does that mean you doubted me at first?"

She laughed. "I didn't know what to make of you at first."

He smiled and drew his arm around her waist. "The feeling was mutual. Believe me." Behind them, the bells of Abbot Hall began to chime, echoing through the ancient village. "Time to go. You ready?"

She threw her arms around his neck and kissed him. Then she leaned back and looked into his eyes and nodded her head.

H arry Shapiro tugged at his ample moustache and then leaned forward on his elbows. "He was there for a month! Can you imagine such a thing? His tour of duty in Korea is over." He waved his hands in the air. "Over! All he has to do is board the friggin' plane and come home. Instead, he wants to come to Nam to see what it's all about. For history! Hah!"

Rebecca smiled. "My older daughter was dumbfounded when he told us."

Harry leaned back. "As well she should be. We were too. You should have seen the other guys in my boat. They thought he was nuts. He spends two weeks with the 25th Infantry Division, one week in Saigon with this guy Finn who works for *Stars and Stripes*, and another week with me rollin' on the river."

Rosario took a drink of his Bass Ale and put it down on the table. "Rollin' is right. The grunts I was with in the 25th had an objective. Finn's work was propaganda, not journalism. But at least there was a purpose to it. Whatever the reason for that reckless joyride up the Mekong River was, it totally escaped me."

Harry took a swig of his Coke. "Don't listen to him, Rebecca. I was one of the few guys on the river who knew what he was doing."

Rosario laughed. "Yeah. Which was what exactly? Trading alcohol, cigarettes, and copies of *Playboy* for Cambodian weed?"

Harry protested. "Nonsense. Those were perfectly legitimate business deals. Culturally acceptable economic transactions. I was simply an entrepreneur at war. Rosario expected some action when he got on board and was disappointed because he never got shot at. Most guys would have been grateful.

Most guys would have appreciated the evasive actions taken by a skillful pilot."

What Rosario had not told Rebecca Scott was that Harry really was a skillful pilot. Two months after Rosario had gone home, the navy decided to use the PT boats to block the Viet Cong's supply lines, and for Harry and his men the jungle trader days came to an abrupt end. The party was over. Now it was time for violence and blood and the ultimate sacrifice men make in war. But Harry, despite his bronze star for heroism, didn't like to talk about those times in front of strangers. He always tried to keep it light, and Rosario always helped him pull it off.

Rosario glanced at Rebecca and shook his head. "All I remember is climbing on board in the middle of the night and spending the next six days smoking dope and drinking beer. Luckily, there was nothing even vaguely military about the operation, for if there had been, it would have been all over. To this day, I have no idea where we went or why we went there. It's been over twenty-five years and he still won't tell me."

Harry grinned and drained his Coke and slid the glass across the table until it clinked against Rosario's beer mug. "Ready to roll?"

Rosario looked at him. "Just about. I have to make a phone call first. A father of one of my kids is all bent out of shape."

Harry laughed. "You gotta let up on those poor kids, Rob. Don't you know that homework hurts their sense of self-esteem?"

"Not in my class it doesn't. Hard work builds character. Remember, Harry?"

"I remember. But I don't think that line of thinking washes with some of the younger parents these days."

Rebecca finished her wine. "It matters to me."

Harry nodded. "That's good. I worry sometimes about these kids. Too many of them are spoiled rotten."

Rosario stood up. "Why don't you take Rebecca down to the dock, and I'll meet you on board *Rabbit II* in five minutes."

Harry looked up at him and smiled. "Are you sure you trust me alone with this ravishing creature?"

Rosario laughed. "It's not her I'm worried about. Watch your step, Harry. Say the wrong thing to this one and she'll toss you overboard."

He held up his hands in mock surrender. "OK, OK."

Rebecca pushed her chair back and slipped her arm through the straps of her shoulder bag. "*Rabbit II*? That's an odd name for a boat."

Harry stood up and ran his hand through his hair. "Well, we won't get into that one."

Rosario held out his hand and Rebecca took it. He pulled her up gently and put his arm around her. "Sure we will, Harry. *Rabbit II* is named after Harry's PT boat."

Harry looked visibly nervous, running his hand through his hair several more times. He lowered his voice. "Come on, Rob. People know me here."

Rosario led them out to the deck overlooking the harbor and pointed down to the lights at end of the dock where Harry's boat rocked back and forth in the waves. A cold wind was blowing in from the northeast but the night was clear and a long shaft of moonlight, an undulating, radiant current, cut across the inky water. "No one can hear us out here, Harry. Did you notice, Rebecca, that Harry drinks nothing but Coke? The man has made it through almost fifty years without beer, wine, or hard liquor."

"A testament to my character."

"Not quite. Remember all the dope everyone smoked in the late sixties and early seventies? Well, Harry smoked about half of it."

Harry snorted. "Bullshit."

"Well, OK. A quarter of it. About 25% of the weed production of all of Mexico."

Harry laughed. "OK. That's a bit more accurate."

Rebecca smiled at Rosario. He put his arm around her again, feeling the weight of the gun at the bottom of her bag. "After about two or three tokes, Harry's eyes…"

Rebecca leaned against him. "Harry has very nice eyes. They're kind of like yours. Very blue."

Harry leaned on the railing and looked out across the water toward the Neck. "But I'm a Jewish blue-eyed boy. So that makes me special." He waved his hand. "With the goyim, blue eyes are a dime a dozen."

Rosario smiled to himself, remembering Rebecca's comment to Jackson Foster's father that doctorates were a dime a dozen. "Yes, well, the only thing is that when Harry got stoned his nose would wiggle and the whites of his eyes would turn bright pink, and with the way that moustache used to droop over his front teeth, he looked just like a giant rabbit in uniform. Whenever he pulled out a joint, the guys in his crew would glance at their watches and bet on how soon Harry Shapiro would disappear and Lieutenant Commander Rabbit would take over. They never had to wait long, believe me. His gunner's mate told me that a week after Harry took command of the boat, they painted a stoned Bugs Bunny on the hull and christened the ship *Rabbit*."

Rebecca looked down at the harbor. "Hence *Rabbit II*."

Harry peered at his watch. "Hence *Rabbit II*. By the way, Robert, if we're going, we have to go now. I've got an early meeting tomorrow morning. You can use the phone behind the bar. We'll meet you on the dock in five minutes."

They came back into the dining room, and Rosario noticed Rebecca shift the bag to her other shoulder as she and Harry descended the staircase. Then he turned and went over to the empty bar and picked up the telephone and punched in the number. "Hi."

"Hi, Rosie. As usual, right on time. Where are you?"

"Harry's yacht club. He just took Rebecca down to the boat."

"What does he think of her?"

He laughed. "He's having trouble keeping his eyes in his head."

"And what about you?"

"What about me?"

"I'm not worried about your eyes, Rob. It's your heart I'm concerned with."

He laughed again, this time out loud, and an elderly couple across the room looked up from their dinner. He lowered his voice. "I thought that's what you wanted, remember? I thought you were worried about my emotional well-being. About whether I had any emotions left. Now all of a sudden my heart is suspect?"

"I'm glad your heart is still working, Rob. I'm glad that you still have some feelings left. It's the object of those feelings that's got me worried."

"Well, old pal, don't worry. I'm too old to do anything crazy."

"What about tonight? Isn't that a little crazy?"

"Not really. It's something that has to be done."

"But by her and her alone. Not with any help from you."

"You got me involved, remember?"

She sighed. "Yes, of course, I remember. And I'm sorry."

"Don't be. You set out to right a wrong and then found out that the situation was a little more complicated than you thought. Do you still believe that what she did was morally justifiable?"

Ursula paused a moment. "Yes. Yes, I do. But there's no guarantee she might not do something like that again."

"Well, you're right on that point. There are certainly no guarantees in life."

"Well sure, but..."

"But what?"

"I don't know. Just take care of yourself."

"That's what David Warner told me."

"Well, he was her husband. He should know."

"Suddenly you're on his side?"

"No, Rosie. I'm on your side."

<hr/>

Rabbit II raced right down the middle of the harbor, its engine roaring behind them and its prow slicing through the black water. Harry turned and grinned and then shouted through the wind and the spray. "Barbary pirates up ahead, Ensign Rosario! Hold on to that fair lady!"

Rosario shouted back at him. "Full steam ahead, Commander Rabbit! Don't fire 'till you see the pinks of their eyes!"

Harry laughed and turned and gunned the engine, and the cold wind rushed into them, lashing their faces and driving Rosario and Rebecca Scott close together. He gripped the rail with both hands and felt her body behind him, her arms tight around his waist and holding fast. They flew past Crocker

Park and the Town Wharf, and as they approached Fort Sewall, Harry waved them up to the bow and shouted out the locations of the islands up ahead. Then he swung the boat to the right in a wide arc, the hull thumping against the waves as they headed out into the deeper waters of Massachusetts Bay.

It was time. He touched her hand and she turned and looked at him and they stared at each other. Then she leaned forward and shouted to Harry. "I'm going to the back of the boat to look at the moonlight on the water! It's beautiful!"

"Take Rob with you! It's slippery back there!"

"I want to go alone!"

"Well, then be careful! Hold onto the rail!"

Then she turned back to go but Rosario followed her and caught her by the wrist. She leaned into him, her head against his chest and he whispered into her ear. "I'm coming back with you."

She glanced past him to make sure they were out of Harry's hearing. Then she looked into his eyes and shook her head. "Sorry, I like to operate on my own. No accomplices. I want to guard against those repercussions we talked about. Especially any repercussions that might come back to haunt two nice blue-eyed boys like you and Harry. It's like you said. All you can do is either act or not act. And I have to act alone."

She pushed him back gently and swung the bag over her right shoulder and walked toward the stern. He turned and went up front with Harry and put his hand on his shoulder. "Thanks."

Harry waved his hand in a gesture of good-natured dismissal. "You know me. I always enjoy a little adventure, especially one with a hint of danger and surrounded in secrecy."

Rosario laughed and squeezed Harry's shoulder. "Whatever happens, there will be no danger in this for you, and in this case, your enjoyment of secrecy is particularly welcome."

"Speaking of secrets, where have you been keeping this one? She's a knockout. Where did you meet her?"

"Cambridge."

"She reminds me a little of Eve. I mean in the looks department. But this one's kind of distant, isn't she?"

"Kind of."

Harry chuckled. "I can see this is not a subject you want to get into in any detail."

Rosario shrugged. "Maybe someday."

"Are you serious about her?"

"I don't know."

Harry smiled enigmatically. Then he glanced at his watch. "Gotta get back." He looked over his shoulder. "Here comes your friend."

When Rosario turned, she was almost there, her hair flying in the moonlight and her eyes fixed on his. He took her hand and *Rabbit II* swung left, pushing the two of them close against each other once again. Harry gunned the engine into full throttle, and they raced away from the open sea and roared back into the harbor. To their left, Marblehead Light shone green and steady, and off to the right in the distance, the lighted spire of Abbot Hall towered over Washington Square and Old Town. Above them, high in the black sky, the moon was big and yellow, and as they sped across the harbor they plunged into a wide, shining, golden path of shimmering moonlight. Harry gunned the engine again and they hit a swell, and for a moment, they were airborne. Then they slapped back down against the water, and as Harry cut the engine, *Rabbit II* made a deep guttural rumble, and slipping slowly past the old fort, glided toward the dock.

She collapsed back on the bed and flung her arms over her head. He waited until she caught her breath and then leaned down and kissed her.

She looked up at him. "Whew. Two orgasms in one week. For me, that's a record."

"Well, stick around. We'll go for a hat trick."

She laughed. "It was really nice of Harry to lend us this condo. I hope we didn't wake that older couple downstairs."

He lay on his side and pulled her toward him. "It's fine. You didn't make *too* much noise."

"Did I really?"

"No. Except for the Brazilian exclamations."

She settled into his arms. "Had there been any exclamations, they would have been Portuguese, not Brazilian."

"I always get my languages screwed up in moments of passion."

She leaned away and stared into his eyes and ran her fingers through his hair. "Is that what this is?"

"I'd say so. For me, anyway."

"And for me too." Then the expression in her eyes grew serious. "But we need to be careful not to let it go any further."

"I know that."

She came back into his arms, her face so close to his that their eyelashes touched. She put her hand on his hip. "The first night we met we told each other we weren't interested in relationships anymore. Remember? You said they were too much trouble and I agreed with you. You see, that's the problem. I'm afraid I would be just too much trouble for you. We need to keep a healthy distance."

He moved his head back an inch. "How's that for distance?"

She smiled and put her hand on his shoulder. "That's not very far, I'm afraid. But be serious for a moment."

"I thought the idea was not to be too serious."

"It is, it is. But what I meant was to listen to me without... without that comic sensibility of yours."

"All right. Consider me tragic."

"Hey, come on."

"OK. Go ahead."

"I know what you're doing."

"What?"

"You're using that sensibility, that attitude toward life, to put off this conversation when you know we need to have it."

He lay on his back and she leaned into him and placed her hand on his heart. Outside on the little cove, the waves rolled in and lapped against the rocks and the sand. He put his hand over hers. "You're half right, Rebecca. That sensibility, as you call it, is an attitude. But it's not quite as conscious as you make it out to be. By this time in life, it comes to me quite naturally. It puts things in perspective. So we can have a long, morose conversation with tragic overtones, or we can just face the facts. And the fact is that we have a choice here. We can choose to be apart or we can choose to be together. But there are other choices too, aren't there? For example, we can choose to be apart *and* be together."

Their window faced the harbor and a cool autumn breeze blew in across their damp, warm bodies. "You mean continue as we are."

"That's right."

"Me in my life and you in yours."

"You got it."

She was quiet for a while. "Rob, I'm so glad I met you. I really am. You've done so much for me. You've made me laugh again. You've stopped me from doing something really awful and..."

"Uh, oh. This sounds like a prelude to something morose and tragic."

She leaned up on her elbow and shook her head in exasperation. "*And*, I was going to say, you've brought me back to life sexually. You've given me these great orgasms. I've never had them like this before. But I can't really let myself get too close to you. It would be nothing but disappointment for you." She slid her hand off his chest.

"Why don't you let me be the judge of that?"

"Listen to me. I know you now. I've learned enough about you in this short span of time to know that you don't want someone like me. Not really. You don't really want a woman who's done what I've done. Deep inside, you want a woman with an edge, but you don't want that dangerous an edge, now do you?"

"Well, at least you give a man fair warning, don't you? You know it's funny, but you just said you knew what I was doing. Well, I know what you're doing."

"And what is that?"

"You're setting the stage for a tragic ending. And guess what?"

"What?"

"I'm not participating."

She laughed and punched him lightly on the arm. "What do you mean, you're not participating? You think we can just *carry on* as we've been doing with what you know about me?"

"It's going to be hard not to, isn't it? It'll be pretty embarrassing bumping into each other in the Square all the time. I don't know about you, but I'm not moving. Cambridge is my home. So unless you take off to Wellesley, you're going to have to put up with me."

"Wellesley! My God!"

REBECCA SCOTT

"Sorry. That's the choice. It's either the suburbs and the soccer moms or me and Cambridge. Take your pick."

She put her hand on his face. "We got too close. A mistake."

"Well, we're only human, right?"

"You are. I don't know how human I am."

"Your kids think you're pretty human."

She pulled away from him and smiled, and then she lay on her back next to him, holding his hand in hers. Outside, echoing over the harbor, the bells of Abbot Hall tolled the hour. He counted to twelve. They were silent for a while, lost in their own thoughts, lying quietly side by side. The little white curtains on the window by their bed fluttered in the breeze, and the smell of the sea filled their lungs. She turned on her side and kissed him on the forehead and sat up. "Well, I think I'm going to go take a shower." She rose from the bed and walked away from him, and the moonlight caught her naked body as she moved across the floor to the bathroom. She went in and closed the door, and then a second later she opened it again and stepped back out. "Hey, Rosario."

Watching her, he felt his voice go husky with desire. "Hey, Rebecca Scott."

"Did you check out this bathroom?"

"I guess I was focused on the bedroom."

"Yeah, I guess you were. Because the shower is pretty big. In fact, it's much too big for just one person. Why don't you join me?"

"Well, now that sounds like a plan to *carry on* to me."

Rosario leapt from the bed and went after her, catching her in his arms in the moonlight. She melted against him, her arms around his neck and her warm body pressed into his, and as he bent to kiss her, somewhere, far back in the recesses of his mind, the warnings of Ursula McGuire and David Warner faded away into a vague and distant recollection.

Made in United States
North Haven, CT
10 May 2022

19064065R00221